Praise for *Game Over*

"Keating has created a female version of the film *Tron*, but with more excitement and realism. The romance is a soul-touching, emotional ride. Both River and Hawk are more than capable of taking care of themselves, but when they come together, they really thrive."

—*RT Book Reviews*

"Keating's debut crosses over to the romance reader who still rolls a mean Dungeons & Dragons d20 die or escapes on her lunch break to the World of Warcraft, yet is easily accessible to anyone who dreams of a true adventure. The somewhat abrupt ending hints that the game and series have just begun, while this well-drawn, dark futuristic world with a dash of magic will appeal to those who like Linnea Sinclair."

—*Booklist*

"Suspense is the background with a perfect trifecta of danger, magic, and romance, making *Game Over* a true page-turner and an instant favorite. Joyfully recommending it is the least I can do while I wait for the next book and next part of the journey for Chase and River."

—*Joyfully Reviewed* (Best of 2010)

"*Game Over* is a fast-paced, roller-coaster ride of a read that flies out of the station house, throwing readers back against the seat rest, taking them on a rip-roaring journey packed with danger and adventure, and not letting go until the car slides back int̶o̶ ̶t̶h̶e̶ ̶s̶t̶a̶t̶i̶o̶n̶ leaving them breathless and panting f̶o̶r̶

"Thrilling action and electrifying excitement fairly pulses throughout *Game Over,* as River and Hawk fight to stay alive. I love this book; it isn't just the nonstop adventure, but also the sexual tension as River and Hawk fight to ignore their attraction, but inevitably they just can't resist each other. I also love that Ms. Keating kept me on the edge of my seat; I never would have guessed the outcome of the story."

—*Night Owl Romance* (Top Pick)

FAIR
GAME

◆

TAYLOR KEATING

TOR®
paranormal romance

A TOM DOHERTY ASSOCIATES BOOK
NEW YORK

FAIR GAME

Copyright © 2012 by Taylor Keating

All rights reserved.

A Tor Book
Published by Tom Doherty Associates, LLC
175 Fifth Avenue
New York, NY 10010

www.tor-forge.com

Tor® is a registered trademark of Tom Doherty Associates, LLC.

ISBN 978-0-7653-6549-1

First Edition: September 2012

Printed in the United States of America

0 9 8 7 6 5 4 3 2 1

To our awesome editor Melissa Frain
and equally awesome agent Ethan Ellenberg.

FAIR
GAME

PROLOGUE

♦

River stubbed her toe on cardboard boxes stacked in one corner of the dark attic and tried not to swear. With a pencil-thin flashlight tucked between her teeth she stood still for a moment, listening, hoping no one had heard her, but the house below remained silent.

She didn't want her stepmother to know she was here. More important, she didn't want Jake to know either. Her half brother was too young for the problems life had thrust on him and it was better if he didn't know about the shit going on in hers.

As River sifted carefully through the contents of the boxes—not sure what she was hoping to find but certain that whatever it was, it had to be here at her childhood home—she tried hard to swallow her worry for Hawk. She would have known if he were dead. She would have felt the hole. But he'd been gone for nearly two weeks, cutting himself off from her so that she could no longer sense his presence or feel his soul next to hers.

He'd said he would return for her, and the feminine part of her had wanted him to keep the promises he'd made to her no matter what.

Which just went to show that a woman could only rely on herself—exactly as she'd been taught by the father who'd raised her.

She had come here tonight in search of answers because of her father. Constable Jim Peters insisted he had been involved in top-secret government experiments. River refused to believe it.

"Trust me," Jim had said to her a few days before he, too, had disappeared. "Your father was no simple farmer." His blue eyes looked tired as he rubbed a freckled hand through his graying red hair and complained about needing a haircut. "Was he overprotective?" he asked. "Did he ever go off without explanation for extended periods of time?"

She'd started to say no to the last because the disappearances had been so rare she'd almost forgotten them, but looking back, there had been at least three. She had no idea if there had been any in more recent years, when she had been less a part of his life. She couldn't deny other oddities either. She had no idea how he'd earned a living. He could fix anything with an engine and four wheels. He'd taught her to shoot a gun, a rifle, and a crossbow, skills he'd later taught Jake. She and her mother had signed up for self-defense lessons and practiced with him. He'd taught them a few moves of his own. These had all been necessary skills in the world she'd grown up in after the war, and they proved nothing other than that her father liked to be prepared.

But neither did they disprove what Jim had tried to tell her, and River wanted Jim to be wrong. She wanted at least one part of her life to be true. If she couldn't believe in her own father, what was the point of believing in anything?

River carefully replaced the last box. She'd found nothing other than the photos she'd already seen, the ones of the poor creature that had died in a mountain cave not too far from the house. She didn't know where her father had gotten these photographs and that was what made her uneasy, although she refused to believe they meant anything bad. The man who had raised her had been honest and caring. Without a doubt he had loved her. He had not, however, always been open. She had to admit that.

As she slid the box farther back on the shelf, she met with resistance. Curious, she reached her hand in behind to see what was blocking it. Her fingers brushed cold, smooth metal. A familiar jolt of energy made her smile and she drew a long cylinder off the shelf.

This was the first toy she and her father had built together. Similar to a kaleidoscope, it could be held to the eye and the tube spun to create images. He'd been far more fascinated by it than she. Anytime she'd played with it, he'd impatiently waited for his turn.

A branch scratched against the windowpane and River started, spooked by the sudden noise disturbing the stillness. She put the toy back onto the shelf.

It wasn't the noise that had unsettled her, she realized, the skin on her arms beginning to crawl. The house was too silent. No matter how quiet she'd tried to be, and she could be very quiet, Jake would have heard her. He had a sixth sense for things out of the ordinary, something he'd inherited from their dad.

She didn't walk to the door. Instead, she used her magic and transported herself across the room so as not to make the floor joists creak. She did not, however, dare jump to the main level because she had no idea what she might find if she did. She opened the door and started down the stairs, carefully stepping where the wood had been nailed to the frame. On the second level she passed the open door to Melinda's bedroom. The room was empty.

She wished Hawk were with her. She might have been taught to look after herself, but there was something to be said for backup. Seriously panicked, and even more cautious, she peered into the other two bedrooms. They were also empty.

A scraping noise came from directly below her, in the vicinity of the kitchen. It sounded like a chair being moved.

She didn't like the thought of having to take that second flight of stairs to the main level because she'd be exposed, but she had no choice. It was either the stairs or go out a window. If she went out a window, she'd have to get back into the house again.

At the foot of the stairs she paused in the darkness to let her eyesight adjust and to orient herself. She turned to the kitchen door and placed her hand on the wood, listening hard but hearing nothing now. A funky smell seeped through the cracks, coppery and rank. Hope died. She pushed the door open.

And jerked her head to the side, her lightning-fast Fae instincts reacting to danger a split second before her brain caught up. The bolt from a crossbow quivered in the doorframe a few inches from where her face had been.

"Jake!" she cried out, knowing immediately where that bolt had originated. "It's me, River."

Her words met with silence and she waited, debating what to do next and not daring to move. He was scared. She could taste his fear, as thick in the air as the unbearable stench. His next bolt might not miss. He was good, and now he had a better sight on his target.

The overhead light clicked on, flooding the room. River blinked a few times, not wanting to accept what she saw. The walls, the floor, even the ceiling were coated in blood. The television had smashed onto the tiles. One overturned chair sat on its side. Two mangled human remains lay near the kitchen table. And Jake, her beautiful, blond-haired brother, not yet fourteen, stood near the exterior door with one hand on the light switch, the other gripping the shaft of the crossbow that rested against his shoulder. He'd jammed a chair under the knob of the door. That was the scraping noise she'd heard.

River didn't ask him what had happened because she already knew. Rage unfurled inside her, sliding through her veins like floes of ice on a swift stream. Bright red dots of fury obscured her vision. Weres had come looking for her, finding her stepmother and youngest brother instead. Only Jake remained.

A stern voice in the back of her head ordered her to

focus on him. Her vision cleared, the rage subsiding but not disappearing. She stored it away, ready to withdraw it at a later time. Right now, Jake needed her.

So did Melinda and Sam. Her throat hurt with the effort of keeping her emotions in check.

"We have to bury them," Jake said, so matter-of-factly he sounded exactly like their dad. River nodded, unable to speak.

They worked through the night. By the time they finished, she had already decided where she would take him. What was important was getting Jake to safety. She had no idea when, or if, the ones who had done this might possibly return.

The psychological damage done to him would have to be dealt with too, but at a later date. She didn't want him to spend his life planning revenge against creatures that had been following orders.

Neither did she want Weres following her and Jake. She had an excellent method of travel that would not leave a scent.

"Hang on, Jake," she said, taking his hand. "We're going for a little ride."

CHAPTER ONE

♦

"Jesus, River. I don't like this. I don't like it one little bit."

Deep inside the guts of the city's abandoned subway, tucked away in a makeshift computer lab, Nick Sutton slicked his hair back from his face and squared his shoulders. He stared straight at River Weston, but she knew it wasn't really her he was seeing.

River's glance raked over Nick in return, analyzing him with clinical precision and taking in everything from the moisture on his pale skin and how he fidgeted restlessly in his seat, to the way his Adam's apple bobbed crazily as if going down for the third count.

Holding off on tapping into his mind—her skin crawled at the thought of it—River briefly turned her focus from Nick to the strings of code on her monitor, then back to him. With his blue eyes blinking rapidly he held his arms stiffly in front of him, groping and catching nothing but air as he tried out River's newest software invention—Hollow Man. Nick had named it after one of the old movies from the turn of the twentieth century he and Tanner used to watch together.

She shied away from thoughts of Tanner, along with the two other dead members of their former software team. Nothing would bring them back. The best she could hope for was that their souls had found peace, something she now knew no one could guarantee.

Deciding Nick wasn't in any real danger and looking instead for some sort of error in the implant she'd given him, she shifted on the rickety folding metal chair that the Demons—a gang of teens who ruled the city's underbelly—had scrounged from one of the deserted apartment buildings nearby. Consisting of a microchip crafted from living tissue and triggered by River's magic, the implant was meant to replace the need for external gaming gear. She'd also added a few enhancements to it that she hadn't learned about in any of her engineering courses.

The implant was working perfectly. What's more, it was perfectly safe. She'd tested it herself. The Demons had test driven it, too.

"What is it you don't like?" she asked Nick.

He made a face, tossing his dark hair out of his eyes. "I don't like any of it."

Hands planted on her knees, River leaned forward and narrowed her eyes at him. "Can you give me details?"

His right shoulder jerked as if he'd accidentally bumped into something, which was more than likely what had happened. He didn't have good control and hadn't yet learned he didn't need to move his physical body. "It just feels weird."

Relaxing, she slouched back into her chair. He was a medic. *Weird* meant there was nothing wrong with her implant, because otherwise, he would be more specific.

"It's an out-of-body experience," she reminded him. "How did you think it was going to feel?"

"I don't know," he complained. "But I was hoping for more orgasmic and less like tripping on bad drugs."

After everything they'd been through she wasn't about to waste her sympathy on something so insignificant. "Level one is pretty easy. Stop being such a baby."

"Just because I don't leap before I look, it doesn't make me a baby."

She tapped her fingers on the keyboard. "Sometimes you have to trust your gut and go with your instincts."

He wobbled drunkenly on his chair. "My gut tells me we don't all have your freaky Fae instincts."

River hadn't quite come to terms with her unusual heritage and the reminder was unwelcome. "*My* gut says we don't all have your instinct for self-preservation," she shot back.

Streaks of red materialized on his cheeks. "I wanted my body back."

She suffered a slight twinge of pity and maybe a bit of guilt. Nick had been shot trying to protect her. The Dark Lord—or Sandman, as Nick liked to refer to him—had captured Nick's consciousness as it abandoned his dying body. River had healed Nick's body with her magic, although too late to save him, and Hawk's consciousness had stepped into it.

Hawk had used Nick's body so he could protect her. Nick had tried to drive Hawk crazy in an effort to get it back.

Maybe she didn't feel quite so guilty after all.

River grabbed Nick's wrist and tugged, impatience lacing her words and making her sharp. "For God's sake, put your arms down. Let your mind control your hologram's movements and make them a little more normal. You look like an idiot and if you're doing this out on the street, I'm sure you're drawing unnecessary attention to yourself."

A sound rose in his throat, a mixture between a snort and a nervous laugh. "And rumor has it the Fae are such gentle creatures." Nick splayed his sweaty hands over his jeans-clad thighs, wiped them dry, then dropped his arms to his sides in helpless surrender. "It feels too much like being dead."

"You're in control, Nick. Just remember that. Once you take charge of your hologram you won't have to do it with me monitoring you. Now tell me, what do you see?"

Nick's arms shot straight out in front of him. "I see people walking around me and keeping their distance."

"That's because you're doing a fine impression of Frankenstein's monster. You don't need to move around, so keep your hands down." Once again, River grabbed his wrists and anchored them to his sides. "Remember, your mind and body are separate."

Nick's nostrils flared, then he inhaled and swiped his tongue over his bottom lip.

"Do you smell something?" she asked, curious about his reaction even though it annoyed her.

"Coffee."

The longing in his voice made her laugh. She glanced at her watch and took note of the time. Tim Hortons always brewed a fresh pot this time of day, which meant Nick was responding well to the implant and it wasn't simply wishful thinking on his part.

"Perfect," she murmured to herself and jotted down a few notes.

"It smells good," he said wistfully.

"Grab yourself a double double. On me."

"Very funny."

River resisted the urge to point out he could grab one if he ever reached level two. Even though they were underground, deep in the bowels of the subway, through her program they could project themselves onto the city streets—anywhere, anytime. Adding magic to the program allowed them to see, hear, touch, and smell. Out on the sidewalk Nick might be nothing more than a hologram, but to those he encountered he was a living, breathing, functioning human being. Her lips curved in a smile. Although a crazy-looking one.

But despite the enhancements she'd added to Hollow Man through magic, she'd also defined limitations. She wanted the Demons to be able to protect themselves, but a part of her shied away from making it possible for them to kill with a program she had created. Magic allowed the Demons to physically strike an opponent to protect themselves, and it was magic that made certain their blows couldn't kill.

The power of suggestion, however, created serious limitations in itself. Level-one beginners couldn't always tell the difference between a blow to their hollow forms and one to their bodies.

Every member of Dan's gang had to learn how to work the program properly so he could be safe. No one was allowed on the street in Hollow form unsupervised until he reached level two. That included Nick.

But Nick, a man whose self-preservation instincts easily surpassed average, hadn't wanted the implant. He'd been the most reluctant to receive it and the last to concede. The Demons, on the other hand, had been practicing for weeks and had gotten so good at it, the level twos could manipulate their holograms and make their opponents see whatever they wanted them to see. River grinned. An ability to project oneself as a "real" demon could do a psychological number on the unsuspecting. A few of them could even project weapons.

She'd have to think about a prototype for a third level sometime soon. Dan had already mastered the first two and was ready for more.

"I've had enough, River," Nick announced.

She tried to be patient. "The Demons are just kids and they didn't kick up this much of a stink after I implanted their programs. They couldn't wait to try them out."

He mumbled something under his breath and River decided to change tactics. He seemed genuinely troubled, and mentally, the time he'd spent sharing space with a Dark Lord couldn't have been easy on him. It was wrong of her to expect him to be tough enough to get past it after a few short months.

He was no Hawk.

"Come on," she said, shooting him an ounce of understanding and lacing it with unrepentant manipulation. "We just need a few more minutes. Who knows what will happen if we haul you out before the program has had time to completely embed itself in your brain?"

Nick cursed. "And therein lies the problem. You should have figured out what could happen before using us all as your guinea pigs. This isn't a video game. This is serious shit, and the Demons are just kids."

Nick had his faults, but he had a few redeeming qualities as well. He cared about the Demons every bit as much as she did. Despite River being a wanted woman, Dan had taken them both in four months ago after they'd blown Amos Kaye's laboratory all to hell and put a serious kink in his bioengineering program. These kids protected them, and helped keep them hidden, and she wasn't about to do anything to hurt them.

But what Nick failed to understand was that she would be hurting them more by not implanting them with the program, because this had once been a Dark Lord's world. Hawk had told her the Guardians would come because of that, and if they were anything like him, they would shoot first and ask questions later. There were other, more immediate dangers, too. Weres had killed her friends and her family. They were searching for her.

And monsters, bioengineered or not, always found their way underground.

"These *kids* are going to help save this world, and probably your ass in the process," she replied. "When the Guardians come, they'll be ready. I can't say the same about you."

She and Nick had forged a truce after the hell they'd been through, and maybe she was being a bit of a controlling bitch at the moment. But for months they'd been waiting, planning, and preparing for the Guardians to arrive, and all of the pent-up energy that had been building in the underground was playing havoc with her normally bright and sunny disposition.

Nick opened his mouth to speak, probably to come back with some smart-assed comment, but a shuffling sound at the door had him slamming his mouth shut. At least she thought it was the sound at the door that caused his reaction. There was something odd in his expression and the way he'd cocked his head to the side, as if he were listening very carefully to some distant sound, and suddenly she was concerned.

"Hey, River, Dan wants to see you."

It was Jake at the door. The haunted look in his eyes was a constant reminder of how much had changed for him over the last four months.

Nick had real concerns for her little brother. "Jake is suffering symptoms of post-traumatic stress disorder," he'd warned her. "He's jumpy and doesn't sleep well. His pain receptors aren't normal. Dan puts a serious shit kicking on him during training, and he gets up and asks for more."

Nick, however, was a chronic alarmist. Jake had always been mature for his age, and while River admitted he'd had to grow up too fast, he was a survivor. Of that, she had no doubt. He was too much like their dad to be anything else.

Jake's worn sneakers scuffed on the cement floor as he took a step into the room. He started to speak but adolescence cracked his voice. He cleared his throat, embarrassed, and pointed to Nick. "Is he okay?"

"Shit!" Distracted by her brother, she'd missed Nick's increasing signs of physical distress. His fingers had curled into fists and he was shaking almost violently. His head was twisting left and right, his chest rising and falling, and a rapid pulse at the base of his neck told her he was in serious trouble.

"River!" Nick bellowed. "What the hell is going on?" The genuine panic in his voice frightened her.

She placed her hand over his and tried to stay calm. She didn't want to escalate the situation. "You have to pull yourself out, Nick. All you have to do is visualize yourself back here. We've been over this."

"I can't seem—" His words fell off and his back stiffened.

Immediately, River pulled a thread of magic and slipped into his thoughts. A second later she found herself standing beside him on the sidewalk outside of Tim Hortons.

"Hey," she said, curling her fingers into his. She kept her voice light despite the worry she was feeling.

Nick turned to her, confusion apparent in his expression. Something wasn't right. It was as if there was a new energy crackling around them. If she listened really hard she could hear it, although she couldn't quite pinpoint its source. Did it have something to do with the program?

"Come on, let's go back," she coaxed him. She sent out a small surge of magic to help guide him along.

Then they were back in the tiny office off the subway platform. She watched his eyes as he blinked a few times before driving agitated fingers through his dark hair. Relief washed over his face as he took in the familiar surroundings, clearly happy to have his body and consciousness reunited.

"I hate that program," he said with feeling, sweat beading on his forehead.

"What happened?" she asked him.

He frowned. "I'm not sure. I knew something wasn't right. I could hear this strange buzz, then it felt like my wires got crossed somehow and I couldn't pull back."

River really didn't like the sound of that.

"You okay, man?" Jake asked him from behind her.

Nick jumped at the sound of the boy's voice and clutched his fists to his chest. Startled, Jake instinctively raised his own in self-defense.

She'd forgotten her brother was in the room. She didn't want him seeing Nick like this. "Tell Dan I'll be with him in a minute."

Understanding that he was being dismissed, Jake nodded and left as quietly as he'd entered.

River turned back to Nick. "What do you think that buzzing sound was?"

"You heard it, too?" His relief was palpable.

"Yes." But this was the first time, and none of the Demons had mentioned it before. She didn't want to alarm him. He was freaked enough.

"Do you think it's the Sandman?"

"No. He's gone, Nick. Andy destroyed him."

Andy had sacrificed herself in order to save River, and not a day went by that River didn't think of her friend.

The buzzing noise was a concern, though. She wondered what it meant. Did it stem from the technical part of the program, or did it come from her magic?

Nick exhaled slowly, then pulled the sticky heart monitor off his chest and with shaky hands rebuttoned his shirt.

"Why don't you go see what Dan wants?" he said. She watched him rise and move to the door, unable to sit still. Tension rolled off him. "Anyone able to go get me a coffee?"

"I'm not sure. You'll have to ask around."

After Nick left the small office, River powered down her program and yawned, sucking in a mouthful of the subway's clammy smell. God, what she'd give to breathe in air that didn't leave an aftertaste like sewer and burning garbage.

As much as she, too, would love to go topside, neither

of them could do so. She'd never risk leading Kaye back to the Demons. She'd seen what his bioengineered Weres could do to a person, and if she and Nick went aboveground, they could be tracked back here by their scent.

No, if Nick wanted to see the outside world he was going to have to get used to his hologram. That had been the carrot she'd dangled to get him to try it.

She suddenly remembered that Dan, the unpredictable seventeen-year-old leader of the Demons, was waiting for her and he wasn't particularly patient.

She stepped from her office onto the platform, then hopped off the side of the platform and onto the tracks. The sound of her sturdy boots hitting the wooden sleepers echoed around her and she kept a close eye out for rats as she followed along the tracks to find Dan.

Her mind raced as she mulled over the strange buzzing sound both she and Nick had heard. The program was working just fine. She knew that. But she'd created the program using skills she'd inherited from both her Fae mother and Guardian father. If the noise was caused by her program, could it be some sort of forewarning that trouble was coming?

Trouble, to River, meant Guardians.

Flashes of Hawk rushed to the forefront of her brain, her body reacting to the vivid memories as if she'd received a physical blow. She crossed her arms in front of her chest and hugged herself as she recalled the comforting feel of his arms wrapped around her. She couldn't help but think of the warmth of his mouth when he kissed her, the energy that poured from her body to his when they made love. Hawk's Guardian instincts were strong, but River was half Guardian, too, and she knew that what was between them went well beyond any sense of duty to protect a Fae he might have.

Electricity trickled through her at the mere thought of him. It had been four long months since she had felt any connection to him, and even though it was slight, it rekindled her belief he was alive. She couldn't imagine what kept him from her. Her body longed for him. So did her heart.

But Earth had once been the home of a Dark Lord, and to him, it was dark. If he came back, Hawk would again try to take her away.

If he did, River had no intentions of going. She was counting on his desire to protect her to interfere with the Guardians' obligation to see a dark world stripped of technology, because without technology, Earth might never recover.

Footsteps heralded someone's approach. She watched Dan descend the concrete stairwell from one of the street entrances above, his large, almost-man-size frame silhouetted in the bright rays of sunshine spilling down the entry and beating against his back.

He jumped the last few steps and reached a hand down to help lift her off the tracks to the platform, carrying the enticing scents of the outdoors with him. She caught traces of lilac and spring grass. They reminded her of new beginnings.

Except today, she feared, could be the beginning of something bad if that buzzing sound in the program signaled a warning.

Dan held her hand a little too long and she withdrew it from his as casually as possible. She knew how he felt about her, but she was ten years too old for him. Besides, her heart was otherwise occupied. She didn't see that changing anytime soon.

"We need to talk," Dan said. He spiked a hank of hair out of his eyes with his fingers, his face even more grim than usual.

River got a knot in her chest that was becoming all too familiar. This was about Jake.

"Jake's had a rough time," she replied, cutting him off. "You're being too hard on him."

"We've all had rough times. The kid's got to learn how to fight."

River didn't know much of Dan's story, although she suspected it was as bad as Jake's. Maybe worse. He'd been on the streets for so long he didn't remember another life, at least not one he'd admit to. But it was Jake she was worried about now.

"He'll get the hang of the program. Nick's having trouble with it, too." She frowned. "He says it's making a buzzing noise."

"Nick's not out on the streets, hanging with the other Demons." Dan's bleak eyes revealed little emotion. "Jake's got to learn how to fight, with or without the program. I'm sorry, River, but if it comes down to a situation where it's Jake or some other kid, Jake's going to lose. His problems are his own."

River's heart shot into her throat. "Don't let anything happen to him."

"If he wants to go topside, he has to look out for himself. The little ones come first. Everyone else pulls their own weight. No one hesitates. You know that." Dan's voice had hardened, the way it always did when he made tough decisions. He wasn't as cold as he let on, River knew. But he was practical. He meant what he said.

"Jake can look after himself," she said, defending her brother.

He'd looked after his mother and little brother, too, ever since their father had died. But losing Melinda and Sam had damaged him. As much as she'd tried to deny it, Nick had been right about Jake. Along with everything else, he had a whole lot of survivor guilt to deal with.

She wished she had someone to turn to. Someone like their father, who would be a positive male influence on Jake.

Someone like Hawk, who had been good with him in the short time the two had known each other.

She hadn't needed another reason to miss him.

"There are monsters in this city," Dan was saying, "and sooner or later, Jake's going to come up against them. When he does he'd better be prepared, because if he's not, no Demon will help him. I'll make sure of it."

Maybe Jake's problems with learning the program

were similar to Nick's. Maybe there really was something wrong with it, as Nick claimed. Right now, River was willing to grasp at any explanation if it would keep Jake safe and take away this awful sensation of helplessness she was experiencing.

"I'll keep Jake underground for a few days," she said to Dan. "I need to run some tests on the program anyway, to check on that noise, and he can help me. If he has a better understanding of how the program works it might help him figure it out."

Dan started back up the steps of the metro, the conversation finished as far as he was concerned. He paused partway up, his hand on the railing as he looked down at her.

"A few days," he warned her. "But the next time he's topside, he's on his own."

CHAPTER **TWO**

◆

After four months spent undergoing relentless observation and psychological testing, Hawk had finally been given approval to take a team to River's world. It might not be the approval he'd wanted, but it was all he required.

He and his handpicked team would be leaving as soon

as the word was given. He had one more meeting to attend, first thing in the morning.

Frustration at even that slight delay had him on edge. He couldn't stop thinking of her.

The elevator whispered to a halt on his floor and he stepped onto thick carpet that silenced his footsteps. He paused.

Someone was in his apartment.

More than thirteen months imprisoned in a virtual world with the king motherfuck of all evil motherfucks had given Lieutenant Colonel Chase Hawkins a sixth sense for these things. He didn't know how they'd gotten past the retinal scanner, or the dozens of other security measures he'd had installed, but they had. It didn't matter. Hawk had been itching to kill something—anything—for four months now, ever since his return.

He hoped they put up a fight.

His entry door slid back soundlessly and he crossed the threshold into the brightly lit foyer. Whomever it was, they didn't seem concerned about discovery or even the element of surprise. That meant his unwelcome visitor was probably government.

Two men, both well beyond middle age, sat on the sofa in his sunken central room. One of them he recognized, and had been trying to contact for four months. The other was a stranger to him, although his peaceful presence and black, casual traveling clothes strongly suggested he was Fae.

And not just any Fae, he realized immediately. This

was a spiritual leader. Serenity wafted off him in waves so thick even Hawk felt compelled to relax. He shook off the compulsion, not liking the subtle attempt at mind control.

At least now he knew how the two men had gotten in. Dr. Spencer Jennings had been given a pass so he could water Hawk's plants for him while he'd been in stasis. The Fae would have jumped—transported himself with his magic—because it was doubtful he would have risked being seen on the Guardian world when he was not part of an official delegation. It wasn't that the Fae wouldn't be welcome here in any capacity. Rather, as a spiritual leader and healer, he would be unable to move freely without being mobbed by the faithful.

Hawk hoped neither man noticed that his houseplants were no longer healthy. The plants had belonged to Hawk's daughter. When he'd moved to this apartment they had come with him, but he didn't have a Fae's magic touch and the plants were suffering from neglect. He slid the knife he'd palmed back into his sleeve.

Dr. Jennings leapt to his feet, clearly uncertain about the welcome he was about to receive. He was slight and wiry, with a boyish face under a trim beard, the kind of man who looked odd with graying hair. He had a true scientist's fascination with life and possessed an air of innocence that couldn't be faked. His entire adult years had been spent in classrooms and labs.

"Spence." Hawk injected warmth into his greeting to put the scientist at ease. He was still pissed about being left in stasis longer than planned—he didn't like being a lab rat—but at the same time, it was how he'd met River, so he was willing to forgive and forget. But only Spence, who had never in his life done deliberate harm to anyone or anything. The rest of the cryonics research world could kiss Hawk's ass.

Spence ignored the hand Hawk extended and instead pulled him into his arms for a fast, surprisingly enthusiastic hug that embarrassed them both. The Fae, who'd remained seated on the white sofa, couldn't quite hide a smile at their male awkwardness in displaying affection.

"I was told nothing about you or your experiences," Spence immediately complained, and then it was Hawk who couldn't hide his amusement. This was the Spence he'd known and called friend. He worried about Hawk first, but once Hawk's safety was established, the data became his total priority. "I was caught bringing you out of stasis without authorization and summarily dismissed. *My notes* were *confiscated.*" Indignation over the lost notes quivered in his voice.

The information surprised Hawk. He hadn't known that his return from stasis was unauthorized. Resentment swelled in him. The bastards. They would have left him in stasis until he'd had just enough of his brain left to be able to tell them whatever they wanted to know. It wouldn't have mattered to anyone but him if he spent the rest of his life with diminished intelligence. They would have given him a pension and called it adequate compensation.

This was one more reason why, after he recovered River, he was taking her to the Fae. The Guardian world was no longer home to him. He didn't recognize anything about it anymore.

The Fae cleared his throat and Spence immediately turned to him in apology. "My manners are terrible. Achala, allow me to introduce Colonel Hawkins. Hawk, this is Achala Ravensfell."

Despite the fact the two men had broken into his home uninvited, and Hawk disliked any invasion of his personal space, he was impressed. He'd known the man was a high-ranking Fae because of the aura about him, but he hadn't suspected how high. This was not any spiritual leader. This was *the* spiritual leader. The Mother's representative.

They were here about River. There could be no other explanation.

Wary now, Hawk did not offer his hand. No one touched a Fae unless he was willing to have his thoughts read, and that was something Hawk would never again permit without good reason. It had taken him the entire four months since he'd been brought out of stasis to regain the ability to sleep uninterrupted, and even now, he sometimes awoke in the night in a blind rage, ready to fight off whatever new mental torture the Dark Lord had decided to inflict on him.

He couldn't help it. He scanned the room for anything out of the ordinary, some sign that this meeting might not be real.

"I'm honored to meet you, Colonel Hawkins," the Fae was saying. "Spence has told me a lot about you."

Well, well. Hawk looked at Spence with new appreciation. He hadn't missed the casual use of his name. The scientist had friends in some very high places, but none of them higher than this.

"The honor is mine, Your Grace." He gestured toward the sofa in an invitation for them to resume their seats. "What did I do to deserve it?"

Achala smiled openly at that as he took his seat, his black clothing and graying curls elegant against the simple white of Hawk's decor. Hawk settled on the settee across from them. The furniture had been chosen by his late wife and he saw no reason to change it. He'd lived in darkness for so long, he wanted light around him.

"You were right," Achala said to Spence. "He is very direct." He turned back to Hawk. "I hope you will permit me to be equally so." His eyes speared Hawk, making him feel like an insect mounted on a display board. Hawk forced himself to hold still rather than squirm. "Did you know you are a demolition man?"

Hawk's initial reaction was one of relief. They weren't here about River after all. They were here about the world where she lived.

He paused a beat to deliberate whether or not to reveal military secrets, then decided to go with the truth since it was more than likely Achala already knew the answer to the question. Otherwise, he wouldn't have asked it.

"Yes. I knew." He did not, however, know why it mattered.

Spence made a small sound of dismay and Achala held up a hand for silence. He continued to watch Hawk as if trying to read him.

Hawk had no fears of that happening. He had denied a Dark Lord. A Fae, no matter how powerful, was no stronger than that. Not even the great Achala Ravensfell could enter his thoughts against his will.

But while he didn't expect a spiritual leader to be happy about the demolition training he'd received, Spence's attitude toward it surprised him. Spence knew what being military meant. Hawk eyed his friend's ashen face. Didn't he?

"I thought demolition men were a myth," Spence said into the awkward silence.

"They're not a myth," Hawk replied. "But the term *demolition* is somewhat misleading."

"Can you explain it to me?" Achala asked. He glanced back and forth between Spence and Hawk.

"It's an old military designation." Hawk wondered where the conversation was headed. "Demolition men are chosen because of their natural ability to withstand stress, and for their survival instincts. They're trained to control those instincts under extreme duress. They then lead teams that have been ordered to defuse worlds that aren't yet ready for the technical advances they've made." He looked at Spence. "You accepted me into your study for those very same qualities," he quietly reminded him.

"Defuse?" the spiritual leader echoed, as if the word left a bad taste in his mouth. "Is there a difference between defusing and demolition?"

Hawk had once had this particular debate with his wife. Cassie hadn't liked the peacemaking part of his job. She'd preferred her role in helping the Fae bring life, and really, who wouldn't?

But not everything in reality was so simple.

"Sometimes a world's technology develops faster than its laws on ethics," he replied carefully. "Not only does it then become a danger to its own population, but also to other worlds. When it becomes a danger to others, it automatically becomes a danger to the Fae. The Guardians then step in and strip it of technology, effectively allowing its ethics more time to develop. That's known as defusing."

A case could be made that defusing was simply a slower form of demolition. Sometimes worlds recovered from it. Sometimes they didn't.

"If you defuse worlds, not destroy them, then why do your demolition men receive special training?" Achala asked.

"The training itself isn't enough to create a true demolition man," Hawk said. "Theoretically, actual demolition would involve a bomb the size of a pinhead that's implanted into the brain, and meant to respond to sharp spikes in levels of a naturally occurring stress chemical. If the stress chemical level rises sharply and then drops, it's a sign the demolition man has lost all hope. The concept of such a bomb was once part of the military's risk-contingency plan in case a Dark Lord couldn't be contained. Worlds that have been touched by a Dark Lord are at a higher risk for underdeveloped laws on ethics, because Dark Lords have no souls and therefore no conscience. Without a physical world to sustain them, their magic becomes harmless.

"But when the last Dark Lord was imprisoned, the bomb was abandoned by the military. I've never heard of anyone ever receiving an implant," he added. "Besides, demolition would be a suicide mission. A true demolition man would volunteer, and he'd travel alone. He'd never endanger his team."

Spence and Achala exchanged a look that Hawk did not miss. Something was definitely wrong.

"Did you or did you not receive orders today to defuse a dark world?" Achala asked Hawk.

"Yes. And I'm taking a team," he added. What he didn't tell them was that in this instance, he had been ordered by the Great Lords to not only defuse the world but destroy a suspected Dark Lord before she reached her full potential. The suspected Dark Lord in question was River.

He supported the first order, although River might not agree with him. Some serious shit had gone wrong on her world. But he'd be damned before carrying out the second order, or allowing anyone else to do so.

His eyes narrowed as a thought occurred to him. He had the means for guaranteeing River's safety sitting in this very room. He had an opportunity that he did not dare pass up on, but first, he had to see how open-minded Achala would prove to be before he told him about her. Hawk would never have thought the Great Lords capable of ordering the execution of a Fae, even one they believed was a Dark Lord. And yet they had. He wouldn't take the chance that Achala shared their beliefs and their prejudices. River could not help whom her parents had been. She was innocent.

She was also unsuspecting, and he tried not to let his fear for her force him to act carelessly. If he gave the Great Lords any reason to believe he wouldn't carry out their orders, his opportunity to lead this mission and handpick his own team would be withdrawn. Then River would truly be in danger.

Achala continued to watch him closely. Hawk met his gaze in return. He had nothing to hide from the spiritual leader in terms of his soul. He was comfortable with his decisions. He had no doubt his handpicked team would feel the same way once they met River. They would guarantee the safety of a Fae, no matter the personal cost to them. It was what they had been trained for.

"And you will defuse this world despite my objections?" Achala persisted.

"Yes." Hawk crossed his legs at the ankles and studied the toes of his boots. "I've seen firsthand the dangerous turn its technology has taken. Better for it to have to start over than progress to a point where it's a threat to other worlds."

Achala was frowning. "Defusing is another unacceptable practice that shouldn't be allowed to continue."

"Then you're free to tell the Great Lords so," Hawk replied. "At which point I will be pulled from the commanding position, because they'll know—or at least suspect—where you got your information. Meanwhile, the fate of the dark world will remain unchanged."

And River's fate would be sealed.

"I want to be perfectly clear about something, Colonel," Achala said, and Hawk heard steel in the older man's voice. "It is unacceptable to the Fae that any world be harmed for any reason. You've never heard of anyone carrying out the duties of a demolition man because the Guardians swore to us with the imprisonment of the last Dark Lord that the practice would end. That is the primary reason the Guardians and the Fae travel together. To uphold an old, but important, agreement." He leaned forward, his forearms braced on his thighs and his long, elegant hands clasped gracefully between his knees. "Do you honestly think a race that can control magic and an ability to jump needs the Guardians to protect them? Why would we need protection when we can remove ourselves from danger?"

Hawk discovered he didn't care for the slight to a duty he believed in implicitly.

"No offense, Your Grace. When the Fae focus their magic, they are indeed vulnerable to danger. They don't pay attention to what is around them." He knew that firsthand. He uncrossed his ankles and planted his feet on the floor, allowing a little steel to temper an inference of his own. "Do *you* honestly think Guardian souls would be lost without the Fae to guide *them*?"

"Gentlemen." Spence, Hawk saw, appeared ready to have a stroke.

He shook himself. What was he doing, insulting the beliefs of a Fae leader? "I apologize, Your Grace. I'm more used to giving orders than in practicing diplomacy."

"No apology necessary," Achala said smoothly. "The fault was mine. I spoke without thinking because I'm angry. We'd assumed the practice of utilizing demolition men had stopped."

"It can't stop," Hawk pointed out, "because it never began."

He had spent thirteen months questioning his reality and his sanity. He already questioned the motives of the Great Lords, and he disliked the increasing number of doubts this conversation was raising.

His goal was saving River and nothing else mattered. He clung to that like a lifeline.

Achala looked at his fingers. "I find myself in an embarrassing situation. I have to tell you something I did that you aren't going to like—"

"But he did it at my request," Spence interrupted, "because I was worried about you."

Hawk had little patience for ambiguity. "Maybe you should just come right out and tell me what you're talking about."

"I entered your thoughts without permission."

A fear of heights used to be his biggest phobia. Now it was of going insane. Speckles of red light danced at the backs of his eyes and Hawk had to remind himself to breathe.

"Impossible." He wasn't that weak.

"It happened while you were still in stasis," Spence added, his eyes begging Hawk for understanding. "The readings on your chamber worried me enough that I wanted to end the study immediately, but Dr. Jess interfered and I wasn't allowed to pull you. Achala agreed to see if you were in danger."

"I understand." And Hawk did. Spence had no way of knowing that throughout those dark months of torture, his sanity had been his one serious weakness. From the look on Achala's face, however, Hawk suspected he did know it, and that while in his head, he'd learned a few other things of interest to him.

While Hawk might understand, he hated the thought that the other man had been tiptoeing through his mind uninvited, picking his memories apart and stealing information.

Something else Spence had said registered with Hawk. Even though he'd been ordered not to do it, he had pulled Hawk without permission and gotten himself dismissed as a result. What had Achala discovered that had made Spence endanger a career that was his whole life to him?

"Crisos," he said, suddenly sick. "Are you telling me I've suffered some sort of irreversible brain damage?"

"What? No!" Startled, Spence looked to Achala for support. "Tell him his mind is fine."

Achala's concern seemed equally genuine. So did his reassurances. "Of course your mind is fine, Colonel. I didn't mean to alarm you. If anything, you were very difficult to read. The only things I picked up on were things you didn't seem to know were even there. Or that you had no control over."

Alarm bells continued to ring. What could possibly

be in his head that he didn't know about? What had Nick and the Dark Lord done to him?

A Fae leader and a respected research scientist wouldn't have entered his apartment without permission and waited for him for no reason. Spence might have nothing left to lose, but politically, Achala had put himself and his people in a very uneasy position.

"If my mind is fine, then why are you here?"

The Fae regarded him for a long moment as if trying to decide how best to approach it. Hawk's uneasiness escalated.

"I suggest you brace yourself, Colonel Hawkins. I discovered two things that are of interest to me. The first is that someone has planted one of those demolition bombs in your head. It can't be activated by accident. It won't even detonate if something violent should happen to you. But the trigger is linked to the levels of the chemical in your brain that you mentioned, and if that trigger is activated, you won't be able to stop it. You would indeed be on a suicide mission. So would your team."

The air in Hawk's lungs turned to lead. He looked at Spence. He could think of only one opportunity anyone would have had to implant such a device.

"I wish I could say it's not true," Spence told him. He looked at his hands. "But I can't. There were other scientists with access to your brain. I can't speak for their professional ethics. Not anymore."

Spence knew who had done it, though. Hawk could see it in his eyes. The real question was, why?

"I can help you control the chemical levels in your brain," Achala was saying. "If you let me into your thoughts I can show you how to do it yourself."

Hawk's entire consciousness rebelled. He didn't want anyone tampering with the thoughts in his head. If he had to, at the first sign of danger he would transport himself into empty space and allow the bomb to detonate there. "Explain it to me instead."

"It would be better if I showed you. I'm sorry. There is no other option."

The spiritual leader's tone was sympathetic but uncompromising, and ice-cold fingers of anger clutched at Hawk's chest. Achala had learned enough about him through his thoughts to know he would refuse, and had come here prepared to do battle.

Hawk would give him one. With or without Achala's help, he would control the trigger and get River to safety. He'd like to be able to control it long enough to kill whoever had placed the bomb in his head as well, but that was of secondary importance.

"I don't need help to control my own mind."

Again, Achala was studying him. "I'm not offering to help you out of the goodness of my heart, or any doubts as to your abilities if left on your own. My offer stems from the second thing I discovered through your thoughts. Someone has created a link to your soul."

He knew about River.

Hawk kept his face and thoughts carefully blank. "I've made no secret of the fact that a Fae is living on the dark world and needs to be recovered. It's in my briefings."

"I know who she is. My concern is for what she may become. That she is linked to your soul is not a point in her favor. It demonstrates her lack of knowledge. Or, of control." Achala suddenly seemed old, and sad. "The Fae are taught how to use their magic from a very young age. Most instruction begins at birth because its use is inherent. The restrictions we've placed on it are there for good reason. Fae nurture life. We help it grow. We don't influence it in any way, and the touching of souls is forbidden to all but the most experienced of spiritual leaders." He pressed a thumb between his brows as if easing a great mental pain. "My soul was chosen for me at birth by the elders. My path in life was always known, as it is for all of the Fae. If this woman has a Fae soul, it wasn't chosen by the elders for her. It means she is random. Worse, she's had no training or guidance. If her heritage isn't 100 percent Fae, then it's another obstacle for her to overcome. Natural instincts for the use of magic in a half-breed can be dormant or nonexistent, and because of her birthright, she has two sides to her nature that are very different. She has the potential to follow a dark path without ever knowing she's on it."

Achala, too, thought River was a Dark Lord. Or at least well on her way to becoming one.

Hawk's chest tightened. He knew the number of Fae souls that could be matched to their offspring was finite, and something was happening to them. He had volunteered for an experiment that created an out-of-body experience so his consciousness could search for those missing Fae souls.

He thought he now knew what had happened to them, and the Dark Lords were only indirectly to blame. The Guardians could also be blamed because they had allowed technology to flourish on a world that a Dark Lord had claimed.

"This changes nothing," Hawk said. "I'll deal with the bomb in my head on my own."

Achala looked away as if wondering what more he could say to persuade Hawk. "I don't wish her any harm," he said finally. "Far from it. She's my granddaughter."

Spence looked as shocked by this news as Hawk felt. He hadn't known either, then.

"I'm sure you're aware of the value the Fae place on family," Achala continued. He stared at the wall as if lost in some other world. "Her mother, Annia, was my only child. She was bright and shining, and my whole life. The thought of her soul being released without the ritual guidance of the elders is sometimes more than I can bear, even though the Fae who travel are trained for that possibility. She had great control over it."

Hawk understood how Achala felt. Even though the Guardians had a very different attitude toward family relationships than the Fae, he, too, had lost a daughter who had once been his whole world. He'd also lost a wife he'd loved very much. But then River had entered his life and things changed. He again had a purpose, and he wouldn't risk her, not even for a Fae spiritual leader who was undoubtedly telling the truth. If Hawk brought River to him, Achala would see for himself that she was Fae.

But until Achala met her and accepted that, and guaranteed her safety, Hawk was taking no chances.

"I'm sorry for your loss," Hawk said, knowing how trite the words truly were because he had heard them himself so many times. "But everything you've told me only gives me more reason to refuse your request. If you're her grandfather, then you are in no position to judge her. You can either explain to me how to isolate the trigger, or you can trust me to figure it out for myself. But I swear to you," he added softly. "She is not dark."

The room was silent for a long time as Achala thought it over.

"Very well," he said finally. "But on one condition. I can follow you wherever you go now because I've touched you. If you ever have any reason to change your mind about allowing me entry, or should come to suspect she is dark, will you call for me?"

Hawk could agree to that. River wasn't dark.

He spent the next several hours following the spiritual leader's instructions for controlling his emotions.

By the end of it, Hawk felt as if he'd had a worse mental beating than any the Dark Lord had given him. Achala did things to exacting standards. And why shouldn't he?

The lives of an entire world were at stake, including the life of his granddaughter.

"He's as strong as you said," Achala admitted to Spence when they were done.

Spence had stayed on as an observer, fascinated as always by anything experimental, although Achala had forbidden him to take notes. Hawk had welcomed the scientist's presence. It gave him more confidence that his reality wasn't being altered without his knowledge.

The two older men prepared to leave.

Spence gripped Hawk's hand and elbow. "I wanted only to save lives with my cryonics experiments," he said. "I'm truly sorry for everything that's happened to you because of me."

"I'm not," Hawk replied truthfully. He didn't like a lot about the way things were handled, but overall, he couldn't be sorry. He'd gained some valuable information. Plus, he'd met River.

Spence left through the front door and Achala simply vanished. One moment he was standing in Hawk's main room. The next, he was gone.

Hawk didn't move, only stood and listened.

Once he was convinced he was truly alone, he turned off the lights and moved to the windows that made up one full wall of his apartment. He drew back the curtains and the room filled with the warm, red glow of a cloudless Guardian night.

The city glittered with lights in the semidarkness below him. Lush gardens, with draping trees and flowers of every color and shade of the rainbow, peppered the landscape. Three red moons, all in various stages of their individual lunar cycles, guaranteed that it was never completely dark on his world, something he'd taken for granted in the past but now found comforting. Every few years, the moons became full at the same time and when that happened, night glowed brighter than day.

The festivities surrounding the event were amazing and steeped in thousands of years of tradition. His daughter had loved the excitement, and so had his wife.

While technology came as second nature to his people, they had long ago discovered that it was the simple things in life such as these that gave the greatest pleasure. They lived as the Fae did, surrounded by nature's beauty. The difference was in the way their natures were achieved. The Guardians created much of theirs with technology. The Fae used magic. But both concentrated on sharing their talents for nurturing life with worlds that needed them in order to thrive.

At least, they had in the past.

Hawk stared out the window for a very long time, absorbing the splendor of the night as if it might be his last. He no longer took it for granted that he would return from a mission.

Although tired, he knew he wouldn't be able to sleep. Not yet. The exercises with Achala had reminded him too much of his days with the Dark Lord, when he'd had to keep mentally agile and rest wasn't an option. If he'd slept, he would never have known for certain what reality his consciousness might awaken in.

A mortal body, however, needed rest or it would die, so he'd learned a few tricks of his own once he'd returned to his physical form and sleep could no longer be avoided. Always, before he closed his eyes, he allowed himself to remember River's face. He pictured her Fae beauty and the warmth of her smile. He thought of how sensual she looked when he moved inside her. Then, when he awoke, he brought the memories back to him, to remind him of where he was and what needed to be done. This was a secret he guarded carefully so that no one would know how he tested reality.

For four long months he had avoided all contact with her. He'd concentrated on keeping his thoughts guarded, afraid that if he let her in, he might inadvertently let someone else in, too. He had been afraid someone might discover how important she was to him, how close their connection, and have a weapon to use against him—or worse, against her. He'd worried he might be excluded from this mission to find her, that he wouldn't be able to protect her, that he might somehow bring harm to her.

These past few months had required far more discipline from him than the entire thirteen months he'd spent trapped in a Dark Lord's virtual prison, resisting his torture. He'd worried over her endlessly. He'd longed for her. He'd dreamed of her every night.

Had she given him up for dead, he wondered. Had she decided he was not going to return as he'd promised? Had she moved on with her life?

His fingers tightened into fists at his sides. She'd cared about Nick Sutton, the bastard. Had she renewed her relationship with him?

He steadied his breathing, forcing himself to relax and think only of River. He couldn't arrive at her door unannounced. Not after four months of silence. Neither could he let her know why he'd been sent. She already distrusted the Guardians. He didn't want her to hate them. Whether she liked it or not, she would have family on his world, too.

The thought startled him. He'd been so focused on the fact she was Fae, he had never stopped to consider whom her Guardian family might be. Whomever they were, they wouldn't welcome her existence. Unease slithered under his skin, setting its alarm sensors on fire. Right or wrong, her father's relationship with a Fae would be viewed as dishonorable. River would be living proof of that dishonor.

River, who was innocent. He closed his eyes. He needed to let her know he was coming. That meant he would have to reach out to her.

Slowly, sliver by sliver, he inched open his thoughts and released a bit of his soul. It was like stuffing a giant pillow through a swollen door with unoiled hinges.

For the longest time, he sensed nothing. And then, there she was.

She was dreaming of him.

Triumph coiled through him. Her thoughts were un-guarded. She had not blocked him out. Then he frowned. She was dreaming of him, but not in his own form. First, he was Sever—the video game character she'd built around him—but the differences were marked. She'd described the character to the illustrator who had de-signed it. That person had not captured him completely.

Next, he was Nick—and having her remember him in connection with a former lover was torture of a far worse kind, even though he had inhabited that body.

No. From this point forward, River would know Hawk

for who he really was. Never again would he wear another man's face when he made love to her. He would wipe those old memories away.

Without any qualms whatsoever, he stepped into her dream.

CHAPTER **THREE**

♦

After several days of dodging River and her relentless testing to find out what had gone wrong with her scary-assed program, Nick had finally had enough.

On edge over the malfunctioning implant and more shaken than he cared to let on, not to mention his desperate need for a coffee that wasn't lukewarm, he was also totally freaking stir crazy. They had spent four months underground, and while Amos Kaye was probably still angry that River had blown up his lab, even that crazy fuck wouldn't hang around for so long. If he'd really wanted to, he would have found them by now.

The littlest rug rats were asleep. The older ones were out terrorizing the neighborhood. River would totally kick Nick's ass if she found him out here, but what she didn't know was never going to hurt him.

He poked his head out of the entrance of the underground subway that he not-so-fondly called home and shot a glance up and down the darkened street.

Finding it nearly deserted and with no sign of the police, he emerged into the deep shadows of night. Even with the change of government, and the increased police presence, most cops avoided the subway, particularly after dark. It was where the infected bodies had been disposed of, locked away and forgotten, during the original outbreak of a viral pandemic that had nearly destroyed the world. The police were as superstitious as the rest of the world. They thought monsters lived underground.

So did Nick. The biggest difference between his fears and those of the others was that he knew the monsters were real. And that they didn't all live in the subway system.

He zipped his nylon jacket as the night air hit him. Warmth generated by the sun continued to radiate from the concrete and asphalt beneath him, even after dark, but the winds off the mountains remained cool. He'd always hated west coast Canadian winters, so he was glad that the overcast days and the damp, bleak season were finally behind them.

A chill chased through his body. It was quite possible that the chill had more to do with River and her latest experiment and less with the outside elements. Something was seriously wrong with her. She'd gone from a fun, hot, sexy software engineer interested in challenging games and a good time in bed to this militant, paranoid chick obsessing about the end of the world.

He'd liked her better when she'd bitched about him being the paranoid one.

He pulled the hood of his North Face jacket over his head to conceal his identity and inhaled deeply, glad to be breathing in something other than the stagnant air of the metro.

The fresh smell of dew-dampened mown grass hit his face, and he took secret, girly pleasure in it until his hay fever kicked in. He buried his nose in the crook of his elbow and sneezed. The sound of the sneeze rang through the quiet streets and he froze, hoping the noise hadn't drawn any unwanted attention. Even though the virus had been eradicated and the world was slowly rebuilding, people remained weird about things like that.

He tugged his hood lower over his eyes as he cast a nervous look around. A black sedan zipped by, kicking bits of crumbled asphalt onto the sidewalk. Their heads down, a handful of pedestrians on the other side of the pothole-riddled street hustled about their business. With the change in government people didn't drag their asses around the city after dark anymore unless they had to, and therefore paid little to no attention to him.

Annoyingly enough, his nose tickled again and he pinched the bridge with his thumb and forefinger to ward off another sneeze. He cursed under his breath until the sensation passed, then shook his head to clear it. Needing to get away from the sudden influx of allergens, he hurried his steps, rounded the corner, and crossed the empty street.

Just up ahead he spotted Tim Hortons, but when his nose started running faster than his feet, he sniffed and rubbed his watery eyes. Christ. First the buzzing noise, now this. He hadn't had an allergy attack since he was a kid, and hoped like hell the immune disorder wasn't kicking back in.

Then again, he'd take an allergy attack over the buzzing any day. That was probably an impending aneurism.

He needed a distraction, something to take his mind off project Hollow Man, the greater purpose River hoped her new technology would serve, and the peculiar way it made him feel when he'd taken it for a test drive. His stomach tightened at the thought of projecting again. He couldn't even remove the damn implant himself. She'd inserted it with magic.

Disturbed by the thought of that, Nick pulled open the heavy glass doors to the coffee shop. The scent of a fresh brew filled his nostrils and helped push back the sniffles. As his nose dried he stepped inside and studied the brightly lit although empty shop, an instinctive response since technically, he was a wanted man and who knew when Supercop might be on the beat? His gaze zeroed in on the bored bleached blonde with the great rack behind the counter. As his glance collided with hers, she perked up and smiled.

Hello.

He'd found his distraction. Her name tag said *Angie.*

Angie leaned forward, offering him a view of her creamy, ample cleavage. Everything about her screamed easy.

He wasn't normally a gambling man, and the fear of his dick falling off from some sexually transmitted disease was usually enough to tame his arousal. But it had been far too long since he'd last had a chance to enjoy a smoking-hot double double. Since River wasn't interested in picking up where their relationship had left off, he was forced to look elsewhere.

There was no denying that he missed sleeping with River. But ever since she'd bedded down with that bastard Hawkins, at the end of the day she no longer had any interest in him. He'd been pretty much walking around with a raging hard-on ever since.

What exactly did Hawkins have that he didn't? The bastard had screwed River using his body. The real kick in the ass was that he hadn't even gotten to enjoy it.

He walked up to the counter. Angie, who looked as if she'd just stepped out of the centerfold of one of the dirty magazines that he'd kept under his mattress as a teenager, gave him a smile full of promise and the peter in his shorts sprouted another inch. He had three emergency condoms in his jacket pocket. He'd been hoping to use them with River, but hey, she'd had her chance.

"What can I get you?" Angie asked. Her gaze shot to his crotch and she lifted a brow.

Angie, he'd bet, was earning extra tips during her downtime. He could spare the change.

He fished around inside his front pocket, grabbed a fifty, and with the tip of his index finger, slid the bill across the polished countertop and thanked God River had taught the little kids how to pick pockets. And that they didn't know what a fifty was.

He let his glance fall to her double-D breasts, which

threatened to pop out of her bland brown work uniform if she bent over much farther, and his pants tented in response.

He pitched his voice low and answered, "Large double double. That's what I like."

He slowly let his glance track back to her pretty face, and the seductive look in her smoldering eyes told him she knew he wasn't referring to the fresh pot of coffee percolating on the heating rack behind her.

She picked up the fifty and slid it into the pocket of her uniform. He wondered how many guys she'd slept with. If he didn't think it would earn him a slap and a lonely night battling a raging erection, he'd ask to see her latest round of blood work. Hell, maybe he'd just dip her in vinegar before he did her.

Her big brown eyes locked on his and she gave him a dirty smile full of promise. He in turn gave her a once-over, looking for any telltale signs of infection. Hot body aside, her shiny blond hair looked clean and well cared for. Her peach skin was clear of blemishes, and she had plump pink lips designed for kissing. Him. Every-where. Now.

She looked healthy, and with the way his dick was doing all the thinking, that was good enough for him. He had condoms.

"What time do you get off?" he asked.

Cupping her chin in her hands, she leaned on her el-bows and eyed him with warmth. "The important ques-tion is, what time do *you*?"

Nick looked around. The place was empty, and judging by the traffic on the street, was likely to stay that way for a while. He was a good-looking guy. He'd bet Angie made certain he got his money's worth.

He lifted the hinged panel in the countertop and stepped through to the other side.

"There's no time like the present."

◆ ◆

After a few frustrating days of listening to Nick complain about having to practice with Hollow Man, River had fallen into the sleep of the utterly exhausted.

Sleep, however, brought its own set of problems. When she was overtired, the way she was now, she dreamed of Hawk.

But never before had she dreamed of him with this level of clarity. The man in this dream tonight was new to her, although not unfamiliar.

She'd seen Hawk before when she'd entered his thoughts to help pull him from a nightmare, but now there were differences. He was tall and broad shouldered, but the haircut had changed. He wore his dark hair in a short, military cut. His face, angular without being harsh, had deeper lines than she remembered etched around a strong, full mouth, as if he'd spent the last months under enormous stress and forgotten how to smile. *Grim,* she thought. He'd brought that quality to both Sever and Nick. It made him look dangerous.

Black eyes filled with heat raked over her hungrily. If she hadn't known him, that look would have frightened her. Instead, it spiked her desire. She'd missed him terribly, and here, in her dreams, she could freely admit it. She braced herself, not knowing what kind of state he was in, not knowing what he'd gone through these last four months. That those months hadn't been easy showed on his face.

"Mellita." The endearment rolled off his tongue like a caress.

Her heart punched into her throat at the achingly familiar sound of his voice. A bone-deep need ripped through her soul. The past few months of worrying and wondering hadn't been easy for her either, but all that mattered was that Hawk had finally reached out to her.

"You okay?" she whispered.

"Yeah, baby. I'm better than okay," he said. "You dream about me."

The male satisfaction in his words made her laugh. It also made her want to bring his ego down a notch or two. Regardless of the reason for his months of silence, she wanted him to suffer for them, at least a little.

"I dream about Red Bull, too."

He reached for her. "Good. Because I know how much you love that stuff."

River had gotten very good at manipulating her dreams into a semblance of reality, thanks to both her magic and her experience with programming games. Hawk, however, was a master.

He pulled her into his arms. As he held her to him,

she felt the walls going up around them. He was building a safe house and blocking everything from it but her. Blackness enveloped them.

Their thoughts had joined, but he didn't want her to see his. What was he hiding from her?

She found she didn't care. The freedom from months of worrying and wondering, of being strong for others, left her limp with relief. His presence scattered her thoughts. The brush of his soul against hers made her melt. This was a dream. She wanted only to enjoy it.

He brushed his lips over her cheek before burying his face in her hair. The tantalizing sweep of his mouth over her flesh elevated her pulse. "We don't have much time," he said.

With a touch that was both commanding and soft, his rough hands raced over her body, pulling her impossibly closer. When his eager lips found hers, her thoughts shattered into fragments. A tremor shot through her as she went up on her tiptoes to meet his mouth.

As their bodies connected, it was all she could do to inflate her lungs. Overwhelmed by his ruggedness, she felt desire twist inside her. She took a moment to absorb the magnificent sight of him, then decided he was by far the most handsome man she'd ever set eyes on. She ran her hands over his sculptured cheeks, his firm lips, and his short, spiky hair, pulling him harder against her small frame. And still, she was unable to get him close enough.

Hawk let loose a low, tortured moan, his undisguised need bombarding her body with unbridled desire.

She needed him, too.

Their warm breaths mingled as sexual tension rippled the air, the scent of their combined arousals teasing her senses, eliciting a shiver from deep within her core. Hawk's nostrils flared as he inhaled the tang, then dipped his head and parted River's lips with his tongue. He spread her knees with his legs, and the hard planes of his body pressed against her as he breathed a kiss into her mouth. His sweet breath fanning her face, her sex muscles clenched.

She could not have programmed anything better than this, not even with magic.

Without conscious thought River gave in to her emotions, and unable to help herself as an overwhelming need careened through her bloodstream and demanded the Guardian's undivided attention, refusing to settle for anything less, she dissolved against him.

Famished from four long months apart, agonizing months of aching to feel his protective arms around her, River eagerly returned the kiss. Moisture broke out on her skin as their tongues touched and dueled, vying for dominance.

Trembling from head to toe, she felt raw hunger claw at her insides, and in turn Hawk deepened the kiss and ravished her body without moderation, his hands pushing, pulling, demanding, claiming, his hips moving and grinding sensually against hers, letting her know in no uncertain terms what he wanted.

Bundled in his strong arms, she pressed her breasts against his chest, the telltale hardening of her nipples in turn letting him know how much she'd missed his touch. His kisses. The feel of his strong, naked body sliding over hers.

She palmed his sinewy muscles, then moaned in protest when he inched back and broke the intimate connection. But when he cupped her face and stared at her with those dark, intense eyes, far more tortured and troubled than she'd ever seen them, her heart trip-hammered. Whatever had kept him from her, without a doubt it hadn't been easy for him.

Her stomach soured and a wave of anger trickled through her blood. The loneliness had been more unbearable than she'd let herself admit. She wanted to know what he'd been doing all this time, why he hadn't come back to her. She opened her mouth, ready to ask the questions that had been plaguing her since he'd shed Nick's body and returned to his own.

The heat smoldering in the depths of his deep brown eyes when his glance locked on hers stole her words. His hands traced the pattern of her face, skimming the outline of her jaw.

"River," he murmured with longing as his lips crashed down on hers, swallowing her ability to formulate an intelligent thought.

As her mind shut down and her body betrayed her, she melted into him, her anger forgotten as it morphed into passion. She could feel his arousal pressing against her stomach, feel the need pumping through his veins and reaching out to her in ways that magically strengthened the powerful bond between them. Her soul wrapped around his and held it tight, and then, nothing else mattered. Nothing but this man and this moment, and her need for him to love her again, the way he did best.

Hawk drew back to study her. Calluses scraped her neck as he brushed her hair from her shoulders, exposing her flesh to his scrutiny. The concern in his gaze as he examined her sent ripples trickling along her spine. His inspection of her face and body was slow, careful, and thorough. Then, seemingly satisfied, he wet his lips and let his eyes drop to her mouth.

His voice hitched. "You're so beautiful, River." An invisible band tightened around her heart and she ached, deep in her core. The need in his tone touched her soul.

"Hawk," she rushed out, suddenly breathless as the heat of his flesh curled around hers with warm familiarity. His hands slid over her skin and want burned a lazy path through her body as his earthy, arousing scent fueled the desire inside her. Instantly distracted by his touch, and dizzy with need, she felt as if she were dreaming, drifting on another plane, and had to engage her knees to keep herself upright. The sensation alarmed her. "What's happening to me?"

Instead of answering, he anchored her to him and said, "I've missed you. By the Mother, how I've missed you." The warm intimacy in his manner spoke of unchecked emotions and she wasn't prepared for the impact his needs would have on her own.

As her gaze panned his face, taking in the turbulence

in his dark eyes, their emotions collided. His burning lips brushed over her face with explosive hunger, derailing both their abilities to concentrate.

His hands went to her clothes. She wore a man's shirt that draped to her knees. One of his, she guessed. She wondered what else he found sexy. There was a lot they still didn't know about each other, even after all they'd been through together.

He tugged at the hem of the shirt and emotions took over where her brain had left off. Her head fell back, lost to his touch, and she let him peel the shirt from her body and toss it to the floor. A lacy white bra followed.

He brushed a thumb over her puckered nipple and she arched into him. Her breasts felt heavy, achy, and when he lowered his head and took possession of one hard nub, greedily drawing it into his hot mouth, she bit back a breathy sigh, positive she'd died and found heaven.

She raked her fingers through his short hair and held him to her, never wanting the moment to end. His hands slipped around her waist and he gathered her into his arms. With his eyes fixed on hers, they exchanged a long, heated look, one that set a fire to her body that only Hawk could extinguish.

He carried her to a king-size bed, one she didn't recognize and could only assume was his. She glanced around the room. It was decorated completely in varying shades of white.

"It was like this when I moved in," he said with a

slight lift of his shoulders when he saw the curious light in her eyes. "I've never bothered to redecorate."

He laid her out and she spread her arms and legs, enjoying the soft feel of cotton sheets beneath her. She rolled and buried her face in his pillow, drawing his distinct scent deep into her lungs.

Hawk gave a low, throaty growl, pulling her attention back to him. Intense eyes stared down at her, so dark and full of desire that it rattled her to her core. She crooked her finger, beckoning him close.

He stood back and ripped his clothes from his body and the sound of River's indrawn breath cut through the silence. He stalked toward her and sat on the edge of the mattress, his eyes cast on her in thorough concentration. River ran her fingers along his arm as he took his time, his dark inspection pausing near her naval.

"Hey," she murmured, her hands lacing with his.

With that Hawk bent and dropped a soft kiss onto her parted lips. "It's been too long," he whispered into her mouth, his voice flooding her with warmth.

"Too long," River agreed.

His muscles bunched as he shifted and a moment later the full weight of his body pressed over hers and for the first time in a long time she felt safe, as if she were home.

Hawk slipped his hand between their bodies and played with the straps of her panties. A tremor raced down her spine and she arched up, impatience thrumming through her. Understanding her urgent demands, he climbed between her legs. He fingered the soft, lacy material and tossed her a sexy grin before stripping them from her hips, leaving her naked, warm, and wanting.

He then pressed his mouth to hers, a slow, easy kiss that lacked the urgency of earlier but was just as powerful and mind numbing. His fingers danced over her flesh, burning her skin and forcing her to draw quick, shallow breaths.

He pitched his voice low as his eyes caressed her with sultry heat. "I need to be inside you."

River widened her legs. "I need that, too."

She gripped his head and pulled him to her. His mouth found hers and they exchanged a needy, passionate kiss before he broke away and ran his lips over her neck and breasts. He made a skilled pass with his tongue, and that first sweet touch to her distended nipple drew a whimper from her throat.

His hands traced her curves and he shifted his weight. With agonizing slowness, warm fingers trailed over her thighs, then he cupped her bare sex. As a surge of need flooded her veins, River sucked in a tight breath. Heat pooled in her body, filling her with a restless ache.

"Hawk, please."

He inserted a finger inside her. He moved it slowly, in and out, in and out, preparing her for his girth. She widened her legs and bucked against him, her sex growing slicker, her body flushing hotly.

"Please what?" His voice dropped to a thread.

Before she could answer his mouth came down on hers hard and she sensed his growing urgency. He positioned himself between her legs and a fever rose in her as she arched up to meet him.

River let out a little gasp as he offered her an inch, but with her body shaking from want, and demanding she answer the urges, she wrapped her legs around him and pulled him in. He growled out loud and threw his head back as he sank into her heat.

Joining them as one he buried himself fully inside her and when she cried out, he began to move urgently over her body. Moisture sealed their skin together as energy arced between them, and the faint peppery scent of sage, River's magic, drifted in the air.

Soft light spilled over their bodies and the look on his face as he made love to her stopped her heart. River threaded her fingers through his hair and brought his mouth back to hers for a deep, soul-searing kiss. His tongue savored the inside of her mouth and his blatant need drove her beyond the brink of sanity.

His hands gripped her hips for leverage as he plunged into her, his need fierce, demanding. River drew deep, gulping breaths as her body tightened, the sweet friction pushing her to the precipice. He touched her in such familiar ways, stirring things so deep inside her that she had to draw on every ounce of strength she possessed to keep herself sane.

When his hand slipped between their bodies and stroked her swollen bundle of nerves, she gripped the sheets and cried out. Her body shuddered, and her sex clenched around his thickness as she tumbled into orgasm.

"Mellita," Hawk groaned, and the tenderness in the endearment produced a corresponding fullness in her chest near the vicinity of her heart.

Her breath left her lungs as she wrapped her arms around him and held him to her, his hard chest pressing against her swollen breasts. He stilled inside her and his mouth found hers as he gave himself over to his release.

He buried his face in her neck, his breathing labored and erratic. River lightly brushed her nails over his back, and he shuddered as she enjoyed the feel of his flesh.

"I missed that," she whispered.

Hawk collapsed beside her, cupping her face with one hand and dropping a soft kiss onto her lips. She examined him greedily. Even though their lovemaking had given them both a boost of energy, and Hawk was the strongest man she knew, the darkness in his eyes spoke of strain. Something was wrong. River snuggled in close, wanting to ask, but as Hawk's body relaxed she could feel his mind drift, sleep pulling at him.

She allowed herself to drift off as well. It had been months since she'd had enough rest.

Heavy knocking jolted her awake.

She jerked upright and cocked her head to the side. "Hawk?"

His gaze flew to her face and in a swift move he put a silencing finger to her lips. She stilled, tasting his tension as it saturated the air.

"Don't answer that," he said. "Not yet."

With a new urgency in his expression he opened his mouth as if he wanted to say something more, but then he fisted his hands and stayed silent.

Their time in the safe house was up.

As sobering reality inched its way back into her brain, she thought of her brother, the Demons, and a world in crisis, and knew she'd been gone for too long. She didn't want whoever was tapping at her door to discover her like this, and knew she needed to make her way back. She extricated herself from Hawk's arms and eased away, immediately missing his touch, his warmth.

Tension visible on his face, Hawk cupped her elbow and held her still. "Don't open the door, River. Not yet."

She met his gaze, undecided. She had so many questions, so many things she wanted to discuss with him. The knock sounded again, louder this time. More demanding. People were counting on her. "I'm sorry. But I have to go."

Possessiveness filled his eyes as she rose from the bed. She felt him watching her as she pulled his shirt over her head and slipped her hands into the sleeves.

"I'm coming for you," he promised as her palm touched the door.

◆ ◆

River's eyes fluttered open, the thick darkness disorienting her as she tried to gather her scattered senses from the effects of her dream. The knocking was now accompanied by the sound of someone calling her name.

She sat up in bed and reached for the lamp. Light flooded the room and she blinked several times as her eyes adjusted. Everything around her reeked of familiarity. She had built this room using magic and creativity, plus a bit of thievery on the part of the Demons. She'd wanted a home for them all, particularly the youngest ones who'd never known the comfort and joy of simple luxuries. The ancient subway system had become a true haven for them.

Jake opened her door. "Are you in here?" he asked, poking his head in.

River smoothed her hair away from her flushed face, patting the loose strands into the braid she wore for sleeping, and hoped the effects of her dream weren't obvious to the world.

Hawk had seduced her from a world away. She was impressed. But so many other emotions were involved as well. Four months of worry couldn't simply be dismissed.

"What is it?" she asked, noting with relief that at least she had on her pajamas.

She saw the worry on her brother's face, and her dream was perhaps not forgotten so much as set aside for later examination.

"Nick has gone topside."

CHAPTER FOUR

♦

Hawk stepped from his apartment building onto the busy street of the nation's capital city. He hadn't slept all that well after his night spent with River.

He hadn't felt this alive in a long time either, so the tradeoff was worth it.

He pushed the memories aside so he could concentrate on the matter at hand. This morning meeting with the Great Lords was overdue. He wanted to be with River again. He had chosen his team, and he believed he had chosen well. He'd been patient, and done everything asked of him, all for the purpose of returning for her. That time had come.

Being hostile with the Great Lords over what they had done to him wasn't going to help speed things along. He could overlook it. For now.

The sun shone brightly. He walked the streets from his apartment to the Hall of the Great Lords, pausing in the center of the square for a blessing from the Mother.

He knelt at the base of the statue of a beautiful woman with an urn in her arms. Water flowed from the urn to pool at the Mother's feet. The water represented life and contained residual properties of magic, a gift from the Fae a very long time ago. The statue reminded him of River and made his lungs ache with longing for her.

He closed his eyes. He loved his home, deeply and with passion. This was a world of peace and tranquillity. The entire time he'd been imprisoned, it had served as a beacon of hope to him. Even in the days after the deaths of his wife and daughter, when he'd thought he would never be able to feel love again, he had not lost his faith in either his people or their purpose.

But at some point, he didn't know when, the Great Lords had lost sight of that purpose. The knowledge that the arrogant bastards had planted a bomb in his head and were sending him on a suicide mission meant he knew where his loyalties now lay.

They lay with the people, both Guardian and Fae. Hawk didn't play in a political arena. He would leave that to Achala. Now that the Fae leader knew of the training of demolition men, and the bomb, the first nail in the coffin of their eons-old alliance had already been driven. If Hawk allowed the bomb in his head to go off and River's world was destroyed, not only would she be lost but the Guardian alliance with the Fae would also be dead. So much was at stake.

He dipped his fingers into the waters of the fountain and immediately felt a jolt of magic, along with an accompanying sense that the Mother was pleased. It startled and disoriented him, and made him uneasy, as did anything out of the ordinary these days, but as he looked around him there was nothing he could see that might cause him alarm. People continued to go about their business. No demons or imps walked among them.

He accepted the blessing and rose to his feet, wanting to linger in the sunshine and the grace of the Mother, but not daring to do so any longer.

He loped up the stone steps of the pillared hall and entered through the arched doors. A page was waiting to escort him to the Great Lords' meeting chamber.

The Great Lords sat at a long table on a raised dais at the far end of a vast, otherwise empty room. The ring of the heels of his dress shoes on the marble floor echoed off the walls and high ceiling, and he made no attempt to dampen the sound. He'd thought it would be easy for him to hide the depth of his anger at their planting of a bomb in his head. Perhaps if he'd learned of it before his time spent with the Dark Lord, it would have been. Or even if they'd been more receptive to River and what she was. Now he found he had to work at it.

One other person had joined the Great Lords at their table. Dr. Robert Jess, the man who had replaced Spence as the head of cryonics research, was well known to Hawk. He sat to the right of the First Lord, a fact that spoke volumes regarding his influence. His attendance didn't surprise Hawk so much as make him wary. To his knowledge, the meeting today had nothing to do with cryonics.

He didn't much care for the man either. It didn't take a lot of intelligence to figure out who was responsible for leaving him in stasis longer than what was considered safe. If not for Spence pulling him, Hawk might be there yet.

"Good morning, Colonel Hawkins," the First Lord said. "I see you have made application to finalize your team." He consulted his notes on the touch pad set into the tabletop in front of him. "Three names. All good people."

They were, and all with different qualifications. Major Faran would be second in command. He was also their virus expert, something Hawk had thought they might need when on a world still recovering from a pandemic.

The other two were captains—Aris and Lilla. Word had it Lilla wouldn't be a captain much longer. She was in line for promotion. Hawk intended to see that she made it back to receive it.

"They've worked with me before." The Great Lords would know that, of course. "Now that the team is assembled, I'm ready to proceed."

"In due time, Colonel Hawkins." The First Lord turned to the scientist beside him. "Dr. Jess, Colonel Hawkins should hear the results of your tests."

Dr. Jess tapped his touch pad and scrolled through his notes, reviewing the data out loud while Hawk stood patiently at ease.

"In conclusion," Dr. Jess finally said, "it's been determined that while physically Colonel Hawkins is in perfect health, his psychological state remains questionable. There are indications of paranoia."

At first Hawk thought he'd misheard. "I'm sorry," he said. He kept his voice calm. To anyone who truly knew him, however, he'd become very dangerous. "Could you repeat that last part to me?"

Dr. Jess appeared ill at ease. The First Lord stepped in, his expression and tone placating. "For four months you have refused all of Dr. Jess's requests to access your memories."

"My brain was monitored closely while I was in stasis," Hawk reminded them all, his gaze sweeping the table. Three of the Great Lords avoided making eye contact, a fact he found interesting. "I've been debriefed on six separate occasions. My security clearance grants me the right to refuse any such requests for access to my memories under these circumstances, because they amount to nothing more than an invasion of privacy. Dr. Jess is a scientist. Perhaps he doesn't understand military law."

The First Lord's expression cooled. "We know what the laws are, Colonel Hawkins. However, we have rights, too. So do the people you've requested accompany you. We have a duty to ensure their safety."

Which is why you're sending them on a suicide mission with me, you son of a bitch, Hawk thought but didn't say. He knew he wasn't going to be refused permission to go on this expedition, not unless they had someone else with a bomb planted in his or her brain. Therefore, he was interested to see where the Great Lords would head with this when he continued to refuse Dr. Jess access. He also wondered what they were after, because it was obvious they wanted something from him.

Was it his memories of River?

"With all due respect," Hawk replied, "the people I've chosen are soldiers. They understand the risks. They were also given the option to refuse this assignment. None of them did." He paused and looked around the table again. "I will not allow access to my memories, not for any reason."

There were a few beats of silence as they gave him a moment to change his mind. Dr. Jess's round, fishlike eyes widened to express disapproval. He looked as if he wanted to say something more but didn't quite dare.

"Very well," the First Lord finally conceded. "You have your team, with the addition of two others. You'll leave tonight."

"Two others?" Hawk asked. He didn't like what he was hearing, although again, he was careful to hide it.

"Major Riley and Major Ever. I believe you know them."

He did. These men were excellent. He might have chosen them himself if he'd worked more closely with either of them before. He also doubted if they'd ever worked directly for the Great Lords. That would be too difficult a relationship for them to hide. And to his knowledge, neither of them had received training as demolition men.

But he could no longer be certain. Hawk hated un-certainty.

Much as he opposed the idea, he was going to have to appeal to Achala to probe all of his team's minds to ensure none of them had been implanted with bombs.

And while bombs were a problem he'd need to inves-tigate, so was the power of suggestion. The Great Lords had given him two team members he could not possibly object to, but who might not share his way of thinking as to who, and what, River was. That meant there were two more people on his team he would need to win over to her side.

For her sake, he would make that appeal to Achala. He had a link to him because the spiritual leader had been inside his head. If Hawk was the one to pursue that link, then he thought he could control it. He wouldn't really know for sure until he tried, and he couldn't very well try while standing in the sunlit meeting chamber of the Hall of the Great Lords.

He had roughly ten hours to make the attempt.

"They're excellent men and I'm happy to have them along," Hawk said to the Great Lords, although from a management perspective, having two more majors on the team could prove to be a handicap. "However, they'll need to understand that Major Faran is my second in command."

"Of course," the First Lord said. "It's your team, Colonel Hawkins." He turned back to his touch pad. "Thank you for your time. We will see you off at nineteen hundred hours."

He had been dismissed. Hawk snapped off a salute and followed the page from the chamber.

Once on the street, he turned as if going to Headquarters. Instead, he ducked into the kaffa shop across the way.

He grabbed a mug of the thick, rich-smelling dark

brew and took it to an empty table in one corner of the tiny shop. It brought back memories of his dead wife, and this time, he found he was able to smile. Cassie would have wanted him to move on. He cradled the warm mug in his hands and wondered if she would have liked River. His smile widened. Probably not. Nobody liked the competition. He hated that little shit Nick Sutton, so why should he expect Cassie to like River?

Hawk was used to the looks he got from people when he wore his dress uniform. They might stare, but they wouldn't approach him. Technically, he was working. No one interfered with a high-ranking officer at work.

No one would suspect him of trying to contact a Fae spiritual leader in such a public place either.

Even though the shop wasn't overly warm, he'd started to sweat under his uniform. Crisos. He was like a child, allowing his phobias to get the best of him. He hadn't chosen this kaffa shop because he was worried about discovery. He'd chosen it because it was familiar, a place with happy memories. He also hadn't wanted to be alone when he tried this. He was too afraid he'd lose himself. Here, he had already memorized his surroundings, and if he had to, he could reorient himself in reality.

He looked into his mug and concentrated on River's face. Then he touched the part of his thoughts Achala had found the most interesting. Once he'd done that, he took a deep breath and sent out the mental equivalent of a shout.

The response was instantaneous, and very startled.
Colonel Hawkins?

Now that contact had been established, Hawk focused
his attention on keeping his thoughts away from the Fae,
granting him access only to the words Hawk wanted him
to hear.

We have a problem.

Achala listened politely and attentively. *What time
do you leave?*

Nineteen hundred hours.

*Meet me in the first-floor men's room of the Academy
fifteen minutes prior to that. Can you make certain the
room is empty? No one must see me.*

Achala broke the connection before Hawk could question whether or not that gave them enough time. He
looked around him, noting with relief the little things
about the shop he'd committed to memory that reaf-
firmed his reality—a sketch on the wall, and a few grains
of sugar on the floor under the counter.

He tried not to worry that he was creating a potential international incident by asking the Fae for help in
this matter. If Achala were caught, he would lose his
standing with Hawk's people. This, too, might signal
the end of their worlds' alliance, but this time, through
the Fae.

Hawk would have to make certain they weren't caught.
He reminded himself that they were doing this to help
set a dark world on a brighter path, and more important,
to save the soul of a Fae.

They were doing this for River.

He drank his kaffa without tasting it. Then he walked from the shop and headed for the Academy.

◆ ◆

For four months James Peters, former police officer, dragged an ass that had surpassed middle age and progressed to old over arctic tundra to make it here—"here" being Ellesmere Island, unless he missed his guess—all because of a man named David Weston and the unanswered questions surrounding him.

River Weston deserved answers to those questions. She was one of the few people trying to do right in the world. He hadn't liked being the one to tell her that her father wasn't all he had seemed.

As Peters stood on the outskirts of the island's abandoned military research and weather station complex, he thought it might be midday or shortly after, based on the noises coming from his stomach. Other than that he had no idea what time of day it might really be. The arctic sun's odd progression in the sky remained an enigma to him.

Twenty-four hours of daylight more than made up for any uncertainty, however. As did the little patches of flowers, colorful mosses and lichen starting their slow spring creep across the wide expanse of gray tundra. The lack of people out here was another plus.

So why he should feel as if he was being watched right now caused him a moment's concern.

He inhaled deeply, cold searing his nostrils, distracted from his paranoia by the freshness of the crisp air and the broad expanse of uninterrupted sky. His breath puffed on an exhale as a sense of satisfaction settled deep into his soul, startling him because of its unexpectedness.

He'd once thought his soul long gone. The fact that it had been returned to him was thanks to River's friend Andy, so he felt he owed her. He'd also been grateful to her.

At first.

Now he wanted to get her out of his head. She was driving him crazy to the point that he was afraid to sleep. Finding himself on Ellesmere Island, admiring the scenery like some drug-hazed hippie, following the trail of a dead man, was a case in point. He was too old for this shit.

Peters shucked the heavy backpack of provisions he carried and eyed the ramshackle buildings. He didn't have fond memories of the military and had no idea why he was feeling all warm and fuzzy right now. The lying bastards had been conducting genetic and bio-engineering experiments on people and animals for decades.

He'd never believed any of the bullshit stories they fed the public about weather studies here on the island. David Weston had been no meteorologist.

He scanned the landscape. River and Andy both thought a Guardian army was coming with the purpose of wiping out Earth's technology. Peters hoped they were

right, because while River didn't get it, Andy had. Someone needed to stop the Amos Kayes of this world.

Let the aliens come. They could start their purge on
Earth's technology right here.

He stretched, arching his back and rolling his shoulders, and almost walked off and left his pack where it was
while he looked around because really, who was going to
steal it?

Then he remembered that the area might not have
human inhabitants any longer, but it did have predators.
Freaking big polar bears, not to mention arctic wolves,
so leaving food around unattended was an open invitation to dinner. He didn't plan on becoming dessert.

He unfastened his rifle from the pack before slipping
its straps over the sleeves of his parka. The patch of skin
between his shoulder blades continued to itch, so he'd
rather have the rifle in his hands.

He counted about twenty buildings, then decided to
start with the largest only because he had to start somewhere. What appeared to be a signal satellite station sat
off by itself on a low mountain overlooking the complex. Peters regarded it thoughtfully. Perhaps the military wasn't really shitting people after all.

Before he gave them the benefit of the doubt though,
he'd have to know what they were trying to transmit or
receive.

That feeling of being watched didn't disappear as he
walked along the dirt road that cut through the complex, and he didn't like being so exposed, but since he'd

be visible for miles if he ran it didn't really make any difference. He shrugged it off as simple paranoia. He hadn't seen any signs of humanity for weeks. No one could exist out here for long, not without a supply chain system. He'd managed to make it here by raiding emergency caches the government had stored in carefully marked cairns across the tundra. Even in its sealed packets and with the added boost of an extended deep freeze, the food had been so old it was barely edible.

He approached the building with caution even though his feelings of happiness and well-being were increasing. Since he wasn't exactly the type of guy to burst into song, this odd sense of euphoria drummed a warning. But Andy had directed him here, and if she'd wanted to finish him off she could have done so long before now.

The building, a big steel-sheeted affair with paint that had once been bright yellow but now bore a coating of dirt, was unlocked. Locking anything out here was pointless. Who would they need to keep out?

Another thing Peters noticed was the lack of rust. Since humidity was low, and the waters around the island thickly crusted in ice, the effects of oxidation were minimal. These buildings, while by no means miracles of modern construction, could stand for decades more, centuries even, under these conditions.

But it was the lack of resistance when he opened the door that threw him off. Even without oxidation, if this station had been abandoned for decades as claimed, he'd have expected the door hinges to be stiffer than this.

He shrugged it off. He was an aging man who had been given a second chance with his soul. If this was how life would end for him, then he would die content. He just didn't want to end up inside something's stomach if he didn't have to. The top of the food chain held greater appeal.

The door of the building opened into a foyer and makeshift security desk. Tiny square windows high on the exterior walls offered the barest of lighting. The foyer divided off into two long corridors, left and right. Peters chose left.

He caught movement out of the corner of his eye, a skittering in the shadows that disappeared into a recess in the corridor, and he jumped. His heart hammered in his chest.

What the hell was that?

He started in that direction, his rifle gripped tight in his hand. Swinging double doors met him as he peered into the recess. Other than that, nothing. Not even a sound to be heard. The doors remained motionless, undisturbed. He started to relax, his heart rate slowly returning to normal.

Then he looked down. Through the wide crack between the bottoms of the doors and the ugly green floor tiling, the shadow of two feet could be seen for all of a second before vanishing. He rubbed his eyes with his finger and thumb. The level of warm fuzzies in his system continued to rise, along with the beating of his heart, as if his body were receiving two very different sets of signals. Perhaps the weeks of isolation were finally getting to him. Even though he wasn't especially outgoing, people as a whole were sociable beings and required a certain level of human interaction whether they liked it or not.

Rattled by the possibility he'd gone nuts, he pushed open the doors, deciding being proven sane would be worth getting eaten.

The room was a lounge. It held four sofas, two pool tables, a beer fridge, an old coffee machine, and a wide-screen television. Doors opened off it in several directions.

Again, he saw no signs of life. He wondered if every impending heart attack victim felt this freaking happy, or only the crazy ones.

He walked into the room, the doors swinging silently shut behind him, his rubber-soled boots squeaking against the floor tiles. His attention zeroed in on one of the sagging sofas. *There.*

He approached it with caution. He stopped alongside it and listened. Still nothing. Then he peered behind it.

He leapt back, his lungs and his heart catching fire.

"Jesus Fucking H. Christ," he whispered, clutching the rifle to his chest in a death grip.

◆ ◆

Hawk, dressed in standard military-issue fatigues intended for field duty, was in the men's room of the Academy a few minutes before the appointed time. The room was empty, as promised. He had put a CLOSED FOR MAINTENANCE sign on the door and locked it behind him.

A few moments later Achala appeared, lean and trim in his black clothing.

The Fae had a definite presence to him.

"Why the men's room?" Hawk asked.

"I have to get close to your team if I'm to read them for you," the older man replied. "The only way I can get close to them all is when they are in the same room. That would be the transporter room, and if I remember correctly, it's directly above this one." The message he telegraphed Hawk was meant to reassure him.

Hawk felt anything but.

"Let's get this over with. We don't have much time," Hawk said.

"In a minute." The Fae regarded him. "First, I'd like something from you in exchange. I want to know a little about my granddaughter."

Hawk supposed he should have suspected why Achala had left so little time in which to examine the minds of his team. He'd assumed the Fae leader had other duties requiring his attention. Instead, Achala intended to use the short time frame as leverage to get information.

"It depends on what you want to know about her," Hawk replied cautiously. "Your Grace," he added belatedly.

The Fae held up one long-fingered, elegant hand. "Nothing that might harm her." His voice softened. "I want to know the color of her hair and eyes. What her personality is like. Is she happy? Has her life been difficult?"

With a start of understanding, Hawk realized the Fae had opened his emotions to him so that he could see how much it meant to him to know something about his dead daughter's child.

Unbidden, unwanted sympathy welled in Hawk. Even though Guardians had a far different relationship with their adult children than did the Fae, they, too, loved and protected their children. The feeling he had that he'd failed his own young daughter would eat at him for the rest of his life.

"River is beautiful," Hawk said, the words pried from him against his better judgment. "Her eyes are blue. She has black hair, and she's small." He measured her approximate height from the floor with his hand.

He might have been profiling a stranger, and he could sense from Achala that his words were inadequate. He tried a little harder. "She has a lot of magic in her, but she prefers technology. She has a talent for both. She's kind, but she's not gentle. She loves the world she was raised on. I'm sorry, Your Grace. I'm not sure what else I can say."

Achala's expression settled into gracious and polite disappointment. "Thank you, Colonel Hawkins."

The spiritual leader of the Fae, a race of people who had guided Hawk's daughter's soul on its way to peace, deserved more than this from him. Achala should see that River, despite her mixed heritage, posed no threat to anyone. She was filled with the light of the Mother.

"I'll show you one thing," Hawk said quickly, before he could change his mind. He drew a deep breath and dredged up an image. It was one of his favorite memories of her, from when she'd moved around a safe house she'd created in the first level of her game.

River had built the room using Guardian technology and a generous amount of Fae magic. It was lush and green, bursting with earthy scents and the energy of blossoming life. But it was the peaceful look on River's beautiful face as she'd glided around the room with her blue eyes alight, absently touching things so that they flowered and grew, that stood out the most in his memories. He swallowed, his throat dry and painful, the memory hurting beyond belief because he'd tried desperately to hide it away for far too long.

He was impatient to leave. One night was not enough. He had to see her again. He needed to touch her and know she was real, and safe.

Achala cleared his throat, his eyes shining overly bright in the overhead light of the small room, and with a start Hawk wondered if he might possibly have shared more with River's grandfather than he'd intended.

"Thank you," Achala whispered. He drew himself straighter and closed his eyes, his mouth settling into a firm line of concentration.

Moments passed.

"I can't wait any longer," Hawk finally said to the

Fae, not liking to interrupt but knowing he was out of time. "They're waiting for me. I have to go."

The Fae opened his eyes. They were filled with worry.

"There are no demolition men on your team," he said. "But each and every one of them believes he—or she—is headed into danger."

Hawk reached for the sensor that activated the door. He caught a glimpse of his reflection in the mirror and saw the Fae's worry captured on his own harsh face. He wiped his thoughts clean.

"They are," Hawk replied. "And that's why we have to get River out."

CHAPTER FIVE

◆

In an old abandoned parking lot on the outskirts of town, Jake squared his Hollow Man form off against the Demons' leader, Dan, while the other young gang members stood on the sidelines and watched the fight unfold. It was early evening, although the sun had not yet set.

Only the older boys were physically present in the parking lot. Jake and the others sat in a circle in the underground subway's improvised training room.

In his head, Jake ran through all the things River had

told him the program could do. Level-one beginners—like him—could only send their projections to places on the city streets familiar to them. Staying in the subway kept them safe because their minds couldn't tell the difference between what was real and what wasn't.

When Dan trained the level ones to fight in Hollow form, they felt every blow. They couldn't die—River had programmed Hollow Man to cut out if their minds thought they were going to—but it hurt like hell when they got hit.

The level twos—like Dan and the older guys—could send their Hollow forms out to explore unfamiliar places. They could create and project any image they wanted their opponents to see. They could also stand inside their projection, as Dan did now, in the parking lot, and use it as a shield.

River said there were more levels to Hollow Man but she refused to teach them to anyone, even Dan, until the first two levels had been mastered by everyone.

Jake couldn't even get the hang of level one. He was holding the rest of the gang back.

As Dan angled his body and raised his arms, he stared at Jake with cool indifference. Jake studied Dan's stance, as well as the scars on his body, and couldn't help but think how much the gang leader resembled a boy from Jake's hometown. But thinking about his hometown only reminded him of the brother he'd recently lost, and as he faced his more experienced opponent, it was a distraction he couldn't afford.

Straightening his shoulders, Jake worked hard not to

think about Sam or the brutal way he'd been murdered. Instead he desensitized and focused fully on the man who was slowly closing the distance between them, the fearless guy more than capable of knocking Jake's head clear off his body if Jake wasn't careful.

Regardless of River, Dan would do it, too. Fine by him. Jake wasn't hiding behind his big sister.

He assumed a fighter's position, prepared to take full advantage of the training session that Dan was offering to him and a few of the other, newest recruits.

Even though he wasn't really outside in the vacant parking lot, and was projecting his thoughts from the safety of the training room, Jake could feel the warm sun on his skin and the beads of perspiration running down his face. When a salty drop landed in his eyes and blurred his vision he used the back of his hand to swipe his hair from his forehead, never once taking his eyes off his opponent. His fierce concentration seemed to please Dan, who'd stopped stalking and was motioning for Jake to come to him.

With slow, careful movements, Jake inched his projection forward, feeling his way with his feet and taking extra care not to trip on any of the broken glass and old beer cans littering the abandoned lot. He raised his arms, prepared to get in a few good hits of his own before Dan kicked his ass.

As he manipulated his hologram program a sudden, strange buzzing noise caught him by surprise and threw off his focus. Jake stopped midstrike and whacked his hand against his ear to stop the piercing sound. Frowning, he turned his head from side to side as the buzzing grew louder. This must be what Nick had been hearing.

That brief moment of distraction cost him. With his attention temporarily diverted, Dan delivered a round-house kick that sent Jake skidding across the hot black asphalt. His ass hit the ground with a thud and he didn't stop sliding until he crashed into a brick wall, his back-bone crunching under the impact.

He sat there for a long moment, working to shake off the daze as he looked at the scorching asphalt and the trail of blood and flesh left by his hands.

"Dammit." Jake's back ached in protest as he climbed to his feet, his hands stinging like a son of a bitch. He held them out in front of himself and tried not to wince when his glance met with slabs of pink meat that re-minded him of uncooked pork.

He gritted his teeth, hauled a piece of jagged glass out of his wrist, and tossed it aside. As it clattered on the ground he reminded himself that it wasn't real. None of this was real. Not the pain, not the blood, and definitely not the excruciating ache running the length of his spine.

So if it wasn't real, then why did it hurt so goddamn much?

Because it was real if he believed it was real. River had explained that to him twenty times at least.

Level twos didn't feel pain. Right now, Jake really wanted that level-two skill more than anything else.

Dan stepped up to him, and even though he'd taken a huge growth spurt a few months ago, Jake still had to look up to face the older boy.

Dark, penetrating eyes that had seen a lot over the years met his. "What happened?" Dan demanded, his voice lacking any kind of warmth. He was a warrior through and through. A survivor. And Jake wanted to be just like him.

Jake shaded the sun from his eyes as he met Dan's dark glare. Feeling foolish for allowing a simple little flaw in the hologram's program to distract him, he began, "The sun—"

"Kid," Dan said firmly. "Don't tell me the sun was in your eyes. You should be able to block it. You're in Hollow form."

"I know. I just haven't had much time—" Jake clamped his mouth shut and instantly wished he could take his words back. He hated the way the pathetic excuse sounded on his tongue, no matter how real it might be. In the underground gang world hierarchy ruled and as the newest member, Jake was at the bottom of the pecking order. Which meant that he'd been the last of the Demons to receive the implant, and therefore he'd had the least amount of time to learn how to manipulate it.

For a brief second Jake thought he saw understanding in the other boy's eyes, but he knew he had to be wrong. A guy who'd been abandoned and left to die on the streets at the age of four couldn't possibly understand weakness or failure.

"Tell me what really happened," Dan demanded, and Jake felt like the older boy was testing him.

He wasn't about to lie this time. Dan would know, and

lying came with punishment. "I heard a buzzing noise in my ear."

A strange look came over Dan's face and Jake wondered if he'd heard it, too, but that look was quickly replaced by annoyance. The hardness in his tone when he spoke made all the onlookers snap to attention.

"Distractions cost," he reminded as he tapped Jake's head with his index finger. "You need to get that through your skull. Your survival depends on it. So does mine."

"I understand."

"Understand this. I can't trust you to have my back if you can't get your shit together. It's a risk I'm not about to take."

Jake lifted his chin. "I won't—"

"Listen kid, just because River is your sister don't think that any one of us would get our asses shot off trying to save yours. On the streets, it's every man for himself. Everyone pulls his own weight. Got it?"

"Got it," Jake said.

"Good." A sword suddenly materialized in Dan's hand and he pressed the sharp tip to Jake's neck as he took on the grotesque form of a demon. "And if River wasn't your sister, I'd have killed your sorry ass by now," he added, his human voice sounding freakishly scary coming from the mouth of a monster. He pushed the sword tight against Jake's throat. "Fight me."

As Jake looked at the pair of red gleaming orbs staring down at him, and the hulking, twisted body standing over his much shorter frame, he tried to remind himself that this wasn't real.

"I said, fight me."

Jake felt the prick of the blade on his skin and briefly shut his eyes to concentrate, trying to morph into a frightening nighttime monster and produce a deadly weapon of his own. Weapons were level two, but if Dan could do it, Jake could, too.

Minutes ticked by and his frustration grew, which wasn't helping matters. Dammit. Jake wasn't about to admit failure. He had to do this. He just had to.

"Time's up, kid."

A split second later he felt Dan's foot connect with his chest, and once again he went hurtling backward. With the wind knocked out of him, he hit the ground and tried to remember how to breathe.

He gripped his midsection, each forced breath paining more than the initial blow. "Wait, I just need a few more minutes."

"I don't have a few minutes." Dan exhaled, morphed back to his human form, and turned his attention to the Demons watching the exchange. "Lesson's over."

Jake gasped for air and climbed to his feet. Dan turned back around and pressed the sword he still held against his neck. "Not you. You stay here until you figure it out."

The level ones disappeared from the parking lot, winking out of existence as they deactivated their implants, leaving Dan and the other level-two Demons behind.

The level twos who'd been practicing using their Hollow forms as a shield let them drop.

"Let's go get something to eat," Dan said to them.

Jake watched the older boys walk from the parking lot. No one looked back.

Once they were gone he paced the cracked asphalt, kicking at broken glass while trying to relax and not sound like a leaky balloon when he breathed. He was pretty sure Dan had cracked an imaginary rib with that last kick.

With frustration knotting his stomach, Jake stepped out onto the street and listened to a siren off in the distance as he leaned against the old abandoned drugstore. He tilted his head and watched a flock of birds fly by, and he wondered if he could morph into one and join them. Or better yet, maybe he could shift into a pterodactyl, like the one from Sam's favorite dinosaur book. That brought a frown to his face. If he couldn't even turn into a simple demon, how the hell was he supposed to turn into a flying reptile?

That last thought had him pushing off the brick wall and returning to the parking lot. Determined to figure out how to manipulate and fight in hologram form, he drew a deep breath and cleared his mind.

River and Dan had explained this to him over and over. She had enhanced the program so that he was here in the parking lot, but not in reality as he normally would know it. He could touch real things, but nothing could touch him unless he allowed it to happen. He had the ability to turn into anything his mind could create.

His sister was a freaking genius. If the ten-year-old Demons could grasp the concepts she had described in order to make the hologram work, there was no reason he couldn't.

He visualized himself as a red, scaly demon with a long tail and forked tongue, holding his hands out in front of himself. When his glance met with bony fingers and chipped, dirty nails, he let loose a heavy sigh and tried again. For the next hour he worked on different tricks, trying to produce a sword, a gun, a baseball bat. But each time he came up empty.

Exhausted, but not nearly ready to give up, he glanced up and caught his reflection in the broken storefront window on the other side of the street.

"Sweet," he murmured, and moved toward the monstrous image staring back.

Once again he held his hands out to look at them, but even though they looked human, the reflection proved he was projecting the demon image from inside his head.

Broken gravel crunched beneath his sneakered feet as he stepped out of the empty parking lot to make his way across the deserted street for a better look at himself, but a snapping sound behind him caught his attention and he instantly spun, fully expecting to find Dan checking in on his progress. What he saw instead scared the crap out of him.

He was in way over his head.

"What the hell?" a man said as he took in Jake's demon image. His fingers closed over the butt of a weapon strapped to his thigh.

Jake held up his fists, hating that he had such little

experience in fighting. Every muscle in his body tightened and his heart began to crash against his chest as he studied the heavily armed group of perhaps a half dozen soldiers who'd stepped out into the street and began circling him.

As Jake watched them it became glaringly apparent that they were no ordinary soldiers, and were nothing like the military force that occasionally patrolled the city streets.

His mind raced. Who were they and where the hell had they suddenly come from? One minute the parking lot had been empty, the next it was filled with armed men and women clad in battle fatigues—and from the looks in their eyes it was clear they wouldn't think twice about putting a bullet in Jake's head. And why should they when he was projecting the image of a demon?

He'd rather be projecting the image of a fearless demon than let them see the scared, useless little piece of shit kid that he was in reality.

The man who'd spoken, the one with the deep voice and dark eyes, stepped forward. Jake instantly pegged him as the leader. As the man's hard eyes took on a cold, deadly look, fight-or-flight instincts kicked in. Tension coiled through Jake and before he could even think about producing a weapon of his own, or shaking off the demon image and getting himself the hell out of there, the man raised his gun and squeezed the trigger. The piercing sound cracked the air and cut through the silence, and there wasn't a damn thing Jake could do to avoid the bullet that tore through his chest.

Air ripped from Jake's lungs in a loud whoosh and his ribs exploded as he dropped to his knees. He closed his hand over his heart and when he felt hot, sticky blood seep between his fingers he pulled his palm away to examine it. Light-headed, he blinked and tried not to pass out. If he passed out, he was sure he'd never wake up again.

It's not real!

He drew deep, labored breaths and gathered a scrap of control as he tried to make sense out of what was going on. Who were these people and where had they suddenly come from?

Jake tried desperately to cling to consciousness and clear his head enough so he could think. He could feel himself slipping, drifting into a fog as his demon image flickered in and out.

No longer able to project the demon illusion, Jake took on his human Hollow form. The burning pain in his chest increased. He met the man's gaze straight on as he aimed the gun at him, and Jake braced himself for another bullet.

Instead the man lowered the gun, startled panic streaking across his face as his eyes locked on Jake's and his jaw dropped.

"Jake!" he shouted, then bolted across the street toward him. He crouched next to Jake and reached for him, his hand cutting through the air and coming up empty. "What in the name of the Mother—"

Jake had no idea who this guy was, what he wanted, or even how he knew him, but after getting shot through the chest, he didn't want to hang around to find out. Back in the training room, his real body began shaking uncontrollably.

Hollow Man's safety guards finally kicked in and his implant deactivated.

◆ ◆

River didn't like it that Dan had insisted on Jake rejoining his training sessions.

Dan was pushing him and Jake wasn't ready.

Locked away in her tiny office, she wearily ran through the hologram sequences for what felt like the millionth time, still looking for the flaw that had caused the buzzing sound. She tried not to think about Hawk.

Her fight with Nick earlier in the day also preyed on her mind. He had dragged himself back to the subway in the early hours of the morning, looking like hell after a hard night of tomcatting. Not that she had any right to cast stones, but his selfish disregard for the safety of others, all for the sake of a cheap and easy lay, pissed her off.

It probably pissed her off because she had done something similar with Hawk. But she hadn't spent the entire day sleeping it off.

She rubbed her tired eyes, no longer worried the buzzing sound had anything to do with the Guardians arriving, because Hawk had taken care of alerting her to that. She knew he was coming for her. Therefore, the problem was with her program. She frowned at the monitor. She could find no errors. The hologram program was better than good. It was great. She drummed her fingers on the desk, trying to concentrate.

It was impossible not to think about Hawk.

He was coming for her.

She didn't know for certain how she felt about that. Relieved he was alive. Excited at the thought of seeing him again. Worried as to what his return really meant. Fear for the worst.

What she felt the most, however, was a strong sense of conviction. Her decision had been made and she knew it was right. No matter how strong her connection to Hawk, or how much she wanted him, she would never leave her world. She had people who depended on her, whether they knew it or not. Jake was foremost among them.

She punched away at her keyboard. The buzzing in the program had to be a technical error. She was missing something important.

Jake's loud screams of distress when they came propelled her from her chair with a gasp, the problem with the program immediately forgotten.

For months Jake had shown far too little emotion, so to hear the sheer panic in his voice had her bolting onto the subway platform at breakneck speed.

A minute later she found him sitting alone in the makeshift training room that she'd used her magic to help construct off the main gate of the platform.

She gripped him by the shoulders, noting his vitals.

"Jake," she said, but when he didn't answer, concern for his well-being caused her to squeeze with more force and give him a shake. Her voice rose, demanding he respond. "Jake, it's River. Listen to me. Whatever you think is happening to you, it isn't real. Pull yourself out of it."

Catching her off guard, his man-child body, already so much bigger than her own, began to shake uncontrollably and the rickety old chair on which he sat shimmied and scraped across the cracked cement floor, each violent convulsion threatening to send them both crashing to the concrete.

Working to summon her calm in the face of yet another crisis, River threw her arms around her brother and released a thread of healing magic. It did little to help soothe or ease his distress. Something was seriously wrong, and for the first time in months, she didn't know what to do. Her magic might be able to deal with this, but she had no idea how to make it do so. Technology, she was good with. Physiology, not so much. She needed help.

She shot a glance over her shoulder. "Nick!" she cried out, hoping like hell his medic training could help where her magic had failed. He had warned her of this. She should have listened to him.

When Jake clutched at his chest near the vicinity of his heart and let out a low, keening wail full of physical pain, River nearly panicked as well.

"Jesus. Nick, where are you?" she shouted again.

Sound traveled in the tunnel and bounced off every wall. Unless he'd gone topside or deaf, he had to hear her calling. But Nick knew better than to go topside again after the lecture she'd given him. So where the hell was he?

With the utmost care, River pulled one lid up and looked at Jake's dilated pupils. Her brother's situation, and the way he couldn't seem to pull himself out, was uncomfortably similar to Nick's recent episode with the program.

She mentally ran through the details and possible causes. Perhaps the buzzing sound had something to do with Nick and Jake's inability to extricate themselves from the program? Maybe there really was some sort of fatal flaw in Hollow Man?

But the Demons had been using the implant for weeks, and nothing new had been introduced to the program.

"Shit." She hadn't wanted to do this. Jake's thoughts were his own and he hadn't wanted to share them with her, but she had no other option. She dropped down on one knee beside him and placed her hands over his, preparing to go inside his head and yank him out of the program, but then his eyes sprang open and he catapulted himself out of his chair, knocking her down. She fell flat on her ass.

His glance darted to his hand, then his chest, and equal measures of relief and confusion flashed over his face as he sank back down into his seat and wrapped his fingers around the armrests.

She got to her feet, her eyes narrowing. He'd torn his shirt in his panic. "Jake, what happened?"

"I got shot," he said, his breath coming in short puffs, and looked around the room as if expecting someone to leap from the shadows and sink another bullet into him.

Her stomach punched into her throat. "*Shot?* Who shot you?" The Demons were gang members with all the associated levels of uncertainty in terms of their behavior, but at the same time she'd never thought any of them would turn on Jake like this. Not even in Hollow training. Jake had become one of them, maybe even more so than she liked.

At first, his story came out jumbled and hard to piece together.

"I don't know," he said. "About a half dozen soldiers came out of nowhere, and the leader stepped forward and didn't think twice about shooting me. I don't know what's going on, or how he knew me by name, but—"

Jake's words broke off as the Demons' young leader came rushing into the room, alerted to trouble by River's frantic shouting for Nick.

River turned on him. "Where were you?" she demanded, the anger inside her needing an outlet. Jake's story might not make sense, but one thing was certain. Dan had been responsible for his training and safety, yet Jake had been left on his own.

"I was with—"

"I don't care who you were with," she interrupted. "You left him alone. A good leader never leaves a man behind."

Dan's glance raked over Jake. Rebellion glittered in his eyes. "The kid's fine."

"You're damned lucky he is." River understood Dan's position, but she had done a lot for him in return. He owed her this much, to keep her brother safe. While Jake might not be one of the little ones, he was new to the city streets.

"If you got something to say to me, River," Dan paused deliberately, "just come right out and say it."

"Don't start with me," she said sharply, not in the mood to spar with him. "It's your job to teach the younger kids and you know it. You said so yourself. Don't leave any of them on the streets defenseless ever again. Not even in Hollow form."

Dan's brows furrowed as he gave her a cool look. "We talked about this."

"I don't care. You shouldn't have left him alone."

Dan squared his shoulders. "He needed to learn."

"No, he needed to be taught." Something ominous and dangerous began churning inside her, something she feared had more control over her than she had of it. It was dark and frightening, yet exhilarating and addictive all at the same time.

Dan, with his sixth sense for danger, must have sensed it. He held out his hands palms up and his eyes searched hers as he said in a low voice, "Take it easy, River. Your brother is fine."

"Don't tell me to take it easy. He's not fine. He ran into trouble out there." Electricity crackled in the air between them and Dan took a step back. He hadn't survived by being stupid or reckless, and her outburst was so completely out of character that it made him cautious.

He should be. She was scaring herself.

She took in a sharp breath and worked to tamp down that burst of mind-searing rage before she did something she'd regret.

She turned back to Jake and that torn shirt. He was watching both her and Dan, anxious distress in his eyes. He didn't like her coming to his defense in front of an older boy he admired.

She worked to keep her voice calm. "You said he knew you. The guy who shot you."

Jake nodded quickly. "Yeah. He called me Jake."

Her mind raced as a crowd of mixed emotions welled up inside her. She cut them down quickly so she could think with her head, not her heart, and stared into her brother's eyes. "But you didn't know him?"

"No."

Her entire body tensed in disbelief as her brain leapt to the most logical conclusion. Hawk knew Jake. He'd spent time with her brother when he was in another man's body. But Jake had never seen Hawk in his true physical form before.

Hawk would never shoot Jake.

River rubbed her thumb between her brows, considering the possibilities and not liking the conclusion she reached. Jake had referred to about a half dozen soldiers. Hawk wouldn't have come here with soldiers if he was coming only for her.

That meant he was here for another reason, too.

Andy had warned her that the Guardians would come. River had been expecting them. She had developed Hollow Man primarily with that purpose in mind.

And Hawk was a military man.

Doubt flickered through her chaotic thoughts. She knew how he felt about her. She also knew how he felt about her world. She'd been foolishly naïve to think he would come only for her.

The thought of having to fight him for her world made her ill. She and Hawk were a team.

Or they had been.

"And he called you by name? You sure about that?" She looked at Jake's chest, to the spot he'd been clutching, then back at him, and she could tell he understood what she was getting at.

He lifted his chin. "I held it together. I wasn't delusional, if that's what you mean."

River stood, giving a slow shake of her head as she used a slight, imperceptible brush of magic to assess her brother's state of mind. No, he definitely wasn't delusional. He had too much of their dad in him for that.

"Okay," she finally said. River twisted around and exchanged a long look with Dan.

"Guardians?" he asked.

They had discussed what the Demons would do if—when—the Guardians came.

"I'm not sure," she said. "But I think so."

Dan gave a curt nod and said, "I'll round up the others."

Before he could leave, and acting on impulse instead of logic, River touched his shoulder to stop him. Dan spun back around. "What?"

"Wait," she said.

"What are we waiting for?" Impatience edged his voice. She could tell he was itching for the Demons to try out Hollow Man in a real fight.

"I want to go out alone first," she said. "Once you've gathered the others, have everyone wait for me."

His mouth tightened as he gave her a long, hard glare. "You really want to go out there alone?"

She nodded.

"Why?"

She didn't want to tell him why. Didn't want to explain that she'd spent months worrying about Hawk's safety, about his mental health, and about whether he was dead or alive. She didn't want to explain that she feared the man she loved had returned to Earth prepared to strip her world of technology and leave it without a future. She didn't want to tell him that she hoped it was Hawk leading those soldiers as much as she hoped it wasn't, because she didn't want them to be on opposite teams.

And she really, really didn't want to explain her deep-seated need to see him again because the dream they'd shared last night simply hadn't been enough.

"Why, River?" Dan repeated, his challenging tone pulling her thoughts back.

After months of planning and preparing for an invasion, she wasn't about to lose her commitment to defending her world. She would talk to Hawk first.

She met Dan's glance straight on as he eyed her suspiciously. "There are a few things I need to confirm." She turned back to Jake and gave him one last careful, visual examination. "You okay?"

"Yeah," he mumbled, shrugging off her concern, and she could tell the whole incident had punctured his pride more than anything else.

"Go get some sleep," she said. "I'll be back soon."

With that, River left the small training room.

Dan, too, took off. He headed down the subway, disappearing into the darkness without saying good-bye to her.

As she made her way back to her office, River tried to fight down her nerves. She hadn't eaten much all day and what she had managed to swallow was churning in her stomach. When she reached her office, she sat in her chair and stared at the cold, gray cement wall. One thought kept flashing over and over in her mind.

Hawk was back. Just as he'd promised.

CHAPTER SIX

♦

Nick followed the voices into the darkness of the poorly lit tunnel.

River had changed, he thought. And not for the better. Not as far as Nick was concerned.

Since she'd freaked on him for going topside in search of something she was no longer willing to provide—and, while he wished that meant she cared, he knew it didn't—he now had to resort to monitoring the activities of some of the littlest Demons for his entertainment.

He didn't really care for the younger ones roaming through the dank subway tunnels on their own, and River had been too wrapped up in her program lately to think about the dangers these little guys faced. Boys were stupid. Was he the only person left in the world who'd read *Lord of the Flies*?

Not to mention the fact that Weres could be unpredictable. Some of them weren't especially finicky in their eating habits. He shuddered. He'd seen the crime-scene photos of what they could do to a human once they'd tasted blood. Imagine what they could do to a kid.

A rat scurried along a pipe above his head. Nick made a face at the bold little bastard. It backed against the wall with its long, naked tail coiled around its pink feet and chittered down at him.

"Hey, Dan," Nick greeted it. "Fancy meeting you here. River's going to hate that form, by the way."

The rat flipped him off and Nick laughed softly. It seemed he wasn't the only one keeping tabs on the kids.

He kept well back in the shadows, not wanting the boys to know they were being followed and only half paying attention to them anyway. There were six ten-year-olds in the group. He'd been a boy once. More than two or three together meant they were up to no good.

At first, following them had been nothing more than morbid curiosity and utter boredom on his part. He'd expected rule breaking, like him not listening to River about going topside unless in hologram form. He wanted to ignore her rules, too, so he completely sympathized.

But it wasn't long before he realized from the overheard snippets of conversation that the rules being broken weren't quite so simple. River had herself a little after-hours, juvenile-delinquent, level-one *Fight Club* on her hands. He wished her well with that because he didn't intend to get in the way of boys being boys. A few bloody noses and bruised knuckles were no biggies. He turned to go.

"Did you see that?" one of them suddenly asked. The tension in his voice stopped Nick in his tracks. Billy, he recalled. That was the kid's name. He'd stitched up a split lip for him a few days ago. Now he knew how he'd gotten it.

"What are you talking about?" someone else demanded. "We haven't even started yet. What's there to see?"

"That." The boy pointed at nothing. Nick pressed his back against the wall and waited for what would happen next. Billy was behaving strangely, but he was a kid. They all acted weird.

"There's nothing there," one of the other kids said, giving him a push. "Quit being a jerk."

"It's right *there*." The boy started flapping his hands. "Get it away from me!"

Another boy grabbed his flailing arms. "Dude. You're seeing things."

The boy shook him off. "I'm not seeing things," he insisted. "It's a zombie. *Right there!*"

A low buzz filled the air and Nick suddenly had a very bad feeling. He recognized that sound. He'd heard it himself not two days ago, but his had been while using his hologram program. The boys hadn't turned theirs on yet.

He looked around for Dan, thinking maybe one of them should be stepping in right about now. River needed to check the safety of her program ASAP, and he intended to tell her so. Billy was seriously freaked. To be honest, so was he.

Especially when the kid started to shriek.

◆ ◆

Shooting her brother probably wasn't the best way to work himself back into River's life.

Standard procedure for Guardians transporting to hostile worlds was to arrive with weapons ready, and to shoot first and ask questions later. Hawk thanked the Mother that the boy had been a hologram and not real. His gaze swept the vacant lot, looking for others.

He doubted if he'd done Jake permanent harm. He certainly hoped not. But why Jake was here in the first place was a serious cause for concern. Hawk had chosen this location for their arrival because it was in the center of the city where River lived, and therefore most likely to stick close to. That Jake, who was supposed to be in the mountains on the family farm, had also found his way here was not a good sign.

Hawk took a few deep breaths to steady himself before turning back to his team. That was one mother of a program River had created. And in only a few months. He was impressed. He was also troubled. If she'd used magic to enhance it, Achala maybe had reason to worry.

At least he was the only one with a ticking bomb in his head. The Fae leader had cleared the other members of his team. That was one less thing for him to worry about.

"What in Crisos was that?" Lilla asked, her eyes wide.

Hawk's mouth kicked up at the corners. Lilla was slight, with white-blond hair and angel-blue eyes, and looked like a little girl's porcelain doll. She also had a mouth on her that could make Hawk blush, which was quite an accomplishment.

"That," he responded, "was a kid disguised as a demon."

A demon. He thought about what he remembered of the area, and all of the places where a person could hide. He thought he knew where River might be, assuming she'd remained in the city.

If so, he didn't want her first real sight of him to be as a team leader. This wasn't a dream. She didn't much like the Guardians as it was. He wanted an opportunity to speak with her alone, to see what her reception of him might be.

He knew what he wanted it to be. He'd missed her unbearably, had worried relentlessly, and to be so close at last made him anxious and impatient. The dream had merely whetted his appetite.

Before he could search for her, he needed to put his team to work. Their instructions were clear. Each member had a packet of supercooled chlorine atoms to be launched into the Earth's stratosphere. Each atom had been individually excited, stimulating its ability to eat ozone and therefore to spread damage. In effect, what the Guardians were doing was exponentially increasing the rate at which the ozone layer thinned, and early spring provided perfect natural conditions for the greatest rate of ozone depletion. Since cold air improved the rate yet again, several of his team would be dispatched to the North Pole.

The planet's surface inhabitants had one final chance for survival, and that was to focus their energies on working together to counteract the reversible effects of ozone depletion. Otherwise, those effects would linger for generations. Climate change would drive the ozone damage around the equator, creating a snowball effect. That climate change, along with the associated disturbances in weather patterns, was also going to make it difficult for anyone to utilize electricity effectively. Magnetic particles from the sun would in turn create disruptions to satellites and cause interference with currents running through the Earth's power grids. Without electricity, Earth would have trouble reversing the damage to the stratospheric ozone layer. Its scientists were going to have their hands full for generations. A new dark age was about to descend.

And if people couldn't work together, within three generations, the only life left on this planet would exist in the deepest levels of the oceans.

Hawk consulted the com-link strapped to his wrist. He tapped in a few readings he'd hijacked from one of the ancient global positioning satellites that circled the planet. They'd divided into three separate teams. Faran and Ever would travel to an abandoned research station in the Arctic, and Riley and Aris would travel to a point along the equator exactly half a world away. Each team member had a kit with a transporter and an explosive attached. When he gave the signal, they would transport the kits into the stratosphere above them and detonate the explosives, releasing the supercooled chlorine atoms. He and Lilla would remain where they were, ready to transport the last two kits that would connect the four others. Ellesmere Island would be first, western

Canada second, and midpoint of the equator, third. Weather conditions thirty-five miles above the Earth's surface would have to be exact for all six kits to work effectively.

Lilla was their meteorologist. That was why she stayed with Hawk.

Hawk read off the coordinates for each of the team members.

"Great," Faran complained. "Riley and Aris get the beaches and babes. We get the tundra and polar bears."

"As long as you get the polar bears first there shouldn't be a problem," Lilla said. She sniffed in disdain. "Trust me, Riley and Aris won't be getting any babes. Not if they wear swimsuits on those beaches. They need to spend more time at the gym."

Hawk thought of the last time he'd come across a bear on this world. The brown bear had been massive, and everything he'd read stated that polar bears were roughly the same size.

"Consider this a hostile world, guys," he reminded them. "It has more than people on it, and you'd do well to remember that."

Faran, a giant of a man with a shaved head and a gold cap on one tooth, pointed at something behind Hawk. His lip curled in distaste.

"I'd take polar bears any day over that thing," he said. "Want me to shoot it and put it out of its misery?"

"Better yet," Riley piped in, "shoot it and put it out of mine."

Hawk turned to see what they were talking about. An orange-furred, catlike creature with long, retractable claws, large green eyes, and a flat pug face cut through the end of the lot, its ragged tail in the air, unconcerned with the ongoing debate regarding its life expectancy.

It was a Tabinese, an imaginary creature from River's video game—a cross between her two favorite pets as a child, a tabby cat and a Pekingese. The Tabinese disappeared into an alley, but not before shooting a last saucy look over its shoulder.

Eager anticipation stirred Hawk's spirits.

"It's got quite a bit of attitude for something so ugly," Faran said, rubbing a hand over his smooth scalp.

Lilla rolled her eyes. "You should talk. Besides, I think it's kind of cute."

"What is it with women and small pets?" Hawk asked, itching to follow the creature but not wanting to look as if he were. River had thought it was cute, too.

He hid a smile. It seemed she still did. And she had come to him first. At the moment, that was what was important to him.

Why had she come?

He needed to know.

"Faran, you take that direction. Riley, that way," he said, pointing. "I want both of you to do some reconnaissance. I'm going this way." He nodded toward the alley. "Lilla, Ever, and Aris, the three of you stay here and guard those kits."

Once out of sight of the others he lengthened his stride

and slid between two towering buildings, stepping over broken glass and empty beer cans as he looked for an open door. River was leading him somewhere.

This time when he got her alone, they were going to talk. He had to make her understand what was going to happen, and why.

Ignoring the wailing pitch of a police siren a block or so away, he ducked inside an abandoned warehouse.

◆ ◆

The warehouse had once been used to manufacture tires. Ribbons of light filtered in through the boarded-up windows and spilled across the concrete floor, the pungent scent of hot rubber still saturating the stale air. Her hologram worked even better than she'd thought. When she was in animal form, smells increased exponentially. She darted behind a stack of packing crates and crouched, making her Tabinese self as invisible as possible.

She tried to settle her heart as she waited, but when she heard the sound of crunching glass outside the building, every nerve in her body sprang into life. Peeking out from beneath a wooden box, she watched the door creak open, hoping to find Hawk alone but prepared for an army just the same.

She couldn't get past that. For all his talk of Guardians protecting the Fae, it was clear to her that Guardians knew nothing of them. Life was a Fae gift to all the worlds. What the worlds did with the gift was not the responsibility of the Guardians. That responsibility fell back to the Fae.

But what of the Guardians' gift to the worlds? her own Guardian half whispered. Did the responsibility for technology not fall back to them?

Hawk's large frame filled the doorway like some nineteenth-century Wild West gunslinger, blocking out the setting sun. One hand pushed the door wider, allowing more light to filter in, and as the metal latch hit the wall with a clang, dust rained from the ceiling and fell in drops to the floor. He lowered his hands to his sides, his fingers inches from his weapons as he studied the room.

River's Tabinese heart pattered in response to seeing him in person for what was the very first time, stealing her ability to think with any sort of clarity. She sucked in air, conflicting emotions careening through her bloodstream. Her dream hadn't prepared her for this. In the dream, she'd seen him through his eyes. Seeing him through her own was a far different experience.

She could hardly believe how much she wanted him. Months of worry over a Guardian invasion made her cautious, however, and she skittered backward, her toenails scratching the floor. When she hit the wall she dropped onto her haunches, suddenly unable to inflate her lungs.

"Here, butt-ugly little kitty, kitty," he crooned, and she might have laughed if her animal form had allowed it. He stepped all the way inside and quietly latched the door behind him, dimming the sounds from the street. "Please, River," he said more loudly, and with less teasing and more undisguised need. "I have to see you. I've been going crazy."

That made two of them. She'd survived a deadly video game with a computer-generated Hawk watching her back, survived the dangerous city streets with him by her side—his consciousness trapped in another man's body—yet nothing could have prepared her for this. She needed a minute or two to recover.

Concealed in the shadows she watched him, watched the way his gaze swept the warehouse looking for her. As she studied the hard lines of his profile, she noted that his expression looked haunted and her heart went out to him. Searching for scars, both mental and physical, River's gaze slid over him, hungrily taking in his powerful body, dark, military-style haircut, bronzed skin and the inky shadows beneath his penetrating eyes.

She crept from under the boxes and morphed into her own form.

The instant his dark glance met with hers, her heart leapt in response. She drew a breath and struggled to control her emotions. With every ounce of strength she possessed, she set aside the powerful pull between them, instead concentrating on the questions racing through her mind. Why hadn't he come alone? What were he and the Guardians preparing for?

She'd heard enough to know they were planning something.

She opened her mouth to ask, but when he inched forward and reached for her, the first words out of her mouth surprised her as much as they did him.

"What took you so long?" she demanded.

A grin softened his features, and the sight of his mouth turning up at the corners tore at her heart. She and Hawk were a team. He had no business siding against her.

"I missed you," he said. "Crisos, how I missed you." His voice hitched as again he reached for her. She could tell he was struggling to interpret her reaction to him, whether it was good or bad.

She wasn't certain herself. If necessary, she wondered if she'd have the strength to resist him. They had a bond between them.

"It's been four months. I had no idea if you were dead or alive." She hated the quiver in her voice. He took another step closer, but she matched it with a backward step of her own.

"Last night should have taken care of that," he replied, his eyes darkening with remembered pleasure. "Perhaps I didn't put enough effort into the evening. Next time believe me I will, because there will be no more doubt as to who I am or that I'm alive. Or, if I'm real."

A thrill shot through her at his words. She wanted to walk into his arms and hold him, and to be held by him. She wanted to feel him and to be touched by him.

If doing so affected only the two of them, there'd be

no question as to where she would be right now. Unfortunately, it wasn't only the two of them anymore. There was a world they had to consider, and it contained people she loved. Perhaps it was for the best that she was meeting him first through her hologram program. It kept her from doing something she would probably regret.

She couldn't speak past the pain in her chest.

"Is Jake okay?" he asked her.

"You shot him." She focused on outrage, hugging it around her for strength. "He's just a little boy."

"I shot a demon, not a boy," he said, correcting her. He stopped, his thoughts shifting direction, and his brows drew together. "About that. Why was Jake disguised as a demon? Why is he here rather than with his brother and mother? What exactly have you been doing while I was gone?"

Telling him about Melinda and Sam was more than she could bear right now. Neither did she like the worry and disapproval she heard in his voice.

She tried to touch his thoughts and discovered he'd blocked them from her.

"Why have you come back?" she asked. *Don't lie to me,* her soul begged. His eyes slid from hers but the flash of guilt she read in them told her a lot could happen in four months.

"The Great Lords have determined this world has been irreversibly damaged by a Dark Lord. We've been sent to defuse it."

She caught back a gasp of dismay.

"But first and foremost, River, I came for you." His eyes softened as they fastened on hers. "Always, wherever you are, I will come for you."

She wanted so much to believe him. "I always thought you would come for me. I believed in you. But I never once thought that you'd lead Guardians against me." The sense of betrayal ran deep. "We were a team."

He drew back as if she'd slapped him. Pain filled his eyes. "We still are. I would never lead anyone against you. We have to talk about this. I need to explain."

Before he had a chance to say more, the bay doors at the back of the warehouse burst open, shards of wood spraying against the walls.

A resounding bang echoed off the warehouse walls.

"Weres," River breathed, her head whipping around. Incredulity had her pulse kicking up a notch. She took a step back to better position herself for an attack. It brought her too close to Hawk.

He grabbed for her, but when his hand touched nothing but air, he cursed. His eyes widened, then narrowed. "Crisos, River. What have you done?"

No matter what might happen between them, she couldn't bear the thought of him being hurt.

"You'd better get out of here," she said. "I'm safe. You're not."

"I'm not going anywhere." The sound of the safety release on his gun reminded her of old times. Her and Hawk, fighting side by side, protecting each other's backs. She couldn't deny that it would feel good to be fighting with him again. She'd missed the adrenaline rush.

She'd missed him, too.

Her blood raced as she studied the forbidding man beside her. She gave a casual shrug, already dancing on the balls of her feet in anticipation. "Suit yourself."

The stink of wet dog hit her hard when three men loped through the broken doors. She pressed her back to Hawk's and they began circling. But what struck River as odd was the way the Weres were behaving. She'd done some research, and Jim Peters had turned out to be an authority on them. Weres mostly acted out of animal instinct, going straight for the throat, but these animals seemed to be organized and using a strategy, abilities she'd given the hellhounds in the third and final level of her video game. She didn't like to think what their behavior now meant.

As the Weres pressed themselves to the wall and began to fan out, Hawk didn't waver. He took aim and fired. The shot, centered between one Were's eyes, instantly dropped it to the ground.

When one of the remaining two Weres pushed off the wall, River ran forward. The Were dove for her but sailed through her hologram, landing on the floor behind her with a thud. As it rolled to its feet, shaking the fog from its head in confusion, River drove her sword through its belly. The safeguards she'd programmed into Hollow Man wouldn't permit her to kill it, but she could do it some serious damage. Sparks shot from the tip of her blade and the Were's eyes blinked in surprise. It scrambled back to safety, then turned and ran.

Wild, dark triumph coursed through her, and for an unsettling moment she lost her sense of self in the excitement. Shaking off the sensation, she repositioned herself next to Hawk and they both stood against the third.

"This one's mine," Hawk said. He seemed puzzled by something, wary almost, but River didn't have the time to figure out what or why.

She aimed her sword, pointing to a spot on the street beyond the door. "What about the pack moving in behind him? Can they be mine?"

"Like hell," came the grim response.

River had no idea how so many Weres had been assembled into a pack, but she knew something about it wasn't right. She also knew she and Hawk were completely outnumbered.

Then again, they'd been outnumbered before.

She looked for a weakness in the pack that might give them the advantage, but before she could find one, the Weres began to retreat as if something or someone had called them back.

Hawk turned on her then, his eyes full of questions, the harsh set of his jaw demanding answers. River braced herself for the coming interrogation.

"What in the name of the Mother were *those*?" demanded a woman's voice from behind them.

◆ ◆

General Amos Kaye examined the fresh strips of bloody flesh dangling from a meat hook in the ceiling. The Were's hands had been tied behind its back and its feet were bound.

If there was one thing he refused to tolerate, it was insubordination. Bane, the result of one of his better attempts at genetic mutation, had brought this on himself by running when he should have stayed the course.

Even though he bore the blame for his punishment, it still angered Kaye that he'd been forced to make an example of him. While their survival instincts remained strong, when cornered Weres simply did not care about physical pain. Neither, however, did they like being unable to fight back. He tossed the whip aside. Bane wouldn't be fighting anything anymore.

"Cut him down and dispose of him," he ordered one of the silently watching Weres before walking from the room. The heel of his shoe skidded in a pool of blood, leaving a sticky smear on the floor behind him. The blood was another form of torture. The scent drove the Weres wild, but they wouldn't dare act on it unless he gave them permission.

Kaye knew any number of little ways to teach these creatures self-control. Some got the lessons faster than others. The slow ones ended up like Bane. Unfortunately, there were far too many slow ones. Even more unfortunately, Bane hadn't been one of them.

He stopped in the men's room to wash his hands. Pipes clanged in the walls when he carefully turned on the taps. His hands and face were still tender from the burns he'd received in an explosion four months ago. He had a little score to settle over that, although it was of secondary importance.

Now that Premier Johnson had been assassinated and a new premier sat in his chair, Kaye doubted if he'd be able to keep his research facilities in the former provincial building much longer. The government was becoming more and more reluctant to be seen supporting "private"—meaning "off the radar"—business ventures with public funds. Keeping a security team for supposedly empty offices was raising questions no one officially wanted to answer.

He didn't trust the new premier. Anderson was an ignorant pup. He had no idea how to create and maintain a public image while continuing to get important work done.

Important work in this day and age meant building an army that would put Canada in a position of power as world leader. Forget nuclear weapons. Everyone had them, and they were too easily defused. Kaye preferred biological warfare. Its effects were immediate, pervasive, and completely debilitating. Mutating strains kept civilian populations occupied for years.

And, with the introduction of private armies made up of genetically engineered soldiers for hire to keep the masses under control, the country with the capability of producing those armies stood to gain financially as well. Technologically, Canada had always been a world leader. It was time for it to become a world superpower.

Insubordination continued to be an obstacle, but Kaye was a patient man. He'd proven genetic enhancements to humans could be made.

He shook droplets of water off his wet hands before releasing a paper towel from the dispenser on the wall with his elbow.

Bioengineering could also be done through melding mutants with machines, but not without a little outside help. The late George Johnson had once persuaded a love interest with unusual abilities to help Kaye in those particular experiments, and then River Weston had ruined them for him.

She had the ability to get them back on track.

He tossed the wad of damp paper towel into the trash and headed to his office to change his blood-spattered jacket, his footsteps loud in the silent hallway.

David Weston had somehow discovered a means of harnessing similar bits of unusual abilities, and Kaye was betting he'd gotten them from his daughter. He suspected Weston, and Johnson's former lover, had been working together on that.

He reached into a drawer of his desk and removed a long metal tube. He held it to his eye and turned the casing, watching the images with interest. River could run, but she could no longer hide. Not for much longer.

He lowered the black metal tube and turned it over in his hands, examining it for the thousandth time, intrigued by the bright, swirling colors and its latent abilities. By thinking of something, or someone, he had discovered quite by accident that he could sometimes—

not always—see them when he looked in this tube. He wondered what other undiscovered properties the tube might have.

As a man of science he didn't believe in magic as such. Results were what he understood. Weston had gotten results. So had the woman Kaye had known as Baliani, but whom River called Andy.

Kaye sniffed the tube. He understood results, and he also remembered their associated, unmistakable smell. Whatever David Weston had been up to, this metal tube had been part of it.

He suspected Weston had conducted a few unsanctioned experiments of his own, and that the bastard had hidden the results. Those results belonged to the Canadian military, and Kaye intended to have them back. He intended to have River, too, because results, without the means to reproduce them, were useless to him.

He replaced the tube in the drawer. This little tube was interesting. The video game, far more impressive. But River Weston's latest experiment, from what he could tell, was what would catapult the country's military defense technology into areas the world had never seen.

CHAPTER SEVEN

♦

Peters closed his eyes and opened them again, but the images didn't disappear. He'd never thought he'd go crazy from extended periods of isolation because he hated most people, but once again, Mother Nature was proving him wrong.

Two little boys, maybe six years old, stared up at him from where they huddled together behind the sofa. Identical in appearance, with incredible, sea-green eyes and fine, shaggy white hair, at first Peters thought he was seeing double.

They didn't move. Neither did he.

"What we have here is called an impasse," Peters finally said. "But sooner or later someone's got to blink."

That earned him no reaction. He wondered if they spoke English. For that matter, he wondered if they spoke at all. Had someone abandoned them out here? If so, how could little kids possibly have survived on their own?

If not on their own, then where were the adults?

Before he could make up his mind about what to do next, another boy, several years older than the first two, suddenly materialized between them. He, too, had white hair and those unusual, vivid green eyes. He glared at Peters, then he reached down and took both of the smaller boys by the shoulder. As quickly as he'd materialized, he was gone. So were the little ones.

What the hell?

Peters shook his head, trying to decide if he'd been hallucinating.

If he was, the hallucinations were pretty real. They also liked to play video games and watch cartoons on DVD, he discovered as he searched the room. The kids had access to a generator and knew how to use it. Or whoever was in charge of them did.

He continued to try to puzzle this out. Normal kids, and even the not-so-normal ones, couldn't simply wink in and out of existence. True, they could vanish like little rats when they wanted, but in his line of duty he normally saw their ass ends as they disappeared. A faintly familiar, peppery scent lingered in the air. Magic. He'd once smelled it on Andy.

The rest of the building was empty. His footsteps echoed loudly and the sound made him nervous. Peters again wondered if he'd lost his mind, but if he had to wonder about it, it probably meant he was fine. He sensed no danger, but that warm and happy glow, so out of character for him, continued to be a source of annoyance.

The urgency that had driven him thousands of miles across an arctic desert now sent him back out into the cold. He walked through the compound to a small red outbuilding at the far end. A massive runway, large enough for a CC-130 Hercules aircraft carrier to be able to land, sat empty and neglected. He'd bet it had been more than thirty years since the last Hercules had touched down in this place.

But no more than six since the last human had done so. Two little boys were proof enough of that.

He entered the red building. It was an office storage area of some kind. Filing cabinets, numbered as per year and filled to overflowing, lined the walls from floor to ceiling. He stared at them in dismay. If Andy had led him here in order to find information, he might die of old age before ever doing so.

That twitchy, uncomfortable sensation of being watched returned. He kept checking over his shoulder but catching nothing except the odd, flickering shadow. He opened a filing cabinet and pretended to study the contents. If they wanted him to play hide-and-seek, they would play by his rules.

Lightning fast, he whirled and reached between two of the cabinets. He caught a thin arm in his fingers and held on tight. A faint burst of pepper tickled his nose, but Peters refused to let go and the scent of pepper quickly dissipated. He knew very little about magic, but if the kids had it, their abilities were limited.

He hauled a child from his hiding place. He squirmed and tried to kick and bite him, but Peters was a cop and he'd been kicked and bitten by bigger and better than this. This boy was perhaps ten, and again had the white hair and odd green eyes. He was also surprisingly strong. As Peters waited for him to tire himself out, another scent, far more familiar, mixed in with the pepper and the dry smell of aged paper. Ignoring the kid's struggles, he drew him closer and took a deep whiff.

The white hair was fur.

"Well, hell," Peters said. The kid was a Were. Which meant so were the others. Cold sweat trickled between his shoulder blades. So much for the warm fuzzies. He'd stumbled on a Were farm. He hated Weres. He didn't like kids either.

"Let go of me, asshole," the kid said. His foot connected with Peters' inner thigh, far too close to his crotch for comfort.

At least the little brat spoke English. And apparently he'd learned it from sailors.

"Front and center," Peters shouted out in command to the ones he couldn't see but knew were nearby. "Now. Or I turn this one over my knee and paddle his backside until he can't sit down until the next moon rising. You have to the count of three. One."

Little faces began to appear. Most wore sullen expressions. A few were openly hostile. All in all he counted seven, including the one in his hands who continued to kick and swear. They ranged in age from the two littlest, who he'd figured were six, to about sixteen. They were all boys, and so much alike they had to be brothers.

Now he knew what he'd been sent here to find. The warm fuzzies were soaring off the charts. If he were a woman he'd be in hormone heaven.

"Who's in charge?" he asked.

The sixteen-year-old stepped forward, his eyes on

the boy in Peters' hands, ready to leap to his rescue if Peters so much as twitched.

"No," Peters said, thinking the boy had misunderstood him. "I mean, who's looking after you?"

"I am," he replied.

"Well, f—" Peters started to say, then remembered these were kids and maybe he should clean up his language and try to be a role model. The thought startled him, and he suspected it came from Andy, because he didn't want to clean up his language and he didn't want to be a role model. He didn't want to babysit Were kids either. He'd once led a small private army of adult Weres during the war, and those had been the scariest months of his life. In terms of self-control, Were kids would be worse.

Something in the cosmos hated him.

"How did you get here?" he asked instead. This kind of genetic experimentation had never gone on at Ellesmere Island. It could never have been sustained. Even he knew that much. It required too many medical supplies and sensitive, specialized equipment. Emergencies would have been impossible to manage. And, too, Ellesmere had been considered a hardship posting. Rotations tended to be on a six- to eight-month schedule, and researchers would have had no continuity with their studies. Geneticists weren't exactly abundant.

Plus, the outpost had been abandoned during the war, more than thirty years ago when monitoring space and the Earth's atmosphere had lost priority status with the

Canadian military. Right about the same time the last
Hercules would have arrived to remove anything of value.
He looked at the overstuffed filing cabinets, which should
have included all of these research notes.

The boy hesitated, then answered the question with
reluctance and only because Peters had tightened his
grip on the kid in his hands. "David brought us here."

Peters could think of only one David who might be
connected with Ellesmere Island, and he led back to
River, who led back to Andy.

And Andy, with her part in the early bioengineering experiments, led back to Weres. Some of the pieces
started falling into place.

"David *Weston*?" he demanded, and wasn't surprised
when the boy nodded his head.

♦ ♦

Hawk started at the sound of Lilla's voice, taking his
eyes off River for a fraction of a second. Too late, he realized his mistake.

River vanished.

With her hand hovering steady over her weapon,
Lilla darted her shrewd glance from Hawk to the dead
Weres, to the spot where River had stood only moments
earlier, back to Hawk again.

"Mutants," he explained in response to her question.
"Genetically altered half wolves." Distracted, he paid

little attention to the captain. He itched to find River. She had to be close by.

Lilla's gaze returned to the spot where River had stood. "What, then, was she?" One pale eyebrow lifted. "No, wait, let me guess. An ugly little cat shapeshifter thing?"

Hawk holstered his gun. The last thing he wanted was for anyone on his team to meet River like this. Not when she was in fighting mode. He'd wanted them to see her gentler side, the side full of kindness and empathy, the side that had cared for him and nursed him back to health, mentally and physically, during his darkest hours. He considered himself a strong man, and yet suspected at the end he never would have survived the Dark Lord or all of the psychological abuse without her by his side.

Lilla, however, had seen River drive a sword through a Were. After that, Hawk could hardly say she was Fae and expect Lilla to believe him.

Achala's words of warning came back to him. *She has the potential to follow a Dark path without ever knowing she's on it.*

His silence wasn't helping satisfy Lilla's curiosity.

"Well, Supreme Leader?" She had a hand braced on one hip, all attitude. "You want to tell me what's going on here?"

Hawk squared his shoulders and pulled rank. "Not really, Captain," he said coolly, and Lilla immediately backed down. "Come on. Let's go find the others."

He shot one last glance toward the bay doors and the dead Weres. He frowned and wondered why the other animals had suddenly retreated. He couldn't deny that he was damn glad they had, although giving them a serious shit kicking might have eased some of his tension, but gut instinct told him that whatever, or whoever, had called them back, in the end it wasn't going to be good.

Shelving that thought for the time being, Hawk pushed past Lilla and stepped outside. The air had grown thicker, heavier, almost suffocating. Dark clouds were moving in from the east, a fitting match for his mood.

He had planned to talk to River, to explain what he was trying to do before introducing her to his team. Hawk didn't like it when things didn't go according to plan.

Thunder rumbled in the distance, swallowing the scraping sound his military-issue boots made on the dry cracked pavement as he stepped out into the clearing. Buildings towered over him and as he breathed deep his skin prickled, warning him of danger. His gaze skated over the rooftops, half expecting to find imps or some other creature from his nightmares ready to pounce.

As dark, haunting memories closed in on him, he scanned the abandoned streets looking for anything out of the ordinary. When he found nothing, he ordered himself to relax.

The rest of his team was waiting in the parking lot with the kits.

Keeping a watchful eye on his surroundings, he considered his options as he jogged across the street. Lilla followed behind him, protecting his back.

He had a pretty good idea of where River had gone. He also had a good sense as to what would happen if he showed up with a team of soldiers. He didn't want to antagonize her. He wanted to resolve matters between them as peacefully as possible.

Considering he was about to strip her world of technology and toss it back a few evolutionary generations, expecting a peaceful resolution might be overly optimistic on his part. But if River had such faith in these people, let them prove her right and him wrong. Seeing was believing.

Unfortunately, what Lilla had seen in that warehouse wasn't something to make her believe River was Fae.

What he needed to do first was disperse his team. Sending them to their designated destinations to complete their tasks would buy him some time. He'd call them back once their kits were in position, and then he'd introduce them to River. He was certain that once they felt her gentle Fae soul, they'd guarantee her safety— regardless of the orders they'd been given for destroying a Dark Lord.

A fierce need to protect River welled up inside him as he and Lilla rejoined the others. On the heels of that overwhelming need came an uneasy sense of foreboding.

Lilla moved in beside him, her attention focused on his face with concern. They'd worked together before and she might trust him, but she'd witnessed the darker side of River and convincing her that River was a gentle Fae might not be so simple. Yet Lilla was the one he'd hoped to convince first.

With all eyes on him he said, "Okay, team, here's what we need to do."

Thirty minutes later, only Hawk and Lilla remained. Now they had to find their way to the subway. That was where River would be.

Heavy rain fell in sheets. As it pelted against their bodies, it plastered their clothes to their skin. Thunder rumbled and Hawk counted the seconds leading up to the next flashes of lightning.

Ignoring the discomfort of his wet gear, he cradled the kit in his arms. Water dripped into his eyes and he blinked away the blur. He threw the backpack over his shoulder.

"Let's move."

They hurried down the deserted street with its cracked asphalt and broken storm drains. Water gushed up in geysers, flooding the gutters.

The subway was too far. Standing in the street with what amounted to a lightning rod in his hands wasn't smart.

"Over there," he shouted to Lilla, pointing to an apartment building that looked empty.

The lock on the security door had been broken long ago. They slipped inside the building. The utilitarian gray carpet in the lobby had seen far better days. The rust-colored bloodstains were old. Moving silently, he placed his hand over his gun and studied his surroundings, searching for signs of danger and finding none.

He motioned with his head to the stairwell. He wanted to check out the top floor for a better view of the layout of the city. He also wanted to make sure they were alone.

Their footsteps on the metal stairs didn't draw any attention from the occupants. They were either indifferent or nonexistent. They reached the top floor. Heavy wooden doors, splintered and broken, hung off their hinges, and he glanced inside each apartment as they moved down the long corridor. The living quarters had been ransacked, most of the furniture gone, the few pieces that remained either destroyed or of no value to looters.

He pointed to a door on his right and they both slipped inside. His gazed panned the small space and he proceeded to do a careful search of the other rooms. Satisfied that they were alone, Hawk lowered his kit onto the floor and wiped the water from his face. His wet boots slipped on the floor, and the brittle linoleum cracked beneath his weight as he stepped to the boarded-up window and peered out through the slats. He tensed when he caught movement out of the corner of his eye, but when he zeroed in on the spot he found nothing.

Lilla kicked a broken chair from her path, the sound instantly swallowed by that of the thunder overhead. "Crisos, from what I've seen so far this planet is a hazard to itself. I'm all for defusing it."

Hawk turned on her. "You haven't seen anything yet."

"I've seen enough. And I can't help but wonder where

we're going." Her eyes challenged him. "You knew that woman. Back in the warehouse. Why didn't you tell the others about her? Or warn them about the genetic freaks that attacked you?"

He scrubbed a hand over his chin and felt the beginnings of a headache hammer the base of his neck.

Lilla squeezed the water from her hair and said nothing more, simply waited. Hawk hated the way she was looking at him. As if he'd lost his mind. Worse, she looked as if she didn't know whether or not he could be trusted. As if he'd disappointed her.

"There was no need to warn them," he said. "You were already told about the genetic manipulation and attempts at bioengineering. That's why we were sent to defuse this world."

"In the name of the Mother," Lilla said, her eyes widening in understanding. "That woman is the Dark Lord we were sent to destroy."

Hawk stood with his back to the window. "Dark Lords are male. Did she look male to you?"

"But the First Lord said—"

"I don't care what the First Lord said," he interrupted her. "River is Fae. When you meet her, you'll see it for yourself."

He was about to say more but slammed his mouth shut as a loud noise, like a heavy metal door being kicked open, echoed in the hallway. Crouching low, he gestured with a nod to Lilla and they both pressed their backs to the wall and crab-walked toward the door. The noise sounded again, and a man yelled out, spouting gibberish that Hawk couldn't follow. Lilla darted to the other side of the doorway and Hawk peered around the frame in time to see a man run toward him. Hawk pointed his gun, but the man stopped dead in his tracks. Crazy, unfocused eyes locked on Hawk's but Hawk had the sense the man wasn't really seeing him. A low, background buzz could be heard.

A second later the man took off, running through the hallway and up the stairwell. But what concerned Hawk the most was the nonsense he was spouting.

"What is he saying?" Lilla whispered.

"I don't know," Hawk said. A heavy door sounded in the distance, then slammed shut.

She pointed upward. "I think he's on the roof."

"We should check it out."

Crouched on the other side of the door, Lilla looked at him, then angled her head and glanced out the window. "Or not," she added. "He just jumped."

Hawk turned for the door. "We need to get out of here."

Moving quickly, they bolted from the apartment and retraced their steps. Hawk darted a glance around to ensure their safety before they stepped outside, but when they did they spotted the man's body splattered on the cement, arms and legs twisted and lying in a puddle of blood quickly diluted by the rain. With a sick, disconcerted feeling Hawk inched toward him, and knelt down.

Hawk looked him over and knew something wasn't

right. He was in his early twenties. His skin was pale—sickly pale—and his cheeks were so sunken he looked malnourished. His flesh appeared to be hanging off bone, wasting away before Hawk's eyes.

His stomach revolted when the scent of human waste and *vinegar* hit him. He instantly leapt to his feet and backed away, pulling Lilla with him.

Common household vinegar. River had told him that was what the cure for the virus had turned out to be.

It hadn't worked for this poor bastard.

His mind dredged up disturbing images that were best left buried. Images of the rows upon rows of desiccated bodies stacked several layers deep—bodies that he and River had stumbled on in the subway's main central station when he'd been stuck in Nick Sutton's body.

Hawk had examined those bodies closely. Had the virus resurfaced? From everything he'd read about the pandemic and what River had told him, the host body wasted away but the mind was left intact.

This man's mind hadn't been intact when he'd jumped from the roof. Hawk's kept coming back to the same question—had the virus mutated again?

If so, into what?

"Hawk?" Lilla asked as he mulled over that worry.

"Cover your mouth and nose," he warned, burying his face in the crook of his arm.

"What in the name of the Mother is going on?" she

asked, scared, her voice muffled by her sleeve. She'd done as he'd told her, which he hoped meant she respected him enough as a leader to accept what was coming.

"That's what I'd like to know," he replied. "Come on. There's only one person I know who might have the answers."

◆ ◆

Achala waited patiently in the hall of the Great Lords for their session to adjourn. He had asked the page not to interrupt them. It gave him time to consider what he intended to say.

He'd thought long and hard before coming here. It went against all of the teachings of the Fae and jeopardized their relationship with the Guardians for him to be entering their thoughts, so admitting to it without reason would be foolish. Even though Guardians had excellent defenses against it, they wouldn't bother to use those defenses unless they felt threatened.

What he had seen for himself in the minds of Hawk's team hadn't worried him. They were honorable, all of the ones who had traveled to Earth, with the best of intentions—even if he might not agree with them. They seemed typical examples of the Guardian people.

Yet someone was responsible for the abandonment of his granddaughter, and he believed he knew whom that might be. What he couldn't understand was why this person would have issued an order to destroy her, along with the innocent people who'd accompanied Colonel Hawkins, without any proof of her darkness beyond the unfortunate circumstances of her birth.

He rose from his seat on the stone bench in the marble hall as the Great Lords filed from their meeting room and bowed to him in greeting.

The Great Lords seemed surprised to see him, although not disturbed. He clasped his hands in the folds of his white robe. He'd chosen his attire carefully. White meant he'd come for informal discussions.

"First Lord," he said, addressing a short man with a mild expression and worry lines starting to show at the corners of his thin mouth. "A word, if I may."

"Certainly, Your Grace," the First Lord replied with an acknowledging nod of his head and an expression of polite curiosity on his face. "Please. Why don't we talk in my private chamber? I can have food and drink brought to us there."

They exchanged inconsequential pleasantries as they walked through the corridors. Gentle probing told Achala that the First Lord was puzzled but unalarmed by his appearance. For some reason this angered him. Had the Fae gained such a reputation for peacefulness that they'd lost all credibility when it came to politics and strategy? Was that why they were not consulted in matters affecting other worlds?

Heartache set his chest on fire. Was that why his daughter had died on a foreign world with no connection to her family to help save her life? Because her people had stepped away, washing their hands of responsibility?

He needed to know if they had let his granddaughter down as well.

The First Lord led him into a spacious room flooded with red light filtered through stained-glass windows high on the walls. Thick carpet and deep, dark, over-stuffed chairs gave the room a casual but comfortable elegance. It constantly amazed Achala, these wonders the Guardians had crafted using their ingenuity. To him this was true magic and beyond wonderful.

"Please, have a seat," the First Lord said, indicating a chair. When Achala had done so, he took the chair across from him. A small stone pedestal table rested between them. The First Lord lifted the top of the table to reveal a concealed touch pad. His fingers flew across its surface, then he lowered the top carefully back into place. "I've ordered us kaffa and a few sweets." He smiled. "At our age it's a bit decadent, particularly at this time of day, but I won't tell your wife if you don't tell mine."

A few moments later a page appeared carrying a tray of steaming kaffa and dainty pastries. He set the tray carefully on the table and left. The First Lord reached for the pot of kaffa and filled two thin china mugs. Achala helped himself to a pastry, more out of polite-ness than actual desire.

"Now," the First Lord said, settling back in his chair with a small plate of pastries balanced on his knee and a cup of kaffa cradled in his hands. He blew gently on the warm surface. "What would you like to discuss with me?"

Achala set his own cup back onto the table. "I realize this is a delicate topic since the information didn't come to me through official channels, but I was led to believe that a team of Guardians is on its way to defuse a planet."

The First Lord took a sip of his kaffa. Achala was careful to stay away from his thoughts, certain he would know if he touched them.

"Your information is correct." He gave a slight smile. "I won't ask how you got it." He settled himself more comfortably in his chair. "This was once a Dark world, home to the last known Dark Lord. Do you remember the stories of how the Fae and the Guardians worked together to contain him in a virtual prison?"

"I remember." The Dark Lord had made the mistake of capturing a Fae soul. Together, the Fae and the Guardians had retrieved it. "But that was a very long time ago. The Guardians stripped the world of its technology then, if I recall the story correctly."

"We did. And after, we watched. We have reason to believe that it has again reached a point where it's a danger to the worlds around it."

"Ah." Achala set his empty plate on the table beside his cup. The room was very warm, but pleasantly so. "Would this be the same world where a Fae and a Guardian went missing some thirty years ago?"

This time, Achala caught the caution entering the First Lord's eyes.

"Losing a Fae soul is not something we care to dwell on, and that, too, was a very long time ago. We learned from the failure. Rest assured we won't lose another, if that is your fear," he said.

Achala had heard no mention of the Guardian or his soul. He wondered why that was. The Guardians, too, valued life.

"While the loss of a soul is not something the Fae take lightly," he replied carefully, "there was a deeper loss in it for me. The Fae was my daughter."

He had no need to try to read the First Lord's thoughts. He was unable to hide his shock at Achala's revelation. It was several moments before he regained speech.

"My sympathies, Your Grace," he finally managed. "I never knew."

"It would have made no difference if you did. Her path was chosen for her at birth. She was meant to bring life to other worlds."

"And instead she lost her own."

"The Guardians lost a life as well, and we mourned his passing, too," Achala pointed out. He didn't quite understand the depth of the First Lord's feelings on the subject, but he knew they were intense and centered mostly on shame. They bombarded him and set him on edge. Something was wrong. "Fae souls are valuable to us, but so are all living things. Our people share a common purpose in that regard."

"We share a goal," the First Lord agreed, staring morosely into his cup. "Our beliefs, however, are significantly different."

"I'm sorry to hear that, and I'm also surprised," Achala said. "As spiritual leader to both our races, I would have thought I understood your Guardian beliefs better than this."

"I've offended you."

"Not offended," Achala gently corrected. "Surprised." And alarmed, truth be told. He'd worried his people had somehow failed Annia and her daughter. Now he wondered if they had failed the Guardian people also. "What makes you think your beliefs are so very different from ours?"

"You believe all life is worth saving. We believe ours are worth sacrificing for the sake of the magic Fae souls bring to the universe."

He hadn't expected a philosophical discussion this evening. To his knowledge the First Lord, a practical man, wasn't prone to them.

"This conversation troubles me." More than troubled him. "The Fae don't expect sacrifices from the Guardians. They expect equality. Complementary skill sets. A partnership as they work to a common goal. Now you are telling me that the Guardians' foremost goal is to protect the Fae?" Achala was appalled and dismayed. "The Guardian gift for technology is every bit as valuable as the Fae gift of magic. You're talking about placing one race above all others, and this isn't acceptable according to the teachings of the Mother. No. I don't believe you," he said. "There's more. I can hear it in your thoughts, no matter how hard you try to keep them from me. This is about what happened to my daughter, and I want to know."

"We have very different beliefs, Your Grace," the First Lord said again. "Whether you want to accept it or not. But one belief we share is that interrelationships between our people breeds Dark Lords. We both know this is true."

"We know it breeds the potential," Achala said. "When that potential was discovered, both our people agreed to discourage it. The Fae then took measures to prevent it. With the guidance of the Mother, Fae souls are selected for our newborns through the spiritual leaders. And from birth on, the Fae are taught to use magic."

"Those measures will work only if a spiritual leader is there at the time of birth to select the soul," the First Lord replied. "What if a child is born to a Fae and a Guardian on a world that has no one to help guide its soul?"

"You know about the child born to my daughter," Achala stated. More than that, he wanted her dead. Fear for River coursed through him. Hawk had been right to worry.

Animosity rolled off the Guardian First Lord who faced him in heated waves.

"Of course I know." The First Lord's skin had gone such a sickly shade of gray that Achala, alarmed, half rose from his chair. "Her father was my son."

CHAPTER **EIGHT**

♦

River blinked her eyes back into focus and found herself in her small office once again, staring at the familiar gray wall. She drew her shoulders together as she gripped the seat of her chair in both hands and took deep breaths.

She hadn't been as prepared as she'd thought she would be to find Hawk with a Guardian team by his side. She hadn't been very well prepared for encountering a pack of Weres either. She'd thought Weres traveled alone. One was disturbing enough. And she'd forgotten the incredible rush she got when she fought with Hawk at her side.

But what had really caught her off guard was the fierce, almost urgent need that rose up in her when she'd come face-to-face—for the first time—with the real Chase Hawkins.

She swallowed her emotions because she didn't have time to think about Hawk or how she felt about seeing him again. Not when he hadn't come back alone.

She knew Hawk. She believed he had come for her. His team, on the other hand, had come for some other reason. The fact that Hawk was with them, and shielding his thoughts from her, was not a good sign.

She spun in her chair just as Dan skidded to a halt in her doorway. He panted as if he'd been running hard, and River realized that the normally fearless leader of the Demons was scared.

River was already unnerved, and her pulse leapt in warning. "What's wrong?"

"It's Billy," he answered. Billy was Dan's unspoken favorite among the youngest Demons. He was small but tough, and always came up swinging. He was one of those kids who couldn't get enough out of life. River liked him. "He's . . ." Dan's brow furrowed as his voice trailed off, unable to find the words. "He's not right." He tapped his head. The hitch in his voice told River that something bad had happened. It took a lot to unnerve Dan, and he was shaken.

She leapt to her feet. "What do you mean, he's not right?"

"Come see for yourself."

Moving with swift agility, his feet pounded along the empty platform and with one smooth swoop, he jumped lightly onto the tracks. River followed after him, her hand on the dagger she kept strapped to her leg. In real life, carrying around a sword was a nuisance. A dagger was the next best thing.

She saved the swords for her virtual worlds.

Darkness closed around them as they moved deeper into the subway. The damp underground air quickly bled through her light T-shirt and chilled her flesh, and River wished she'd grabbed her jacket. Sidestepping the live rails, she peered through the dark and studied her surroundings. Nothing seemed out of the ordinary, but as she left the security of the platform farther and farther behind she could hear the faint sounds of people up ahead.

When Dan starting running she, too, picked up her pace, but came to a sudden halt when he turned the corner and stopped short in front of her.

She smacked into his back with a thud and the air left her lungs in a whoosh. Dan shot her a quick glance but didn't bother to offer a hand as she braced her palms on her thighs and sucked in a breath.

Once her lungs reinflated, she moved in beside him and followed his troubled gaze upward. The rusty lights embedded in the walls flickered on and off, providing her with enough light to see Billy peering down at them through a manhole. His voice was high, almost hysterical, and he was shouting some sort of gibberish about zombies and flesh-eating monsters that River couldn't quite follow.

Nick was there. So were several of the youngest Demons. They crowded silently around him, their eyes wide as they watched the performance.

"We are so going to talk about this later," Nick said to her, his voice grim.

"What is he babbling about?" River asked.

Nick shook his head. "I have no idea."

His tone said he didn't want to know either. Whatever was happening, it wasn't going to end well.

"Maybe you should take the kids home," she suggested. He nodded. He, too, realized where this was headed.

As Nick rounded up the protesting kids and hustled

them out of sight, River studied the boy for a moment, then stepped under the manhole opening and called out to him. Rain began to pour in earnest. Drops of water splashed off her skin.

"Hey, Billy. Why don't you come down from there? Dan lifted some chocolate. Dark—your favorite. He's been saving it for you." She softened her tone, trying to coax him. "Please, Billy. You're scaring everyone."

Billy stopped his gibberish and for a second she thought she might have gotten through to him, but less than a heartbeat later, he started ranting and boxing his ears with enough force to rupture his eardrums.

Tuning out the background noises, she listened carefully.

There. There it was.

A buzzing sound, barely audible to the human ear from this distance, was emanating off Billy, rolling along the cement walls and charging the underground air. Dan heard it, too. He cocked his head and frowned, his eyes troubled.

Almost afraid to move, let alone breathe, River angled her chin slowly and whispered through barely parted lips, "Can you hear that?"

"Yeah."

River struggled to think what it could mean. Nick had been affected by a buzzing sound, but that was when he'd been struggling to use the hologram. If it was caused by the hologram, they shouldn't be hearing any buzzing sound now because Billy was functioning outside the program. It didn't make sense.

"Have you ever heard it before?" she questioned Dan.

"Jake and I heard it when we were training."

She searched for commonalities. Like Nick, Jake couldn't pull himself out of the program. She tried not to panic. Nick and Jake both heard the buzzing when they were using the program. This was different.

Nick and Jake were fine.

"Why didn't you tell me you heard a noise in the program?" she asked Dan, then wished she hadn't said anything when he stiffened. He would blame himself for this, although he'd admit that to no one.

"Didn't think it was important." As Billy continued to slap his hands to his ears, Dan narrowed his gaze and asked, "What do you think it means?"

"I'm not sure yet."

Dan stared at her, his cool expression telltale. He didn't believe her. But instead of pressing, he gestured with a nod, already accepting the inevitable. "Can you help him?"

River didn't know what to think as Billy danced circles around the open manhole.

"First I have to figure out what's wrong with him." The only way she knew how to accomplish that task was by entering his mind. She was about to send out a light brush of magic when one of Billy's feet skidded from beneath him and he almost came toppling down on top of them.

Dan cursed under his breath, twisted around, and started for the platform. Impatience laced his voice as he announced, "I'm going up to get him."

Every instinct she possessed shrieked a warning, and without conscious thought River grabbed Dan and spun him around to face her.

"I don't think that's a good idea," she said.

Dan opened his mouth to argue but didn't get the chance. His eyes widened and a split second later she found herself in his arms, rolling along the subway floor and crashing into the cement barrier.

What the hell?

The tunnel blurred before her eyes and her hand went to her head where a lump had immediately started to form. When her eyes were again able to focus, she spotted Billy lying across one of the live rails. The smell of charred flesh filled her nostrils and she started to gag.

"Jesus," she murmured, letting the dry heaves pass before climbing to her feet. Wobbling slightly, she braced her hand on the cool wall for balance.

Dan still wasn't moving. She quickly pulled herself together and reached for him. "You okay?"

He didn't take the offered hand. Instead he climbed to his feet and put on his best hard-ass face when his glance met hers. "You want to tell me what happened to him?"

"I don't know. But I'm going to get to the bottom of it." River ignored the pain running the length of her spine. From deep in her belly, she drew a healing breath and let the soothing magic spread through her aching body to repair her. She thought about offering the same to Dan, but knew from experience the Demon leader would simply see it as a sign of weakness.

"What were the boys doing down here?" she questioned him. Her eyes narrowed. "And how did you know something was wrong?"

"They've been having a little fun with their holograms," he said with a shrug. "I followed them to keep an eye on them. Nick followed them, too," he added, defensive.

Meaning everyone had known something was going on but River. The defensiveness meant it wasn't anything good.

"Define *a little fun* for me," she said.

"They get together in real time with their holograms and use them as a sort of smoke screen. The hologram gives them the illusion, but standing behind it means their characters can pack a real punch."

River was outraged. "And you allowed this?"

"Yeah," Dan said. "I did."

What was it with guys? She had deliberately created the program to prevent them from getting hurt, and yet the first chance they got they worked around its safety features. Now one of them was dead, and she needed to examine him. She tried not to cry because she didn't want to make this harder for Dan.

The closer River came to Billy's twisted, smoking body however, the more her skin prickled in warning. The boy before her bore no resemblance to the one who'd been prowling the subway as little as two days ago.

The hairs on River's arms lifted as she took in his sunken cheeks and pale, stretched skin. Her stomach lurched.

"River, what is it?"

The room around her faded and no longer was she standing in the subway. Time flashed backward until she was sitting in a squeaky rocking chair in her childhood home in Hammonds, feeling helpless and afraid as she kept watch over her mother's sickbed. The once vibrant woman had deteriorated into a shell of her former self until River no longer recognized her, in much the same manner as Billy.

Except it had taken her mother months before she'd reached this stage, yet Billy, less than two days. A wave of terror moved through her. This couldn't be happening. Not again.

Nick and Jake are fine. Nick and Jake are fine. She repeated the thought over and over. They had heard the noise in their Hollow forms, but they weren't delusional.

Not yet.

She pressed her mouth into the crook of her elbow and grabbed Dan's arm to haul him back.

"What is it?" Dan asked again. He pushed past her. His back went ramrod straight and his shoulder blades drew together when he took in the boy's body. He stepped back, and from the look on his face, it was clear that he'd come to a similar conclusion as River. He wasn't old enough to remember the virus, but everyone knew the symptoms.

Now, new symptoms seemed to be manifesting. Hallucinations, for instance.

"Holy shit," Dan murmured under his breath, and took a step back as equal mixtures of fear and disbelief brought color to his face.

"We can't leave him like this," River said. "Think of the children."

She was startled by how quickly Dan returned to business. "I'll go get gloves and a bag. You stay here and make sure no one touches him."

River didn't know whether to be impressed by his fortitude or feel sorry for him. This was no way for a teenager to be spending his life.

The echo of his boots faded as he disappeared around a bend in the tunnel. As she stole another glance at Billy, she fought down the fear. Could her world withstand another pandemic like the last?

There were so few survivors.

As she waited for Dan to return, she spotted an open wallet lying next to Billy's body. Since it hadn't been there before she could only assume it had fallen out of his pocket. Hoping it might hold answers, River kicked it away from the body and with her boot nudged it under one of the emergency lights.

She glanced at the photo ID of a well-groomed, nice-looking man in his early twenties. He sported short brown hair, cognac-toned skin, smoky, intelligent eyes. She read the identification. The name didn't ring a bell. She passed him off as a government employee who should have known enough to stay away from the underground. She loved the Demons but they had sticky fingers. She supposed she was to blame for that since she and Nick had taught them how to pick pockets without getting caught.

On the opposite side of the plastic ID card was a picture of a bleached blonde, a large-breasted young woman with a toothy, flirtatious smile on her pretty face.

She looked familiar, River thought. She wondered if the owner of the ID or his girlfriend had anything to do with what had happened to Billy. The original virus had spread through contact, although each time it mutated its characteristics changed.

River wrapped her arms around herself, wishing again that she'd remembered her jacket, but the chill of her thoughts sank a little deeper than that of her skin. Billy had gotten sick too fast, and not just physically. His mind had been affected, too. The high-pitched buzzing sound was another cause for concern.

If this was the virus and the virus had mutated, she was suddenly afraid that a few cuts and bruises were the least of the program's safety problems.

She'd given the program to Billy. Her concern escalated. She'd given it to Jake and Nick, too.

She'd given it to all of the Demons.

♦ ♦

It might be spring in the Arctic, but that didn't make it warm. Peters swung his arms, keeping the circulation moving as he walked around the weather station.

The Were kids followed him, tumbling about in the dirt, scuffling and wrestling. A sharp command from the oldest boy, Logan, brought them back under control whenever the play got too rough.

From everything Peters had seen so far, Logan had these kids well in hand. They'd apparently spent the day in the tundra, learning to hunt, and he'd interrupted evening play time with his arrival. He had no idea what they were calling evening because the sun never set. From what he gathered, they slept when they felt like it.

For that matter, so did he. He adjusted the rifle on his shoulder. The kids didn't appear concerned for their safety, but he liked having backup.

The other thing he'd noticed was that the little guys could do the same crazy thing with plants that Andy had shown him. He'd thought the plants had started early this year, considering the season. Now he noticed something he should have picked up on before. The vegetation wasn't spreading inward the way it should, from the warmer areas on the outer edges of the arctic desert to the colder inner region. Instead, plant life was spreading outward—from the remote arctic outpost.

That was just plain freaky.

One of the boys suddenly vanished and Peters nearly leapt from his skin. His breath puffed in the cold air as he took a step back and shook his head, trying to clear his vision.

"F-frig," he said. Cleaning up his language was going to be a problem. "Can't you make them stop doing that?"

"Doing what?" Logan asked, his odd green eyes, puzzled, shifting to Peters' face. The boy who'd vanished reappeared at his elbow and he slapped Logan on the back before running away, giggling. "Oh," Logan said, following Peters' gaze as he tracked the kid's zigzagging movements. "That." He shrugged. "They need to practice. Otherwise they freeze when they're in danger, like John and Seth did."

John and Seth being the two youngest boys Peters had found hiding behind the sofa.

As a cop, he was used to hard-luck cases. Abandoned children were nothing new in this world, but these boys had lived on their own under some pretty harsh conditions for a very long time. Grown men had cracked under the strain of living out here, and they'd had a supply chain to fall back on.

But the two youngest would have been in diapers when David had died, and Logan, no more than ten. And yet they'd survived without any help from the outside world. Morbid curiosity made him ask. They were Weres after all, and meat would be their dietary staple. "Were there ever any more of you?"

"Nope. Just us."

Peters hadn't intended to judge. People did what they had to do in order to survive. But he did think he'd sleep a little easier knowing cannibalism wasn't going to be an issue. "Did you ever wonder why David stopped coming?"

Again, Logan shrugged. "If he'd been able to come, he would have. After a while we knew."

Peters wondered what it was like to have such faith in another human being. River'd had the same faith in her father that Logan did. But despite everything he'd seen in his life, Peters truly believed, deep down, in basic human decency. If he hadn't, he would have quit law enforcement a long time ago.

Okay, then. He'd believe David Weston was basically decent. So what had he been up to?

"Did David keep any papers here?" he asked. "Whenever he came, did he have an office he worked out of?"

"Over there." Logan pointed to the outbuilding where Peters had found the overflowing filing cabinets, and his heart sank. Damn it, he'd be here forever if he had to sift through all that shit. Then again, it wasn't as if he had anywhere else to go.

He caught movement out of the corner of his eye. An unmelted patch of snow to his left shifted its tail. He stopped, and Logan stopped with him. Keeping his eyes on the patch of snow, he eased the rifle off of his shoulder.

The patch of snow rose to its four feet, turning into an enormous arctic wolf. Peters viewed it with awe. It stared at him with head up and ears erect, curious but not yet threatening. He tried to figure out where the little Weres were without taking his own eyes off the wolf. Thank God they could vanish. He wouldn't mind having that talent right now himself. It was breeding season and if this was a female with pups nearby, he was screwed.

The Were kids didn't appear concerned. That indicated

this wasn't the wolf's first visit here. Peters wondered what else it meant, or if it viewed him as a threat. That wouldn't be good either.

It started to circle, padding on paws the size of his hands. Jesus, but the thing was big. The white fur and the bright, sea-green eyes told him where the DNA for the Were kids had come from. His faith in Weston slipped a little. He would have hoped he'd be against this experimentation, not for it.

Another wolf appeared.

"Don't move," Logan said from beside him. "They don't like you being here."

No shit. Peters was starting to get the same impression. He wondered if Logan understood something else about wolf behavior. In this little group of Weres, Logan was almost mature. He was the alpha. That might not be tolerated by the adult wolves for a whole lot longer. What would happen if he were challenged?

The wind picked up and the damp cold bit through his clothing. He'd left the zipper on his outer shell undone.

A third wolf appeared.

"What do we do?" Peters asked Logan.

"I'm not sure."

This wasn't good. The boy wouldn't know what to do because he'd never been in this situation before. And Peters, as much as he liked shooting at things, wasn't all that crazy about killing animals for being animals. Especially not in front of little kids.

"Take the others and get out of here," Peters said.

"If I do that, they'll kill you for sure."

He'd already suspected as much. He was prepared to take a few of them with him. But not in front of the kids. "I'll take my chances."

Logan hesitated, then barked out a command. The children disappeared.

Peters steadied the rifle, trying to keep the one circling behind him in his line of vision. He backed up, wishing he was closer to one of the buildings. The one time Andy's voice in his head was silent was the time he could really use her guidance. That it wasn't forthcoming didn't bode well. With any luck he'd be too old and stringy for them to develop a taste for human flesh. He wiped his nose with the back of his gloved hand.

His finger started to tighten on the trigger. He didn't want to do this, but he couldn't see any way around it. More wolves were gathering. He counted seven.

He squeezed off a warning shot. As he did, two men appeared out of nowhere, directly in its path. The bullet breezed past one man's head, so close Peters could have parted his hair if he'd had any.

The man turned his own weapon on Peters. Peters waved him off. "I'm not shooting at you," he said impatiently. "Look behind you."

The two men turned. "Crisos," one breathed.

"Please, Jesus, tell me you're the aliens River keeps talking about," Peters said. "And that you have some suggestions, because right now, I'm a little stumped."

CHAPTER NINE

♦

They had spotted three more delusional people, all show-ing symptoms of illness, and Hawk was now scared. He freely admitted it. If not for River, he would have or-dered his team to withdraw.

As it was, they were probably too late for it to make a difference. The entire team faced months of quaran-tine when they returned home.

"Don't touch anyone," he ordered Lilla. "Don't fight. If anyone comes at you, you're to run or transport home. Do you understand?"

Lilla nodded, as spooked by what they were seeing as he was. He needed to get in touch with Faran. He was the disease expert on the team, which was one of the reasons Hawk had chosen him.

The rain eased to a dreary drizzle as they splashed through the deserted streets, making their way in what Hawk believed to be the direction of the subway. He had a good memory for details, and the city's layout from when he and River had negotiated these same streets hadn't changed.

He slowed when he spotted the familiar stairwell leading underground.

He motioned for Lilla to stop so he could think of their best approach. Perhaps they should look for an-other entrance farther up the street, although from what he remembered, most of the entrances had been blocked off by city residents using them as convenient garbage dumps.

The thought of children living under the conditions he'd witnessed in the subway saddened him, although he understood how it had come about. This world had been brought to its knees by war and pandemic, and it continued to struggle. Societies could be measured by the way they treated their young and their elderly, and the people with the power on this world had somehow taken a very wrong turn on their road to recovery. By taking away its technological and scientific capabilities, it was a Guardian hope that moral decency would re-emerge.

A figure emerged from the stairwell. He turned his head and Hawk zeroed in on his face. Was that Jake?

The streets were no place for a thirteen-year-old boy, especially not with whatever had killed that poor bastard obviously spreading, and he couldn't imagine River putting her brother in danger. What the hell had happened here in the last four months?

Hawk wondered if he should approach him. Was it really Jake? Or was it another hologram?

The boy glanced in their direction, his hand positioned over his leg as if ready to draw a weapon. He scanned the streets and the rooftops. A moment later, he lowered his head and disappeared back into the safety of the underground.

Lilla stated the obvious. "He saw us."

"Shit." Hawk rubbed the back of his neck. So much

for the element of surprise. Thanks to River's new program, in order to get to her he'd have to go through a gang of kids who could kick his ass without any harm to themselves.

By mixing magic with technology, she had created another reason why this world needed to be defused. He hoped she would understand that, but knew from experience that her programs were built with the best of intentions and she would do anything to make them work.

He considered what he should do. If he followed Jake into this street entrance rather than searching for another, at least Hawk knew what he and Lilla would be facing. He thought about the dead man's diseased body, splattered on the street, and his lips thinned. Getting a shit kicking by a bunch of kids was nothing compared to what was happening aboveground. He needed to talk to River, to find out if she knew what was happening, and if not, to warn her.

"Wearing anything red?" Hawk asked. Lilla looked at him strangely. "We're going in. We need to be wearing their colors if we want to get out alive," he explained. He didn't bother adding that even then, it was no real guarantee.

"Turn your back," Lilla said.

A few minutes later, Hawk had a scrap of red lace in his hand. As he fingered the nonregulation, delicate camisole he didn't quite know what to say. The look on her face dared him to say anything.

Wisely, he remained silent. He tore the camisole in two, then tied the strips around their forearms.

They dashed across the street. Moving with careful deliberation he descended the first two steps, listening for movement. Heavy footsteps sounded from the tunnel below him.

Instantly, he readied to fight.

Three massive, bloodred ugly monsters with arms like steel made his gut clench, the sight of them bringing back memories from his days trapped in a virtual prison.

Get a grip on yourself, Colonel. These are nothing but projections.

Magically enhanced projections.

"They're just boys, right?" Lilla asked, seeking confirmation, tension in both her words and her body. She had her hand on her weapon.

"Stay here," Hawk ordered her. Mentally, he prepared himself. "No matter what, don't interfere. They're going to beat the crap out of me, but they can't kill me." He hoped that was true. He based the assumption on his knowledge of River, and how she hadn't been able to kill the Were in the warehouse even though she'd driven her sword through it. But she'd definitely used the sword so that it would hurt. Hawk did not doubt he was about to get his ass handed to him.

If putting his ass on the line got him to River, then it would be worth it.

The Demons closed in around the foot of the stairs.

Running footsteps heralded the approach of reinforcements. Hawk could have retreated. Instead, he carefully moved down the stairwell and took a quick step to the side, wanting to get his back to the wall for protection.

The first blow came out of nowhere as a Demon materialized on the step beside him. The force drove his head back, and his boots slipped on the rain-soaked concrete. A curse cut the air as he hit the ground with a thud. The curse came from Lilla, a few steps above him. Fortunately his ass broke the fall, but his head hit the railing hard enough to fade the world to black for a second.

A knee slammed into his back and he slid the rest of the way down the stairs. The bony knee pressing into his spine, and the dull ache in his skull, made it difficult to remember that these were boys.

They were also gang members in a world with almost unenforceable law. That was important to remember, too.

A Demon stooped down beside him, its face swimming into focus near Hawk's. River had gone all out. These kids had managed to replicate the monsters from his nightmares too realistically for comfort.

"What do you want?" the Demon demanded.

The prepubescent voices killed the illusion. Relief washed through him as he held up his hands in surrender. "I'm looking for River."

"You're looking in the wrong place," someone said.

This boy wasn't wearing a demon form. *Jake.*

"Get Dan," Jake said to a Demon standing nearby.

He didn't recognize Hawk. Worry seized him. Jake thought he was someone from this world, and hunting

River. Of course he would think that. And he would protect her, even to the point of killing anyone he thought might bring her harm.

He was in deeper shit than he'd expected.

Hawk tried to lift his head, only to have it slammed back to the ground. His teeth clicked together. Dark boots circled his head, splashing dirty rainwater into his face. He tasted it, along with a drop of fresh, coppery blood that trickled from his hairline.

"Jake, it's me," he said. "Nick."

It nearly killed him to say that but he didn't know how else to explain.

"You're lying."

"Tell me you haven't noticed what a complete and total asshole Nick has become over the past few months," Hawk said. "My real name is Chase Hawkins, and I'm here to protect your sister. I had to borrow Nick's body for a while in order to do that." He tried to get a good look at Jake, to read what he was thinking.

Whatever he was thinking, it didn't bode well for Hawk.

"I don't believe you," Jake said. He released the safety on the gun in his hand. "I'm all the protection she needs." The gun trembled, but Hawk had no doubt the boy was going to use it. He might be young, but he had backbone. Hawk closed his eyes. He heard a scuffle on the stairs and knew that Lilla had realized, too, that Jake was about to kill him.

He had failed River. That was his only regret.

"I don't like him either, but I'm not sure your sister's

going to be too happy about this," a familiar voice said. "Shooting him in front of the K-I-D-S sets a really bad example."

Hawk would never have thought that hearing Nick's voice again could make him this happy.

"Do you know him?" Jake demanded. The gun remained aimed at Hawk's head. Hawk figured this could still go one of two ways.

"Believe it or not," Nick said, "he's a character from one of River's video games."

Crisos. Hawk was a dead man.

A fireball ricocheted off the tunnel wall somewhere above him, then landed on the tracks and connected with one of the live rails. An explosion of blue sparks shot to the ceiling.

The ensuing silence was deafening. Then another fireball hit the wall, this time uncomfortably close. The heat scorched his exposed skin.

The Demon pinning him down released him, and Hawk blasted to his feet. Relief quickly turned to caution as he discovered two things in rapid succession.

River had arrived. And she was angry.

◆ ◆

They had dared to touch him.

Fury drove River forward, another fireball in her hands. He was hers, and they had hurt him. The sight of blood on his face fed her anger.

A boy stood beside him. He had a gun in his hands. Somewhere, in the back of River's head, a warning shouted out that she couldn't hurt this child. His name was Jake and he was important to her.

She did not, however, like the gun he held. He'd threatened Hawk with it. Her eyes narrowed, and the gun in Jake's hands started to glow red-hot. He dropped it, his eyes widening in surprise and fear, and she knew she should be ashamed for causing that fear but she wasn't.

The gun blew apart as it hit the ground, fragments firing in all directions. The voice in her head barked out an order for her to protect the children. As quick as the gun exploded, the fragments turned into harmless droplets of water.

But she was by no means finished. She wouldn't stop until Hawk was safe. She called up her magic and a funnel of wind spun around him, forcing the boy and the others to back away. They held their arms over their faces against the spray of dirt and debris the wind funnel created.

The magic singing through her veins felt good. She felt alive. Her fingertips crackled with it, and the hair at the nape of her neck caught on fire.

Her vision cleared. Demons stood on the subway platform. Magic throbbed in the air around her. She breathed it in, and released it again through the pores of her skin.

She mustn't hurt children. But demons needed to learn that no one touched Hawk.

◆ ◆

Hawk pushed at the wall of air, then tried to drive his fist through it, but it was no good.

River thought she had sealed him off from danger. Instead, the danger had multiplied. He struggled to keep his spiking panic under control, mindful of the bomb hardwired into his head. He forced himself to think of his options. He had to get through the wall of air, he had to control the chemicals in his brain, and he had to stop River from doing things that could never be undone.

As black waves of anger rolled off her, he reached for her thoughts, brushing them very lightly, and found them in chaos. She'd been agitated even before she had seen him. The threat to him had been like a lit match to a keg of dynamite. Something had happened to her, and whatever it was, it was bad. And it was dark.

He should have come sooner. He would never forgive himself, no matter that he'd had no choice. He should have found a way.

Hawk needed help. And that meant he had only one option. He opened his thoughts to Achala and called to him.

The connection with the Fae was surprisingly strong, even across the empty distance of space, making Hawk uncomfortably aware that River had not even begun to tap her full potential.

Achala's response to his call was immediate. One moment the wall of air cut Hawk off from what was happening around him, and the next, it was gone.

He crouched defensively, quickly assessing the situation, searching for any immediate danger. A few of the Demons remained in their hologram forms, and considering what was happening around them, Hawk was impressed. It would take a great deal of concentration to hang on to their illusions.

Jake had pressed back against one of the tunnel walls, his eyes on his sister full of guarded concern. They also held calculation. Hawk worried the boy would try to approach her, and it was by no means safe for him to do so. As yet, River had very little control over herself and her actions. The last time he'd seen her like this, she'd burned down a subway station. And she hadn't been nearly this angry.

Nick stood nearby, indecision also etched on his face as if he didn't know which way to turn. A small group of children gathered against him, their eyes wide and afraid.

The gray-haired Fae leader, Achala, had positioned himself between River and the children. He'd wisely avoided coming between her and Hawk, allowing her to see for herself that Hawk was unhurt.

If anyone could calm her, it would be Achala. He had absorbed much of the magic around her. Its peppery scent permeated the air, curling through the tunnel.

He was speaking to River in words Hawk didn't understand, but that she seemed to be listening to carefully.

Then Hawk understood. Achala was speaking to her soul. He could feel it through his own. That was why he didn't understand the words, but she did. It was the language of Fae souls.

And slowly, tentatively, hers responded to it. She crumpled, her slight form buckling at the knees as her eyes rolled back in her head. Hawk started for her. Achala got there ahead of him.

Nick and Jake both rushed forward as well, their concern for River overriding their fear. Hawk allowed Jake to pass. He needed to see that his sister was fine, and that Achala meant her no harm. The Fae leader could take care of himself in this situation.

Nick, Hawk turned to intercept. As he did, he saw that two of the demons continued to hold Lilla back, kicking and swearing and telling them what they could do to themselves. It would be interesting to see her reaction when she saw for herself that the demons holding her really were just kids. That alone would be worth the price of admission.

Hawk blocked Nick's path, eyeing him with contempt. Even though he'd just saved Hawk's life, he hadn't forgotten the mind games the little shit had played with him. And okay, maybe he was more than a little jealous that Nick had spent the last four months with River and he hadn't.

"Get out of my way," Nick said, his attention on River and Achala. "She needs me." He tried to push past Hawk, but Hawk blocked him again. "Quit being a Neanderthal, you moron," Nick said impatiently. "I've had medical training. I can help."

Hawk's lip curled. "The spiritual leader of the Fae hardly needs help from you."

"I get it," Nick said impatiently. "You're holding a grudge. But listen, pal. You were inside *my* head, remember? Not my problem what I had stored in it. Now I'm willing to let bygones be bygones." He waggled his fingers at Hawk. "Friends, okay? So step aside."

Hawk itched to hit the sarcastic bastard.

"Stop it!" River cried. She was back on her feet, shaking from head to toe. Both men made a move toward her, their argument forgotten. She backed away, clearly not wanting either one of them to touch her.

"This might not be the best time to interfere," Achala warned them. "She's far from calm. Please, let me handle it." He looked around. "First, let's get rid of the audience. River, *liefeling,* shut down the holograms, please," he said to her gently.

The holograms disappeared. Only a few very surprised young gang members remained, and most were too small to pose any real threat. Hawk recognized Dan, but he seemed content to stand back and watch without interfering. If anything, his attention was solely on the children. Since they were out of harm's way, Hawk didn't worry about them.

He had a bigger problem. Nick, idiot that he was, stuck one hand into his pocket. Lilla, now free from the holograms who'd been restraining her, took it as an act of aggression against Hawk. She rushed forward and nailed Nick in the back with her shoulder. As he crumpled, she caught him in the stomach with her knee. He fell to his knees, then onto his side, and curled in a ball, gasping for air.

"Put your hands where I can see them," she ordered him.

Nick, who was having difficulty breathing, didn't immediately respond. Then he held up one hand with a sliver of tinfoil in it. "Gum?"

The Demons whose hologram forms had disappeared now came pounding around the bend in the tunnel in their mortal forms to join Dan. With reinforcements at his side, Dan and the Demons moved to surround Hawk and Lilla. As Nick lay breathless on the ground Lilla pressed her boot to his neck and held him down, her weapon aimed at his head.

She spoke to Dan. "Come any closer and I'll kill him."

"She's lovely," Nick said to Hawk, wheezing past the pain. "If you're bent on destroying worlds, you picked the right partner."

Achala frowned at Lilla and Nick. "Do something," he said to Hawk.

What did Achala expect him to do? He was all in favor of letting Lilla shoot the bastard. But Nick had stopped Jake from shooting Hawk. If Hawk stopped Lilla, they'd be even.

"Hello," Nick said again, still pinned to the ground by Lilla's boot. "Normally I can appreciate a good dominatrix, but I don't think this is going to end up the way I like. Can somebody get her off me?"

"Let him up," Hawk ordered Lilla. She hesitated, her reluctance to obey the command obvious. "Do it."

Slowly, her boot lifted. Nick pushed her foot away and scrambled to his feet. The Demons pressed closer.

"Stop it, Dan," River said, and all heads turned in her direction. Jake had his arm around her waist. She was pale but in control again, and Hawk's heart twisted with the need to be near her.

After her recent display, Dan knew better than to blatantly threaten Hawk. That didn't mean Hawk felt safe.

"I don't trust him," Dan said to her.

"I don't trust him either," she whispered back, her eyes never leaving Hawk's. "But leave him alone."

Hawk felt her words like a slap, although he understood. He was the interloper here, and he hadn't exactly made a peaceful entrance.

That seemed to appease Dan. He edged to the left, allowing Hawk room to approach her. Hawk pushed past him only to be faced by her brother.

Achala drew Jake aside with a few murmured words that left the boy's face dark from a mixture of rebellion and resignation.

Two seconds later, River was in Hawk's arms. Immediately, the sense of rightness washed over him as a brilliant white light slammed into his soul. She was with him once again, and for the first time in four long months, he felt whole. He wondered if she felt the same way, but didn't dare open his thoughts to her in order to find out. He had things in his head he didn't want her to know about. Not yet.

First he would have to earn back her trust. And then he would have to earn her understanding, because her world needed his help whether she liked it or not. Her beautiful blue eyes kept wandering to his face as if she couldn't really believe it was him, and his heart ached for everything she'd been through and for everything that was about to come.

The warmth of her magic surged through him, healing the cuts and bruises the Demons had delivered. He accepted it without complaint, because doing this gave her pleasure.

He was all about giving River pleasure.

He bent his head to kiss her, then remembered with a start that they weren't alone, and that one of the members of their audience was her brother. Another was her grandfather—and that was another bit of information he wanted to keep from her, because it wasn't his secret to share.

Achala couldn't take his eyes off of River, and he was frowning slightly as if something puzzled him. He didn't appear overly alarmed by whatever it was, so Hawk didn't worry.

"River," he whispered to her. "*Mellita*. I need to speak with you. Alone."

For a heart-stopping moment he thought she'd refuse. He could sense her indecision. He felt the brush of her thoughts, and her surprise, then suspicion, when she found the door firmly closed against her. He pretended he hadn't noticed her prying.

"Come with me," she finally said. Jake made a sharp sound of protest. "We're going to my office," she reassured her brother. "You can stand outside the door if you want."

"I do," the boy replied. The set of his chin indicated to Hawk he wouldn't be standing there patiently either.

"Good," Hawk said. "I want someone I trust standing guard." He saw the confusion in Jake's eyes, then the flicker of recognition. Hawk had said those very same words to him once before, when they'd first met, and both he and River were afraid to sleep. He'd hoped the boy would remember that.

Hawk looked to Achala, an unspoken question transmitting between them. Was it safe to take her away from the Fae's watchful presence?

"I think that's a good idea," Achala confirmed, although he sounded distracted and continued to frown.

Hawk, however, couldn't leave the older man unprotected. He now had the safety of two Fae to consider.

He turned to Lilla. "Stay with Achala," he said, then pointed to Nick. "And keep an eye on that one." He would have liked to add that she could kill him if he gave her a reason, or even if she wanted the practice, but he didn't dare give that order in front of a Fae.

Nick blotted the blood from his cheek with his sleeve while Lilla watched him with cool, quiet dispassion.

River led Hawk deeper into the subway. Jake trailed sullenly behind them.

It didn't appear quite as dark and dirty in the subway as it had the first time he'd been here. From the enhanced lighting to the small rooms off the platform, touches of River and her magic existed everywhere.

As they walked the platform to the farthest end they passed an empty body bag, a shovel, and two pairs of gloves. She kept her face carefully averted.

The body bag reminded Hawk uneasily of what was happening aboveground. Had disease touched the Demons?

He wouldn't question her. Not when her magic continued to hang thick in the air, pulsing with unspent energy, despite what her grandfather had managed to absorb. Her loss of control indicated to Hawk the enormous stress she'd been under, and also the extent her magic had grown. Her knowledge of how to use it hadn't kept pace and he was seriously concerned about that. He thanked the Mother that Achala had come so quickly.

River opened the door to what appeared to be an office. Hawk turned to Jake, who hung back uncertainly.

"I promise you," he said to him, his voice low and intense, "that I will never harm your sister."

Jake looked him straight in the eye. "Do we really know each other?"

"I know that you can kill a bear with a crossbow," Hawk replied. He grinned. "And that you can be a smartass."

Jake didn't return the smile, but he did step back and allow Hawk to close the door.

Hawk clicked the latch firmly. Something was wrong with Jake—something serious. The kid had *trauma* written all over him. But Hawk could only worry about one Weston at a time, and right now, his primary concern was River. An unforgiving fist squeezed his heart as her pain and sadness wrapped around his soul and choked the air out of his lungs.

He leaned his back against the door and scanned the room. It was definitely River's work space. Computer screens, cables, and keyboards cluttered all the flat surfaces, whether horizontal or vertical. A can of Red Bull sat on her desk. She preferred it to coffee, mostly because it gave her twice the caffeine. She was practical about things like that.

Her personal space, on the other hand, would be much like the safe houses she'd designed, filled with lush vegetation and warm, earthy tones. That was why he hated seeing her living down here, even if it was undoubtedly the safest place for her considering what was happening above.

Now that they were finally alone, she looked ready to jump from her skin. She was also so beautiful his eyes stung. He wondered how he'd managed to survive without her these past months. He stared at her hungrily, allowing a touch of that hunger to seep into his expression.

"Well?" he said to her.

Her brows knit together over the bridge of her delicate nose. "Well, what?"

He spread his hands wide so she could examine him. "Tell me this isn't my best body yet."

She examined him slowly from head to toe. "I'm not all that crazy about the haircut," she finally replied, "and you're no Sever, but you'll do."

"I'm glad," he said. "Because this is the real me and the last version you'll ever have to get used to."

She wasn't very big, but she was fast and she was strong. She had his face in her hands before he knew what was happening, drawing his mouth to hers. A single tear seeped from the corner of her eye and he wiped it way with his thumb.

"I thought Jake was going to kill you," she said, resting her cheek against his chest.

"So did I," Hawk confessed. His fingers curled around her hips, dragging her tighter against him. "But in all fairness, I had it coming. I shot him first."

"From now on, no one is shooting anyone."

"Except in the arm or the leg," he agreed. "Or in Nick's case, the kneecaps."

She laughed, the sound making him breathe a little easier and lessening the constriction around his chest. "Not *anywhere*."

He held her, soaking in the feel of her as she slowly unwound. He liked the sex. A lot. But there was something to be said for moments like this.

"How long have you been living down here?" he asked her. Looking around him, he suspected quite awhile.

"Since not long after you left," she replied.

He wasn't prepared for that response. "Four *months*?" he said, dismayed. His beautiful little Fae, who loved life and needed greenery around her, had been holed up underground for four months. "What in the name of the Mother have I missed?"

She told him everything then, the words tumbling over each other, and his dismay grew. She spoke of Sam and Melinda, so now he knew what had happened to Jake.

And to River, too, because even though Hawk had also lost his family, the evidence had been kept from him. He couldn't imagine what seeing it would have done to him, and he'd witnessed some awful things in his line of work. River and Jake were innocents in comparison, even considering the world where they'd been born.

She wasn't quite so forthcoming when she spoke of the hologram program, although Hawk could read between the lines on that one. She wasn't simply giving the Demons a means of protecting themselves. She was building an army.

He paled at that knowledge. She really had no idea what could happen if the program she'd developed fell into the wrong hands, because it never occurred to her that she could be forced into giving it up. Perhaps she couldn't. After what he'd witnessed today that was undoubtedly true, but by boosting her technology with her magic, morally she was on very slippery ground. He thanked the Mother again that Achala had come.

But it wasn't until she started to talk of a boy named

Billy that Hawk truly became afraid. It sounded a little too much like what he and Lilla had witnessed on the streets above.

It also explained the body bag and why she'd already been so on edge.

"Nick blames me for Billy," she said, tears sparkling in her eyes. "He warned me that the hologram had some glitches that needed to be fixed, but I couldn't find any." With her rising frustration, Hawk again felt the shift in her magic. "I should have listened to him."

There was something about what River had just said that Hawk knew should mean something to him, but his concern at the moment was for her.

"That's crazy talk," he said. "No one should listen to Nick. Not ever." The bastard. River Weston would never willingly put anyone in danger. Her sole purpose behind the video game she'd designed had been to bring back a quality of life to those who'd lost the will to live. It was her way of giving them the ability to move, and play, even if only through their minds. She was Fae, and even with untutored magic, she was a gift to Earth and all those who walked it.

She had been too long underground. Hawk needed to take her away from here, to remind her of who she was and what life was about.

"I have something I want to show you," he said to her. "But it's not here. You told Dan you don't trust me, and I understand why you don't. But you have in the past. Do you think you could trust me enough to jump with me? If I promise to bring you back here?" He offered the warmth of his soul to hers, relieved and encouraged when she didn't push his away but allowed them to mingle. "I also promise you, it will be well worth your while."

CHAPTER TEN

♦

Nick's already fan-fucking-tabulous day had taken a nosedive for the worse.

He watched as River disappeared with Wonder-Dude. His hopes of ever getting her back vanished along with her.

The glower on Dan's face said the Demon realized his chances with her—which had been even lower than Nick's—had also plunged from zero to beyond.

"Watch the kids," Dan snarled at him. "I've got some damage control to take care of."

Nick forgot about River. "What do you mean, damage control?"

"The kind that involves rubber gloves and a shovel."

Nick's ears started to ring. *Billy didn't make it.*

"Jesus," he said.

"Yeah." The juvenile delinquent didn't look at him. "I'll be back in a few hours."

Nick wasn't overly fond of Dan. The guy was a thug, two degrees away from becoming a contract killer, which was most likely how he'd end up, but at the same time, he was still a kid. "I'm coming with you."

"I don't want the little ones wandering around. Some- one needs to keep an eye on them."

He was right about that. They didn't need to stumble on Dan as he disposed of Billy's body. Nick hesitated. No way would he ask the blonde to keep track of them. She'd probably bake a few in her gingerbread oven.

"The old guy seems harmless," Nick said. The youn- gest boy was already all over him, hanging onto the dress he was wearing and talking his ear off. To give the geezer credit, he was listening as if the kid was telling him something incredibly fascinating.

Dan shrugged. "Whatever."

"Hey," Nick said to the old guy, interrupting some long-winded story that threatened to drag on all night. "Can you watch the flock until River comes back?"

The man in the long shepherd's robe looked at him. Nick had the uncomfortable sensation his brains had just been picked. It served as a reminder that the old guy had stopped River in her tracks when the rest of them had been ready to crap in their pants.

"Certainly," the man said, a flash of kindness and sym- pathy accompanying the single word. A slight smile tugged at the corners of his mouth, as if he knew a secret that he found entertaining. "Although my name is Achala."

Damn it all to hell. Nick shivered. Getting probed by Achala was right up there with a prostate exam. He felt violated. Nick hoped She-Ra, Princess of Power, couldn't read his thoughts, too. Those ran more along the lines of

bending her over the stair rail and doing her from behind, because she was really hot, but that would be the
only way he could be sure she didn't try to bite off his
head after she'd orgasmed.

And oh, yeah, baby. She would orgasm.

Dan was already gone. Nick started after him, only
to find She-Ra hot on his heels.

"Excuse me," he said politely. "This is a "men-only"
excursion. If you know what I mean."

"No," she replied, swishing the blond ponytail over her
shoulder, "I don't know what you mean. I don't care either.
Hawk told me to keep an eye on you. So I'm coming."

Nick wanted to make a comment about that, but decided he liked his head right where it was. "Suit yourself. But he also told you to stay with that old guy."

She-Ra shrugged. "I'm fairly certain the spiritual
leader of the Fae will be fine with a group of children for
a little while."

"As long as he keeps one hand on his wallet," Nick
muttered. "And doesn't close his eyes or turn his back.
But suit yourself. Got a name, sweetheart?"

"Lilla." She didn't crack a smile. She didn't crack his
skull either, so Nick figured he was good.

He started to jog down the track. "Well, Lilla, stay
away from the center rail," he warned her. He didn't want
to have to bury a second body in one night. "It's live."

Dan was already standing beside what was left of
Billy by the time Nick and Lilla caught up with him.

Lilla let out a small gasp at the sight of the boy's broken and wasted body.

"What?" Dan challenged her with his customary charm and winning ways. He was spooked and upset, and wouldn't want her to know it, so he was going to be an asshole. "Never seen a dead body before?"

"Plenty of them," she replied, bending down to examine the remains more closely. "This is the fifth person I've seen today with these particular symptoms." She looked up at the open manhole. "And the second jumper. Was he hallucinating, by any chance?"

"Don't touch anything!" Nick interrupted sharply. He had started to sweat. He didn't know what the hell was going on, but he knew the signs of an outbreak when he saw them. Everyone did. Damn. "Dan, stand back and switch over to your hologram form. You can use it to help me bag him up."

"What about you?" Lilla asked him. She slipped her hands under her arms in an unconscious gesture to keep them from becoming contaminated, and her face was tense, so Nick knew she'd figured it out, too.

He swallowed hard. A few days ago, he'd stitched Billy's lip for him. He tried to sound casual. Unconcerned.

"I've already been exposed."

◆ ◆

Did she trust Hawk?

River wanted to, so much it hurt. But she wasn't certain she should. He was hiding his thoughts from her, and that meant he had things he didn't want her to know.

But she could read his sincerity and he meant it when he said if she went with him now, he would bring her back. And she was so tired. Months of worrying and planning had kept her awake when she should have been sleeping. The lack of sun also meant her days and nights had blended together. Her latest temper tantrum hadn't helped.

And, truthfully, her slipping grasp on her temper and her magic was a serious concern. Too often of late she'd been sharp with Nick, Dan, and Jake in particular. She could have hurt someone today. The thought frightened her.

She felt like two different people. One she knew. The other was a stranger to her. Technology had always been a part of her life and her world, and a skill her parents encouraged she use. Magic—although when she looked back it had been with her as well—wasn't something she'd ever tried to understand or control. She'd had no encouragement because it wasn't a part of the world she'd been born into.

Hawk, more than anyone, understood this about her.

She wanted very much to say yes to him.

"Do you promise?" she asked, still wary of his intentions and not liking it that she had to be. Neither did she like avoiding what waited for her outside of her office, including the Fae with the gray hair and kind eyes whose magic had overwhelmed hers. But she needed some time to confront the ugly seed of darkness she'd felt germinating inside her.

Hawk had secrets he was keeping from her. River wanted to keep this one from him for as long as she could, because no matter what she did, when he looked at her, he saw nothing but light. Perhaps that would be enough to drive the darkness away.

He held out his hand and his eyes smiled at her. He looked very much like Sever, the character she'd created, and she wondered how deep the connection between them truly went for her to have captured him so well.

"I would promise you the world if I thought I could give it to you," he said to her.

He'd already given her far more than he could possibly imagine. She took his hand, and its rough warmth sifted into her soul. She closed her eyes.

Immediately, a balmy wind carrying the aromatic fragrance of a cross between lilac and honeysuckle billowed over River's flesh. The sound of water lapping against land reached her ears and she turned her face into the breeze, pulling the heavenly scents into her lungs to savor the sweetness.

She opened her eyes, then felt them widen. They stood on the lush shore of a black-glass-surfaced lake, the reflection of three gorgeous red moons as the sun slipped from sight immediately transfixing her. Streaks of pink and purple bruised the skyline.

She absorbed Hawk's heat as he pressed against her

and she relaxed into him, accepting the warmth and comfort he offered. She sighed, exhaling slowly, and allowed his tender touch to help push back the darkness in her.

"This place is beautiful." River bent forward and without thinking, touched a tightly knotted red flower bud with the tip of her finger. Her Fae magic glittered and swelled in immediate reaction, and as the flower's soft petals unfurled before her eyes, a delicate perfume filled the air. She looked up at Hawk in surprise. "That hasn't happened for me in such a long time."

"You're Fae," he said simply, as if that explained everything. His gaze was on her, not the flower. "You bring life. No matter what, you can't ever forget the importance of that. Here. Let me show you something." He leaned past her and gently pinched the blossom from its stem. River made a small moue of protest and dismay. "Open your mouth." She did, intending to voice her opinion of his careless destruction, and he dropped one of the flower's petals onto her tongue.

The taste was beyond description. She allowed the petal to slowly dissolve, rolling the flavor around in her mouth before swallowing.

"What is it?" she asked, looking at the flower in his hand with entirely new respect.

"We call it Mother's Milk. It was a gift from the Fae," Hawk explained. "It has everything in it required to sustain a person's life, and it's often given to babies as a supplement. They can't choke on it, and there's nothing in it to harm their immature digestive systems. Look around you," he added, sweeping his hand to encompass the black lake and its fiery surroundings. "None of this is natural. The Fae gave us life, but it was up to the Guardians to find a way to maintain their gift."

She absorbed his words, examining them carefully. She'd always assumed her skills with technology were what she could bring to her world. Perhaps she had more to offer it than she'd thought. A bit of the darkness within her receded.

Hawk slipped his hands around her waist and lifted her to her feet, then locked his arms over her stomach with her shoulders pressed to his chest. He rested his chin on the top of her head.

She wondered if she could survive being parted from him again. She'd barely survived it the first time. She didn't think she truly had. Not if her loss of control today was any indication.

"It's all so beautiful," she whispered again as a fat speckled fish, gleaming red in the moonlight, leapt clear of the rippling water to snatch at a black-winged fly before plunging back beneath the surface.

Hawk brushed her hair from her shoulders and grazed his lips over the sensitive curve of her neck. "So are you."

She tilted her head to lay her cheek against his shoulder and he brushed his lips over her tingling flesh. His touch was so achingly tender and intimate an unexpected curl of heat licked over her thighs. She took a breath and concentrated on the growing sensations. Her lids fluttered shut for a moment and she knew there was no way she could fight the way he made her feel.

She didn't want to. Not any longer. Not ever again.

As he held her tight, his sweet breath hot on her flesh, she could sense his barriers soften, could feel him opening himself up to her.

"Why did you shut me out for so long?" she asked, overtaken by a sudden sadness for their loss of time together.

"To protect you until I could come back for you," he answered softly. "And to protect myself. Because I thought I might lose my mind from not being able to touch you."

He slipped his hand down her arm, seized one of her hands, and tugged. Heat whispered through her blood as he turned her to face him. A muscle in his jaw tightened, blatant hunger darkening his eyes. He drew her closer to the water's edge and kicked off his boots.

"Join me," he invited, dropping a soft kiss onto her mouth.

She loved the water and he knew it. There had been a river in her game that they'd had to cross. She'd modeled it after the one near her home, and they'd talked about her childhood and how her father had found her near there as a baby.

He didn't need to ask her twice. As his warm lips moved over hers and his familiar earthy scent teased her senses, hunger for him clawed at her insides. She kissed him back with ferocious need. Hands racing over his body, she tugged at his clothes, desperate to touch him, to feel his skin pressed against hers. She wanted to see this man—in his own body, in his own flesh—standing naked before her, hers to do with as she pleased. Moisture pooled at her mound as she ached to join with his.

He caught her hands. "I've been yours from the moment we met," he said to her, his voice low, ragged, and intense.

He'd read her thoughts. Of course he had. She'd made no effort to hide them from him. And she was never very good at blocking them anyway.

As excitement raced through her, his eyes clouded with longing and his gaze dropped to her mouth. His tongue snaked across his lips as he lightly brushed one thumb over her cheek. A moment later his lips reclaimed hers, and as his tongue slipped inside her mouth, she moaned and moved restlessly against him, her sex craving something far more intimate.

Lost in a haze of desire, she didn't miss the strong tremble that ran the length of Hawk's body or the way he'd sucked in a sharp breath as her tongue tangled with his. She absorbed his tremor and remembered something he'd said to her in passing a long time ago, when they were trapped in her game and about to cross the raging river—*When a Fae uses magic involving love it's the strongest by the lake or a river.*

There was no doubt she loved him. She didn't need magic to show him how much.

That thought triggered an instant reaction from him. "I want you naked, sweetheart. I need to see you."

She'd never heard such desperation in his voice before.

When she nodded, Hawk tugged her T-shirt from her jeans and peeled it over her head. Then he made short work of her lacy bra. She watched his chest rise and fall as he lightly brushed the underside of her breasts. As her body beckoned his touch he ran the rough pad of his thumb over her swollen, achy nipples. River moaned and arched into him.

"Beautiful," he murmured and ran his tongue around her areola before he dropped to his knees. He slid his hands around her waist. He drew her close and clung to her, holding her so tight she could barely breathe. Everything in the way he was holding her screamed possession and there was a part of her that found solace in that. As he meshed their bodies and opened himself to her, she brushed his mind. When she felt his fear—fear that she was going to slip from his grasp again—she swallowed hard and choked back the tears. Their time apart had been equally as hard on him.

River closed her eyes against the flood of emotions and raked her fingers through his hair. She shivered as his possessive touch shot through her.

He tilted his chin and looked up at her. The look in his eyes spoke of want, need, and possession.

He unzipped her jeans and buried his face in her pelvis. He breathed deep, pulling the scent of her skin into his lungs and River wiggled, wanting more, wanting to be naked with him.

Attuned to her need, he removed her boots and

slipped her pants down her legs. After he shed her jeans his dark, stormy eyes locked on hers again. The scent of her arousal saturated the air as he toyed with the lace on her panties, running the fabric through his fingers before he ripped them from her hips. With one strong tug he tore the material and tossed it away, then he went back on his heels to take in her nakedness.

She loved the way he looked at her, with such un-abashed desire and need in his eyes. No one had ever looked at her quite that way before. As heat moved through her, she touched a shaky finger to his chest to hold him at a distance.

"Your turn," she whispered.

Hawk grinned, stood, and discarded the rest of his clothes. Once finished he stepped toward her, both of them naked under the red moons and happy to be to-gether at last as the warm lake water lapped at their feet.

"You're the most beautiful man I've ever seen," River said.

Gaze riveted, he tugged her to him and guided her into the water. As the waves washed over their naked skin, and a breeze blew over their bodies, his lips found hers. His kiss was so full of emotion and tenderness it was all she could do to remain upright.

They waded in deeper and Hawk pulled her under the water as he kissed her, their hands holding each other, bodies clinging desperately. When they came up for air and he smiled at her, her entire world shifted and she knew she was lost to him forever.

He slipped his arms around her waist. "Put your legs

around me." The heat in his hushed voice seeped under her skin and brought on a wave of desire.

With both her arms and legs secured, he backed her up until she was pressed against the smooth surface of a boulder. When he loosened his hold, she lowered her legs and ran her lips over his chest, tasting his warm, salty skin and inhaling his scent. He gripped her head and lifted her mouth to his. As he kissed her, his erection pressed heavy against her stomach. Pleasure raced over her as she felt how much his body wanted hers.

"Talk about being caught between a rock and a hard place," she whispered into his mouth and pushed against him, stroking his erection with her body.

His edgy chuckle curled around her and eyes full of tender want and intimacy shot to hers. He groaned low in his throat and ran his hand over her breasts. Continuing downward, he stilled his hand between the apex of her legs.

He pressed his thumb to her swollen nub and she whimpered for more. "Speaking of hard," he teased in return, as warmth filled his eyes. Then he slipped a finger inside her, and let loose a low, guttural moan as his eyes slipped shut. "And wet," he growled, and she could tell he was fighting for control as her heat squeezed his finger. "I love how responsive you are to me, baby." He stroked her deep and she nearly came undone in his arms. No matter how he appeared or where they found themselves, the man certainly had a talent for knowing how to touch her.

She pushed against him, rocking her hips and trying to force his finger in deeper. "Please, Hawk," she heard herself beg.

"Are you ready for me, River?" he asked, his voice a strangled whisper.

She widened her legs. If she was thinking with her head she'd think he was the hottest, sexiest man she'd ever met. But right now she was thinking with her heart. "I've been ready for a very long time," she assured him, falling so hard for him the world as she knew it would never be the same again.

As raw need passed over his face, he gripped her hips, lifted her up, and drove home.

The sweet stab of pleasure made her gasp, and as she wrapped her legs around him, hot desire shot through her. Hawk's breathing grew shallow, and there was a note of desperation in his tone when he said, "Crisos, I've missed you. I've missed being inside you."

She tightened her legs around his waist as he pinned her body between his and the rock wall behind her.

Her whole body quivered as his wide girth stretched her and her fingers bit into his shoulders. "Yes . . ."

He buried his face in her shoulder, cupped her backside, and began moving his hips, burrowing deep as he ravished her with dark hunger.

River was mad with desire, her tension mounting and heat flashing in her veins. She gyrated, meeting his every thrust as her muscles squeezed around him. Her blood pulsed hot, and small ripples pulled at her core.

He stroked deeper, controlling the pace, depth, and rhythm until she writhed and cried out for more. She gasped in ragged breaths and savored every delicious stroke.

He pumped faster, riding her hard and deep, his cock searing her as though leaving his mark, claiming her. Her taut nipples slid over his wet chest as she held on tight, letting him take charge of her pleasure.

In no time at all her sex muscles clenched and vibrated. A whisper escaped her lips. His body crushed hers and he increased the pressure, knowing just what she needed and just how to give it to her.

"You feel so good, River."

Frantically, he pounded into her, hard and fast, and she sensed he was seeking more than release. She knew that feeling all too well. Together they established a rhythm, giving and taking, pushing and pulling. She squeezed her sex muscles, wanting desperately to keep him inside her forever.

They'd made love before, but she'd never experienced anything quite like this, never felt such a deep intimacy, such an array of powerful, overwhelming emotions. Perhaps it was because they were surrounded by water, or perhaps it was because this was the first time she'd ever made love to Hawk in his own form. Whatever the reason, it played havoc with her emotions and she knew there'd be no coming back from the power of this union.

When his dark, intense eyes met hers, sensations ambushed her and she gave herself over to the need pulling at her. Taking deep shallow breaths, she dug her nails into his shoulders and shifted, taking him impossibly deeper. Pressure brewed and her muscles tightened.

"That's it. Come for me," Hawk urged her, rotating his hips.

Her orgasm hit hard, causing her body to pulse violently.

"Yes!" she cried out as her sex clenched with the hot flow of release. The muscles along Hawk's jaw tightened as he watched her and she could feel the pressure building inside him, feel the way he was holding back. Changing tactics he slowed his pace, fighting off his own climax so she could nurture hers, prolong the pleasure and ride out the waves of ecstasy.

When her body stopped shaking, he pulled out of her and in one swift move plunged back inside. River gave a broken gasp as he threw his head back and splashed his seed high in her.

Panting, he stayed inside her. River tightened her arms around him, needing him to hold her, to keep them joined as one.

A long while later, after he grew flaccid, he pulled out of her. He dropped a soft kiss onto her forehead, nose, and then mouth. He inched back and his eyes moved over her face.

An unexpected chill made River shiver and immediately, Hawk gestured toward the shore. "Let's get out. You're cold."

They swam back and dropped to the ground, reenergized from their lovemaking. Months of sleepless-

ness and overwork vanished from River as if they'd
never happened. Hawk draped his jacket over her, and
settled in beside her as she stared up at the three moons,
fascinated by them and the exquisite beauty of her surroundings.

"Is this really all artificially maintained?" she asked
him. She'd heard stories of lush oases on her world that
had been carved from the desert and kept alive through
technology, but that had been before the war. Once the
money ran out, the desert had reclaimed the land within
a decade.

Here, they were talking about an entire world. It was
difficult for the mind to grasp, but she'd had to grasp
some fairly far-fetched realities of late.

"It really is artificial," Hawk assured her, stretching
out on his back and resting his head on his folded arms.

"Do you come here often?" She felt a twinge of envy
at how magical and romantic this little oasis of his
was. She wondered if it had been a special place for
him and his wife, and she tried not to be jealous. She
would never begrudge him his family, or their place in
his heart. She had a special place of her own. That was
all that mattered.

As he rolled into her, draping an arm over her, the
smile fell from his face and he turned serious. "You're
the only one I've ever brought here." He brushed her wet
hair from her cheek. It never failed to amaze her that this
strong, powerful man could be so gentle and tender with
her. "The truth is that most people have forgotten the
value of places like this. They live in the cities, close to

other people. Our cities are very beautiful," he added. "But sometimes it's nice to be alone, especially when you need time to recover."

He'd probably come here often in the days after he'd lost his wife and daughter. Still, she didn't sense the same sadness she once had in him. It was there, but it no longer haunted him.

He was offering to her the same peace this place had once given him. She rested her head on the heel of her hand and stared into his dark brown eyes, touched by his kind thoughtfulness. "Thank you for bringing me here."

"My pleasure."

River trailed her fingers up and down his arm. "So where exactly are we?"

"My dad and I built this place when I was a kid. We had father-and-son bonding time over it."

Talk about an ambitious project. River thought about some of the things she and her own dad had built, and they didn't come close to comparing. She missed him, suddenly and sharply.

"What happened to your father?" she asked, not wanting to think of her own.

Hawk looked surprised by the question. "Nothing. He and my mother moved to the city years ago. We drifted apart after I finished school and joined the military. Kids grow up and get their own lives, River," he said gently, seeing her distress. "People move on."

"We're talking about children, not puppies." River couldn't imagine it. "They just cut you out of their lives?"

He laughed. "Not at all. But we don't share common interests or lifestyles. Even this," he added, indicating the lake and its setting, "is something my father did with me because I enjoyed it. It was never for him."

"I can't believe your parents haven't been a part of your adult life." She couldn't get past that. Had there been no one for Hawk to turn to when his family had died?

The thought made her heart ache for him.

He was looking at her with concern of his own now. "You're getting the wrong idea," he said in a rush to reassure her. "We have different relationships with our parents on this world than you do, just as the Fae have different relationships with theirs. Here, let me show you."

He took her hand in his and opened his memories to her. Her heart tightened.

"Are you sure?" she asked, wanting him to clarify that he was giving her permission to enter his thoughts, and he nodded encouragement.

He sucked in a breath as she wrapped herself around his soul. As they stared at one another for a long moment, his features softened. "See?" he said. "I'm not in need of therapy. I was never abandoned."

The last of his barriers disappeared. He was right. She didn't find any memories of a traumatized childhood.

But what she found instead had her surging to her feet in alarm.

CHAPTER ELEVEN

♦

"The virus is back."

The tension in Premier Anderson's voice made Kaye sit up straighter in his chair.

"Impossible." He gripped the phone's receiver more tightly, splaying the fingers of his other hand on top of the papers he'd been reading at his desk. "The mutations haven't been released yet."

Anderson's voice rose a notch. "Then how do you explain the people dying in the streets?"

The man couldn't handle stress. Kaye tried not to reveal his impatience. "They're dying in *our* streets?" he inquired in polite disbelief. "We certainly wouldn't release the mutations here. We'd targeted the Netherlands." Its dense population and proximity to other borders made it a prime candidate. Not to mention, it had retained peaceful relations with North America when the rest of the world had closed its doors. *Paranoid foreign bastards.*

"You're certain the vaccine works?"

"Positive." Kaye drummed his fingers on the faux wood laminate desktop. He wished the asshole hadn't already been inoculated, but he'd insisted on it the instant he'd learned of its existence. Kaye would have had him killed except that, after Johnson's recent assassination, it would have looked too suspicious. "I'm telling you, whatever is happening, it's not the virus. A few days ago, everything was fine. Now you're saying people are dying in the streets? The virus isn't that volatile. Its incubation period is months."

"Something is killing people," Anderson insisted. "And word is spreading. I've already had phone calls from the U.S. and Mexican consulates. You can rest assured they've reported back to their governments. They don't want to be blamed for another outbreak any more than we do."

This was precisely why Kaye had never wanted to form a coalition with them in the first place. Good fences made good neighbors, particularly when the neighbors were nosy.

"I'll look into it," Kaye assured him. "Whatever's happening, it will be contained. I'll send out the Weres. They're immune to the virus. If they get sick, we'll know it's something different."

He hung up the phone and sat back in his chair, deep in thought. Perhaps one of the paranoid foreign bastard countries had beaten them to the finish line and released a mutation of their own. He intended to find out.

A few hours later he had an answer, but was no further ahead in finding a resolution. People were indeed starting to die with disturbing frequency and speed. However, the Weres reported that the corpses carried a common, unusual smell. They reeked of sage, a peppery scent the Weres didn't like. They also claimed that

the illness involved hallucinations. Kaye found that of
particular interest, and entirely too coincidental on several fronts.

The release of the first virus had been meant to coin-
cide with the development of a bioengineered superarmy,
a combination of his Weres and robotic technology. The
defection of his top research scientist, who'd taken her
abilities and research with her, had set the plan back several decades and made it change course. He couldn't
replicate something when he didn't have the necessary
tools, and his superiors had not been happy over the
years of wasted money combined with an international
disaster.

River Weston's video game had shown excellent military potential. It had taken him months to get government buy-in on that one, and Johnson had facilitated it,
but now Johnson was gone. So was River, although Kaye
had found her again.

And when he'd received reports that she was working on a new project with the promise of even greater
military application, he'd decided to let her run with it
to see where it went while he still had government backing. He was moderately disappointed that her projects,
too, involved certain . . . proprietary tools that couldn't
be replicated. The military preferred to build using
consumer off-the-shelf products. On the other hand,
exclusivity meant no other country could replicate her
experiments. Not unless they had a River Weston of
their own.

He peered thoughtfully out of the small window of

his third-floor office, overlooking the quay fronting the city's wide expanse of river. The white tips of the mountain backdrop gleamed in the morning sunshine.

He doubted if it was a coincidence that River's hologram program and the hallucinations of sick people had manifested at the same time, and both the scientist and the physician in him were excited by the possibilities. What he needed to find out was if the sickness associated with the program was caused by the same strain of virus that had once nearly wiped out the world.

Because if it was, and it could be contained, then the government had itself a very interesting weapon with wider ranging military application than anyone could have hoped for.

Nick Sutton had a very good understanding of military requirements in relationship to software programs.

Kaye went back to his desk and searched through a drawer for a file. Perhaps it was time he renewed that old friendship.

♦ ♦

Nick's back ached from bending over a shovel most of the night. He hadn't been able to bring himself to take Billy's body topside and abandon him somewhere for the authorities to find for several reasons. He hadn't wanted anyone touching what was most likely an infectious body.

And he hadn't wanted to abandon a child in a place

where no one would care. Better for him to be buried down here where his friends would at least be close by.

But dang, the ground was hard around the tracks. She-Ra hadn't made things easier. He hadn't wanted her touching anything, but at the same time having her staring at him all night as if she didn't know quite what to make of him hadn't been a whole lot of fun.

He patted down the last of the dirt and gravel on the top of the gently mounded grave. It wasn't as deep as it should be, but on the other hand they were below the frost line already so it didn't have to be six feet.

He tossed the shovel aside and rubbed the small of his back. She-Ra didn't say anything, but her expression was kinder than he cared for.

"I'm going to bed," Dan announced. His hologram flickered and disappeared, and Nick and Lilla were alone together.

If she said something nice to him now, Nick thought it entirely possible he might burst into tears, and he didn't like the idea of bawling like a baby in front of the pint-sized amazon. He didn't care that she could totally kick his ass, but he wanted to retain at least some bit of manly dignity.

He had to get some fresh air. And maybe, too, he wanted to check on Angie. He covered up the little niggle of growing concern by thinking about her amazing breasts.

He started for the ladder that led to the manhole above. When he got to the top of the ladder, he looked down and saw that Lilla was right behind him.

"Where do you think you're going?" he said, annoyed. "Shouldn't you be checking on Grandpa? Those kids probably have him tied up and set on fire by now. There's a reason they're called Demons."

She didn't say anything, just looked at him, and that annoyed him even more, but short of knocking her off the ladder he didn't see that he had much choice other than to let her tag along.

He popped his head out of the manhole and looked up and down the empty sidewalk. The sun hadn't yet risen, so the street lights remained lit. The pale yellow glow did little to brighten the area and he took note of all the shadowed areas where danger might lurk. The Demons weren't the only lawbreakers roaming the streets, and they were far from the most dangerous.

Kaye's Weres had that honor wrapped up and Nick did not doubt for a second that they were out there somewhere, watching. River thought she was safe in the subway. Nick suspected Amos Kaye was simply biding his time. Without a doubt Kaye had lost a fair bit of skin in that lab explosion she and the cop had rigged, and that would have slowed him down.

He was probably pissed about it, too, but Nick had spent so much time living in terror over the last few months that he'd pretty much shut down in the fear department. Terror tended to generate numbness after a while.

He hoisted himself onto the street, straightened, then with long strides started off in the direction of the coffee shop. She-Ra hauled her ass out of the manhole and darted along behind him, her hand on the weapon holstered at her hip as she scanned the shadows.

Cool. He had himself a bodyguard.

Tim Hortons was open twenty-four hours. Nick often wondered what their business model was based on, because it sure as hell wasn't the population.

He pushed open the heavy glass door and stepped back to allow Lilla to enter. She looked around the brightly lit room with its Formica tables and bright red chairs, curiosity on her face.

It was a shame she was so totally lacking in femininity, because she was truly a gorgeous little woman.

Angie wasn't behind the counter. He fingered the change in his pocket and wondered if he had enough for two cups of coffee. The tiny amazon could probably use one, too.

"Have a seat," he said to Lilla. "I'll get the drinks."

She sat in one of the red chairs, her blond ponytail swinging as she continued to take note of the room. She kept one hand carefully in her lap, not far from her holster. Nick sighed and turned away.

The boy behind the counter wasn't much more than a kid, freckle-faced and nervous. At least he looked healthy, Nick noted with relief.

"Hey," he said. "Two extra-large double doubles." As the boy filled the order, Nick drummed his fingers on the countertop. "What time does Angie come in?" he asked when he was handed the drinks.

The boy paused in the act of scooping Nick's change

into his palm. "Angie's not coming in," he said, glancing up to meet Nick's eyes. "She died early last night."

Nick's hands shook ever so slightly as he clutched the hot paper cups. "How?"

"I'm not sure," the boy confessed. "But people are talking about some sort of fast-acting sickness spreading through the city the last few days. A lot of the old people think it's the virus." He said it like he thought the old people were crazy.

Then Nick wondered how the kid was defining *old* because he thought it was the virus, too. What he couldn't figure out was how it had mutated to such an extent, and so abruptly.

He'd been exposed to Billy.

And Billy had been exposed to him.

He thought about the money he'd passed to the kid behind the counter and felt a little dizzy. Then he looked at the cups in his hand. He tossed one into the garbage before joining Lilla at the small table.

He tried to sound indifferent. "Sorry, Lola, I forgot you shouldn't be touching anything I've touched."

One of her blond eyebrows shot up. "Lilla."

"Whatever." He pulled back the tab on his cup and took a long, loud sip. Tension coiled through his stomach and he hoped the coffee stayed down. He had a tendency to throw up when things got really scary, and perhaps he wasn't as numb as he'd hoped. He pointed toward a vinegar dispenser on the wall near the exit. "Keep your hands away from your face and wash them with that stuff before we leave here. You need to rub them together for at least ten seconds."

She examined his face with cool, unreadable blue eyes. "Are you trying to scare me?"

"God forbid." Nick took another long drink, burned his tongue, and decided he was too tired to think straight. Let River and the body snatcher sort this shit out. He wanted to pull the blankets over his head and sleep for a month. He pushed his chair back with a loud clatter in the otherwise silent shop. "Let's get the hell out of here."

He tossed his unfinished drink into the garbage and went to the door. He blocked the exit when she would have followed him out to the street.

"Hands. Now," he ordered her, and she obediently turned to the dispenser. The smell of vinegar filled the air as she pumped it into her palms, and she made a face.

"The stuff stinks."

"Too bad. The stuff works. Ten seconds," he added as a reminder.

After ten seconds passed, he opened the door.

A hint of cobalt blue now tinged the skyline along the ridge of mountaintops, and Nick took in deep breaths of the fresh air. It was funny how he was learning to appreciate simple little things like this.

He should have been paying more attention to the shadows.

Lilla called out a warning and reached for her

weapon, but it was too late. A heavy fist caught Nick in the side of the head and he dropped to his knees, his face in his hands. The coffee came back up through his nose as he retched from the pain.

He heard Lilla's grunts as she landed a few solid blows against his attacker, and he made an effort to get back on his feet to help her. He was far from a fighter, but she had no idea what she was up against. He did. He'd caught the unmistakable odor of dog when the assailant had hit him. Now it was all he could smell, thanks to the blow on the head.

Lilla, a blond whirl of pint-size arms and legs, clearly well trained, was holding her own, but she wouldn't be able to keep that up for long.

Nick could only think of one thing to do. He activated his hologram, hoping desperately he could hang onto its form long enough to scare the Weres off. Two more of them had arrived, he noted with sinking hope.

At least it would be a faster death than what Billy and Angie had experienced.

The high-pitched noise from his hologram program hurt his ears and he could tell by the way they drew back that it bothered the Weres as well. What else would irritate the little bastards?

River's Tabinese was about the ugliest thing Nick could imagine. If he made it twice the size of a Were and gave it fangs, it might at least make them stop and reconsider.

"Don't draw blood!" he said sharply to Lilla, hoping

she was listening. Blood would only encourage them. If that happened, they were dead. Anyone else the Weres met on the street would be as well.

The hologram shimmered into place around him, a freaking large monstrosity with an ugly, whiskered pug face. Nick lengthened the teeth and added a bit of dripping saliva. He hadn't helped develop video game characters for nothing. The experience was paying off big time.

But this, however, was a far different experience from sitting in a chair in the subway while his hologram wandered the streets. Nick had a greater sense of control. He could reach through the hologram and use the creature's paws to deliver harder blows with greater impact.

This was freaking awesome. Not much wonder the little kids got off on it so much.

He knocked the Were circling Lilla flat on its ass. It scurried backward, not quite certain what to make of the slobbering, fanged monster that had taken Nick's place.

If it surprised Lilla, she gave no indication. She never slowed. Instead, she went straight after the downed Were. A kick to its head from her black-booted foot laid it out cold.

Nick, however, hadn't counted on the Weres' keen sense of smell. He'd surprised them, but it only took the remaining two Weres a few seconds to regroup and realize he was inside the hologram. They stalked him, forcing him back until the brick wall of the Tim Hortons shop blocked his retreat.

"Run!" he shouted at Lilla.

Lilla, however, had other ideas. At last, she'd gotten her hand on her weapon and she aimed it at the Were closest to Nick. Before she could fire it, the Were she'd knocked unconscious recovered. She had her back to it and Nick yelled out a warning, but she couldn't turn fast enough to avoid its attack. A heavy foot caught her in the small of the back, and with a cracking sound Nick hoped hadn't come from her spine she crumpled to the pavement and went still.

"Lilla!" he shouted, and distracted by the sight of her as she went down, he lost control of his hologram. It vanished, leaving him facing three angry and agitated Weres.

He threw his hands wide and exposed his neck in a show of submission. He hoped they'd at least make it quick.

◆ ◆

The wolves appeared unbothered by the sudden appearance of two alien men.

Damn. Peters had hoped it might scare them off. Instead, they merely seemed curious.

He hoped he wasn't mistaking curiosity for hunger.

He and the two other men stood silently, surveying

the wolves, the landscape, and each other. Peters tried
to decide if he could bring himself to shoot one of the
newcomers if they threatened him. He'd had no problem killing George Johnson, but that bastard had it
coming. Killing a man based on a suspicion didn't carry
the same kind of absolution.

"We're going to have to kill at least one of those
things to get the rest of them to back off," the shorter of
the two aliens finally said.

The big bald man with the gold-capped tooth dropped
to one knee and sighted his weapon at the largest of the
white wolves.

Logan flashed into position in front of him, blocking
his shot, and the big man swore under his breath.

Peters swore, too, but his was a little louder. He couldn't
let them do this with Logan watching. Not when Logan
was looking at him with such pleading in his eyes.

"Forget it," he advised the other men. "I don't know
what it is, exactly, that's bothering these wolves, but
they've been looking out for a bunch of kids for a number of years now. Maybe they think we're a threat to
them. We can't just start shooting. Not unless they attack
us first," he added, directing that comment to Logan.

"We have to get out of their way," the boy replied as
if stating the obvious.

Peters saw the two men examine the wolves, the boy,
and then look at each other. He could tell the exact moment when suspicion entered their heads, followed by
conviction. They knew what Logan was.

Or at least where some of his DNA had originated. It

wasn't hard to tell by looking at the kid. Not if someone was familiar with gene manipulation. And according to River, these people were the bomb when it came to science and technology.

If so, then they could help get him the hell out of this situation.

"I'm going to make a wild guess here," Peters said, "and assume I'm the only one of the four of us who can't just decide he wants to play leapfrog into another part of the universe. So I have a suggestion." He kept an eye on the wolves. They hadn't gained any ground but remained openly restless. The building Weston had used as an office was the closest to him, although it might as well be a million miles away under the circumstances. "If the three of you stay still and keep me covered, I'll move slowly into that building over there. Once I'm inside, you can follow me."

The bald-headed man nodded agreement. "Go."

Peters had never liked putting his life in the hands of other people. It was one of the biggest reasons he'd always worked without a partner. That, and the fact he didn't like most people. But he was willing to forgo his prejudices right now if it kept him alive.

He began the slow process of edging toward the building. Logan, to his credit, remained calm. Peters had no doubt that the boy's presence went a long way toward keeping things from going completely to hell.

Being stared at by those unblinking, feral eyes and anticipating the worst was an experience he never cared to repeat. While it probably didn't take as long as it seemed, eventually, the stainless-steel doorknob was within his gloved grasp. He twisted the handle and the door swung open.

The hell with caution. He darted inside and slammed the door shut behind him. Within seconds, giving him no time to rejoice, Logan appeared, and then the two strangers.

Shit, he wished he could do that.

"Go check on the others," Peters said to Logan.

Logan disappeared.

The bald-headed man rubbed a hand over his scalp as if seeking warmth, which was undoubtedly the case. It was cold in this part of the world.

"What in the name of the Mother was that?" the big man asked, indicating the spot where Logan had stood.

Peters went to one of the grimy windows and peered outside. The wolves hadn't left. Instead, they'd settled down as if ready to wait him out. It looked as if he'd be stuck here awhile.

He might as well make the best of it. Somewhere in this mess, David Weston had left notes. With any luck he had himself a couple of willing research assistants.

"That," he replied, turning back to the men, "was a Were. A wolf boy. So. Who are you, and what are you doing here?"

CHAPTER **TWELVE**

♦

Achala enjoyed the company of children. They worried about no one's opinions but their own and were quite frank in voicing them.

He was also impressed with the almost absolute authority the boy called Dan had over these particular children. They trusted and respected him. That meant Dan, although brusque and hard, had redeeming qualities.

Their trust and respect in River, however, had taken a bit of a beating. They'd seen a side of her they might have suspected existed, but never had reason to fear before.

He'd spent the evening in one of their bunks in some sort of underground dormitory, listening to them whisper to each other in the darkness as they tried to sleep. He'd done and said nothing to ease their concerns over River because he didn't yet know if he'd be helpful by doing so. She had good in her. A lot of it.

But there was darkness as well.

Once the last of the littlest had fallen asleep, he'd gotten out of bed and gone off in search of the shaggy-haired boy called Jake, the one River thought of as her brother. He was hungry to learn more about this woman who looked so much like her mother it made his heart ache from the sharp, jagged edges of a pain he'd thought time had worn smooth.

He walked through the tunnel, his footsteps making soft scuffing sounds in the silence. This place was a far cry from the luxury he lived in, but it wasn't the worst he had seen. He wondered that River, although she'd obviously added many comforts and necessities, had made no effort to turn this underground haven into a home. Perhaps she wanted better than this for these children.

Or she didn't care.

He found Jake sitting propped against a closed door, his cheek resting on his drawn-up knees, sound asleep. He looked exhausted and very young.

Achala started to turn away, not wanting to disturb him, when the boy spoke.

"They aren't in there." Jake lifted his head and looked at Achala, his eyes surprisingly sharp considering he'd been asleep just seconds before. "I don't know where they are."

The news pleased Achala. He'd been worried. That they were gone together, and Colonel Hawkins hadn't seen fit to let him know they were leaving, or their destination, was a good sign.

Let them have this time together. It was obvious what the situation between them was. It was equally obvious, if River's other grandfather's reaction to her existence was any indication, that Colonel Hawkins had a serious problem on his hands. Neither the Guardians nor the Fae would welcome her. The Guardians believed her to be dark. The Fae would see her soul as damaged because it hadn't come to her through the Mother's spiritual leaders. He had seen nothing yet to fully contradict either view, other than that Colonel Hawkins, a man with a strong mind, found her worthy of his love.

Politics aside, Achala's primary concern was for his granddaughter. To the Fae, life and family were everything. Strong family ties nurtured the soul. He wanted to protect her, but he could only do so up to a point. Her situation was not normal, and her path in life wasn't his to choose.

"I doubt if they've gone far." Achala smiled at Jake to reassure him, but the boy didn't smile back. Gentle probing told him he, too, had a strong mind, quite resistant, but it also warned that he'd experienced serious distress in recent months. "Do you mind if I join you?" Jake shrugged, so Achala lowered himself carefully to the concrete beside him to rest his back against the door. "Tell me about your sister."

"There's nothing to tell."

Nothing that Jake was willing to tell him, at any rate. Very well. He wanted to ask questions, but he didn't want to reveal things to Jake that he might not want to know.

"You look nothing alike," Achala observed carefully. "And she's a lot older than you. Is she your sister by birth or through adoption?"

"She's my half sister."

Shock pinched his lungs. Was her father still alive, then? That Annia was dead was a fact beyond doubt. Her passing had left a hole in his heart. It hadn't occurred to him that the Guardian had somehow survived her death and perhaps made a home for himself on this world.

The shock must have registered on his face.

"My father and his first wife found her when she was a baby," Jake added reluctantly. "My mom told me that. Dad never said a word."

Achala understood what the boy didn't say. Their father had loved her as if she were his own and nothing else mattered to him. That Jake loved her, too, was equally evident. Relief overwhelmed him. He'd already failed Annia and her daughter. He hadn't realized how important it had been for him to know that River's life hadn't been completely harsh.

Jake glared at him. "Are you going to take her away?"

Something warned him that his answer to this question was vitally important. The boy was smart and he'd known River for a long time. He would recognize that Achala shared certain abilities with his sister. It wouldn't take a large stretch of imagination to come to the conclusion that there was a connection between them, whether through blood or simply by nature.

"I can't make her do anything she doesn't want to do," he replied carefully.

"She won't go with you."

Achala smiled at his defiance, but he suspected the boy was correct. From what he'd seen, River had a deep, Fae loyalty to this world and she wouldn't give that up easily.

Jake's glare turned to a lost look of uncertainty. He was tall for his age and rapidly becoming a man, but

Achala caught a glimpse of the child within that expression.

Jake jerked a thumb at the closed door behind them. "She can't. She's already gone with him."

Now Achala understood the true source of the boy's concern. He was afraid River had abandoned him and nothing Achala said would convince him otherwise, because in Jake's mind, Achala didn't know her.

Jake, however, did know her, and he seemed to think abandonment was a real possibility. Perhaps it was. River was an adult and Jake was little more than a child. She'd probably come and gone in his life for years. He'd mentioned his mother, so River hadn't raised him.

But he wasn't with his mother now, he was with his sister, and given what Achala suspected about trauma in the boy's life, this was a recent circumstance. It seemed as if the two siblings only had each other.

Until now. If Jake was River's brother, and their father had accepted her unequivocally as his own, then it stood to reason that Jake was also Achala's grandson. He found he was charmed by the idea. Adoption was rare in Fae society, not because it was unacceptable, but because there was little need for it. The Fae aged but they didn't sicken. When off world they were well protected by the Guardians, and with their speed and sound instincts, fatal accidents were all but unheard of.

Jake didn't need an unwarranted worry added to his troubles. She would return to him. "Did she say goodbye to you before she left?" he asked the boy.

"No."

"Is it normal for her to leave without saying good-bye to you?"

This time Jake's response was slower and more thoughtful. "No."

"Then it's safe to assume she'll be back." Achala settled himself more comfortably and closed his eyes. By showing he was prepared to wait for her, too, he hoped Jake could finally relax.

Because while Achala believed River would be back, he suspected it wouldn't be quickly. Not if the starved expression on Colonel Hawkins' face when he'd stared at her was anything to go by.

◆ ◆

As he stared at the empty space where River had stood only seconds before, Hawk couldn't believe how stupid he'd been.

It had seemed like the most natural thing in the world to open his thoughts to her. Instead, she'd found far more than he'd intended. The red glow of the moons reflected off the shining black water, spreading across the rock and the foliage to touch his bare feet. How could he have forgotten about the bomb in his head?

He had to go after her, and he had to explain. He dressed quickly and gathered her clothes. She was naked. Unless she'd improved her ability to jump in the time he'd been gone, her options for destinations were limited.

But he already knew where she would go.

The transporter that Guardians wore under their skin at the small of their backs was easily controlled by their thoughts, hardwired to their brains through their neurological systems. By calculating the coordinates he wanted to reach through the communicator on his wrist, his brain picked them up and transmitted them in turn to the transporter.

Within seconds he stood on the bank of the river near her childhood home. She wasn't there. Panic threatened before he realized there was one other place she might be. His lips thinned. She was alone in a hostile world, unprotected. It didn't matter that she had been on her own and unprotected for months. He was back, and he intended to stay close to her from now on.

He found her in the attic of the old farmhouse, staring at the shelving along one wall. The room was dusty, cramped, and bitterly cold, but she didn't appear to notice. He hoped it wasn't because she was about to spout flames again. The house was old and its wooden frame tinder dry.

He held out her clothes to her, a sort of peace offering but also an attempt to gauge her state of mind.

"I thought you might need these."

◆ ◆

The sound of Hawk's voice had River spinning around. Startled, even though she'd known he would come, she sucked in a tight breath and wondered if she'd ever get used to the fact that he could jump, too.

There would be no more privacy for them from each other. Not unless they were both willing to grant it. The knowledge thrilled and alarmed her.

She took in his posture and the way he had his back to the wall, with his legs spread wide, his hands braced by his side never far from his weapon. He was in full military mode, always ready to protect her, but did he realize that he himself posed a threat?

Her Guardian, a man who had sworn to protect her, was a living time bomb. He either didn't know it, or hadn't wanted her to know. She suspected the latter since he'd kept his thoughts carefully guarded.

She reached for her clothes and silently dressed. A sick, apprehensive knot tightened in her stomach as she tugged her shirt over her head and surveyed the room, more to avoid looking at him than to actually check her surroundings. "I'm not sure why I jumped here."

Hawk pushed off the wall, watching her carefully. "You reacted instinctively to a threat, and your Fae soul automatically sought out the place it feels safest."

He had known about the bomb, and now he knew that she knew. She wasn't ready to go there, or to find out what it meant.

Instead, she thought about the last time she'd jumped here and what had awaited her. As she dredged up the painful memories, ones she'd worked hard to keep under wraps, she began to pace. "This place isn't safe anymore.

I knew that already. So I'm not really sure what prompted me to come here."

Hawk took two steps and closed the distance between them. He placed his hands on her arms to still her, then pulled her to him. "I'm sorry for what happened to Melinda and Sam."

Her stomach clenched as he spoke their names. Melinda and Sam were dead because of her. So was Billy, and who knew how many more to come, because she was really afraid she'd created something deadly out of something she'd intended to use for saving lives. She'd only ever wanted to help. Why was that proving so difficult?

He dipped his head and spoke more softly. "I can only imagine how hard this has been on you and Jake."

She tried to block out the images of Melinda and Sam's shredded bodies, and the look on Jake's face when they'd had to bury them. She'd never liked Melinda, but her stepmother hadn't deserved to die like that. Neither had sweet-natured little Sam, whose last moments she couldn't bear to contemplate.

Hawk held her tight, his touch both firm and strong. He grew quiet. "Jake needs help to deal with this, River. He's still a kid. He needs to find his place again, and gain a sense of control, before the stress debilitates him and he loses his sense of right and wrong."

"I know," she replied. Her glance moved over his face, and the look in his dark eyes, the unspoken message flitting through them, told her what else he wanted to say. That she, too, needed help.

They both fell silent until finally, River broke away from Hawk and his protective embrace. Her feet scuffled on the floorboards as she crossed the small room and dropped onto a bare cot, the blankets that she'd used months ago folded neatly and placed at the foot, exactly where she'd left them. The old springs groaned in protest at the same time a crow cawed outside the window. It cut through the deep quiet of the evening and had her thinking of Jake and how a few short months ago he would have been trying to catch it and turn it into a pet, not hiding in an underground subway with her.

Hawk was right, her brother did need help, but getting him help was a moot point if the virus continued to spread through the Demons. She was pretty damn sure common household vinegar wasn't going to cut it this time, which begged the question: what was it going to take?

She planted her elbows on her knees and followed a streak of pale, watery light from the rising moon as it cut through the grimy windowpane and lit a path along the scratched and scarred floorboards. Her glance came to rest on cardboard boxes, all neatly lined in straight rows on the metal shelving unit at the back of the room. As she examined those boxes, the hairs on her nape tingled from a strange sense of unease.

Hawk picked up on it immediately as he followed her gaze. His body tightened, his hand moving closer to his weapon. "What's wrong?"

"I don't know." She angled her head, unable to pinpoint exactly what was bothering her. "I can't quite put my finger on it." At first glance everything appeared to be in its place. The boxes were neatly aligned, stacked exactly the way she'd left them. "It feels like something's missing."

"You think someone's been up here?"

River couldn't say for certain, or even if it mattered. She'd been through those boxes herself and had come up empty-handed. Then again, she'd had no idea what it was she'd been looking for. Someone else might have been looking for something more specific.

She hated the thought of strangers rifling through her family's possessions. What if they'd been watching and waiting while she and Jake had been busy burying the remains of their loved ones?

The idea filled her with helpless fury. She needed an outlet and Hawk was the nearest target. Her eyes narrowed.

"Why don't you tell me what you and your team are planning to do?" she asked.

The shift in her mood and the turn in the conversation caught him off-guard. Then caution shuttered his expression, and he appeared to be trying to pick his words carefully.

He finally opted for bluntness. "The plan is to defuse your planet," he said. "As it was all along. You knew that. I never lied to you." He took her hand. "And I promise, I won't start now."

He then told her about his team, and how they had

dispersed to specific locations on Earth to plant devices meant to take out the protective outer ozone layer, and how that would lead to total technological breakdown.

"It will give this world another chance to change its course of evolution. If nothing else, it will slow down and disarm the crazies like Amos Kaye, who know far more about science and technology than is good for anyone."

She remembered the bioengineered mutants—a mixture of man, animal, and machine—and how Andy had once tried to use her magic to tie souls to them. River's own attempts at offering technological advances to her world were proving equally disastrous. First her video game, and now the hologram program.

Hawk's solution, however, was far too extreme. Without technology, civilization would be lost. But he truly believed in his cause, and as she listened to him speak, the sick feeling in her stomach mushroomed. She wondered if she was fighting a losing battle.

That didn't mean she was going to sit back and do nothing. She thought of the parents who had raised her, and done what they could to make this a better place for people to live in. Her birth parents, too, had come here intent on saving this world. Did all of earth have to suffer for the actions of a few?

"I won't let you do this," she said.

"River." He spoke her name with a great deal of patience, and it irritated her. "Whether you believe this or not, your world is dying. Stripping it of technology will give the ethics of its leaders a chance to catch up with their knowledge."

Even though a small part of her agreed with his logic, the Guardian half of her shuddered. She couldn't imagine a world without technology. People would be defenseless in so many little ways. Against illness. Starvation.

Each other.

What he was suggesting was inhumane, although she knew he didn't see it as such.

"What about the bomb?" she asked quietly. That was what made no sense to her.

Concern reflected in his brown eyes and he deliberated over his next words even more carefully before delivering them.

"The Great Lords believe you're a Dark Lord, or at least on the verge of becoming one. And any planet that's home to a Dark Lord is considered a danger to others—most important, to the Fae."

She started to laugh. Unlike Hawk, she had never expected the Guardians to welcome her with open arms. She was the half-breed offspring of a union forbidden by both races. But the ludicrousness of the accusation was beyond breathtaking. She'd met a true Dark Lord through a glitch in her video game and he had totally kicked her ass, time after time. She'd been no match for him.

Yet a tiny voice reminded her that she'd felt a small seed of darkness take root inside her, just as she'd once sparked a seed of light inside Andy's soul. And she summoned magic when she was angered.

But the gray-haired Fae had effectively contained that magic, she argued with herself. She had been no more a danger to him than an imp was to a full-grown demon.

Hawk was watching her, trying to assess her reaction. It was her turn to be blunt with him. "So you plan to blow up my planet, and everyone on it, including yourself and your team? Because of me?"

"I'm not suicidal," he assured her. His gaze gentled, settling warmly on her face. "Not when I have so much to live for. I didn't know about the bomb until a few days ago. Now that I do, I know how to contain it. No one is going to hurt you."

Her eyes widened in awareness. "But that was your Great Lords' plan. To get rid of me and my world. You and your team weren't supposed to return either." A low noise crawled out of her throat. "Nice leaders you have there, Hawk."

"Somewhere along the way, a few of them have lost sight of their purpose," he agreed softly.

She swallowed, her throat aching painfully. "The Fae you summoned? Does he believe I'm a danger, too?"

"Achala is here because he doesn't approve of the measures the Great Lords have taken to protect the Fae. He believes they've overstepped boundaries."

He hadn't really answered her question.

She lightly brushed his thoughts, examining the bomb, and he didn't try to block her but waited patiently. There had to be a way to get rid of it. He sucked in air as she let loose a bit of healing magic, but when she couldn't find a way to remove the bomb—to safely relocate it—fear for him overrode everything else. Nothing mattered to her more than Hawk. The knowledge was frightening. She would always continue to do what she knew to be right, but without him, she would be empty inside. It would be duty, nothing more.

"Achala taught me how to isolate the trigger," he said, his eyes never leaving hers.

River couldn't believe this was happening. "What is the trigger?"

"A naturally occurring chemical in the brain," he explained. "If the chemical's production is stimulated in a particular sequence and to a certain level, it will detonate."

She thought about what *stimulated* could mean, then asked, "So you're telling me that as long as you don't lose control of your emotions, it won't go off?"

"Something like that," he said.

River studied him. "And if you do lose control?"

"Then I'll transport deep into empty space so no one gets hurt."

The thought horrified her. "*You'll* get hurt."

"It won't go off. I can control it."

"For now." She noted the lines under his eyes that told a slightly different story. She knew he was strong-willed, incredibly so, but this was taking a very big risk and she didn't like it. "Is there no way to remove it?"

He gave a quick shake of his head. "Not that I know of, but it's not my priority. Right now, we have another crisis on our hands. Something has kick-started a new strain of the virus and we have to figure out how to prevent it from spreading." Hawk stood, the springs of the cot sighing with relief from the release of his weight, and reached a hand out to her. "I have a viral research expert on the team. He's gone to a place called Elles-mere Island, and I need to bring him back."

Ellesmere Island.

River wondered why that name sounded so familiar.

But then Billy's little face, twisted in death, filled her thoughts and she knew Hawk was right. The virus was their priority. She'd have to trust him when he said he could control the bomb, because she didn't want any-one else to die the way that boy had. If Hawk and his team could find a way to stop the virus, then she would gladly do whatever she could to help them.

Because she was very much afraid that she'd been the trigger to set off this particular bomb.

◆ ◆

Jim Peters slid the last of the filing cabinet drawers closed and rubbed his tired eyes. What passed for night on Ellesmere Island had long since expired.

His two newfound friends, Faran and Ever, had proven excellent at research once they got past their ini-tial excitement at seeing so much paper in one place, although *excitement* wasn't the word that first sprang to mind when he looked at it.

While Peters and Ever had gone through the cabinets methodically, quickly scanning the files and setting aside anything that looked interesting, Faran had reviewed what they found and created several more carefully or-ganized piles.

And what they'd found was astounding in both its scope and its completeness. The three men had done a lot of talking through the long night hours, waiting for the wolves outside to get tired and hungry enough to move on. David Weston had been a risk taker who had gone to great lengths to ensure his risk taking would go undetected. Then he'd documented everything and hidden the evidence in a place cut off from the rest of the planet.

"This is one dark, messed-up world," Ever said. He was a young man with light brown hair and serious, dark gray eyes. "What does it all mean?"

Peters didn't like to tell him that what they were seeing was the tip of the iceberg. So to speak.

"It means that early on, someone in the government distrusted General Amos Kaye enough to put a watchdog on him," Peters replied, speaking mostly to himself as he sorted it all out in his head.

That watchdog had been River's father. Weston might not have had the authority to put a stop to Kaye, but he had a reason to want to continue to monitor him even after he'd been called off. The reason was his daughter. River had played a part in all of this from the very beginning, whether she knew it or not. Peters suspected she didn't. How big of a part was the question.

He ran through what he'd already known.

Amos Kaye had started off by crossing wolf DNA with human DNA to create an army of genetically modified soldiers. He'd then dabbled with bioengineering experiments, modifying living bone and tissue to meld with mechanical frames. A woman named Baliani had been integral to those experiments. She'd tried to bind souls to the bioengineered results in the hope that they'd be easier to control, but with limited success. Then Baliani had had a change of heart about her involvement in the research, and fled to become a woman named Andy. When she disappeared, the program had been forced to close.

Then, Peters sorted through what the files had revealed.

David Weston had found River as a baby. Not too long after that, Andy had appeared on the scene. Andy had told him a fantastical story of magic and other worlds, and claimed that River's soul was in danger. Weston had assumed Andy was River's birth mother and that she was unstable. It wasn't until River was five or six years of age that Weston had started to question the truth of what Andy had told him, and that was when he'd begun experiments of his own. It was also when he'd managed to get himself reinvolved with Kaye's genetic modification experiments.

Peters held up a drawing. It looked like a detailed blueprint of a kaleidoscope, which made no sense to him whatsoever. A kaleidoscope was a child's toy. It didn't require a blueprint. A six-year-old could make one.

But what could a six-year-old who possessed magic manage to make?

He rolled the drawing carefully and tucked it into an inside pocket in his parka.

Ever and Faran were watching him. They'd already seen the drawing and dismissed it as nothing of importance, at least not to them. Peters wasn't so sure. Weston had gone to a lot of trouble to hide these files, the drawing included.

Frustration filled him. Chunks of research were missing. They hadn't yet found out how these Were kids factored in. Weston had brought them here to hide them; Peters felt certain of that. He doubted if Weston had meant to abandon them, but unfortunately, shit happened. Usually at the worst possible time.

"This can't be all there is," Peters said out loud.

"Maybe there's more at the signal tower," Ever suggested.

Peters had to think for a moment about what he meant. Then he remembered the tower on the nearby mountain ridge. "How do you know all this?" he asked. "I thought you were aliens."

"We do a lot of research on hostile worlds before we travel to them," Faran explained.

Peters wondered how they managed to get that research. Then he thought of all the government space programs back in the good old days, and the number of aging satellites circling the earth. Many of those satellites continued to provide communications worldwide. And apparently beyond. "So you guys are the peeping toms of the universe?"

Ever cracked a slight smile. Faran looked pained.

"We're Guardians," Faran said, frowning at Ever, whose smile quickly faded.

"I know that," Peters said. "I've met Chase Hawkins." Although the circumstances had been unusual in that

Hawk was wearing Nick Sutton's body at the time. Not that the two of them could ever be confused. They were nothing alike, not in mannerisms or in beliefs.

But Andy had liked Nick and been lukewarm toward Hawk, so Peters had a bit of a mental war going on over Guardians in general. River, too, harbored a distrust of them.

Hawk, however, would never do anything that might hurt River. Both he and Andy knew that for a fact.

"Why would you care about an old signal tower?" Peters asked, suspicious. Hawk might not do anything to hurt River, but there were a lot of other innocent people on this world. The Were kids were a good example. None if this was their doing and they needed protection. "For that matter, why would you be interested in an abandoned military base that's hundreds of miles from what's left of civilization?" He rubbed a hand through his graying red hair. "River thinks you're here to shut down technology. Please tell me she's right, because this"—he swept his arm wide to encompass the filing cabinets in the room—"has to end. If I had to guess—and assuming I've read these notes right—I'd say those poor little kids were intended for bioengineering, and Weston brought them here to save them. But why would Guardians come to Ellesmere Island, where Were kids just happen to live? And why the interest in a signal tower?"

The two men exchanged looks.

"I agree that Weston most likely brought the children

here to save them from further experimentation," Faran said slowly, dodging the real question as he pointed to Peters' parka and the blueprints he'd pocketed, "and believe me, we had no idea that they even existed, but evidence indicates he was doing some experimenting of his own. Your little Were friend Logan reeks of magic.

"And magic belongs to the Fae."

CHAPTER THIRTEEN

♦

Nick tried not to think about how much his head hurt. At least he knew he wasn't dead because he'd been dead once before, and it hadn't hurt at all. Death was boring but pain free.

If he kept his eyes shut, maybe the pain would go away.

Or not. The last thing he remembered was a Were taking a swing at him. He could still see the hairy fist coming at him, replaying like a bad video over and over against the backdrop of his eyelids.

Then he remembered Lilla. When he thought of her, he heard the crack of her spine as one of the Weres kicked her in the small of her back.

Damn it all. Now he had to open his eyes because he had to find out what had happened to her. First River, now the pint-size Princess of Power. When had he developed this unwelcome soft spot for women with aggression issues?

Against his better judgment, he pried open one eye. He found pale, creepy, unblinking eyes staring back at him. Nick's bowels loosened.

That was General Amos Kaye, all right. He was hunkered down on his heels, staring him in the face. The overhead light reflected off his shiny scalp. Lilla lay on the bare floor behind Kaye, her hands and feet trussed together behind her back, her body forced into an unnatural arch. Her chest rose and fell, so at least she was breathing. He had no idea for how long. Nick's own hands and feet were tied, although not looped together like hers.

That was how much contempt Kaye had for him. A girl required tighter security.

"For months now, I've been trying to figure out how you could possibly have survived a bullet to the chest at close range," Kaye said, his tone light and conversational. He stroked a trim gray goatee. "The scientific conclusion is that you couldn't. Which leads us to a rather unscientific conclusion, wouldn't you say?"

The last time they'd met the crazy bastard had shot him. If not for River, Nick would be dead.

"Yeah. Your aim sucks," he replied, trying to keep his attention off Lilla and on Kaye. He didn't want him to know he was worried about her. "I've got the scars to prove it." He had a jagged, puckered hole slightly above his heart. Another one, from an uglier and messier exit wound, marred the skin beneath his left shoulder blade.

Really, he had died. He remembered the experience in vivid detail. He supposed he should be grateful to the Guardian who'd stepped into his body so that River could heal it, and to the Dark Lord who'd snagged onto him, because Nick's subconscious had recognized that death was approaching and run like hell.

Everything about him was chickenshit. Normally that didn't bother him. At the moment, it did. Kaye already knew River was one of his weaknesses. He didn't need to know that Lilla was another.

Nick had to find out what Kaye was after. If he'd planned to kill him again, he'd already be dead. So why would Kaye want him alive?

River.

"If you're planning to torture me to find out where River is," he said, "then I can save you the time and trouble. I'm not all that good with pain. Why don't I just tell you?"

Kaye chuckled softly. "I don't need to torture you for that information. She's been hiding in the subway with a bunch of street kids. So have you." He tapped a finger against his lips as if considering his choices. "I think I'd rather know more about the hologram program she's been working on."

"The name kind of says it all, don't you think?" Nick hedged, stalling.

"For every time you give me a smartass answer," Kaye replied slowly, "I'm going to break one of the pretty little blonde's fingers. So think carefully before you say anything more."

Lilla didn't move or give any indication that the threat bothered her, making Nick wonder how alert she was. It would have bothered him if he were in her position. Unfortunately she was about to get a finger broken, because he couldn't let on that Kaye's threat affected him. If he did, a few broken fingers would be the least of her worries.

"That won't be any fun. She looks like she's in a coma."

"She's awake." Kaye seemed very certain of that.

"You should rape and beat her, then," Nick advised. "That's what the bad guys do in the movies."

The general turned, leaning over Lilla. The sound of the bone in her finger snapping rang in Nick's ears, magnifying his headache a thousand times, and his stomach heaved. Lilla, however, never flinched, so he swallowed the bile. If she could take it, so could he. He thanked God their roles weren't reversed. Physically, he was confident she was tougher than him. He really didn't like pain. But from what he'd seen of her, controlling her temper might be a problem.

He could stay calm. He was good at that.

"She's not my type," Kaye replied.

The smile he gave Nick made him break out in a cold sweat. He didn't want to think about what Kaye's type might be. If his lab experiments were anything to go by it most likely involved large woodland animals, but he wasn't going to risk another one of Lilla's fingers by saying so.

"What makes you think I'm a bad guy?" Kaye added curiously.

Because psychopaths weren't known for kindness, but pointing that out wasn't worth a broken finger either.

Before he started spilling his guts, Nick wanted to find out what information he should keep to himself. Whatever Kaye wanted, Nick didn't intend for him to have it—but he was going to have to give him something.

"What do you want to know about the hologram program?" he asked.

"How does it work?"

That wasn't something he intended to share. If Kaye knew Nick had an implant in his head that River had created, he'd find himself on the wrong end of a scalpel.

"Don't tell him anything," Lilla said fiercely, her eyes open now. She glared at them both.

"They're her fingers," Nick said to Kaye with an apologetic, *what-are-you-going-to-do* roll of one shoulder. "If she doesn't want me saying anything, my lips are sealed."

"Fair enough."

Kaye broke another one, on the opposite hand this time, and tears burned like acid at the backs of Nick's eyes.

The seconds ticked away. Finally, Kaye sighed. "I didn't want to have to do this." He drew a small but sharp-looking knife from a sheath strapped above one ankle. "The three Weres who brought you in are the more advanced ones I keep around me. I have a fourth who's a bit lower on the evolutionary scale, and he doesn't have the same level of control over his natural instincts. If I make a cut here"—he drew the blade down the side of Lilla's neck—"and another one here"—he touched its tip to her exposed midriff—"how long do you suppose he could keep his appetite from getting the best of him?"

Nick risked another finger. "Can I have a few minutes to think about that?"

"Tell you what." Kaye slapped his hands to his thighs and levered himself to his feet. "Why don't I give you the rest of the day to think?"

The heavy steel door clicked shut behind him as he left them alone. Seconds later, a dead bolt shot home.

The cold bastard. Nick now had hours to think about watching Lilla get eaten alive. He remembered the crime-scene photos of what a Were had done to the other three members of his and River's original software development team.

Then he looked around the stark, narrow room for something to throw up in.

◆ ◆

River hadn't wanted to sleep in the attic of the house that no longer held warm memories for her, but Hawk had insisted. She'd been too long without undisturbed sleep, and even with magic to temporarily sustain her, to continue to ignore the needs of her body was foolish. A mortal body, even a Fae one, needed to rest.

Hawk had slept with her on one of the narrow cots, his solid, comforting body draped around hers, a blanket of warmth against the chill night and even chillier dreams.

"My mind is safe," he'd assured her. The confident smile he wore when he spoke reminded her very much of Sever, the video game character she'd first fallen in love with. Somehow, when she'd created Sever, she must have known Hawk was out there in the universe, waiting for her to find him.

Because Hawk had been able to sleep, River had, too. He would never have done so if he thought there was danger. Consequently she'd slept far better than she'd expected. The past hadn't returned to haunt her. She hadn't dreamed of the troubled soul who'd once wandered the woods near this house. She hadn't dreamed of Melinda or Sam either, or of her dead friends. She hadn't dreamed at all.

They slept until midday.

Now they returned to River's office in the subway. She stood in the gray concrete room, really seeing it for the first time as more than a place where she worked, and decided she hated it. Her whole life she'd surrounded herself with bright light and lush plants. When had she let her personal world grow so dark?

The day Hawk had left it. Now he was back, and she wasn't going to live in the dark anymore. They would isolate the virus. She would find a way to convince him to help save her world. Then she would deal with the monster who'd been stalking her.

But first she would have to face the children. She'd frightened them, and that was no easy accomplishment considering how they lived. She couldn't bear the thought of them fearing her, but it was Jake she worried about most. She was all he had left, and she wished she could offer him a normal family life, but that was impossible.

Someday, perhaps.

"Ready?" Hawk asked, his expression soft as he reached for the office door, and she nodded.

Hawk turned the knob. Jake, who'd been seated on the other side of the door, rolled backward and onto his feet in a smooth, continuous motion of recovery.

The gray-haired Fae, Achala, who'd spoken to her soul and contained her magic so completely, stood behind Jake. His eyes met hers with warmth and kindness, and more important, without judgment. If it hadn't been for this man and the way he'd injected her with calm, she would have done things she could only regret.

An unspoken greeting passed from him to her, but communication through thoughts and emotions with anyone but Hawk felt awkward and foreign, and far too intimate for comfort.

"Thank you," she said to him out loud, and he seemed to understand her reluctance.

Hawk's hand was at the small of her back, offering reassurance and less-than subtle encouragement as he propelled her forward when she would have hung back.

"Jake," he said to her brother. "I'm starved." He took up his kit bag from a corner of the office and held it up. "Want to share something to eat?"

Refusal firmed Jake's mouth. He wasn't yet ready to

fall back into familiarity with Hawk, or to leave his sister's side. He also knew when people were trying to get rid of him. River sent him a look that pleaded for cooperation. Whatever this gray-haired man wanted to speak to her about, she didn't want Jake to overhear. Not yet, before she had a chance to explain things to him in her own way.

Jake shrugged, detachment settling over him as he led Hawk onto the subway platform and toward the common area.

Hawk sent her one last look of encouragement over his shoulder, accompanied by a sexy grin that silently reminded her of how they'd spent the evening and made her face burn, before disappearing with her brother. She listened to their fading voices, then turned to the Fae.

Hawk was mistaken if he thought the Fae could persuade her that she had a duty to his people. Her duty was to her own.

Achala gestured toward the two empty chairs in the office behind her.

"Do you mind if we sit?" he asked. "My age is catching up with me, I'm afraid."

She sat down to face him and waited.

Achala, however, said nothing for long moments as he stared at her. She, in turn, sized him up. She wouldn't be swayed by anything he said, but she would hear him out. She owed him that much for protecting the children.

He was a handsome man, despite his advanced years, and carried himself with an easy dignity that spoke of much practice with people. Deep blue eyes probed hers and she tried not to squirm. A deep sadness seeped from him, increasing her discomfort.

Long moments passed.

"Forgive me," he said with a sudden start, as if only just realizing that he had been staring. "But you look so much like your mother."

River had never anticipated meeting anyone who'd known either of her birth parents, and therefore was unprepared for the shock that scorched her face and limbs at his words. Light-headedness blurred her vision and hampered her hearing, and she wondered if she'd somehow misunderstood. This was a revelation she hadn't expected and her body tightened as her mind jumped to an ugly conclusion.

He thought to use her mother as a means of getting her to do something he wanted.

Her vision cleared. "This is my world, and these kids are my family. I'm not going to leave them, and I'll do whatever it takes to protect them."

"I understand. They're charming, although they seem quite able to take care of themselves." His smile was so full of warmth and friendliness it crept under her skin and soothed her edgy nerves. River wasn't sure how she felt about that.

A rat scurried past the open door and she shuddered, distracted. Even though they were living creatures and the underground was their home, she couldn't learn to like them.

Achala's soft chuckle curled around her. "Your mother never liked creatures who dwelt in the dark either."

That was his second reference to her mother. River thought often of the bright and shining presence that had risked its soul to protect both her and her birth father. This conversation was taking another unexpected turn. She blinked hard, her throat suddenly tight, wondering if it was headed in the direction she suspected. What was Achala's relationship to her mother?

"She didn't like darkness," she corrected him quietly. She cleared her throat. "It sounds as if you knew her well."

"I knew her very well, River." He leaned toward her, his eyes sharp as if gauging her reaction without trying to read her mind. "She was my daughter."

Hawk had known this. That was what he'd been hiding from her. She supposed she should have considered the possibility, but she hadn't until now.

She didn't blame Hawk for keeping his silence. More than anything else she felt an overwhelming relief. This was between her and her . . .

Grandfather. The word seemed strange as she rolled it around and tested it out. She'd never had grandparents before, not even human ones. Eventually she'd have a million questions for him. But not yet. Now, she was too numb and wanted simply to absorb what he was trying to share.

River studied him more closely. As she examined his features she took the liberty of brushing his thoughts, just enough to sweep the outer edges, and was a bit surprised to find how far he'd opened them to her. She discovered sorrow for the daughter who had died, a blossoming, hopeful love for the granddaughter he hadn't known existed, and a deep caution regarding who—or what—she turned out to be. She wished she knew the answer to that herself.

She made no attempt to hide the thought from him, but waited instead to see how he'd respond to it.

"I know that you're special, particularly to me." Humor curved the lines of his mouth. "And to Jake, and Colonel Hawkins as well."

"I'm also dangerous," she said. Bitter pain sliced at her heart with the admission of a fear she'd tried hard to bury. "We can't forget that."

He folded his hands and didn't deny it. "There are some who can be forgiven for thinking it." An eyebrow went up, daring her to argue. "You're certainly different."

She didn't want to be dangerous, or thought of as different. She'd only ever tried to help those who needed it most. "What do you think?"

"Why don't you tell me what *you* think?" Achala suggested.

She didn't know the answer. Perhaps it was because no one, not even Hawk, understood what she was. She wasn't Fae. Neither was she Guardian. She was a combination of the two, and despite all her best intentions, no good ever seemed to come of that.

Perhaps she truly was a Dark Lord, or well on the path to becoming one. Would she be the last one to know if she were?

"What if you are?" Achala asked, curious but not

judgmental. "What if you discover that your path is dark, and well and truly set?"

Hawk was willing to transport himself into deep space at the first indication the bomb he carried had become a threat to others. She had those same protective Guardian instincts in her, as well as a Fae reverence for life.

As she searched her own soul, the answer became clear to her. The moment she felt her magic stray from the light, she would make the same decision Hawk already had.

"No one's path is set in stone," she replied. "Paths are chosen."

He was regarding her closely. "The Fae believe their paths are set at birth, when a newborn's Fae soul is chosen for it by the Mother's representatives."

"I'm not Fae."

"No," he agreed, slowly and thoughtfully. "You are not. But neither are you truly dark. Let's hope that if you're ever put to the test, you're indeed able to make the right choice."

Did no one other than Hawk believe in her ability to do so?

The possibility depressed her at first, and then she wondered why it should matter. She believed in herself.

"Can you tell me a little about my mother?" she asked Achala.

He laughed a little. "It seems so strange to think of her as your mother. The last time I saw her, she was younger than you are now." He held out a hand to her. "Why don't I show her to you instead?"

She stared at his hand, her throat tightening almost painfully. She understood the implications, understood what he was offering. She also understood he wasn't forcing her to accept him, merely making the offer, and it was up to her whether or not to accept.

Hesitant at first—she really wasn't keen on examining anyone's thoughts too deeply—River touched him, the desire to know and understand more about her birth mother overruling her inner fears.

When his hand closed over hers, she felt as if she'd been struck by a lightning bolt. Adrenaline coursed through her blood, providing a rush better than a shot of her favorite drink. She sucked in a sharp breath as images of a young girl played out in her mind.

Entranced, River watched and absorbed the entire picture show. A man came into view, and River instantly recognized him. It was Achala, only younger, which meant the little girl with the golden curls and big blue eyes was her mother, Annia.

River's heart crashed against the walls of her chest as the images changed, the child growing older, maturing. When the girl smiled, River smiled in response. When the girl cried, River cried with her. She watched her mother's short life fly by in fast forward.

When the show ended, River opened her eyes, but the room was nothing more than an unfocused haze, blurred from the liquid pooling in her eyes.

"You loved her very much," she whispered.

"Yes."

"And you're worried about her soul. That it might have been damaged somehow."

There was a longer pause as she felt him struggle against an intense wave of guilt and pain. Then, "Yes."

River withdrew her hands from his and placed them in her lap. Her throat threatened to close over as she remembered those few special moments she'd had with what had once been Annia, at the graveyard, before both the Fae soul and its magic departed.

She looked at the ugly cement floor and stared blindly at the cracks. "She died trying to protect me, and her soul was captured trying to protect my father. She spent a long time watching over him, but now their souls are at peace. Her soul is undamaged."

Another long pause. Then, "Thank you for that, *lief-eling*." He smoothed his robe over his knees with the heels of his hands and added, "It saddens and shames me that I never got to know you, or spend time with you the way a grandfather should."

River couldn't help but feel sad for that, too, even though she had no regrets about the parents who had raised her.

Then, taking her by surprise, he held his hands out once again. "May I?" he asked. "I would like to know a little bit of your life. Only what you would share."

Warily, still not quite comfortable in sharing her thoughts with anyone but Hawk, River slid her hands into his and offered him memories of her own. He held her fingers tight, and she watched the play of carefully controlled emotions as they crossed his still-handsome face. A long while later he pulled back, his blue eyes contemplative as they met hers.

"Your soul is different," he said.

She'd been hearing that a lot. "In what way?"

He paused as if sorting through questions brought on by her thoughts. "It's a nurturing one, very powerful. But Fae magic has rules. You need to learn them."

Her mood darkened. In her surprise over discovering that he was her grandfather, she'd forgotten that he'd come here for a reason. Everyone thought they knew what she should do, and what was best for both her and her world—the Great Lords of the Guardians, Hawk, and now, even her Fae grandfather.

Her human father, on the other hand, had always encouraged her to do what she believed in, but he was gone and no longer able to help support her decisions. She missed him fiercely.

"Why would I need to learn Fae rules?" she asked Achala, her eyes narrowing with renewed suspicion. "What do you want from me?"

Before he could answer, one of the Demons, a thin girl of about twelve, skidded into the room, her eyes wide. She hesitated for a split second when River turned to look at her, but then quickly overcame whatever reservations she may have had.

"Dan told me to get you," she said to River, her eyes darting between them. "People out on the streets are acting all weird."

CHAPTER FOURTEEN

♦

Jake had walked away from him the moment they were out of River's sight.

Hawk considered going after him, then decided to leave him alone. The boy was tired and irritable, and that was never the best time to try to reason with a teenager.

Besides, Hawk had other things to worry about. Not necessarily more important things, because Jake was certainly that, but definitely pressing. What had happened to Lilla?

Hawk frowned. She wasn't responding to her comlink, although that might not be so unusual. They were underground, which could disrupt the signal. So could River's hologram program.

He had searched everywhere, however, and it wasn't like Lilla to simply disappear. Not when she'd been given an order. He tried to remember what that order had been. At the time, his attention had been focused entirely on River.

He'd told Lilla to stay with Achala, but to keep an eye on Nick. She wasn't with Achala. His jaw set. Therefore, of course she'd be keeping an eye on the asshole, and only the Mother knew where he might be. Trouble followed him like the stink off a wet dog. She could take care of herself, but still.

A gunshot rang out, the sound distorted by the tunnel's thick walls. Hawk stiffened. Another shot cracked the air and he started cautiously in that direction, his hand on his own weapon. These might be kids living here, but they were far from innocent. Regardless of whether they were creating it or receiving it, those shots indicated trouble and he couldn't ignore them. He had two Fae now to protect.

When he rounded a bend in the tunnel he found Jake, crouched on one knee, a gun cocked and balanced on his forearm. He was dressed in a pair of broken down sneakers, jeans and a North Face nylon jacket similar to the one Hawk had seen Nick wearing. Crisos. Of all the men the kid could have chosen to emulate.

A quick scan of the area told Hawk the boy was alone, so he pressed back in the shadows to see what he was doing with the gun.

It took him a few minutes to figure out that Jake wasn't exactly himself. Every once in a while his image flickered, and when it did, a faint buzzing sound could be heard. The noise wasn't quite the same as what Hawk had heard coming off the sick people on the streets above, but it was close.

Was Jake in the early stages of disease, or was this something else entirely?

Hawk watched him take potshots at rats creeping along the pipes crisscrossing the tunnel ceiling overhead. Seeing him shoot at small animals bothered Hawk. He didn't especially care about the rats. They spread disease and posed a health hazard, particularly to the smaller children, but it was the purpose behind Jake's activity that had him concerned. Hawk had once been a boy himself so he understood that Jake was just being a boy, doing what boys do, but he couldn't forget that Jake had been going to kill him.

Psychologically, Jake was walking a very fine line. This was how serial killers began.

"You shouldn't be doing that," Hawk said.

Jake spun around, his gun redirected at Hawk. "Doing what?"

"Shooting rats. Or using your hologram when there's something wrong with it," he added. "You should have River check out that noise."

The boy shrugged but didn't lower his weapon. "I can't hurt them. It's a safeguard in the program. And River knows about the noise. Nick's got it, too. She'll fix it."

So technically, Jake wasn't killing the rats. Good to know. And something to think about.

He stopped. Nick had the noise in his hologram, too?

Before he could ask about it, another rat scurried by. Jake lowered his gun.

"Why aren't you shooting that one?" he asked.

He grinned, his chin edging up a notch. "Because I know better." Jake's hologram flickered out completely, startling Hawk by the unexpectedness of it. "If you're worried about me using my hologram, don't be. If I was going to get sick, I'd be sick by now. I heard how fast it hit Billy."

It didn't take long for good news to spread.

Jake's voice came from behind him now, and he turned to face him. The rat disappeared down the tracks and Jake started back toward the platform. A few long strides had Hawk at the boy's side, then keeping pace as Jake trudged in silence along the sleepers with his head down and his lips pressed tight.

Since the kid wasn't going to give him an opening, Hawk finally cut the quiet himself. "Do you remember when we first met? We talked about how River is different."

"She's good with computer programs," Jake replied, refusing to be drawn into discussion. "She got a little carried away with the one she's been working on, that's all." His tone dared Hawk to disagree.

Hawk couldn't. It was a fairly accurate assessment—only she'd gotten carried away with the magic she'd used and not her technology. But Jake had it explained to his own satisfaction, and that was what mattered. River was his sister and he believed in her.

So did Hawk.

A sliver of guilt wormed its way into his conscience. Jake only had River left. Soon, he wouldn't have her either.

"I'm sorry about your mom and Sam," he said. Awkwardness made him sound abrupt and inside, he winced.

Jake stiffened, ever so slightly. "Yeah, well, thanks, but you only met them once. You didn't really know them."

"No, I didn't," Hawk agreed. "But I know what it's

like to lose my family. I lost my wife and my ten-year-old daughter in an accident." He still found it difficult to talk about them, particularly his daughter. "They waved good-bye to me one morning, and that was the last time I ever saw them." The excitement on his daughter's face at the thought of her first off-world trip would forever tear at his heart. But this wasn't about him or his loss, this was about Jake. "Do you like being a Demon?"

"Dan is still teaching me how to fight. Only the guys who can kick real ass get to be Demons."

The envy in the boy's voice had Hawk worried. "Dan might be teaching you how to fight, but is he teaching you what to fight for?"

An odd look came over Jake's face. "Nobody has to teach me that. I know what I'm fighting for."

"You sure about that?"

He drove his hands deep into his pockets. "Did River tell you what they did to my mom and brother?" he asked, his voice dark and dangerous as he kicked at a pebble. It ricocheted off the concrete wall, skipping a few times. "Whoever did it are the ones who'll be sorry."

Fresh scars on Jake's forehead indicated to Hawk that he'd been training too hard and with far too much purpose, and that Dan wasn't holding back on him either.

"Your mom and Sam are gone and nothing will bring them back," he said carefully. "Life is for the living. If you're going to fight, fight to keep the little kids safe."

He let him think about that for a few moments before adding, "You're River's brother. Whether you like it or not, that makes you different, too. You have to make good choices, and set a good example for the others. The little ones look up to you."

"Dan looks down on me."

And the older boy's opinion was important to Jake.

"That's only because he knows what I know," Hawk said.

"What's that?"

"That when you start believing in yourself, and understand the strength you have in here," Hawk stopped to prod Jake's chest, "you're going to be a leader. He doesn't want that to happen."

Jake shook his head. "You're wrong. About me and Dan."

"What if I'm not?" Jake continued to stare straight ahead, his face expressionless. "The only person who you have to prove anything to is yourself," Hawk added, leaving it at that.

They walked in silence for a long time, Hawk giving the boy a chance to think. When they reached the main platform and the living areas, Hawk glanced toward the stairwell and the long streams of sunlight from above.

He had to find Lilla. Something was wrong.

Jake started off for the training room.

"Jake," he called after him.

He turned back, his eyes bloodshot from lack of sleep. He looked young, and Hawk felt sorry for him.

"Yeah?"

"If you see Lilla, tell her I've gone out looking for her, and tell her to stay put until I get back."

"What makes you think she'll take orders from me?"

"Because you tried to kill me," Hawk said. "She knows better than to mess with you."

Jake rubbed one tired eye with the heel of his hand. "About that."

"Don't worry about it."

Jake's face relaxed, and the tiny fist of unease in Hawk's stomach unclenched. That craving for approval meant Jake cared about the difference between right and wrong.

"You should stop giving me reasons to shoot you," Jake said.

Hawk laughed as he made his way up the stairs. He poked his head cautiously over the rail at the top and looked up and down the empty street. He frowned. This wasn't the busiest part of the city at the best of times, and yet he couldn't shake the smell of shit gone bad.

Where was Lilla?

◆ ◆

The nausea passed.

Nick pulled himself together, trying to think. He wanted to tell Lilla he was sorry for getting her into this mess but wasn't quite sure how to go about an apology.

Besides, he'd tried to tell her to stay in the subway but she'd refused because Captain Courageous had told her to keep an eye on him. This should teach her a lesson about blindly following orders.

The room they were being held in was empty of furniture except for one bigass flatscreen mounted on a wall, and the color of the paint was definitely blah, but the sun was shining brightly so it had to be at least mid-morning, maybe later.

When he sat up he could see a wide swath of the river and white-tipped mountains in the distance from the large, black-tinted window. He recognized the skyline. They had to be in an office building on the city's main quay. The compound where he used to work on a video game project with River was near here. He could think of only one building on the waterfront with black windows, which meant Kaye was keeping a torture chamber in the government building. Nice to know how tax dollars were spent.

And he'd thought the bioengineering programs were a ballsy use of public funds.

The dark windows meant no one outside would be able to see in, so jumping up and down and waving for help wouldn't do them any good.

Lilla still hadn't moved, and that had him worried.

"Are you okay?" Nick asked her.

"Two broken fingers are nothing."

They weren't nothing and he knew it, but he didn't say anything more about that. "How's your back?"

"My back?" She turned her head to look at him, surprise in her eyes, so apparently it was fine.

"You took quite a hit outside that coffee shop," Nick explained awkwardly, uncomfortably aware that she'd come to his rescue and yet he hadn't been able to do anything for her in return. "I thought I heard something break."

"It was my transporter," Lilla replied. She swore a little. "They're implanted under our skin. I'll have to get Faran to fix it. Otherwise they'll have to go home without me and send someone back to repair it, and no offense, but I don't want to stay here any longer than necessary."

"None taken." Talking would get her mind off the pain and his off the Weres, so Nick was willing to keep the conversational ball rolling. "Who's Faran?"

"He's what you'd call a doctor, I suppose." Lilla tried to loosen the knots on the ropes binding her hands and feet but with no luck. The broken fingers weren't a lot of help. "Look," she said patiently, "I don't mean to be rude, but I'd like to point out something. You can use your hologram, correct?"

"Not very well," Nick admitted, "but sort of."

"And it's used as a weapon, so you can hit things with it?"

"Again yes, but not very well."

"Then you should be able to use it to untie us both, right?"

He couldn't think of any response to that other than yes.

"Sorry," he said, feeling stupid. "I'm not used to it, so that never occurred to me."

She didn't say anything smartass or obnoxious like he would have if he were the one in her position. Instead, she said encouragingly, "Try your best. We've got all day."

If she believed that, then she wasn't so very much smarter than him. Kaye was messing with their heads.

He tried to think of something easy to project, something with strong fingers. In the end he settled for an image of Lilla because she was right there in front of him, so he didn't need to think too hard about it.

"Crisos. That is so amazing," she breathed as she watched an image of herself appear in the room. Her expression darkened with amused reproof and she rolled her eyes. "But my breasts aren't that large."

"No time to be picky about the details. Your ass isn't that small either," he replied, although her real ass was very nice. He'd checked it out several times. He frowned in concentration. This wasn't easy for him. He didn't know why he found it so hard. A ten-year-old had better control than he did.

"Should we be worried about that buzzing sound?" Lilla's glance shot to the door.

"We should be terrified." And not only because someone might hear it. Nick was really afraid of infecting her. He didn't think the virus could be spread through the hologram's touch. He was fairly certain it had to be true physical contact, but he wasn't positive. He wouldn't be taking this risk if he didn't know for a fact that Kaye didn't bluff.

When he came back, the freak was going to feed her to a Were.

Hollow Lilla picked away at the knots on real Lilla's bindings. She was patient while he worked, staring at a spot on the ceiling. Nick lost his focus and had to stop several times to rest. The better part of the day passed before she was finally free.

The real Lilla shook off the bindings and swung her arms to get the circulation going, which ate up more time.

When she was able to, she moved toward Nick, reaching for the knots on his bindings, but he rolled out of her reach.

"Don't touch me!" he said sharply. Her broken fingers were too swollen. More important, the buzzing sound was almost unbearable now and he didn't want her to get sick. He hoped Kaye caught it, though. Nick tried to remember if Kaye had touched him. The Weres had, but they weren't 100 percent human. From the reports he'd seen, they'd been immune to the virus the first time around.

Lilla rocked back on her heels in frustration. Her worried eyes told him she didn't want to wait for Hollow Lilla to try to untie the knots. It took far too long. "Can you send the hologram for help?"

He didn't see that he had a whole lot of choice other than to try, although he did feel better knowing that she was free. She'd at least have a fighting chance. "No problem," he said, lying.

But whom was he going to ask for help? It couldn't be River. That would be giving Kaye what he wanted, and Nick wasn't about to do that. He couldn't ask the Demons either. They were kids, and no match for Kaye and his Weres.

That left Chase Hawkins.

Nick sighed. Then he concentrated. River was always harping at him to practice and now was a good time.

Hollow Lilla leapt through the window as if passing through water and hit the ground running.

◆ ◆

Peters paused at the base of the low mountain ridge and unstrapped his snowshoes from his backpack, the cold wind whipping grit and chunks of ice in his face. Snow had not yet receded from this side of the mountain face. While the sun now skimmed the skyline it wouldn't set, so the men had all grabbed some sleep before setting out, knowing that darkness wouldn't be an issue.

Faran and Ever, even though they had a far more efficient means of travel, had chosen to hike across the tundra from the weather station with him, curious to check out the landscape. Other than a herd of shaggy brown musk oxen and a surly wolverine that Peters had to warn Ever to stay clear of, the trip was uneventful. The wolves had withdrawn, at least for now, but if they continued to show aggression, Peters worried what the future might hold for the young Weres. Weston might have been trying to protect those kids but he hadn't thought it through.

Faran and Ever had told him pieces of their plan, although probably not all. They intended to launch chlorine atoms into the stratosphere and knock a bigass hole in the ozone layer that would grow over the coming months. That hole would take out a significant amount of the Earth's technology, because anything operating on any kind of a frequency, or with an electrical current, was going to have its signals disrupted. Something to do with sunspots.

He'd had mixed feelings about it all day. Fantasizing about an all-out Armageddon, and having the day of reckoning actually arrive, were very different things. The ozone layer would eventually repair itself. Governments had been talking about that for decades, and now they were going to have to pool their efforts and put their money where their mouths were.

But this setback was going to seriously test an already weary world. The virus had wiped out close to 80 percent of its population and started a war of epic proportions, causing entire countries to literally disappear off the map. The newly formed Union of North America was a case in point.

On the other hand, this might give Amos Kaye, the Monster Man, something better to do with his time. The Were kids would be safe. So would River.

That thought had Andy tap dancing in his head

once again. Jesus. He slid his boots into the fittings of his snowshoes and clipped them in place.

The mountain ridge wasn't high or especially difficult to reach. The snow had thinned enough to expose any hidden crevasses, and the summit was clearly visible, as was the signal tower, butted against an outcropping of rock that formed the zenith.

"Let's go," he said, and started trudging upward.

A few hours later they reached their goal. Built somewhat like a domed observatory, the base of the signal tower remained sheltered by rock face, but its rounded top rose slightly higher than the summit's peak.

"What's with the lock?" Faran asked, examining the heavy padlock on the door.

"Maybe they were worried about an alien invasion," Peters deadpanned, and Ever had to choke back a laugh.

"Then they should have factored in this." Faran pulled a long, thin piece of metal from his pack and set to work on the lock. Within moments they were inside.

Peters looked around in disappointment. No filing cabinets. Therefore, no research notes. The tower was empty except for the biggest freaking telescope he'd ever seen, and it rose about twenty feet to the roof. Bitter cold chilled the room, and his breath puffing like smoke in the air, he swung his arms to keep the circulation moving. He'd made the climb for nothing. At least the return route was all downhill.

Ever examined a large, stainless-steel tubular object he found on the floor beside the telescope.

"What the hell is that?" Peters asked, immediately

forgetting his disappointment. It looked a lot like the drawing of the kaleidoscope he'd tucked into his pocket, only giant size.

"It's a finder scope," Ever explained absently, his attention on the long tube. Clumsy welding marred its seams. "It's a mini version of the main telescope. It sees more of the sky so it can pinpoint the area you want to examine more closely." The finder scope's viewfinder was twisted into an awkward angle and looked as if a piece might be missing. "Although unlike anything I've ever seen before. It's got a black lens. And I have no idea what it's doing on the floor. It could be a dud, an experiment somebody tried but didn't work. Only one way to find out." He glanced up at Faran. "Help me lift this into place, will you?"

The two men grunted beneath the weight as they fitted it into sturdy clips mounted on the side of the main telescope.

Peters watched as Ever fiddled with the viewfinder, trying to figure out the correct angle. Andy had gotten very quiet in his head, but an air of expectancy told him this was something else she'd sent him to find. He leaned over, craning his neck to see.

"Crisos," Ever suddenly said. He'd gone completely still, the color slipping from his face. His chest rose and fell as if he struggled for air.

Faran pushed him aside and put his eye to the viewfinder. Ever dropped to the cold, knotted, pine-planked floor and rested his head between his knees.

This couldn't be good. Andy remained silent, so

Peters had no way of knowing for certain. "What is it? What's wrong?"

Faran didn't answer him, but continued to look silently at the sky above for a long time. Peters tried not to show his impatience.

Finally, Faran stepped aside. "Take a look," he invited. "But don't adjust anything. The sun is still in the sky and you don't want to damage your eyes. That explains the black lens."

At first, Peters didn't see anything. As far as he could tell, the black lens wasn't a help. Then, gradually, billowing rainbows of vibrant colors became discernable in the lens-darkened sky, swirling like the eye of a hurricane until they massed into a giant cloud in the finder scope's field of vision.

The burning, peppery scent of sage seeped into the signal tower. Peters became aware of it at the same time as the two Guardians. He took his eye away from the viewfinder in surprise. He recognized that smell.

"Quick!" Ever cried. "Unfasten it. Shut it down."

Peters leapt out of their way as the two men rushed to lift the finder scope from the clips. Once it was free, they eased the scope gently to the floor and backed away from it as fast as they could, as if they'd committed some deadly cardinal sin.

The whole tower reeked of sage now, so thick in the air the men could taste it. Rather than taking ten years off of his life, Peters had the sense of ten years being added. He hadn't felt this alive since . . . forever.

"Something is seriously wrong on this island," he said. The two men looked at him as if he'd stated something so obvious it bordered on stupid. He felt stupid, so that was okay. "Anyone mind explaining what we were seeing in that thing?"

"Those are Fae souls," Faran replied, his voice bleak. He glanced at the com-link on his wrist, startled. His face twisted in confused disbelief. "Crisos. Now Hawk wants me. This world is one disaster after another." He tossed Ever his pack. "Make yourselves useful. Peters can help you get these set in place, but don't either one of you do anything or leave here until I've had a chance to get some direction from him on this."

Then, Faran winked out of sight.

◆ ◆

To say that people were "acting all weird" wasn't an accurate description. That they had disappeared completely was closer to the truth. The streets were empty.

River hadn't expected that, and she found it alarming. When people felt threatened their initial response was to stay close to the safety of home. It wouldn't be long, however, before they'd be forced to emerge. They'd need food and other basic necessities. Disaster was coming.

Despite the certainty, this was the first time she'd been outside in her physical form in more than four months, and she breathed deeply, taking in the smells of spring and new life. Warmth and light sprang from her soul in response. She'd been starving for this. She hadn't realized how much.

Dan had opted to use his Hollow form. She stayed close to him as they walked, just as he'd ordered, not because it made her feel safer but because it put him in charge. She had encroached on his territory, not the other way around, and she wanted to be more respectful of that.

She'd refused to use her own Hollow form, however. The virus and the program were somehow related and the link between them had something to do with her. Until she figured out what, she wouldn't expose anyone else. The thought that she was responsible for such terrible deaths, even unintentionally, was unbearable.

She had to fix this. In order to fix it, she had to determine what had gone wrong.

Silently, she followed Dan as he led her through several back alleys. They headed up the mountain streets, away from the downtown core of the city and the waterfront quays. They finally emerged in a small park, the kind of place where mothers took small children to let them play with their friends. Although shabby, and in need of an experienced gardener, someone had made an effort to keep it tidy.

River looked around, curious, her fingers itching to dig in the dirt in search of seeds that she could encourage to grow. A small city park filled with sandboxes and swings wasn't a place where she would have expected Dan to hang out. Then, she understood.

This tough guy, who would kill anyone entering his territory and not wearing his colors, brought the littlest ones under his care here to play. He continually surprised her, and yet this side of him was why she had instinctively turned to him when she'd needed somewhere for Jake.

The park was empty.

"Over here," Dan said. He beckoned River over to a bench. Behind the bench, a woman's body lay twisted in death. Her wasted remains indicated she'd died of the virus. An empty stroller sat nearby, a diaper bag swinging from its handle.

The sight of that empty stroller made River grab onto the back of the bench for support. It was unlikely this young woman had come here alone.

"I took the kid home to the subway for now," Dan said shortly, seeing the stricken expression on her face.

She didn't need to know any more than that. He would have made certain the child was safe.

"From what I've seen," he continued, "babies don't seem to be catching this. Her little girl is probably about a year old, if that." His eyes went flat, hiding all emotion. "But it happened fast. The mother looked perfectly healthy when she got here. Maybe a little high strung."

A baby's mind wasn't well enough developed to work the hologram program, so it was possible they couldn't be infected with hallucinations. River's breath caught. Did that mean there would be a number of tiny, defenseless orphans once the first wave of sickness had passed?

"Who did the mother come into contact with?" she wondered out loud.

Had Dan talked to her? Touched her? Picked her pocket? Was that how she'd gotten sick?

"No one that I saw," he replied. "And no," he added as if reading her mind, "I was nowhere near her. I came here to think, not steal. She never saw me. All at once she started screaming about strangers trying to steal her baby. While she was fighting off whatever it was she thought she saw, I grabbed the kid."

An empty coffee cup rolled across the ground, disturbed by a puff of wind, and Dan picked it up. It was another interesting character trait of his that he worried about litter. Nick thought Dan was the next best thing to a psycho, but what would he have been like if he'd had a different start in life?

"Was that her cup?" River asked suddenly. It looked new, as if it hadn't been here long.

"Yeah." He threw it into a nearby trash can.

She watched Dan, her mind half on him, the other busy with the virus. They needed to follow the virus's trail, to see if it led to anything important. At the very least, she might find out how far it had spread.

"The woman stopped for coffee on her way here," River pointed out. "Where's the closest Tim Hortons?"

CHAPTER FIFTEEN

◆

Hawk searched the nearby streets and empty buildings with caution, not wanting to disturb any trigger-happy squatters or victims of delusional illness.

The body count was rising. He'd found a few more, some obvious suicides, others who'd fought to the death. What they'd been fighting was known only to them, because there was no evidence to support that anything physical had attacked them.

He could well imagine what these people had suffered. For more than a year, he'd lived with the fear of losing his mind.

A television had been left on in one of the buildings. Hawk caught the tail end of a news report. Word of the virus was out. The panic had started.

He had to get River and Achala away. Perhaps Achala could make some suggestions for convincing River to go. If it came down to it, maybe they could take Jake as well and deal with the fallout of that later. But deep down, Hawk knew it was never going to happen. Not as easily or cleanly as he'd like. Could he bring himself to use force with her?

He had that nasty little explosive surprise rolling around in his head. Trying to use force on River wasn't likely to be good for those stress chemicals in his brain.

Lilla would have no problem using force if she had to. Maybe it was time Hawk started to delegate. First he would have to find her. For the life of him, he couldn't imagine where she would go.

Maybe he needed to think like Nick, not Lilla, because wherever she'd gone, she would have been following him. So where would a selfish bastard worried only about his own skin go?

He wouldn't travel far from safety. He'd need a hole to scurry back to. That meant Hawk should focus on the areas around the different subway entrances.

He moved several blocks down the street toward the city's center and the next subway entrance, since he hadn't yet searched in that direction.

The day was progressing well into night by the time he finally saw something that caught his undivided attention.

River.

For the love of the Mother. That had better be her hologram he was staring at. It wasn't though. He knew it instinctively. He rubbed his forehead with the back of his hand. What had possessed her to come out on the streets in the middle of a potential epidemic?

Dan was with her, but when Hawk looked closer he could tell that he was a hologram. Little things in the details he was projecting weren't true to life. The real Dan wasn't that muscular or tall.

From Hawk's perspective, having Dan in his hologram form was for the best. He couldn't kill anything this way, but if he had to, he could defend River.

He held back, wondering what they were up to. River walked up to the main entrance of a nearby coffee shop and tried the door. It was unlocked, although the store's interior lights hadn't been turned on despite the fact that streetlights now sparkled throughout the empty city. Hawk frowned.

"Don't open that door!" he shouted, running out of the shadows toward her. A well-aimed knife narrowly missed his head. "Hey!" He rounded on Dan, who'd thrown it at him, and thanked the Mother that the little bastard really couldn't kill him. "Was that necessary?"

The boy shrugged. "You took me by surprise. Now that the cavalry's here," he said to River, "I'm out of here. I'm starving."

He disappeared.

"He makes me nervous," Hawk said, eyeing the spot where Dan had stood. "You should hang a bell on that kid." He scowled at River. "What are you doing out here?"

"Following the virus," she replied. "From what Dan could tell, a young woman got sick and died in a very short period of time. She'd stopped for coffee at some point before that. We found an empty paper cup on the ground beside her." She crooked dark strands of her long hair behind her ear with her forefinger, smoothing it absently. Then she shrugged in defeat. "It was a long-shot. So far, we've been wasting our time."

A noise around the side of the building made both him and River turn their heads. Someone was hiding in the shadows. Hawk drew his weapon.

River laid a small but firm hand on his arm to stop him.

"Do you remember the innocents in the game?" she asked, her voice soft so as not to be overheard.

Hawk hesitated, then nodded. The gamer had to approach the innocents to ask for directions. True innocents gave clues to finishing the level. Others turned into werewolves or demons that had to be killed. Killing werewolves and demons gave the gamer energy to continue. Killing an innocent, however, came at a heavy cost.

Her fingers tightened on his arm, encouraging him to be reasonable, then she released him. "Why don't we try asking some questions first?"

Fair enough. "I'll ask."

"Or," she suggested, rolling her eyes, "I can ask the questions and you can cover me. I'm faster than you are, but you're a better shot."

"Tell you what," Hawk said. "I'll get the conversation started. Hey," he called into the shadows. "Whoever's back there. Come out with your hands up or I'll kill you."

River punched him in the kidney with her knuckles. It hurt, but not much. "You don't get to go on many peacekeeping missions, do you?" she demanded.

A teenage boy wearing a brown and tan coffee shop uniform emerged from around the corner of the building, his raised hands shaking. Hawk examined him. He looked healthy enough, although scared half to death. Hawk slid his weapon back into its holster.

"Definitely an innocent," he muttered to River. She ignored him, her attention on the boy.

Hawk was discovering that when she wanted to, River could use her magic to her complete advantage. After only a few hours with her Fae grandfather she'd already absorbed his ability to calm other people. The boy relaxed under her gaze. When his eyes flickered back to Hawk, however, panic filled them.

Hawk stepped a little away from her so that the boy wouldn't feel so threatened, but he didn't go far. He'd allow her to handle this, but he did not intend to run the risk of her coming to harm.

"Hi," River said to the boy.

With those brilliant blue eyes and a disarming smile filled with compassion, no one would guess she could slay a fanged, drooling Feral with a single blow from her sword. Or summon fire- and windstorms at will.

The kid, however, wasn't in a trusting mood. He looked ready to crawl out of his skin. He reeked of vinegar, the sharp smell thick in the air around him.

"Be careful, River," Hawk warned her quietly.

The boy's gaze shifted to him. "Everyone should be careful," he replied. His hands shook harder and his face crumpled. "The whole world's going crazy. Are you crazy, too?"

Pity swelled in Hawk's chest, tightening to the point of pain, and River tucked her hands under her arms. Not for warmth, he knew, but because she was trying to resist the urge to comfort the kid. Crisos, what a shame. Whatever had happened had damaged him.

"No," Hawk said. "Neither are you."

"Why would you think we were crazy?" River added.

The boy's eyes widened in horror. "If you aren't, then stay away from me or you will be. I think I did that to them."

"Did what?"

Hawk listened as she pried it out of him, bit by bit. Four people had come into the shop that day. The first two had seemed fine when they left, but the third, a young mother, had started to worry on her way out of the shop about strangers stealing her baby. The fourth was a man, and he'd been completely delusional. The boy had followed him, trying to calm him, but he'd screamed about rats in the alley eating him alive.

It didn't take a genius to figure out what had happened next. The shadows of that building hid the body of the fourth person. But how was the virus spreading? And why had the boy not caught it when everyone around him was sick?

"Why do you think you're causing whatever this is?" Hawk asked him. "Why couldn't they have gotten it from someone else? A lot of people have been getting sick." His jaw set. A *lot*.

"I probably couldn't have given it to everyone," the boy agreed. "I'd never even seen that d-d-dead guy before. But Angie got sick when we changed shifts the other morning," he explained. His lower lip began to tremble. "She kissed me good-bye when she left. Then she d-died a few hours later. And Ben never showed up to take over for me today. We worked together yesterday for a few hours. The woman with the baby started acting all paranoid after she got her coffee from me. I think I might have touched her when I gave her the change." Confusion drew his eyebrows together as he puzzled it over. "The couple who were here first thing this morning seemed okay though, although the guy made the girl scrub her hands with vinegar before they left." He held out his own, palms up, then flipped them over, examining them front and back. "He sounded like he knew what he was talking about so I've been using it, too. It can't hurt to try." His eyes filled with tears. "Do you think it's too late?"

The couple that'd been in first thing that morning could very well have been Nick and Lilla.

Hawk's stomach plunged as he started to connect some of the facts he should have pieced together before now. Four months ago River had stood watch while he'd examined the desiccated, virus-infected bodies that had been disposed of in the central subway station during the early days of the war. He had been wearing Nick's body at the time. Now, Nick was hearing noises in his Hollow form.

And people he'd been in contact with were getting sick.

The coffee shop was close to one of the subway entrances. Nick would have had to pay for the coffee, and money carried all kinds of germs. That was one of the reasons why the Guardians relied on an electronic system of currency.

"The couple—was the guy about this tall," Hawk held

his hand shoulder height, "skinny, with scraggly dark hair and a narrow face like a ferret?" River shot him a look that said she wasn't impressed by the description, which he pretended not to see. "And did he have a short blond woman with him? Pretty, like a doll?"

The boy nodded. A fine mist of rain had begun, and he wiped his damp hair back from his pimply forehead.

"Did you hear a buzzing noise around any of them?" River asked. A dead leaf skittered past her ankles, rattling unnoticed down the sidewalk.

He nodded. "The last guy."

Hawk felt the faint, familiar tug of her magic and caught a soft whisper of its peppery odor as she sowed gentle reassurance into the boy's thoughts. She looked at his name tag.

"Liam, if you haven't gotten sick by now, you aren't likely to catch it. I don't think you're spreading it either. You don't have to worry about getting home safe, but if you can, stay away from anyone acting unusual. If they're hallucinating, they might try to hurt you."

Liam took off at a run and never looked back. River and Hawk watched him disappear into a dark curtain of drizzle.

"What do you suppose the odds are," Hawk said slowly, hooking an arm around River's neck and hauling her close to him, "that I introduced the virus into Nick's body when we were at the subway terminal and it somehow got mixed into your hologram program?"

She was silent for a really long time. He could feel

her thoughts as she ran through the things he already had, sorting them out in a chronological order.

She pressed her forehead into his chest and slid her arms around his waist.

"Too good to bet on," she finally said. "If you and I started this virus," she added, worry on her face as she tipped her chin to look up at him, "we have to find some way to stop it."

He closed his eyes. He'd hoped she would have another explanation.

He hadn't come here for this. He'd intended to set off the kits, recover River, return her to the Fae, and leave this world to deal with the aftermath of ozone depletion and the major disruptions to its power grids.

This new virus was not of human making. It had been created by a Guardian and a Fae, through technology and magic, and no one on this world stood a chance against it. Not unless, like Liam, they were naturally immune. Or Nick, who appeared to be a carrier.

Jake might be a carrier, too. And who knew how many others?

His conscience would no longer allow him to walk away. Neither would River's.

He thanked the Mother that River and Achala were Fae. Fae didn't get sick. But Guardians did, and Hawk had a team to worry about. One of those team members was with the person most likely spreading the virus. He reached for his com-link.

It was time to call in some help from an expert.

◆ ◆

Wandering the streets in Hollow Lilla form was an interesting experience.

Nick cupped his hands around her breasts, surreptitiously adjusting them under her—his—shirt. Lying on the floor in their prison, he was rubbing his own chest with his bound hands. He could feel both his and Hollow Lilla's at the same time. It was the weirdest experience ever.

It was also very cool. River totally rocked at bending reality.

"Hey!" he heard Lilla say sharply, reminding him that she was sitting beside him and could see what he was doing.

He dropped his hands. "Sorry."

The buzzing noise that accompanied his program was going to make it difficult to move through the streets unannounced. On the other hand, the streets were empty. People had hunkered down. He'd thought the world had already gone through the plague stage of the Apocalypse, but apparently not.

He now knew for certain which building he and Lilla were being held in downtown. He had to let Hawkins know how to find it. A slight complication was that Nick had trouble holding onto the hologram. He was getting better at it, but one minute he was walking the streets and the next, he was staring into Lilla's worried eyes. It slowed progress.

Eventually, though, he found himself back in Demon territory. There was no sign of any of them lurking around, so even those nervy little bastards had stayed underground. How bad had things become?

The sound of familiar, hushed voices near the Tim Hortons shop carried to him and he stopped, listening carefully. One was Colonel Dickhead. The other was definitely River.

What was she doing out of the subway?

His lips pressed together. She'd better be in Hollow form.

Right now, though, he had a more pressing concern. Lilla didn't have that much time left. He'd hoped to get Hawkins alone, but he should have known the two of them would now be conjoined.

Nick managed to jerk his Lilla hologram around and started off in the direction of their voices. There was no sneaking up on them, not with the buzzing in his head announcing his approach. Colonel Dickhead sprang into full macho mode, pushing River behind him.

"Nice," Nick said. "You bring her out here and put her in danger, then act like everyone else has the problem."

Two blank, surprised faces stared back at him.

"Nick?" River asked, pushing from behind Hawk for a closer look.

He'd forgotten that he was in Lilla form, and for a bizarre moment he got what it must have been like for Hawk to live in someone else's body.

The guy was still an asshole.

"What's happened to Lilla?" Hawk demanded. His

hands had balled into fists at his sides. Worry etched his face.

"You wouldn't hit a girl, would you?" Nick asked, eyeing those fists. He kind of hoped he would. Thanks to the hologram program, it wouldn't hurt him a bit. Or very much. He was getting better at level two.

"Lilla?" River reminded him, placing a restraining hand on Hawk's arm.

"She's right here beside me. Relax, Rambo," he added, because Hawk looked ready to blow a jugular. "She's fine for now. But we've got a problem."

As he explained the situation, Hawk's face grew even more grim. River caught back a little gasp when he told how Kaye had broken Lilla's fingers.

"He wants River," Nick said to Hawk. "That means she has to stay behind. Good luck with that, because believe me, I know quite well how much she loves diving headfirst into a battle." It had been his job to monitor her progress as she'd worked through the levels of her video game. She'd constantly pushed the safety limits, both physically and mentally.

"But what is Kaye planning?" she asked, bewildered.

From the very first, when River had pitched her idea for a game to a group of investors that had included representatives of the former Canadian government, this had been about her and her unique abilities. General Amos Kaye had recognized them immediately. Nick had been placed on the team of software developers to keep an eye on his investment.

He'd never pretended to be upstanding.

"You have to think more 'mad scientist' and less normal," he replied. His program flickered like crazy for a second and he had to stop and concentrate before he could continue. "He wants you to pick up where Andy left off. The crazy bastard intends to build a super army of bioengineered monsters. Whatever it was she was doing, he thinks you can do it, too."

Nick had never quite understood that part of it. He knew Andy had once been a scientist, which had come as a surprise, but the bigger surprise was that she'd had magic. He would never in a million years have suspected it of the quiet tavern owner. She'd never given any indication of her abilities.

If he had magic, he'd be doing all kinds of awesome things with it. He'd be rescuing Lilla himself right now rather than having to beg a dickhead to do it. "So are you coming with me or what? And you aren't invited," he said to River before she could speak.

She turned to Hawk. "If you go without me," she said to him, her voice low and fierce, "don't bother coming back. Either we're a team or we're not."

"If you let her go with you, you're not half the man I thought you were," Nick said. "Although my opinion wasn't all that high to begin with."

The fine mist of rain had stopped. The moon made a feeble attempt to appear. Nick's Hollow form flickered again.

"Stop it, both of you." Hawk rubbed his temples. "It kills me to say this, but River, he's right." He looked at Nick. "How much time do we have?"

"Not much." In truth, it could be six minutes, six days or six weeks. It depended on what kind of torture Kaye wanted to inflict. He enjoyed psychological pain as much as physical.

With her palm extended, River bent down and touched the ground. At once, a tree shot upward, unfurling its branches with lightning speed. In less than a minute, a maple tipped the surrounding rooftops. In her other hand a fireball appeared. She tossed it upward where it exploded, igniting the night sky with a sparkling fireworks display. Seconds later, a tunnel of wind whipped around them.

The wind died away and the silence and darkness were again complete. The two men gaped at her.

It took Nick a second to find his voice. "You're in," he said.

"She's not." Hawk took River by the arms and looked into her eyes. "*Mellita*. Sweetheart. There's too much danger for you. Lilla is trained for this."

Nick recognized the stubborn set of River's jaw even if Hawkins didn't. She was going to win this argument, and he was wasting valuable time.

"If you don't take her with you, she'll go alone," Nick pointed out. "I don't like to keep harping on this, but Kaye's a freaking psycho and Lilla's only got eight fingers left. Actually," he corrected himself, "six fingers and two thumbs. You'd be surprised how defenseless that makes a person."

"If you come," Hawkins said softly to River, ignoring

Nick as if he weren't there, which in truth he wasn't, "can you promise me to keep control of your magic? To remember that it is for bringing life, not taking it away? Because Kaye isn't the only danger to you." He frowned. "Perhaps I should take Achala instead."

Past the buzzing in his head, Nick heard the tread of approaching footsteps. He might have missed them if a part of his brain hadn't been on standby. They were coming from outside the room where he and Lilla were being held prisoner.

He had to shut down the hologram. That buzzing noise would be audible to whoever was outside the door.

Lilla heard the footsteps, too, and whispered a warning.

"Time's up," Nick said. Fear returned, churning the bile in his stomach. He lowered his voice as he gave River and Hawk the address, the words tripping off his tongue in his haste.

Then he was blinking his eyes against the sudden brightness of an overhead light.

Lilla stood by the door, a wastebasket in her hands hoisted high over her head.

◆ ◆

River turned to Hawk. The fear over what was happening to both Lilla and Nick made her ache. "We have to jump."

"Can you control your magic?" Hawk insisted again. "This is important, River. It could cost you your soul." His eyes, dark and worried, were intent on her face. "You have an obligation to your soul that is far greater than any to Lilla and Nick. I don't believe you fully understand the importance of that."

She ignored the tiny dark seed that made her, too, question her ability to control her magic, because when it came to Hawk, she had no doubts whatsoever. She would protect him from anything, even herself, whatever the cost.

"You are tied to my soul," she replied. Her hands cupped his face and she kissed the harshness from his mouth. "I would never do anything to harm you. For you, I can control my magic."

His fingers tightened on her hips. Then, he released her. He punched a sequence of numbers into the com-link on his wrist.

Seconds later, an enormous bald man appeared on the street.

"Faran," Hawk greeted him. "This is River."

The bald man looked River up and down, then flashed her a grin that glittered in the streetlight. He had a shiny gold cap on one of his front teeth. "Hello, beautiful."

Hawk glowered at him. "She's Fae."

"She's . . ." The grin faltered. Something unspoken passed between the two men that they kept carefully hidden from her. River intended to ask Hawk about that later. "She's the one," Faran finished awkwardly, seeing that she was watching him.

The one, what? River was definitely going to ask Hawk about that. Right now, she was far more worried about Nick and Lilla.

Hawk quickly explained the situation to Faran while River danced with impatience.

"You need to get into River's office in the subway," Hawk finished. "Once there, look at the program she's created. Achala can help you. Somehow it's picked up a human virus that's highly contagious." He adjusted the settings on his com-link. "If you hear a buzzing noise around a person, don't touch them. Don't go anywhere near them. That's an order."

River reached for and removed the strip of red lace Hawk still wore on his sleeve. Standing on her toes, she quickly tied it around Faran's massive bicep. "You'll need this," she explained as she did so. "You'll never get past the Demons without it."

Faran shifted uneasily as if afraid of her touch. "When you get back," he said to Hawk, his eyes flickering briefly to River, "we have another situation that requires your attention."

Hawk went still. "Can it wait?"

"For now."

River got the impression that whatever it was, it wasn't going to wait forever.

Hawk didn't question him further. He reached for River's hand. "We extract Lilla first. If anything should go wrong, my kit is with Achala." Another unspoken message passed between the two men. He turned to River. "Ready?"

She nodded, and curling her fingers around one of his, they jumped.

CHAPTER SIXTEEN

♦

Jake shoved his hands into his coat pockets and crept carefully down the street under cover of the shadows. He blinked drizzle from his eyes as he scanned the darkness. He'd followed a group of full-fledged Demons in Hollow form but lost them. Or rather, they had lost him.

Crap. That made him feel even more like part of the gang. Not.

Tall shadows stretched below towering, empty-eyed buildings, and homesickness washed through him. He missed the mountains and the woodlands. He wished he had his crossbow with him, but River wouldn't let him carry it in the city. She said she worried he'd kill somebody with it by accident, but he knew the truth. She worried he'd kill somebody on purpose.

He'd almost killed Hawk—would have done so without a second thought—and it made him stop and question himself and where he was heading for the first time.

Killing Hawk would have been a mistake that he might never have known. And it would have been a mistake that could not be undone.

A dog barked nearby, making him jump, and a cat hissed in response, the high-pitched sounds amplified by the empty streets and damp night. The sewer drains below, poorly maintained and overflowing from last night's heavy rains, gurgled and sputtered.

Jake continued as quietly as he could, the rubber soles of his sneakers silent on the pavement. The Demons didn't want him, so he didn't know why he continued to tag along behind. Maybe because he had no one else. Now that she had Hawk, River no longer needed him.

He heard a faint scuffling behind him and his heart leapt into his lungs. Survival instincts kicking into high gear, his body turned in the direction of the noise, his eyes scanning the night for signs of danger.

His hand automatically went to his back pocket where he kept his jackknife, but his heart settled back into a steadier rhythm when he saw Dan emerge from the shadows. His leader's long legs ate up the sidewalk as he closed the distance between them. Jake shoved his cold hands back into his coat pockets and glanced around to see if Dan had come alone.

"Hey," Jake greeted him, trying to keep his voice even as uneasiness closed in. An overhead streetlamp flickered and his gut warned of trouble. Jake tensed, not at all sure what was going down, but sensing danger nonetheless. The pale, overhead light showcased the dark, dangerous gleam in his leader's eyes.

"What are you doing out here?" Dan demanded, his voice low, his eyes shooting daggers as he darted a glance around to assess their surroundings. Jake wondered where he'd been. He hadn't seen him all day. Then he saw that Dan was in his Hollow form. Jealousy surged. Would he ever be able to use his program as well as that?

With a flip of his chin, he gestured to the empty street behind him. "Just taking a walk."

Dan's black eyes narrowed and Jake tried not to squirm. "Why aren't you with the others? You're not supposed to be out here alone."

The last thing Jake wanted to do was admit to Dan that he'd been ditched by the Demons. "Got tied up, is all."

Dan let that go, although Jake doubted he bought it.

He leveled Jake with a glare. "What do you know about this guy Hawk and what he was doing out on the streets?"

Jake knew Dan had the hots for River, just like Dan knew he'd never stood a chance with her. He didn't need to take his pissiness at Hawk out on Jake.

Jake shrugged. "Nothing, really. He was looking for his captain."

That answer obviously didn't cut it. "Did he say anything to you?"

"About what?"

"About anything."

"No," Jake answered. He wasn't discussing River and Hawk with Dan. It wouldn't improve his mood.

Dan eyed him suspiciously, cracked his knuckles, then said, "I don't trust him, and if you had half a clue, or even a shred of street smarts, neither would you." He grunted and added, "Then again, what can I expect from a country boy like you?"

"River trusts him," Jake blurted out, stung by the *country boy* remark, then instantly realized his mistake. Shit. Now Dan was mad. He braced himself for a beating.

"Yeah, well your sister's a nut job," Dan snarled. "You saw the way she went off. She's from another fucking planet."

No one, not even Dan, was going to get away with talking about his sister like that. Jake opened his mouth, ready to come to her defense and take the ass kicking that was sure to follow, then he realized that Dan's attention kept shifting off in the direction he'd come from.

Something was happening back there, and it better not have anything to do with River. He'd let down his mother and brother. He wouldn't let her down, too.

"What's going on?" Jake demanded, worry for his sister trumping any fears over a beating. "You're being a dick, even for you."

"River and I were tracking the virus most of the day. It's starting to spread pretty fast." The older boy looked past Jake's head into the darkness. "Get back underground. I'm going to round up the other Demons. No one's wandering the streets until things settle down."

Dan had blown off the dick comment, so Jake knew

things were even worse than they sounded. But if Dan had been with River all day, where was she now?

A high-pitched buzzing, familiar to them both, steadily approached. Dan grabbed Jake by the arm and yanked him into the shadow of an old hardware store.

Seconds later, the blond-headed Guardian came into view. Jake's heart thudded in his chest as they listened, waiting for her to pass. Her jerky movements and the buzzing indicated she was either sick, or this was a hologram program used by someone whose skill level was far worse than Jake's.

Dan released his arm. "Come on."

Jake was too scared not to obey. They held back enough not to be noticed, although he couldn't imagine she could hear them over the buzzing.

She'd heard something, though. Her head snapped around and she suddenly changed direction. They followed. A few minutes later they spotted River and Hawk standing on the street outside of a coffee shop.

Jake made a move for River, worried about her being exposed to whatever sickness this was and ready to shout out a warning, but Dan caught him and clapped a hand over his mouth. He struggled, but his hands and feet went right through the older boy's Hollow form.

"Cut it out and listen." Dan's voice was little more than a soft whisper in Jake's ear, but carried an unmistakable note of command.

Jake did as he was told, but as he listened, he learned more than he liked. The blonde turned out to be Nick in Hollow form. Wow. Nick really sucked with the pro-

gram. Jake felt a lot better about his own lack of skill.
But the talk of bioengineered monsters and magic put
things out there that he would rather not have known.
River didn't help matters any by showing off the things
she could do. It made him uncomfortable to think those
things couldn't easily be explained. It made it look as if
Dan was right when he said she was from another planet.
That maybe she didn't belong here.

It made him feel completely alone.

Nick disappeared. Then a third man showed up out of
nowhere. Jake vaguely recalled him from the parking lot
where he'd had his first run-in with Hawk. He rubbed his
chest, remembering how much it had hurt to be shot. He
frowned. Or at least, how much it had seemed to hurt.
Since it hadn't been real, he couldn't know for certain
how it felt.

Dan didn't like it when River gave the bald guy a
strip of red to help him get into the subway. Jake didn't
like how the bald guy acted afraid of her.

Then River and Hawk disappeared and the big bald
guy headed for the subway entrance.

"You follow the bald guy," Dan ordered him. "Keep
an eye on him and tell me what he does. I'm going after
River."

"Keep an eye on him yourself," Jake retorted. "She's
my sister. She's not going anywhere without me." He
waited for Dan's fist to strike, his knees shaking a bit, but
he wasn't backing down. Dan would have to beat him
into submission and that would take too much time. Besides, whoever was after River was responsible for the

deaths of his mom and brother. He wasn't letting what happened to them happen to her. He wanted a chance to make the bastard pay for it, too.

Dan's blow caught him on the side of the head and he staggered, his ears ringing, but managed to stay on his feet.

"The next time I tell you to do something, you'd better do as you're told," the older boy said, stepping close to get in his face. He gave him a push. "And if you're coming, you'd better be able to keep up."

◆ ◆

"What are you doing?" Nick asked.

Lilla raised the wastebasket higher, resolve firming the line of her jaw. She didn't get a chance to answer him because the door opened as he spoke, drawing her full attention. She brought the wastebasket down hard, but an elbow blocked it and threw her off balance. She recovered, but not quickly enough to dodge the hand jamming a needle into her arm. Her eyes rolled back in her head as she slid to the floor.

Nick struggled against the knots binding his hands and feet, but he'd been lying on the floor in one position for several hours now and the pins and needles of pain as he shifted nearly blinded him. He was useless to her.

Kaye stepped through the door and stooped over her still body. He lifted one of her eyelids and touched a fingertip to her eye. She didn't react. He slipped a hand under the collar of her shirt, presumably seeking a pulse. Jesus, Nick hoped she wasn't dead. Although it would be far better than getting eaten alive.

He thought about that. Kaye didn't make empty threats. That was part of his charm. So she wasn't dead, but he had a feeling he was about to wish that he was. With any luck Nick could keep Kaye talking until Hawkins arrived.

"You stay just where you are," Kaye murmured to her. He rose, stepped over her body, and crossed the room to stand over Nick.

"So," Nick said. "How was your day?"

Kaye kicked him, the toe of his shoe catching him under the chin, snapping his head back. His eyes, already watering, started to stream. That *hurt*.

But Lilla was completely defenseless, and he figured if she could suffer through two broken fingers, he could survive a little pain, too. Never mind that it was scientifically proven that women had a higher pain threshold.

He swallowed blood. Saliva made it seem like more than it probably was, but no way was he spitting it out to see for sure. Not with Weres in the building.

"My day wasn't nearly as busy as yours," Kaye said to him. He crouched down to meet Nick's eyes. "You've been holding out on me, my friend."

Nick remembered the way Lilla had stared at the ceiling as he'd used the hologram to untie her. She'd spotted the surveillance camera immediately. No doubt she thought he was stupid because he hadn't.

He tried to think of some way to stall Kaye, but his jaw ached, his mouth hurt and his limbs were on fire. The sight of Lilla lying so silent distracted him. Where were Hawkins and River? Had they stopped for coffee?

"Is she alive?" he asked, nodding at Lilla. Maybe he could kick Kaye in the head with his feet as he turned to look at her.

Kaye didn't cooperate by looking. "She's fine. I've given three times that amount to a Were, but I wanted to see how big a dose I could give to a woman her size. The side effects of an overdose can be nasty. What happens to her after this depends a little on what happens next," he added. "I may need her alive. But if I don't, I'd like to see how different her anatomy is from ours. The last chance I had to study one of her race, the guards at the lab damaged his body too badly when they killed him for it to be useful. The differences may be subtle so I'd like hers to be fresh when I examine it, and I don't have any autopsy equipment here."

"You'd kill her just to see how she ticks? Don't you have a medical degree?" Nick goaded him. "Didn't you have to take the Hippocratic oath?"

Those freaky eyes showed a brief flash of puzzlement, the first sign of true emotion from him that Nick could ever recall. "She's not human." His tone added, *idiot.*

Nick hadn't actually been serious with that remark about the Hippocratic oath because Kaye was crazy and probably hadn't taken it too seriously in the first place, but his response was chilling nonetheless. Nick didn't want to know how he defined "human" because his criteria were likely sketchy and not in anyone else's favor.

"What I really want to know is how the hologram program works," Kaye continued. "But first, why don't you tell me where you went and who I can expect to come charging to your rescue?"

While he might not be the bravest or the smartest person on Earth, Nick was a definite contender for the world's best liar. The trick was sticking close to the truth and dodging direct answers.

"I went looking for her commanding officer." He gestured to Lilla. "But I couldn't find him."

"Are you trying to have me believe that you didn't find anyone else you thought might be able to free you?"

"Who else would I tell?" Nick asked. "I wouldn't go to River. She's the one you're after. You own the police, the streets are empty because of this virus, and I live with a bunch of kids who might think they're tough but couldn't fight off a single Were even if they all tackled it together. Hawkins was my best bet."

Kaye examined his words with careful consideration. "Then that's who I'll expect. I think I'll expect the Fae as well."

Damn it. He should have said he'd gone to Dan and the Demons instead. Hawkins was going to have to take care of himself and River, because Nick had enough shit of his own to deal with.

"Now. I want to know how the program works. More

important, I want to know how she crossed a human virus with a computerized program." He tapped his chin with the steepled fingers of his clasped hands. "She would have needed a host for the human virus. But she's been underground for months."

This was the part that Nick hadn't quite puzzled out. River had given the program to all of the Demons. Billy was the first to get sick, but he'd had the program for a while and Nick had heard the buzzing right after River gave it to him.

Nick stitched Billy's lip right before he got sick.

Son of a bitch. Nick was the host.

But how?

"She hasn't crossed a human virus with a computer virus," he said. "That's impossible."

"For you or me, maybe. But here's what I think," Kaye replied. "I think the host has to be someone she's been in daily contact with. Someone she gave her program to." He leaned in closer. "She's obviously given the program to you. And I think that if you don't tell me where she implanted it, I'm going to start carving your body apart, starting with the places I think most likely."

Nick's crotch started to sweat. He'd never before thought of being torn apart by a Were as a mercy killing. "If I turn out to be the host, and you do that, you run the risk of infecting yourself. It's spreading through touch. You can't get one of the Weres to do it for you either, because they can't handle the smell of blood. They'd probably go nuts and swallow it by accident."

"True enough," Kaye admitted. "I'd thought of using

your little friend over here as a test case by having you touch her and see if she gets sick, but I'd rather not damage her, at least not yet. And while I was immune to the first strain, there's no guarantee I'll be immune to this new one. So now I have a bit of a conundrum."

"I hope you aren't expecting me to offer suggestions for figuring it out," Nick said, "because I see that as a conflict of interest on my part."

"Don't worry, my friend. You're safe enough for the moment." Kaye stood. He walked over to the monitor on the wall and turned it on, the screen flashing to life. Nick could see the street at the front of the building. Seconds later, he saw the back. The whole exterior was being monitored. So was the inside of the building.

"It's River I want," Kaye continued, his attention on the screen. "And if she's coming, she'll be coming any minute now."

♦ ♦

Hawk and River touched down on the street outside of a gray, granite-stoned building, probably six stories high, with their bodies exposed and vulnerable to attack. This was far from a strategic position and he drew River across the street to the derelict building that faced it. He preferred having his back protected and the cover of darkness.

The brightly lit sign on the front of the building they watched proclaimed it to be PROVINCE HOUSE. Hawk caught movement inside its front foyer. Several guards milled about, talking into small black com-links secured to their shoulders. He thought it likely that they were Weres, but without getting close, it would be impossible to tell.

The office windows in the building were black. He couldn't see through them, but he could tell which ones had the lights on. Lighting suggested the rooms were currently occupied. He counted three. Those were the rooms they would check first.

He wrapped his arms around River, nestling her back to his front while he weighed the pros and cons of their next move. Even though he knew she could take care of herself—and of him when the situation required it, which sometimes it did—he didn't have to like it. But he'd learned that there was no stopping her when she made up her mind, and he was slowly learning better than to try.

What complicated matters was the bomb in his head. He had to worry about keeping the chemicals in his brain at manageable levels, and she didn't make it easy for him. He wasn't about to draw her attention back to it either.

He'd been thinking about that. If the time should come when he needed to transport himself into deep space, he would need to keep his thoughts guarded from River. He couldn't do both if the chemicals in his brain were disrupted.

He felt River frowning. Never a good sign.

She pointed to one of the windows. "There's something in there."

"Something?" he asked, leaning his head down and placing his cheek against hers so that their breath mingled. "Something . . . what?"

"I don't know," she admitted. "But it's important."

As anxious as he was to find Lilla—and to a lesser extent, Nick—and get them to safety, if River thought it important, then he would follow her Fae instincts.

Unfortunately, her instincts weren't always 100 percent Fae. He double-checked his equipment to make sure everything was in working order. His weapons were replicated according to what was available on the worlds he visited to help them blend in with the locals. Their communications devices were less of an issue.

He briefly considered passing River the gun in the holster strapped to his thigh, then decided against it. There was little point in arming her. She'd take off a Were's head with a virtual sword without giving it a second thought, but the last time he'd armed her for real, she'd thrown the gun at her target. In reality, magic was her weapon of choice.

"Ready?" He touched her arm, unease twitching again as he brushed her mind and found it practically dancing with anticipation. Crisos. So much for being Fae. Sometimes she had the soul of a street thug. He gripped her elbow harder in warning. "If you find yourself in trouble I want you to jump."

She tapped his head in return. "Don't worry about me. You're the one who needs to keep it together."

Since she spoke the truth, he let that slide. "Let's go."

They dashed across the street to the wrought-iron

gated alley beside Province House, dodging the spot-
lights illuminating the entrance. He boosted River over
the gate, then vaulted it easily.

She took up position beside him, her penetrating blue
eyes scanning the ground and rooftops for danger, but
the streets remained quiet.

He shifted, running his hands along the exterior wall,
wondering if he could find enough finger- and toeholds
to climb to the upper levels where windows were less
likely to be locked. He hoped they could find an entrance
through a ground-floor window. He wasn't good with
heights.

Not far away the soft, gentle rush of water could be
heard. If he remembered correctly there were several
quays along a wide expanse of riverfront. The building
must sit near one.

The ground-level windows were barred. Hawk dropped
to one knee to test them, hoping that time and neglect
might have weakened a few, but they didn't budge. He sat
back to think. He didn't like the idea of jumping into a
building. There was too high a risk of landing in a con-
fined space without enough room to fight.

River rested the palm of her hand on his shoulder.
"Allow me."

Hawk straightened and stepped back, curious. This
should be interesting.

The bars melted into a wet puddle of metal on the
ground at their feet when she touched them. Freed of
support, the rotting wooden window frame sagged, pull-

ing loose from its concrete foundation. The pane of glass popped out, shattering on the floor inside, and Hawk winced. River froze beside him as they listened for any sounds of movement. After a few agonizing moments it became apparent that either no one had heard the racket, or no one cared enough to investigate.

As he poked his head inside the gaping hole, River suddenly whirled away to peer into the night. Hawk cracked the back of his skull on the window frame in his haste to find out what had distracted her.

"What is it?" he asked.

"It shouldn't be this easy."

"It's only easy because Kaye wants it that way. It's a trap, and Nick and Lilla are the bait. He's hoping that you come for them." Otherwise, they'd be dead already. Nick had known that. It was why he hadn't wanted River to come. And naturally, exactly why she had.

He felt her breath quicken. "Nick and Lilla aren't the bait."

"What?"

"He took something from my parents' house," she said. Her eyes went to the upper levels of the building again. "It's in here somewhere. I know it."

And he could see that whatever it was, she wanted it back. Resignation settled over him and he almost sighed. It would be faster to get it for her than to argue. It was the reason behind Kaye taking it, however, that made Hawk wary. Whatever it was, it wouldn't be good.

"First, we find Lilla and Nick," he said to her. He

placed his hand on the small of her back and gave her a nudge toward the window.

He lowered her through the broken frame, hanging tight to her forearms until her feet were safely on the floor inside. He followed, landing lightly, then waited a moment for his eyes to adjust.

They'd entered some sort of storage closet. The room was musty and smelled of disuse. Boxes filled with files and papers lined one wall while tall metal filing cabinets ate up another. If he took a deep breath he could pass between them. It never mattered how far computer technology progressed. There was something about paper that people couldn't seem to give up. Hawk itched to investigate, but they didn't have time to stop and look.

He nodded to the stairwell across from the storage room door and the black-domed security camera in the ceiling above it. There was no point in shooting the camera out. If anyone was actually monitoring it, they would already know that he and River were inside.

They entered the stairwell and climbed silently upward until they reached the third floor, and the first of the rooms that had the lights on. Hawk pushed open the heavy steel door and scanned the long, narrow hallway. It was empty. He counted the doors in his head, matching their locations to the overhead lights he remembered seeing from outdoors. The fact that no one had come to check on them might mean the security cameras didn't work. That would be good.

River made a move to slip past him, but he stopped her. "Me first."

He thought he heard her mutter *asshole* under her breath and he grinned as he stepped from the stairwell, gun steady in his hand. He inched along the wall until he reached the third door, which was partly open, and darted a quick glance inside.

A blood-crusted meat hook, the kind found in the freezers of abattoirs, hung from the ceiling. Stains darkened the tiles on the floor beneath it. A funky smell, like death mixed with disinfectant, settled on the back of his tongue. He tried to block River's view, but she'd followed right along with him and he couldn't keep it from her. The look on her face when her eyes flew to his told him she thought the worst.

He sent her a silent message of reassurance. *The stains aren't fresh.*

That wasn't the true source of her distress however. River could sense the loss of space left by souls when they departed their mortal bodies. She'd once likened it to a black hole. Something—someone, maybe more than one—had died here.

He tested the next door on his mental list of potential prison cells and when he found it locked, he bent down and examined the knob and its mechanism. Nobody had ever intended for this lock to keep anyone out who was serious about getting in, or for that matter, anyone inside who wanted out. Lilla could have tackled this with no trouble—if she'd had the full use of her fingers. He suspected Kaye's decision to break them hadn't been random.

He fumbled with the holster strapped to his leg. The

buckle on it had a sliver of metal long enough to rake the primitive lock.

River, however, placed her hand over his and shook her head. *The room is empty.*

She pointed to another doorway at the far end of the hall, just past the men's room.

Lilla and Nick? he mouthed, but she shook her head again. By the look of determination firing her eyes, he knew the room contained something she wanted. She started for it.

He grabbed her arm and she tried to shake him off. He refused to give in. He would do anything for her to keep her safe, but whatever she wanted in there, it would have to wait.

He wasn't convinced entering that room was safe for her anyway. He didn't know what she thought was in it, but by the way she was acting, whatever it was had a powerful attraction for her. That meant it was a trap. It also meant they were expected. Without a doubt, someone had been watching them from the moment they'd entered the building.

First, Lilla and Nick, he reminded her.

She cast a last, longing look over her shoulder before allowing him to draw her back into the stairwell. Together, they scaled the next flight of stairs.

The first room they checked was empty. Then, jackpot.

The door was closed but Hawk could hear muffled movements inside as if something heavy was sliding across the floor. As long as it wasn't a dead body, they were good. He looked at River. She didn't have that look on her face she got when she came across a place where someone had died, so whoever was in there either wasn't dead or hadn't died there.

River looked at him, the expression in her eyes warning him that she wanted inside and wasn't about to wait much longer. He thought if he went into the office next door, he might be able to ease off one of the ceiling panels so he could see in.

Before he could pass on his plan to River, she lost patience. She drew back her foot and kicked the door. It exploded inward, the frame splintering, then dangled from one of its hinges.

He sometimes forgot that she was a lot stronger and faster than one might expect from someone her size. He dove for her, taking her to the floor and covering her with his body, rolling her out of the line of fire in case someone on the other side of that shattered door took exception to her knock.

"Get us the hell out of here!" Nick shouted from inside the room. "It's a trap!"

"What kind of trap?" Hawk called back. "The kind that blows up or the kind that shoots?"

There was a brief moment of stunned silence. "Does it make a difference?"

Whatever the danger was, it wasn't immediate. Nick didn't have that edge of panic in his voice that people got when they were about to die. Hawk's mind raced. River could jump and take someone with her. Hawk couldn't do that. She could save Lilla.

He, on the other hand, was stuck with Nick.

But they were all going to have to hurry.

He peered around the broken door frame. Lilla lay unmoving on the floor, slivers of broken wood on her clothes. Nick was nearby, his head pointed in her direction as if he'd been crawling toward her. That must have been the sliding noise Hawk had heard.

River pushed past him and rushed to check on Lilla, her Fae instincts taking over at the sight of someone in distress.

"She's alive," Nick said, tension crackling in his tone. "But we've only got a few minutes. Whatever he gave her, he was testing the dose. He's trying to see how much he can give River without killing her."

"Grab Lilla and get out of here," Hawk ordered River.

It was the instinctive reaction of the Fae to obey the command of a Guardian in a dangerous situation, and she moved to comply as she had on a number of other occasions. It was inevitable, however, that she would eventually overcome that innate response.

She froze. Then her chin lifted. "We're all leaving together."

"Kaye wants to cut Lilla up to study her anatomy," Nick said. "He wants to find the Hollow Man chip you gave me, and he plans to start searching with a sharp scalpel at my ankles. He wants you to show him how you crossed a human virus with a computer one. And you," he said to Hawk, "he just doesn't like. Now can somebody cut me loose?"

"Don't touch him," River warned as Hawk reached for the knife at his ankle.

"He's already come in contact with both Lilla and me," Hawk pointed out. "I agree that he's spreading it, but he hasn't infected us."

"I wonder if it's because you belong to a different species," a voice said from behind him.

Hawk recognized that voice. He'd once heard it through a telephone line in Nick's apartment. He spun to meet colorless eyes examining him from a monitor mounted on the wall beside the door.

The situation reminded him far too much of his months spent in the Dark Lord's prison, helpless to defend either himself or any of the other captured souls trapped along with him. His heart skipped a few beats in response to those memories.

But he'd found an infallible way to remind him of what was real and what wasn't. He reached out for River—or more accurately, her soul. It was right there with his, warm and bright and reassuring.

He scanned the images on the monitor, taking in as much as he could in case he needed to draw on it later. Kaye sat at a desk in an otherwise empty office. Hawk caught a bit of the room's reflection in the black window behind him. He appeared to be alone. There was something in his hand, hidden from view under the desk, but Hawk couldn't tell what it was. The man's body partly obscured it. He wondered at first if it might be a weapon of some sort, but then Kaye lifted it to the desktop.

It was a long, cylindrical tube with a viewfinder on one end. River's small gasp of recognition and outrage told Hawk that whatever it was, it held a great deal of significance for her. With a sinking sensation settling in his stomach, he knew. This was the bait.

He should have listened to River's instincts and gone for the door she'd chosen on the second floor when they had the chance.

Kaye held the cylinder at eye level between his two index fingers and examined it closely. The lack of expression on his face as he did so was chilling.

"Now what do you suppose your father was doing with this?" he asked River, as if this was a normal conversation and they were colleagues, or even friends. "It seems to have some interesting properties."

"That's mine, you bastard!" River cried at the screen, her voice quivering with poorly contained anger. Her eyes narrowed.

"And I want it back."

CHAPTER **SEVENTEEN**

◆

The area around the building Nick had given the address for was being patrolled.

Jake and Dan watched from partway up one of the steep side streets, looking down at the waterfront. Dan was in his Hollow form. Jake, however, was there for real. He tugged the collar of his jacket higher and tried

not to let on that he was damp and cold, not wanting
Dan to think he was being a baby.

Every few minutes, two figures passed beneath the
streetlights at the front of the building below.

Dan swore softly, pressing back into the shadows and
pulling Jake with him. "Those are Weres. If we get any
closer they're going to smell you."

Deep down inside, Jake started to tremble. Weres had
killed his mother and brother. He hadn't seen the initial
attack, which he was grateful for, although he often
thought if he'd been there he might have been able to do
something to save them. Instead, he had come in at the
end. He'd seen what Weres did once they'd tasted blood.

"Do you have a gun?" Dan whispered.

"No, but I have a knife." He drew it from his back
pocket and Dan shook his head in disgust. Jake's stomach pushed into his throat. A jackknife might not seem
like the greatest idea, but he knew how to use it. His
dad had been big on hand-to-hand combat.

As he held his knife out, the light from the lamppost
glittering on the blade, Jake couldn't hide the slight
tremor in his hand. He quickly tried to shake it off, but
the look in Dan's eyes told him he'd caught it, too.

"Have you ever seen a Were before?" the older boy
asked him, his eyes narrowing. "You know, up close and
personal?"

"I know what they can do." Jake swallowed bile.
He'd tried to block out the memories for months.

"Then get your shit together, kid," Dan growled under

his breath. "Otherwise, you're going to get both of us killed."

They continued to watch in silence, Jake waiting for Dan to tell him what they would do next.

"Have you?" he finally asked, inching closer to the other boy and keeping his voice soft.

Dan never took his eyes off the street below them, timing the movement of the Weres. "Have I what?"

"Have you ever seen one?"

Dan nodded without looking at him. "Yeah. They used to hunt Demons in the subway for sport."

Taking in Dan's expressionless mask, Jake knew better than to ask any more questions about it, but had a flash of understanding. Dan was every bit as scared as he was. He simply hid it better.

Knowing Dan was also afraid made his own fear more bearable. He wasn't helpless. He was a skilled hunter, and back home, he'd single-handedly taken down a brown bear in River's defense. Hawk's, too. A brown bear was a lot bigger than a Were and every bit as dangerous. It might not be as smart as one, but then a Were wasn't as smart as a human.

"Something's wrong," Dan whispered abruptly, his head going up. "They aren't walking around the building anymore."

A shape came hurtling out of the night, ramming into Jake and knocking him to the ground. Knees pinned his shoulders. The smell of damp fur slapped him in the face. He felt the hot breath as it went for his throat.

He didn't have time to think. He rammed the jackknife he held in his hand into the Were's stomach and yanked upward. Wet heat gushed over his hand and down his arm, then onto his jacket.

The Were went still with shock and surprise, then with a muffled sigh, toppled over. Dan grabbed the Were under the arms and hauled his body off Jake.

Jake rolled free, then promptly threw up. The sticky warmth on his hand and jacket quickly turned cold in the night air.

Killing was ugly and messy, and not nearly as satisfying as he'd expected after months of looking forward to a moment like this.

"All this blood isn't a good thing," Dan said grimly. "It's going to attract others, and now you're covered in it."

Jake wiped his mouth with his clean sleeve. "He was about to—"

"I know what he was about to do," Dan interrupted. Running feet could be heard thudding on the pavement toward them, and Jake tensed, clutching the slippery knife. "Relax," the older boy said. "That's me."

Jake's head started to spin as he tried to puzzle that through. Two seconds later, real Dan skidded to a halt beside them, breathing heavily, and Hollow Dan winked out.

"I am never going to figure this program out," Jake said, impressed beyond measure that Dan could control his hologram to the point that his real body moved independently of it. Did River know he could do that?

"On your feet," Dan commanded. Jake did as he was

told, then started to unzip his jacket. He hated the smell. It sat on his tongue, too. "Keep that for now," Dan added, stopping him. "We don't have much time and they can follow the scent anyway. But you'd better figure out your program in the next few seconds because we're about to have company, and with all this blood everywhere, we're going to need all four of us to handle it."

Hollow Dan reappeared as the second Were came at them from behind. Hollow Dan and the real Dan immediately flanked it. The Were hesitated, taking in all three boys and not certain at first which ones were real.

"Nice trick." The Were raked shaggy hair off his forehead and made a threatening move toward Dan's hologram.

Hollow Dan produced a sword, and he laughed in response. Then, catching both Dan and Jake by surprise, he walked straight into it. Jake's heart nearly stopped. Animals had healthy self-preservation instincts, and one would never walk into a sword if it thought it could kill it.

Which meant the Were knew better.

Still, that sword had to hurt. Hollow Dan was holding it, and as long as it was attached to the projection, whomever he struck with it would feel some sort of blow.

Surprise made Hollow Dan flicker. The Were jerked free of the blade, then went after real Dan. With lightning speed he drove his head into Dan's stomach, sending him crashing backward into the brick side of a building. The Were tossed his head back and laughed, then slowly started to stalk him.

What the hell?

How had he known the sword wouldn't kill him? How *could* he know?

"Do something, Jake!" Dan yelled, scrambling along the brick wall.

Think, Jake, think.

His mind raced. What if the Were came up against a weapon it didn't recognize, one rarely found on the city streets, but something Jake knew well enough to make look good?

He knew just the thing.

He fired up his hologram. If he stood inside it smelling of blood, this should appear pretty close to real. He called up a crossbow and took steady aim. He didn't want to give the Were too much time to think about it. "Hey, Muttface. Over here."

The Were turned and Jake, crouching low in his human form, shot a bolt into his heart. The Were staggered backward, his arms flying wide, stunned. Jake knew it wouldn't kill him thanks to the safeguards River had imposed on the program, but the power of suggestion was going to make the pain feel real enough.

As the Were tried to recover from what had just happened, Dan burst away from the wall and ran. He shoved Jake into action as he passed. "Move it!"

Dropping his hologram image, Jake took off after him.

As they cut through what used to be a small park,

Jake slowed long enough to tear a branch off a sapling, then followed after Dan until they found an old apartment building with a broken entry lock. Dan shouldered open the front door and they bolted inside.

The heavy front doors swung shut behind them and Jake looked around for something to block them with. He shrugged out of his jacket and quickly tied the metal door handles together. That wouldn't stop the Were, but it would slow him down.

"Nice thinking," Dan said with approval.

Jake stole a quick glance out onto the street through the glass doors and cursed under his breath when he spotted a shadow moving toward the building.

Dan saw it, too. "We need to get out of here."

They ran up the first flight of stairs. "Let's split up and run up and down as many stairs and hallways as we can for five minutes, then meet back here on the second floor," Jake suggested. "That should confuse him."

Five minutes later they regrouped in the hallway. They touched all of the doors for good measure, testing the knobs, and opened the first one they found unlocked just as they heard a smash and a bang from below.

The apartment smelled bad and was clearly unused.

A light from the parking lot filtered through the boarded-up window. Jake pulled his jackknife from his back pocket and placed it on the cracked kitchenette counter. A table with rusted chrome legs had been pushed into one corner to free up space. Jake flipped it over and began removing the screws on the legs.

"What are you doing?" Dan asked.

"Making a weapon."

"What for? By now he knows it won't kill him," he snapped, sidestepping broken glass as he carefully walked across the ratty laminate to take a look out the window.

"That's the point," Jake said. "This one's real. He won't be expecting that."

Dan turned to stare at him, a strange expression on his face. "You sure you can make something that will really kill him?"

"You see another way?"

Dan looked around and shook his head. "No."

"Then hold these." Jake passed the chair legs to Dan. As he kicked off his own shoes, he gestured toward Dan's boots. "Give me your laces."

A second later, with his equipment in hand, Jake tied the legs together to form a T, then strung a bow with the bendable branch he'd grabbed in the park. "Look around and see if you can find anything sharp, anything I can use as a quarrel. All I have is my knife."

Dan opened and closed cupboards, drawers, and closets, but paused in his search when a dark, menacing voice sounded on the stairs.

"Come out, come out, wherever you are."

The Were was in the building.

"Find anything?" Jake asked, trying not to panic.

"Not yet."

The banging of doors echoed through the building, and Jake positioned his knife on the stock. "Then I guess we only get once chance at this." He searched the floor of the dimly lit apartment. "Here, hold this for a second."

Dan examined the homemade bow. "What exactly is this?"

"This," Jake said, scattering bits of broken glass near the door, "is what you can expect from a country boy like me."

"Come out, come out, wherever you are," the voice crooned again, this time from the end of the second-floor corridor.

Jake took the bow from Dan and positioned himself across from the door. He tried to quiet his heartbeat as he steadied his weapon and waited.

The Were poked his head into the apartment and sniffed at the air.

"The young ones are always the best tasting," he said.

Jake centered the weapon on his forehead, but the Were kept on coming. Glass crunched beneath his feet as he stepped into the room and he looked down, just as Jake had hoped. When he looked up again, Jake released the knife. It whirled across the room and drove into the Were's head, catching him between the eyes.

He blinked, once, twice, then dropped to his knees.

Dan ran across the room and planted the sole of his boot on the knife's hilt, driving the blade all the way into the Were's skull. He kicked him in the ribs for good measure.

"Nice shot. Now let's get out of here before any more of them find us," he said to Jake.

Relief made Jake weak at the knees. "I'm with you on that. Let's go find River."

Dan pulled up short on his way out the door, his hand on the frame.

"Sorry, Jake," he said. "There's no way we can get past any more Weres. Not with you covered in blood. River's on her own this time."

◆ ◆

Ever had explained to him what the kits contained and how they worked, but Peters wasn't quite grasping it.

"So you flip a switch and these little doodads launch into the stratosphere and cause all kinds of technical problems around the globe?" he summarized.

Ever looked as if he wanted to smile, but he managed to keep it to himself. "Something like that."

Between them they had set up two metal containers on what appeared to be aluminum tripods, but seemed a great deal sturdier. Ever was spending a lot of time playing with the settings on the sides of the long tubes. They contained liquid, Ever told him.

"You're going to launch them from indoors?" Peters asked. He felt like a kindergartner. And not the smartest one either.

"*Launch* isn't quite the right word," Ever explained, looking up at him. "They transport, the same way we do." He turned back to his task, frowning in concentration.

"Everything has to be timed just right so that they all go off together."

"You do this for a living? Defuse worlds . . . is that what you called it?"

"Hardly ever," he replied. Peters could tell he was only half listening, but this was his world they were talking about and he wanted to understand what would happen next. "I'm trained for it, yes. All of the Guardians are. But what we really do is escort the Fae to other worlds so that they can restore life. Guardians provide basic technical knowledge to help primitive people sustain what the Fae begin. Sometimes the worlds we visit are completely barren. Then the Fae start life growing, and over time those worlds take care of populating themselves."

"So in the entire universe, only the Fae have magic?"

Ever rocked back to sit on his heels. "The universe is a pretty big place. I wouldn't go so far as to say that only the Fae have magic, but we've never found anyone else who does. And we've traveled a lot, for a very long time."

"Those little guys back at the base have magic. The Were kids," Peters clarified. He could almost hear Andy applauding inside his head, so he knew he was on the right track about something. "Don't you think it's a bit coincidental that Were kids with magic happen to be in the same place Fae souls are hanging around? Could they have picked magic up from them somehow? Through osmosis or something?"

"Do you even know what the word *osmosis* means?"

Ever muttered, rubbing the back of his neck. "Never mind," he said more loudly. "The answer is no. Fae magic is tied to their souls, and their souls are reborn to the Fae. If any of those souls are lost, they're lost forever. Without the Fae, life as we know it would eventually cease to exist."

While he might not have traveled the universe, in Peters' opinion the Guardian was being a little closed-minded on the subject. He'd lived through a lot of shit in his own little corner of it and he didn't believe in coincidence. Andy had once been involved in experiments that tried to tie souls to bioengineered monsters. She'd led him here. He didn't know how Weston had managed it, but he strongly suspected he'd been running similar experiments on his own.

Those little kids were the result. And from what he could tell, they were good enough people. Better than most. If he was right, then maybe whatever Weston had done wasn't so bad.

"So what will happen to those Fae souls hovering around out there," Peters asked, pointing to the ceiling where the giant telescope captured images of a sapphire-blue, midnight arctic sky, "if you're ordered to set off your little stratospheric interference anyway?"

Ever quit rubbing his neck. The patient half smile he'd been wearing disappeared. "Son of a bitch."

◆ ◆

River was pissed.

Fingers of rage clawed at her insides, climbing, seeking cracks in her control to allow it release. The man on the monitor was responsible for the years of torture her birth parents' souls had endured. He'd used Andy to create monsters and tie Fae souls to them. He'd killed her team of gamers, Jake's mother and little brother, and he'd shot Nick, all in pursuit of her.

And now he had her kaleidoscope, a toy she had built with her father as a little girl. She had poured bits of her energy into it, wanting to share it with him, although until now she hadn't fully understood what she'd been doing. Her energy was magic, and magic was tied to her soul. He had loved the swirling bits of color she'd created. It had been important to him.

She hated for this man to be holding these tiny connections to her soul that she'd once given her father.

Yet if she gave in to her anger, she knew the situation could very well become hopeless for them all. The trigger for the bomb in Hawk's head was linked to a sharp increase, then a drop, of the chemicals in his brain, signaling desperation followed by hopelessness—the emotions of a man who faced death, realized it was inevitable, and accepted the outcome. He would experience those same intense emotional responses if anything happened to her.

And Kaye, in his insanity, didn't have a clue that by taunting her, he had his finger on the red button that would blow up the world.

So she had to get herself under control.

She tried to think, to focus, but all she could concentrate on was the rising fury building inside her as Kaye peered into the kaleidoscope.

"If you want it back," he said, holding it up, "you have to give me something in return. I want Hollow Man."

"Don't do it, River," Nick warned. "He's not going to give you anything."

Hawk was watching her intently. Past the overwhelming anger, she felt the faint brush of his soul and the unspoken urge for her to trust him. "Do as he says."

She hesitated. Hawk would never tell her to do something that might harm her, but she wasn't as certain that what he asked wouldn't bring harm to others. She wanted to trust him. The program had safeguards built in. Whatever Kaye wanted to do with it, it was doubtful he could override that security. It was tied to her Fae magic. Hawk knew that.

"I'll give it to you," she said to Kaye. "But I need to touch you to do it." She met his cold, colorless eyes, holding her temper. "And you'll have to give my kaleidoscope to Hawk first."

"Is that what this is?" Kaye asked, sounding faintly surprised. Then he looked thoughtful. "I suppose it is. But it's so much more than that, too." He leaned back in his chair, splaying the fingers of his free hand on the desk in front of him. "Very well. Lilla!" he commanded. "Use your syringe on River."

Lilla surged to her feet, and lightning quick, she drew a syringe from the open neck of her shirt.

River's instincts were good, as was her speed. Hawk's

rivaled hers. But they were both taken by surprise, their attention on the monitor and their backs to Lilla, and although River twisted to the side and managed to bring the wiry blond woman to the floor with her, Lilla jabbed her in the thigh through her jeans with the needle.

River gasped as ice shot up her leg to her spine. Her hands went numb and her tongue thickened in her mouth. Hawk jerked the needle from her flesh as he thrust Lilla aside, then his face hovered anxiously over hers. His lips moved but she couldn't make out his words. She closed her eyes.

One voice sliced through the fog.

"Don't go to sleep, little Fae," Kaye ordered her.

Her lids, too heavy to hold less than a second before, snapped open. Blind panic filled her, telegraphing itself to all who could hear it. Kaye had gained control of her body, but he didn't understand.

Now nothing had control of her magic.

◆ ◆

A commotion at the entrance to the subway platform interrupted Achala's story to the children.

"He's wearing red," he heard one of the older boys say.

"We should kill him anyway."

"Does anyone care that River and Hawk sent me?" A stranger's voice, unusually deep, interrupted the debate.

The stranger sounded unconcerned. That worried Achala. While he enjoyed the children immensely, he wasn't blind to what they were. These children were damaged. They had very little empathy for anyone other than their own small group. They were far more dangerous than this man seemed to realize.

He strode quickly to the platform, the little ones following behind him, their curiosity evident. Achala planned to speak to Dan about what the little ones were being exposed to. He understood that they needed to learn to protect themselves from the world they lived in, but he doubted if Dan understood he was raising cold-blooded killers. They were far too young for this.

Hologram demons surrounded an enormous, bald-headed man standing near the foot of the stairs. The lights mounted on the subway walls created long, dancing, demon shadows. Achala frowned. Not much wonder the little ones had nightmares.

He recognized the man. He was one of Hawk's Guardians.

"Did he not tell you that River sent him?" he asked the shadows, sending out silent waves of calm on his words. The calmness wasn't directed at the holograms. He sent it to the nearby room where the real Demons sat when they projected their Hollow forms. River had indeed created a marvelous program for them. The Demons simply needed to be taught some restraint. "He's not a danger to you. Let him go."

He felt resentment as they released their holograms, but they did as he said.

The Guardian looked considerably less comfortable in Achala's presence than he had when surrounded by demons.

"Your Grace," he said, bowing his head. "I'm Major Faran. Colonel Hawkins sent me to find you." He glanced at the children standing behind Achala. "He has something he needs us to do for him."

Something he didn't want the Demons to know about. Achala was fascinated by Guardian subterfuge. It was something the Fae rarely engaged in because it was difficult to hide things from each other. It was why they most often left politics to the Great Lords.

Faint anger, foreign to him, stirred at the remembrance of his last conversation with the First Lord. He wouldn't be leaving politics to the Great Lords in the future. His daughter hadn't called to the Fae—or to him—for help because she would have trusted the Guardians to protect her. The Fae had sadly neglected their responsibilities and bore an equal measure of shame in these matters. Ignorance was not a defense.

"I don't think River will mind if we use her office," Achala said to Faran. He turned to the little ones. "Go and ask Sarah if she will tell you a story." Although still a child herself, Sarah was very good at keeping the younger children entertained.

He led the Guardian to River's office. A lot of its contents had no meaning for him so he'd never paid much attention to them. Major Faran, however, drew up short in the doorway and stared.

"In the name of the Mother," he whispered, then suddenly seemed to recollect whose presence he was in. "Apologies for my language, Your Grace."

He quickly forgot about Achala again as he crossed to examine the assortment of computer equipment mounted against one wall. Large monitors covered most of another wall. Faran touched one screen and immediately a white glow of light filled the room.

"Colonel Hawkins wanted us to do something?" Achala said, gently prompting Faran's memory.

Faran looked up from a tiny piece of flat board with a disproportionately large assortment of colored wires sprouting from its surface. The wires seemed to lead everywhere and nowhere.

It took him a moment to focus on Achala. "Hawk believes the virus that's spreading is a cross between a human and a computer virus," he said, dragging his attention away from the piece of technology in his massive hands. "The only way that's possible is through magic. What I need to do is find the virus in the program and see where the connection to the human virus could happen. Once I isolate it, I'll need you to show me how magic could connect it to humans."

"I wouldn't recognize a virus—human, computer, or otherwise," Achala said. "I'm not a doctor."

Faran grinned, flashing his gold tooth. He sat down at River's desk, his giant frame dwarfing her tiny chair. "But I am, Your Grace. I'll share my thoughts with you. Think of yourself as a nurse."

Achala watched in silence for the next several hours as the big man muttered to himself while he figured out River's hologram system.

"I think I've found it," Faran finally said. He tipped his head back and rubbed his reddened eyes, then rolled his shoulders as if working out stiffness. "But if she'd had the proper technical training and wanted to hide it, not even magic could have followed this trail." He sounded deeply impressed. "The woman has talent."

"But it happened by accident?" Achala asked. "The crossing of the viruses?"

Faran's movements stilled, his eyes reflecting his surprise at the question. "Without a doubt. It's very complex. All it would take is a single distraction and the right circumstances. She hasn't tried to hide anything. If she had, I could sit here for months and not find it."

Achala felt a tightness inside him relax. It was a relief having someone without any interest in his granddaughter to confirm it. He'd wanted to believe in River's goodness, but his objectiveness was colored by their relationship. Hawkins couldn't be considered objective about her either.

Faran, however, was a stranger to her.

"Are you ready to search for the connection?" Faran asked him.

Achala nodded, and Faran opened his thoughts.

The process was long and painstakingly slow. Every few minutes Achala had to stop and ask for an explanation of what he was seeing, but Faran was very patient. They ran through sequences of coding, often interrupted by Faran's detailed description of the structure of the various human viruses that might fit.

"Viruses are reliant on host cells," Faran explained as they sifted through his memories. "They're opportunistic and parasitic, moving from cell to cell, altering them as they go. Eventually they run out of cells, or they alter too many, and the host dies. Computer viruses require an electrical current to reproduce but the result is essentially the same. I've isolated the error in sequencing that triggered the computer virus, and the interruption that allowed the human virus entry, but the human virus would need to have the same basic structure as its computer counterpart and that's impossible. What magic has done, essentially, is forced a square peg into a round hole and given it the ability to replicate itself. If we can interrupt the replication, then we've found the cure. But first," he added, "we have to find the hammer that drove the square peg. Then you have to show me how we can stop it from continuing to force the pegs into the holes."

Achala thought about that. "Fae magic encourages growth. In someone like River, who sees technology as being as much a part of herself as magic, it makes sense to me that her magic would respond to it in the same way it would something alive. But are you certain it's magic that continues to hammer the virus beyond its initial germination? Why can't it be the electrical current? The brain has synapses, does it not? Isn't electricity a part of chemical responses? What if an electrical current is feeding the virus?"

Achala felt Faran's growing excitement. "You could be right," he said. "I think—"

Jake tore into the room at that moment, covered in gore and reeking of death, and whatever Faran was about to say was forgotten. Achala broke off the connection between their thoughts.

"Jake," he said, his tone filled with dismay. "What have you been doing? Are you hurt?"

Jake ignored his concern. "River needs our help." He shot a look of disgust over his shoulder at someone just outside the door. "Dan wouldn't let me go after her."

Achala put a hand over his nose to block out the coppery, acrid smell of blood. "Dan was probably correct. Where is she?"

"She's—"

A panicked cry from River reverberated through Achala's thoughts and he clutched at his head in response, Jake immediately forgotten. Dimly, he heard the sound of a chair toppling nearby, and then Faran's anxious voice in his ear. "Your Grace. What is it? What's wrong?"

Before he could answer, another call, this time from Hawk, entered his head.

Achala! I need your help.

CHAPTER **EIGHTEEN**

◆

I've got you, River, Hawk said to her, over and over, until he finally got through past the panic. *Never worry, mellita. Nobody orders you around but me.*

That really got her attention.

He had to work not to smile because the last thing he wanted to do was tip off the crazy freak on the monitor to the fact that he might not have as much control over the situation as he thought.

Hawk had to admit, however, that it surprised the hell out of him how Kaye had managed to snag Lilla. Drugs or not, mind control on a Guardian was a difficult thing to accomplish.

His heart squeezed. River, unfortunately, didn't have the same amount of training or experience.

Achala was with him now, offering his own reassurances to River and helping to calm her. The Fae leader didn't ask for explanations, he merely gave his support, which was good. Hawk needed to concentrate on what was happening in the room.

"What did you put in that syringe?" he asked Kaye, truly curious. It would be good knowledge to have for the future.

"The government invested a lot of time and money on mind-control experiments, starting around the middle of the last century," Nick said, speaking instead. "Nice," he congratulated Kaye. "Isn't it amazing what adding a lit-tle bit of crazy to immoral experimentation can accom-plish?"

It worried Hawk that Nick could be so close to River and yet so well informed about things most people wouldn't know.

Kaye's cold, pale gray eyes fixed thoughtfully on Nick. "The key ingredient turned out to be a chemical in the brains of pack animals that makes them respond to the commands of the alpha. You should have stayed dead," he added.

Nick yawned, shifting one shoulder. "It was boring." He looked at Lilla standing quietly nearby, immobile and with no discernible expression on her face. Hawk thought he caught a flicker of anger in his eyes as they touched for a second on her swollen hands. "Someday," Nick added softly, addressing the monitor, "one of your experiments is going to turn on you. I'd like to stick around to see that."

"Lilla," Hawk commanded. "Kick Nick in the nuts and make him shut up."

She never moved.

On the monitor, Kaye appeared amused. "The alpha is the first person who issues an order after the drug is ad-ministered. It was intended for military use. We couldn't have mechanically enhanced weapons turning on com-manding officers. River," he ordered. "Take those pieces of rope on the floor and tie up Colonel Hawkins." He folded his arms and addressed Hawk again. "If you re-sist, I'll have her throw herself out of that window."

She wasn't going to cooperate. Hawk felt the tiny thread of stubborn resistance in her, as well as Achala's hesitation. A black curtain of panic overwhelmed her again, but he brushed it aside. *Do as he says,* mellita, he encouraged her. *Don't let him suspect you can disobey.*

She stooped and gathered the pieces of rope that had once bound Lilla. She gave no outward indication, no hint whatsoever, that he was in her thoughts with her as she bound his hands and feet, then laced them together so he couldn't bend forward.

Hawk tested the bindings. She'd done a good job. If he hadn't been so certain of her, he would be very concerned right now.

The monitor went black.

"Nice going," Nick said. He held up his own bound hands. "Great rescue."

"Shut up," Hawk said. Footsteps could be heard, faint at first, approaching in the hall. He wanted to know where Kaye was coming from because when this was over, he intended to get that kaleidoscope back for River.

First, though, he was going to kill the bastard. But he was going to have to rely on Nick and Achala to help.

Achala, he thought, carefully keeping River out of the connection. *River is going to implant him with the hologram program. When she does, do you think you can make him believe he has the virus as well?*

Beyond a doubt, the Fae assured him in return. *Major Faran has discovered how to force a square peg into a round hole.*

Hawk had no idea what that meant, but if Achala said he could mimic the virus, that was good enough for him. The virus should cause Kaye to hallucinate.

Hawk prayed to the Mother that Nick was smart enough to know how to play along as General Amos Kaye stepped into the room.

He was a smaller man than Hawk had anticipated, but his presence dominated the room nonetheless. He radiated an air of confident, intelligent authority. This was a man used to getting his own way, and Hawk didn't underestimate him, but Kaye had never come up against two Fae and a Guardian before. The man might be smart, but that didn't make the rest of them stupid.

Kaye wasn't underestimating Hawk either, however. He kept the gun in his hand trained on him from the instant he entered the room. The rest of his attention remained focused entirely on River.

"I want the implant," Kaye said to her.

Hawk thought it only right to give him fair warning of what to expect if she did. Not for Kaye's sake, but for the sake of the two Fae. Neither were killers.

"If she gives it to you," Hawk said to him, "you're a dead man."

Kaye cocked the gun. "If she doesn't give it to me, so are you."

"Either way," Nick chimed in, "we're all going to die."

Hawk didn't wait for the reaction to those words that he knew would be coming. The only reason the rest of them were still alive was because Kaye wanted bargaining chips to maintain control over River in case the drug didn't work as well as he anticipated. He launched himself forward, knocking Kaye off balance so that the shot he fired at Nick went wild.

Kaye staggered into the wall, then swung the butt of the gun and caught Hawk in the side of the head as he fell, not hard enough to do damage, but enough to hurt.

"Son of a *bitch*," Hawk swore, his eyes watering as he rolled to his feet. His bound hands and ankles left him unable to break his fall and his shoulder ached where it had struck the floor. Nick's smart mouth wasn't helping any of them. He glowered at him. "*Now* will you shut up?"

Kaye had regained his balance and brought the gun back around to Hawk. "Why don't you both shut up?" He spoke to River. "I want that program. Now."

So far, Hawk knew, only Achala's presence in her thoughts had held River back. She was a keg of gunpowder, and any little spark could set her off. The Guardian in him rebelled as she stepped close to the bastard who'd stalked and threatened her for months, possibly years. The possessive male in him growled as she lifted her hands and placed them on another man. Only the knowledge that Kaye had to be stopped kept him from blindly reacting.

Achala's calming presence helped them both keep their control.

Hawk eased back, allowing the Fae leader greater access to River's thoughts as he felt her use her magic to carefully take bits of tissue and nerves from inside Kaye's head and twist them into living microchips.

Achala guided her at several points. Hawk sensed him consulting with Faran as he did.

Through it all, Kaye had no idea that anyone other than he had control over River. When she finished installing the program for him, her hands dropped to her sides. The expression on Kaye's face was nothing less than beatific.

"Show me how to use it," he commanded her, bracing his back against the wall as he tried to keep a watchful eye on his prisoners. The gun in his hand remained steady.

You're certain the program will mimic the virus? Hawk questioned Achala, tension hardening his lungs. It was tempting to try to take advantage of Kaye's distraction, but not if it endangered River. And as a Guardian, there were things he needed to learn.

Absolutely.

Slowly, carefully, the hologram of something not quite human began to appear in the center of the room. With the snout of what might be a wolf, or even a bear, and great hulking arms and shoulders, the torso narrowed to a man's hips and overlong, but still human, legs. Hawk had seen something similar in a cave not far from the home where River had been raised, and also in the lab where the souls of her birth parents had been kept captive. Underneath the layers of flesh on the monster, he suspected he'd find pieces of machine melded to bone.

"Oh, shit," Nick whispered from beside him. "He wants River to give those things life."

They had all forgotten about Lilla, who'd been standing passively nearby. Suddenly, without warning, she darted forward, and crouching low, fumbled for Kaye's ankle with one of her damaged hands. He whirled on her, but his attention had been so focused on the hologram he'd been trying to create, his reflexes were sluggish. She yanked a small knife from its sheath and rolled out of his reach.

The hologram Kaye had created firmed, gained more substance, and started for her, its beady eyes angry and red. She dodged it easily, but rather than getting out of its way she ducked and dove once more for Kaye. She slashed clumsily at him with the tiny blade. A trickle of blood appeared on his sleeve, and on a shout of pain and anger, Kaye's hologram blinked out.

That gained him more control of himself. The barrel of the gun he still held whipped around toward Lilla. Bound as he was, Hawk was too far away to be able to help her.

And then Kaye stopped. He turned his head. A low buzzing noise cut through the room. "Who gave you permission to come in here?" he demanded of something Hawk couldn't see.

Hawk turned to Nick. "Quick! What do you think he might be afraid of? And do you think you can copy it?"

Surprise, then understanding, flashed across Nick's face in rapid succession. The buzzing in the room doubled in volume. Within seconds, he'd built a hologram of a Were.

Hawk knew that Were. Its name was Bane. The last time he'd seen him, he'd been running into the mountains outside of Kaye's lab. He might look like a man, but on the inside he was pure animal. This was the tool Kaye had used to kill River's gamer friends. Hawk had once seen him rip out a man's throat.

Kaye wasn't yet affected enough by the virus not to realize that something was wrong. He looked at the hologram of Bane. "You're dead," he said sharply.

"You're bleeding," Bane replied in return, and looking hungrily at Kaye's arm, he licked his lips. He flicked long black hair out of his eyes in a signature gesture. "How does it feel to be fair game?"

Hawk had been counting on this. Nick designed video game characters, so he understood the importance of detail. He also knew what buttons to push to drive someone completely over the edge. He'd tried it on Hawk in the past.

He was doing an admirable impression of Bane's gravelly voice now, too.

River had gotten out of the way and stood quietly near Lilla on the opposite side of the room from Hawk. Achala was showing her how to nullify the effects of the drug in her system with her magic.

Hawk tried to block out as much of what was happening in the room from her as he could, but he couldn't hide it all. He bent his knees to reach for the knife he kept at his own ankle, keeping his spine arched so as not to tug on the bindings. Within seconds, he was free.

Kaye's head swiveled between the two holograms—
one of Bane, and another that only he could see. Stark
panic lit the whites of his odd, colorless eyes as Bane
steadily stalked him. So, apparently, did the invisible
image only Kaye could see.

"Ever wonder what it's like to be eaten alive?" Bane
asked, continuing to stare at the blood on Kaye's sleeve.

Kaye's back hit the wall, his head connecting with the
corner of the monitor and knocking it sideways. Trem-
ors wracked his body. His chest rose and fell, the pulse
throbbing at his neck plainly visible.

The panic suddenly vanished from his eyes and
awareness settled in. He looked to Hawk and let out a
soft laugh. "Nicely done," he congratulated him. "I'm
assuming there's no cure."

He lifted the gun. River screamed as he fired, covering her face with her hands. Blood and brains spattered
the wall where Kaye's head used to be.

The buzzing noise ceased abruptly. Bane disappeared.

Hawk dove across the room in an effort to reach
River, but Lilla got to her first.

She plunged the knife she held into River's chest.

◆ ◆

The pain in River's chest was nothing compared to the
pain she felt pouring from deep in Hawk's soul as she
slid to the floor.

She tried to speak, to tell him she was fine, but no words would come.

She was floating, watching the room from above. Hawk bent over her, his hands on her chest as he applied pressure to a wound that bled very little. River knew that was bad. Lilla lay crumpled on the floor not far from her, a deep bruise darkening her temple where Hawk must have struck her. What remained of Kaye's head splashed one wall and the floor beneath it, while his body half slouched in a sitting position where it had fallen.

Hawk tossed his knife to Nick, who cut himself free. Then he, too, was bending over her.

River, however, was distracted by the things she could sense happening outside of the room. She felt the passing of Kaye's soul and made no move to stop it. He'd caused nothing but pain in this life. Perhaps in another he would do better.

Hawk continued to call to her. So did Achala, holding her back so she couldn't drift away. But even though she wanted desperately to stay with Hawk, other voices called to her as well.

Fae voices. Thousands of them. They swirled in the night sky, brilliant flashes of color, so beautiful that River watched them in awe. They didn't want her to join them. They wanted her help. They needed a Fae to welcome them into this world.

Everyone wanted something from her. Needed her. It made her so tired.

Except for Hawk, who wanted and needed her, yet made her feel strong. Without her, he would die. So would many more. Less than 20 percent of the world's population remained, and thanks to a virus she and Hawk had unleashed, that number would dwindle again.

Thousands of Fae souls, and billions of humans, had suffered far worse than she. Hawk, too, had suffered in an effort to save others. She had no right to be tired.

She did, however, have a right to be angry.

The dark seed inside her cracked open, and then she was back in her body. Her eyelids flew wide and she blinked against the sudden influx of light. She stared up into Hawk's anxious face.

Somewhere in the back of her mind she felt Achala pulling her power, trying to absorb it, to control it. She wouldn't let him. Not this time. This time she was going to hold it tight. Use it.

It wouldn't use her.

"Run!" she cried to Hawk, trying to push him away. She couldn't hold back for much longer, nor did she want to.

"Take Lilla and get the hell out!" she heard him yelling to Nick.

The swirling anger surged onward and outward as wind curled around the room, gaining momentum and power. It flashed in her mind. Seconds later, white-hot flames licked up the walls and chaos erupted.

You hold both light and dark in your magic, a woman's voice, soft and compelling, spoke inside her head. It was unfamiliar to her, and yet River new instantly to whom it belonged.

Achala, too, had heard the voice. She felt him draw

back in reverent surprise. Then he was gone, and she and her magic were free.

Which Path will you choose?

♦ ♦

Despite River's warning, Hawk had no intention of going anywhere. He did, however, intend to get her kaleido-scope for her before she blew the building to pieces.

He lifted her in his arms and dashed from the burn-ing room just as the sprinklers came on. Rusty, stagnant water sprayed over them before he could kick the door shut. A loud alarm went off, the noise nearly deafening him. She paid no attention to any of it, and he'd been blocked from her thoughts.

Leave her alone! Achala warned him sharply. *This is her battle, not yours.* Then he, too, withdrew.

The hell he would leave her alone. From the moment he'd met her, their battles were joined. He dashed down the stairs to the second floor, then set her on her feet. The crackle of fire filled the air as smoke rolled in billows down the stairwell from the burning room above. He only had a few minutes to get her from the building.

He jogged down the hall, trying each doorknob as he went. He finally found Kaye's office and ran inside. The kaleidoscope sat on the desk. He grabbed it, sprinted back into the hall, and stopped in dismay.

River was gone.

♦ ♦

River knew Hawk could get out before the fire destroyed the building, but she couldn't hold back any longer.

She jumped to the street below. The Weres standing guard had fled when the fire alarm sounded. That was good. She had no desire to hurt them. She had no desire to hurt anyone.

She did, however, need to find an outlet for her energy. It had been bottled up inside her. Now it wanted out.

She walked toward the riverfront and stood on the quay, the night and the chill wind embracing her. Sparkles of light from the city danced on the water.

She channeled all of her energy into its depths. A fountain of water shot sky high in response. She made it dance, spinning and swaying, then added flame to its core. The fountain lit up the night. She walked to the edge of the wooden quay, near the street, and dug her fingers into the dirt. Seeds sprouted in response. Within seconds, she'd crafted a garden of seedlings and shrubs that spread thousands of feet down the street in either direction.

When her energy was spent, she turned to find Hawk standing directly behind her.

"Now *that* is a temper tantrum," he said with a grin. He opened his arms wide and River ran into them.

"I choose light," she said fiercely as his arms closed around her.

CHAPTER NINETEEN

♦

"Lilla was following orders, as she's been trained to do," Achala reminded Hawk as they spoke in quiet tones outside of River's bedroom. "The drug didn't help."

Hawk had convinced River to lie down. How long she would stay there without him was anyone's guess.

"I know that." He did. His anger with Lilla had evaporated, although if River had died, he might be feeling differently right now. "What I don't understand is why the order was given in the first place. We already had our instructions. Once we had proof she was a Dark Lord, we were to act. River has done nothing to convince Lilla of anything other than that she has magic."

Achala was silent for a long moment as if struggling with his conscience over something important. "She wasn't ordered to kill a Dark Lord," he said finally. "She was specifically ordered to kill River."

Hawk couldn't speak. Lilla was an excellent captain. A very good soldier and leader. She could have come to him if she'd been given orders she didn't believe in, and morally, in any soldier's mind, such orders would have been wrong. But she hadn't come to him. "Why?" he asked after finding his voice. "And by whom?"

Again, that hesitation. "I spoke with the First Lord after you left," Achala replied. He looked at his hands. "It turns out River's father was his son."

And with blinding clarity, Hawk understood. Guardians had a far different attitude toward family than the Fae, and even humans. This was about honor and pride. The First Lord's son had disgraced him and whether she was a Dark Lord or not, River wasn't going to be allowed to live. Her life meant nothing but dishonor to the First Lord and his opinion on that would never change.

The bomb in his head suggested to Hawk that somehow, the First Lord had known of River's existence all along. It would have had to be implanted while Hawk was participating in a cryonics experiment involving out-of-body travel.

Had the First Lord's son tried to contact his father all those years ago? Had the First Lord refused help to his son, and therefore, to a Fae?

The thought sickened him.

"River doesn't ever need to know," Achala said quietly. "I would rather she didn't. But I thought you should know why this world is the best place for her to remain."

If she remained, then Hawk remained with her. But could he survive on this half-dead, backward planet?

The selfish, unbidden question wracked him with guilt. He'd had no qualms about asking River to give up all that was familiar to her. He could do the same. He'd been so certain that his world, and that of the Fae, were far better than this one. Instead, they were simply in a different stage of decline.

But if he stayed, danger stayed with him.

"Faran believes he knows how to eliminate the bomb

in your head," Achala added, correctly interpreting at least part of Hawk's silence. "But it will involve River's cooperation."

◆ ◆

"Absolutely not," she replied when Hawk presented the solution to her. "We'll find another way. I'm not infecting you with the virus."

He hadn't liked the idea either. Not at first. The last thing he wanted was anyone messing with his head. But they already had, and of the few people he knew who might be able to fix this, he trusted River the most.

He sat on the edge of her bed, watching with distraction as she stretched the sleep from her lithe body. There were things he'd far rather be doing than argue with her, he thought with regret.

Later, perhaps.

"You're not infecting me, you're infecting the bomb," he patiently explained. "Faran and Achala believe the virus is spreading through electrical impulses. The virus can enter the bomb. Then, when we set off our kits in the stratosphere, static interference should break the connection. It's an effect similar to sunspots. When that happens, you can use your magic to grab the bomb and transfer it into empty space. That's just a precaution," he added hastily, seeing the look on her face.

She tucked a strand of black hair behind her ear. "It's not good enough."

He bent down to kiss the spot on her neck she had bared. When she turned her face and tilted her head for him, Hawk dropped another soft kiss onto her mouth. He lingered, their gazes locked in a silent exchange of intimacy.

He sighed, conquered temptation, then stood and held his hand out to her. She allowed him to pull her to her feet, then nestled her body against him. She slid her arms around his waist.

Hawk let loose a heartfelt sigh. "Remember this moment, because when this is over I want you back in this room and here in my arms." He tightened his hold. "Just like this." Then he released her and crossed to the door. He held it open for her. "But right now, Faran and Achala are waiting for us."

They walked to her office.

Faran sat in front of River's monitor. Achala balanced on the edge of the desk, watching him.

"She has a few reservations," Hawk said to Faran, who looked up when they entered. He deliberately kept himself between Faran and River. He had no way of knowing how many orders the First Lord had given out, or to whom.

"No need to worry," Faran assured River. He rubbed his temple with the tips of his fingers. "We can solve two problems at the same time. The virus will interrupt the bomb's ability to react to stimuli. An atmospheric disruption will sever the electrical impulses that appear to be spreading the programmed part of the virus. No impulses, no ability to spread, and no exploding bomb. Magic will take care of the rest."

"I don't like it," River said. "There has to be a better way. How do you know it won't set the bomb off instead?" Her glance darted between the three men, unable to find an ally. "The virus is picking up speed." She cast a finger in Hawk's direction as she zeroed in on Achala. "He could be dead before the kits are ever detonated."

Achala placed his hand on her arm. "As soon as we implant it, Hawk will give the signal to detonate the kits. The virus won't have time to do any damage to his brain. This will all take place within a matter of minutes."

Her stubborn protectiveness warmed Hawk's heart. "This could be our only chance. We may never get another."

Her chin quivered. "Don't ask me to do this."

Hawk pulled her to him. She twisted his shirt in her fingers and murmured into his chest, "I don't want to lose you."

He put his mouth close to her ear and breathed conviction into his words. "You'll be saving me."

Achala pushed himself off the edge of the desk. "Perhaps you two need some time."

Both Achala and Faran left the room, the door clicking tightly shut behind them.

River hated this plan and everything about it.

"Hawk," she whispered, fear making her desperate. "Please."

She wasn't sure who moved first, but the next thing she knew his mouth was on hers, kissing her with a passion and ferociousness that had her head spinning and set her heart on fire. She dragged her fingers though his hair and held him tight. His muscles quivered in response.

"River," he murmured into her mouth with a raw need and urgency she'd never heard him use before. His hands raced over her body and his lips moved hungrily, as if he was unable to get enough of her. Breathless, she pressed closer, her needs and fears mingling and overwhelming her senses. Her heart kicked up a notch, the rush of blood making her dizzy.

When he inched back and buried his mouth into the hollow of her neck, her body moistened with unabashed need and she murmured, "I need you." Oh, God, how she needed him. In her life, her arms, her bed, and was sure she couldn't survive without him.

Unguarded eyes met hers. "I'm yours, *mellita*." His voice, deep and primal, flooded her with longing. His hair brushed against her bare skin and his hands tightened around her, squeezing so hard it took effort to breathe. "You won't hurt me," he repeated. He trailed kisses around her jaw, then once again his lips found hers. His tongue thrashed inside, seeking, searching, ravishing her like a man starved.

Shaky hands stole up her shirt and warmth spread over her skin. She let loose a sob and urged him closer as she gave in to her needs. Hawk unfastened her buttons, baring her breasts.

His voice trembled. "I want you. Now."

"I want you, too," she managed to get out as she tore at her jeans. Hawk unzipped his fly and dropped himself down onto her chair as she wiggled out of the tight denim.

He reached for her, his burning eyes leaving her face to track her body. "Come here," he said, and dragged her to him. She moved quickly, needing him inside her more than she needed air.

His tongue flicked over her nipple as she wrapped her legs around his. She felt the wet tip of his arousal at her opening. With desperation fueling her, she tried to insert him, but he gripped her hips and held her tight.

As she hovered over him, his eyes met hers and everything in the way he was looking at her felt more intimate than a caress. He slipped a hand around her head and drew her mouth to his. His warm breath wafted across her cheeks and when he finally urged her to lower herself onto him, to join them as one, Hawk deepened the kiss, his mouth rough with emotion as he guided her to him.

As he pushed open her tight walls she drew a shaky breath. Hawk groaned out loud and wrapped his hands around her waist, stilling her movements. They held each other tight and when their gazes collided, she saw love shining in his eyes. Her throat closed over as love rushed to her own heart.

She began rocking against him and Hawk followed the motion, powering his hips upward while gripping her hips for leverage. He guided her up and down, up and down, until she was burning from the inside out. The look on his face told her he was fighting for control, because they both knew this encounter wasn't about sex, not for either one of them.

Need consumed them both as they came together and forged an intimate connection, one that went well beyond the physical, one that took two halves and made them whole again. Hawk had taken up residency in her heart, he was under her skin, a part of her, and to lose him now would shatter her into a million tiny pieces.

His grip grew tighter, his thrusts more frantic and she could tell by the look on his face that he was searching, seeking more than simple release as he gave her a piece of himself.

In no time at all she felt an orgasm pulling at her.

"Hawk," she cried out, frantic, her nails clawing his skin.

His voice thinned to a whisper when he said, "That's it, *mellita*. Let go."

He reached between their bodies and pressed his thumb to her nub, stimulating the tight bundle of nerves and raising her passion to new heights. Her entire body shook from the onslaught of ecstasy and when he drove into her again, she gave herself over to that pleasure and tumbled into orgasm.

Hawk gripped her hips and buried himself deep inside her as he, too, let go. Breathing hard, she wrapped her arms around him and could feel his pulse hammering at his neck as she held on.

After he depleted himself, large hands gently cupped her head and brought her face to his. Her heart swelled with emotions. He watched her for a moment before saying, "I love you, *mellita.*"

A sob caught in River's throat as he echoed her sentiments exactly. "I'm not going to lose you, Hawk," she whispered, although every instinct in her body warned of the possibility.

◆ ◆

Nick finally found her.

She'd taken up guard duty at one of the entrances to the subway, a forlorn little blond Princess of Power who looked as if her batteries had finally run out of juice. The kit bags sat between her knees.

Hawk, the douche bag, had taken quite a strip off her with a lengthy lecture on military ethics. In Nick's experience, *military* and *ethics* were mutually exclusive terms, so as far as he was concerned, Hawk had been blowing hot air. To top it all off, River had healed Lilla's fingers. He suspected that had pissed her off even more than the lecture.

"Hey," he said softly, and Lilla jumped, so he knew she wasn't really guarding anything, only hiding. He'd thought long and hard about what he should say to her. "Sooner or later you're going to remember you forgot to thank me for saving your life, and then you'll be sorry. So let's get it over with."

She told him to do something to himself that was totally unladylike and anatomically impossible. Shit, he really liked her.

There was something seriously wrong with him.

"Tell you what," he said, sitting down beside her on the stairs. He hadn't given her the virus, not yet anyway, so he guessed she was safe, possibly immune. "I'll show you how it's done." He placed a hand over his heart. "Thank you for tackling three Weres on my behalf, even though I didn't need your help. I could have handled them myself if you'd given me the chance."

She smiled a little. Then her lower lip started to shake, and Nick drew back in alarm. He couldn't handle tears. He was okay with his own, as long as he was in private, but women crying made him nervous. Lilla especially. It was most likely steam leaking and meant she was about to explode.

"Thank you for getting my fingers broken," she replied, and he relaxed.

He crooked an elbow around her neck. "There. Was that so hard?"

"You really are an ass," she told him.

"It's part of my charm." Nick settled his back against the cold concrete stairwell and folded his legs along the length of the step so that Lilla sat at his feet. "What are you doing?"

She patted the kit bag. "Waiting for orders."

Nick didn't especially care what those orders might be. General Amos Kaye, the boil on his ass, was gone— and he'd had a hand in it. He was sitting in the sunshine

with a really gorgeous woman who, with a bit of encouragement, might grant him a few favors. There was
only one way to find out. "Mind if I wait with you?"

She studied him carefully, although he pretended not
to notice. He closed his eyes.

"Suit yourself," she said with an indifferent shrug,
and inwardly, he smiled. Life didn't get any better than
this.

The com-link on her wrist flashed. She pressed a
button.

"What in the name of the Mother has happened to
everyone?" an irritated voice demanded. "Has Faran forgotten he left us on a mountaintop, freezing our asses
off?"

◆ ◆

"I have something for you," River said to him.

They shared the chair in her office, River straddling
Hawk's hips with her knees, her hands on his face. They'd
straightened their clothes, although in his opinion, that
was a pity.

She dropped a light kiss on his brow, then reached
into a desk drawer and pulled out the kaleidoscope he'd
recovered from Kaye's office for her. For a moment she
cradled it, rubbing her fingers over the smooth black
finish, then she pressed it into his hands.

In all of the earlier commotion he hadn't gotten a

chance to examine it. He turned it over and over now, admiring the sleek fittings, then held it to his eye.

If she hadn't been sitting on his lap he would have tumbled from the chair. Spinning bits of colored light danced in a display similar to fireworks on a 3-D screen. Before he could draw a second breath, brilliant tendrils of light disengaged from the multihued mass, piercing the dark tunnel of the viewfinder and forging a connection directly to Hawk. He felt magic, smelled it, and knew instantly it belonged to River.

Bits of her soul had been tied to this toy. The magnitude of the offering overwhelmed him. He wondered if she understood the significance of what it contained. An ugly thought overrode his initial pleasure. The original gift had been to her father, who must have known she was special. Had he understood what she'd given him? If the answer was yes, then what had he done with the toy?

The fact that it had caught the attention of someone like Kaye meant David Weston had undoubtedly done something.

River was watching him, a frown forming between her lovely eyes, obviously disappointed with his reaction to her gift and trying to hide it. He set the kaleidoscope carefully on the desk beside them, then laced his fingers through hers. His voice thick with emotion, he said, "You can't imagine how honored I am that you would trust me with something you value so highly."

The frown vanished. Her eyes darkened to cobalt

blue. "I don't value a toy as much as I do you. Please don't ask me to do something that will hurt you."

The truth was, after spending more than a year trying to get back to his own body because of a cryonics research project gone bad, he wasn't anxious to allow anyone to mess with his head. He'd certainly never expected the next person who tried to be River. But he had no other choice, not that he could see, and if he was going to trust anyone, it would be her.

And if anything went wrong, although he didn't expect it to, he would transport himself as far away from River and her world as possible. Guardians had done enough damage here.

"I bet I can fight off the hallucinations twice as long as anyone else could," he said in a bid to relax her. He admired the flush still infusing her cheeks and was glad they'd made love. They were going to need all that stored energy, and then some. "The teams are on standby, waiting for me to give the command. As soon as the virus infects the bomb, you can start passing out sunscreen." She didn't look as if she found him funny so he kissed her. "It's going to be fine," he added, drawing her close.

Her brows knit together. "I'm afraid, Hawk," she admitted. "What if I make a mistake?"

"You won't." When she glanced away he added gently, "We can't leave a bomb in me forever. This might be our only chance to get rid of it. If we don't, the Great Lords might decide to detonate it on their own." Hawk no longer trusted them. It was entirely possible they had another trigger.

"If they do try, and it doesn't detonate, will more of the Guardians come?"

It was a good question and he wasn't certain of the answer. He thought of her Guardian grandfather and his determination to kill her. Pride was a terrible thing.

"Let's let Achala worry about that. He has a lot more influence than you might think. Right now," he added, sliding his hand over the rounded seat of her jeans where she balanced on his thighs, trying to ease some of her tension, "I'd like to get on with this before he and Faran come back. I don't want anyone else around for it." While his trust in Achala had risen greatly, he was far more comfortable with River as the only witness to any meltdown he might have.

She knew how important his sanity was to him. She caught her lip between her teeth as if still undecided. "If I blow us all up, do you think your soul will remember that I love you, too?"

He took her tightly clenched fist in his palm and held it over his heart. "It couldn't possibly forget," he said, smiling into her eyes, "because our souls are joined."

She smiled in return.

"Then let's get this over with," she said, gritting her teeth. She placed her palms on either side of his face and seconds later, a strange click sounded in his head. "Think of someplace familiar," she said, "and imagine yourself there."

He thought of the empty lot where he and his team had arrived. It was to be their rendezvous point.

Immediately, there he was. He spun around in a circle

on the cracked asphalt, automatically checking for danger, wobbling like a toddler taking its first steps. It seemed surreal. Part of him was with River. He could feel her, and see her if he concentrated. Another part of him stood in a vacant lot. It was as if he'd stepped into a 3-D movie. His stomach lurched, dragging his attention away from her. Unease crawled over his skin and he sucked in a tight breath as he listened for a buzzing sound.

"You okay?" she asked him, concern in her voice.

"Fine," he answered, looking up and trying to focus on her. "Just not really liking the whole out-of-body experience."

Her hands leapt away from his face. "We can stop."

"No." He grabbed her wrists and replaced them, liking her touch and more than a little comforted by it. As long as she was in control, he would know what was real.

He lifted his arms and his hologram groped its way forward. Sitting on top of him, with her cheek pressed to his, she made a sound of amused disgust that helped ground him.

"What is it?" he asked.

"You're acting like Nick."

"There's no need to kick a man when he's down."

He felt the smile in her tone as she answered. "When he first tried the program he was walking around like Dr. Frankenstein's monster, too."

"Crisos. Who is this Dr. Frankenstein, and how many monster makers do you have on your world?"

"Never mind."

Hawk felt the light brush of magic as she examined

the bomb inside his head. He blinked and pulled himself out of the hologram. He focused on River, shaking off a sudden unease.

"How do you feel?" she asked.

The truth was he felt a little disoriented, but passed the dizziness off as nothing more than the virus integrating itself into the bomb's circuitry. At least they weren't hearing a buzzing sound. And he hoped like hell they wouldn't.

Instead of answering he asked, "Can you tell if it's working?"

Warmth moved through him as she released a bit of her healing magic, taking her time to pick her way gently around the bomb. He felt her relax. "It's doing just what you said it would," she finally answered.

"I told you everything was going to be fine." He turned his attention to his com-link. "I'll tell the others to prepare to launch, and we'll meet Lilla in the parking lot before I give the order."

He pressed the com-link, but nothing happened. "We'll have to go outdoors," he said to River. "Something in the tunnels must be interfering with our communications signals." It was most likely her program. He could think of nothing else on this world that could cause interference.

Someone banged a fist on the door. Then it flew open.

"Change of plans," Faran said, thrusting his head into the room, one hand braced on the doorframe. "We can't set off the kits. We'll have to find another way to disrupt electrical signals."

CHAPTER TWENTY

♦

"I'm sorry, Hawk," Faran said for the tenth time after explaining about the Fae souls he, Ever, and Peters had discovered over the Arctic. Lilla stood behind Faran, her face pale and still. "I didn't think about the kits doing damage to the Fae souls." His expression grew hopeful. "It's possible they won't, but we need more time to find out for certain."

The room grew small, claustrophobic, and breathing became difficult for River as she listened. Jim Peters had been following her father's trail. The moment Faran had mentioned his name she'd known where that trail now led. From the virus, to the concentration of Fae souls, to the arrival of the Guardians, everything had happened because of her.

"It's too late," she said. Faran and Lilla looked at her. Hawk tried to silence her with a dark look and a shake of his head, but she continued anyway. "I've already infected him—"

"I can fight it," Hawk interrupted. "A Guardian has never been infected before. Our brains are wired a little differently." He grinned at everyone, acting as if this were nothing at all for them to be concerned about. "I think Lilla proved that when she shook off Kaye's drug."

Lilla and Faran believed him, River saw with a knot of alarm. She wanted desperately to believe him also, but she knew him too well. He might be able to hide his fear from the others but he could never hide it from her.

But she also knew he was strong. Perhaps he could hold off long enough for Achala to help.

Achala, when consulted, remained noncommittal on Hawk's ability to do so. His face when he learned of the Fae souls, however, reflected a growing excitement and concern.

"Fae souls are sent out into the universe until it's time to call them home," he said. "Newborns and souls are carefully matched through a series of ceremonies and rituals." He lifted his hands in a gesture of helplessness. "Something has called them to this world, to what would seem like an abundance of life to them, and I'm not certain they would listen to me."

While River understood the importance of these souls to the Guardians and to the Fae, nothing was more important to her than Hawk. She picked up the kaleidoscope from her desk and rolled it absently in her hands, wishing she knew what to do for him.

"Where did you get that?" Faran asked her abruptly, his gaze fixed on the kaleidoscope.

The others turned to see what he referred to. River looked to Hawk for an answer.

"She built it," Hawk said.

"Then I think I know what called the souls to this world," Faran said. "Or who." Rather than dismay, his eyes filled with speculation and a cautious respect. He looked to Achala. "And I may have a plan."

♦ ♦

As far as plans went, River had heard better.

It was dusk. She shivered in the cold wind whistling across the darkening parking lot, although it wasn't the cold that bothered her. She didn't like the uncertainty. Not when it came to Hawk's life. So far, however, he'd shown no obvious symptoms of the virus, although he was guarding his thoughts from her. That worried her, too.

He came up behind her and crooked his arm around her neck, drawing her head against his chest. She snaked an arm around his waist. "Everything will be fine," he assured her. "The kits are almost set, including the ones in the Pacific. As soon as Lilla gets this one ready, you, Achala, and I will head to Ellesmere Island. Achala feels confident that between you, you can disperse the Fae souls." One of Hawk's eyebrows shot up. "It's not as if it's the first time you've released them."

That was true. She had released one poor, tortured bioengineered soul, and she'd released her parents. She bit her lip. For them, she'd had Andy's help. This time, they were talking about many, many more.

"Your grandfather is one of the greatest Fae spiritual leaders," Hawk reminded her, reading her thoughts easily.

"I don't know him the way I knew Andy."

Nick and Lilla knelt side by side on the asphalt, unpacking a kit. Nick was complaining, as usual, and making the humorless little blond Guardian smile. Faran and

Achala stood apart, discussing the telescope and how River's kaleidoscope must fit into the finder scope. Dan and Jake hovered in the shadows at the far end of the lot, thinking they hadn't been noticed.

Hawk kissed the top of River's head, then started across the lot to exchange a few final words with Faran and Achala.

As he did, a low sound cut through the air.

Buzzing.

They all heard it at the same time. Lilla paused in the act of showing Nick how to help set up the kit, her hand in the air above one of the controls. Nick froze, too.

River saw both acceptance and defeat cross Hawk's face. Nevertheless, he continued to walk toward Faran. "Round up the team, take the kits, and go home," he ordered the Guardian. "This mission has failed. The only favor I'd ask is that you all do what you can to protect River."

The big man nodded, his face grim, and River looked wildly back and forth between them, trying to figure out what was going on. Comprehension slowly trickled in. When it did, she was furious. He'd decided he was already dead. He planned to transport himself into space.

She wouldn't allow it to happen.

"No," she said, running after him. "Please don't make me the cause of your death. Not after everything we've done to keep each other alive."

He gathered her into his arms. The buzzing grew steadily louder. "This is my decision to make for my team," he replied. His eyes gentled, memorizing her face. "I knew there was a risk, *mellita*. I did this to me, not you. You have to find another way to end the virus. I have faith in you."

"Then have faith in me a little longer," she urged him. She gripped his shirt with fierce determination and refused to release him. "Otherwise, where you go, I go."

He tried to pry her fingers loose. "You don't understand," he said. He drew a deep, body-shuddering breath. "I'm afraid that any moment now, any second, I might turn on you. If I wait any longer to do this, it will be too late. I won't know for certain that I'm doing what's right."

"Then let Faran make the decisions," she said. She looked to Faran and Lilla for help. "You both heard him. He's no longer rational."

Outrage and a sense of betrayal rolled off Hawk, wounding River deeply and forcing blood to pound in her ears. She'd played on his biggest fear, and now his agitation increased the level of danger to them all. They no longer had time to jump to Ellesmere Island so she and Achala could communicate with the souls there.

She would have to welcome them to this world here instead.

"She's right," Achala, who'd stood quietly aside until now, interjected. Lilla murmured her own assent, and Faran, a muscle working in his cheek, reluctantly nodded as well.

At the far end of the lot Dan and Jake watched them in worried confusion, unable to hear what was being said. The bigger boy was holding Jake back, and for that, River was grateful. She didn't want him to know the end of the world was coming if it turned out she'd made a mistake.

She danced quickly out of Hawk's reach. Too quick for him to react, she drew energy from deep in her core, more than any she'd ever drawn before, and let it rush through her body until her entire nervous system was alive and crackling. Fire arced from her fingers, static lifting the hair on her head. Desperation fueling her on, River released the energy into the sky. A stream of brilliant white light shot skyward.

Her entire body trembled but she stayed on her feet, sending out light and calling the Fae souls to her. One of them brushed over her, warm and loving, and she nearly sobbed from the emotions it brought out in her. She felt the presence of her Fae mother's soul, along with the kindness of Andy's, wrap around her own before Hawk threw himself at her and knocked her to the ground. She landed on her back with a hard, lung-bruising crash, her body pinned beneath his.

He'd thought she was under attack.

Drained, and unable to breathe as her already deflated lungs begged for air beneath Hawk's added weight, River looked into a sky spinning with color, so gloriously bright it turned dull dusk into radiant day. She threw her arm across her eyes to shield them.

The swirling colors dropped from the sky to surround and embrace the group of people on the ground. Then they vanished in all different directions, scattering on the night wind.

Faran found his voice first. "Now!" he barked into his com-link.

Lilla rushed forward and launched the kits while Hawk slid off River to lie on his back beside her, both of them staring at a sky that was empty once more.

Sheets of lightning streaked across the heavens as the kits detonated.

Hawk gulped in air as the buzzing sound silenced abruptly. "That was unexpected."

She ran her hands through his damp hair and held him to her, releasing a wave of healing magic as she slipped inside his head. She choked down relief when she found no lingering signs of the virus.

The bomb, too, had gone dead. She seized it with fingers of magic and crushed it to powdery dust. The particles of dust, she sent spinning into space.

She withdrew from his mind, sliding her hands around his waist and gripping him tight. Tears spilled down her cheeks. "I thought I'd lost you."

Hawk rolled toward her to brush the tears away. "How many times have I told you not to take risks for me?"

She smiled. "When are you going to realize you can't tell me what to do?"

Hawk laughed, a sound so rare from him, it made her tears flow again. Another thought struck her, a dark one this time.

"What is it?" Hawk asked, seeing the sudden change in her expression.

"I've called souls to me. Does that make me a Dark Lord?"

He hooked long strands of hair from her face with his finger and pressed a soft kiss to her temple. "You're about the farthest thing from a Dark Lord imaginable. Remember when you made the water in the river dance?" She nodded. "And you said you chose light, as if you were challenging the Mother herself to contradict you?" She nodded again, her heart starting to smile, sensing where he was going with this. "That makes you a Bright Lord, my love." He kissed her mouth. "And you're all mine."

"You may to have to share her," Achala said from close by, his words laced with amusement. "She has a grandfather and a brother who would like some of that brightness as well."

River had forgotten their audience. Hawk had, too. With a somewhat embarrassed grin on his face, he climbed to his feet and offered her his hand.

As River stood, a pair of familiar blue eyes fixed on her with ill-concealed concern. She reached up and ruffled Jake's shaggy blond hair. He'd had another growth spurt recently, and she'd failed to notice.

"I'm okay," she assured him.

His eyes narrowed. "Are you sure?"

"Positive." But this was hardly the time to celebrate. They had simply traded one disaster for another. The coming years would be hard ones. The remainder of the world's population would need to head underground to survive.

She was Fae. She brought life. She couldn't abandon her world.

Her glance found Hawk's. Emotions clouded his dark eyes as he looked at her with all the love inside him. She wrapped her soul around his, binding them together, and when his eyes slipped shut, her heart thudded against her chest. She loved him so much it was as frightening as it was exciting. He planted a soft kiss onto her mouth.

"I'm going to be here for you," he whispered into her ear. "Together, we'll make this world our home." Relief overwhelmed her. She hadn't wanted to consider their parting, or the pain it would cause. "Although I never thought I'd end up with a bunch of little Demons for family," he added, sounding both amused and resigned at the same time.

That brought her up short as she considered his words. Of course they were family. Her mother and father hadn't needed any blood relationship to consider her a part of theirs. And as long as she and Hawk had family by their side, they could face whatever was coming.

She slipped her hand into his and squeezed.

"Well thank God the fun's over," Nick said, breaking the sudden quiet as he dusted dirt and debris off the knees of his jeans.

Hawk and River exchanged a look. Contrary to what Nick thought, the fun was far from over.

This was just the beginning.

EPILOGUE

♦

River gazed around the old military base, at the steel buildings and the cracked runway, and breathed deeply of the crisp, fresh air. The roar of the nearby bay could be heard, its icy waters lapping sluggishly at the shoreline.

She had read about the Arctic, but she'd never experienced it before. The sun, ever present, had come as a surprise. Peters said that in the winter the sun wouldn't rise above the horizon, but at the same time it never became totally dark either. Not the way it did at home.

"It's more like a very long twilight," he'd explained. "This is a desert region, too, so there isn't much snow, but whatever we get is going to last until spring."

Children's laughter rang out from behind one of the buildings. Hawk was playing hide-and-seek with the boys. River couldn't think of them as Weres. In her mind, Weres were animals. These boys were beautiful and good-natured.

"Don't let that one fool you," Peters replied sourly when she said as much. He pointed at a little boy with shaggy, white-blond hair, who reminded her too much of her late brother, Sam, as he rounded the corner of one of the buildings. "He bit me hard enough to break the skin. And he swears like a sailor."

The boy stuck out his tongue at Peters, then grinned at River. River grinned back. She loved little boys, but there was something about these ones in particular that warmed her heart. Andy used to tell River that she was good for her soul. River got that same sort of feeling from these children.

Later in the day they walked across the tundra—River, Hawk, Achala, and Peters—and climbed the mountain to the telescope. They could easily have jumped, except all of them wanted to see more of the Arctic landscape.

The souls were long gone, called by River and dispersed throughout the world.

"What does it mean?" she asked her grandfather as Hawk fitted her kaleidoscope back into the finder scope slot her father had made for it.

"It means that Fae souls have been welcomed into this world, and now they are free to choose their own hosts," Achala replied.

She didn't miss his slight frown. "Have I done a terrible thing?"

His graying brow cleared. "Not at all. Change is inevitable, even for the Fae. Who is to say that this wasn't planned by the Mother?" He placed a light hand on the shoulder of her parka. "I can't say I'm unhappy with the choice your soul made when it chose you. And now this world has a strong Fae connection. It's safe."

He believed the presence of Fae would protect her home from the Guardians ever returning. Hawk did, too. She hoped they were right.

She also hoped the new generation of Fae would help restore life on her world. If the children in this place were anything to judge by, she suspected they would.

That night, as she crawled into a sleeping bag next to Hawk, she asked him what he'd discovered about her father. He had been going through the filing cabinets with Peters, the two men comparing notes as they searched.

He put his mouth close to her ear and breathed soft words of reassurance. "Both Faran and Peters believe he was protecting these children, River. That's good enough for me."

It was more than enough for River. That was the father she remembered—a man filled with kindness, love, and a desire to do right by the world, someone who could never abandon a child in need. She wanted Hawk to think well of him, too.

Hawk rolled to his side and propped his head on his hand so he could look down at her. Light filtered in through the high windows of the small, barracks-style room where they slept. He stroked the backs of his fingers along her cheek, his eyes darkening, before he leaned over to kiss her.

"I've survived some of the darkest days of my life because of your presence," he whispered. "When I close my eyes, I no longer fear what reality I'll wake up to, because always, deep in my soul, I know you are with me." He kissed her again, with more passion this time, and River's arms slid around his neck to draw him close. He rested his forehead on hers.

"And now, thanks to you, the brightest days are ahead."